How to Mend a Broken Heart

How to Mend a Broken Heart

Anna Mansell

bookouture

Published by Bookouture
An imprint of StoryFire Ltd.
23 Sussex Road, Ickenham, UB10 8PN
United Kingdom

www.bookouture.com

ISBN: 978-1-78681-024-3
eBook ISBN: 978-1-78681-023-6

For Grace: anything is possible, if we try.

Prologue

Sun scorches my skin. There's no breeze, no respite, just the comforting discomfort of prickling pain. Heat-softened tarmac warms my body.

I'm alive.

Despite this, and some discomfort, I've found a strange kind of peace. Peace amongst the rising panic in the voices around me. Peace amongst the rumble of queuing cars, engines running on standstill, the buses, the immaculate Chelsea tractors. Sheffield's buzzing suburbia, brought to a dramatic standstill.

Yummy mummies leave the coffee shop, passing my vacated table, with spent coffee cup now stained with froth and sprinkled chocolate. Their necks crane as they push Bugaboos by the scene. Chubby hands reach for tiny, sockless toes and something somewhere, deep in my subconscious, recalls a feeling. A past.

I stare at the endless, denim-blue sky. There's a whisper of cloud in the distance; a plane dawdles its vapour trail from east to west. A face obscures my view.

'Hello.'

Rough, sweaty hands cup my face. It's a man wearing the green shirt and trousers of a paramedic. 'Can you hear me? I'm John, I'm here to help you.' His eyes seek mine for a response. Beads of sweat form across his *forehead. He wipes them with his arm; his shirt soaks up the dew. 'Can you tell me your name? Can you tell me what happened?'*

But I can't tell him. Or I won't tell him. Because, really, what's the point? I close my eyes and dream of a Grimm tale without the Disney ending.

Apparently this summer's going to be a long one. Like 1976. I suppose it would have been a shame to miss it.

Chapter One

KAT

'So the only other thing to tell you about is Susan.'

'Susan?' I reach for my tea, wishing I hadn't let it go past the point of perfect to drink. I hate lukewarm tea. It's unnecessary. An affront. A crime against hot drinks. It's also possible I overthink it.

'Susan Smith. Female, fifty-six. Had an argument with a bus down Ecclesall Road and lost.'

I frown, pushing my new glasses back up my nose. They feel heavy on my face, out of place. I probably shouldn't have been talked into them by the Gok Wan-lookalike assistant at the optician. New hair. New glasses. A new wardrobe at home with every item still carrying the price tag. Belts to accentuate my waist. Also Gok's fault – the real one. Can you have a mid-life crisis at the age of twenty-eight?

'These are great, by the way,' says Emma, circling the air in the general direction of my face. 'Tres Geek Chic.'

'Yes, that's me. Geek and indeed chic,' I say, fiddling with them again. I can hear my tone; it's definitely approaching grumpy yet I don't have the strength to buck my ideas up.

Emma adopts a bad, Irish accent. 'You remind me of a young Nana Mouskouri.'

'A who?'

'Greece's finest export!' she exclaims. 'Well, Nana and feta.'

The blank look I give her in response forces an optimistic nod of encouragement, as if that answers everything, then a swift roll of her eyes when she realises I've no idea. 'Come on, misery. If we didn't laugh we'd cry,' she goads, followed swiftly by, 'You don't have to be mad to work here…'

'Don't!' I say, my hands shielding my ears, stopping her before she can finish. There's a pause in our chat, a pause filled with the warmth of a friendship that can transcend my mood. I crack a half-smile. She's someone I need right now. She gets me.

I drain my mug – lukewarm is better than none at all – and place it back on the table, waiting for Emma to finish our holiday handover while I resist a second biscuit; it's barely 9 a.m.

'So, Susan Smith, then,' she continues. 'She was in with that new consultant in charge—'

'Ooh, Mr Just-Call-Me-Mark Barnes!' says a bank nurse pushing laundry past our station, dirty bed sheets overflowing. 'I wouldn't mind being *in* with him,' she says, gurning like Vic Reeves, minus a thigh rub.

'Leg brace and everything!' Emma shouts after her with a giggle and a snort.

'Leg brace and everything?' I repeat, shaking my head. 'That doesn't even make sense, Emma. I thought this was Sheffield's finest teaching hospital, not a remake of *Carry On Nurse*.' I frown again. 'A few days away and you lot have gone rampant.'

I'm no longer approaching grumpy. I'm right there, wearing its heavy cloak. A cloak smattered with the gentle whiff of Eau de Post Break-Up and Still Not Over It.

'Don't tell me you haven't thought about "Just-Call-Me-Mark" even just a teensy bit?' Emma looks shocked. Like maybe I'm not a real woman or something.

'No, actually, I haven't.' I glance over the rim of my glasses to labour my point. At least they're good for something. '*Mr Barnes* doesn't do it for me at all.' Which is true. He's not my type. I wouldn't say he was a cad – because I'm not from the 1950s – but he's borderline. Borderline cad. He's also a consultant. Attractive? I suppose, if you like that sort of thing, but a consultant all the same.

'He did it for you once upon a time...' mutters Emma under her breath.

I stare down at paperwork, opting to ignore her. I admit, when I first met him, we flirted. But that was purely whilst in the comfort and security of a long-term relationship – a cheap thrill if you will. But things have changed. Not least my Facebook relationship status. And besides, nurse gets with consultant? Like that's not a massive cliché. 'He's from Manchester, anyway,' I say suddenly. Emma looks confused. 'Wrong side of the Pennines.' I offer it up as a legitimate excuse, then I remember she's a born and bred Mancunian, so wiggle my eyebrows as if I was just trying to wind her up with some Sheffield versus Manchester rivalry.

'He may not do it for you, but you definitely do something for him,' she nudges.

True. Apparently. But since Daniel, my boyfriend of five years, thrust his hand into my chest and ripped out my heart, I've sort of gone off men.

Apparently, by now, I should be over it. He doesn't deserve me. I'm better off alone. Et cetera. All of which is easy for best friend Lou to say, given that her wedding is imminent and unlikely to be suddenly, nay brutally, called off.

Not that I had an imminent wedding as far as Daniel was concerned, but in my head it was a given. Neither Lou nor Emma can feel the pain in my heart. And when either suggest I date, meet people, start afresh… Well, they don't see how the very idea of re-entering the dating game, if and when I choose, makes the pit of my stomach fall through my shoes. The thought of first-time sex with someone who hasn't grown to love my stretch marks… Though perhaps, on reflection, Daniel didn't love them as much as he said he did when trying to extract me from my pants... Well, anyway, the thought of it. Ugh. And besides, what would they make of my plain black, in-a-long-term-relationship-and-can-admit-a-thong-is-in-fact-a-crime-against-one's-nether-region pants? Emma clears her throat and I pull myself together. 'Can we stop talking about Mr Barnes and get on?' I say, taking a deep breath to lock back up the tears that now sting the backs of my eyes. I waft authority and my paperwork in her face. 'Your shift finished twenty minutes ago.'

'Alright, mardy bum. Who got you up on the wrong side of bed this morning?' She winks and I glare, just long enough for my eyes to fill and Emma to spot we're hurtling towards a line neither of us wants to cross. 'Okay, okay.' She surrenders, hands up. She backs off to the light box, attaching an X-ray. 'Susan Smith then. According to eyewitnesses, Susan got up from her seat outside the coffee shop and walked straight into the flow of moving traffic. It was Ecclesall Road so, you know, busy. She was flipped by a motorbike undertaking a bus. Frankly, she's lucky to be alive. Her notes are all here.' She passes me the file. 'Along with these.' We study ghostly images of before surgery and after. A clean break, set and plastered. 'She'll need physio on her left arm too,' continues Emma. 'It's pretty badly bruised, though no break there. Her pain relief seems to be working and there are no latent signs of additional damage.'

We stare vacantly at the image, heads tilted slightly left in perfect unison. The clock ticks above me, snapping me out of a daze, and I snatch the images from their clips. 'Sounds like an avoidable accident, surely. Have we talked to her about how it happened?' I file Susan's X-rays and papers, then reorganise the desk into my preferred system. Emma watches me with a wry smile. 'What? It works better this way…' I try, feeling caught out.

She grins. 'It works perfectly well the other way too,' she says good-naturedly. 'Anyway, yes, we did ask, but getting Susan's story is proving to be a problem.'

'Why?' I move to study the rota, getting to grips with today's team.

'Well, she isn't answering our questions. She won't actually talk at all. We offered her a pad and pen to make notes, in case it hurt her to talk, but she wouldn't take it. We haven't been able to identify a next of kin either. There was some ID in her handbag, one of those old paper driving licences, but little else.'

'She's not communicating at all?' I ask, my hand resting on a pile of files stacked high on the desk. 'Have we tried everything? You said notebook and pen?' Emma nods. 'Signing?' She nods again. I try thinking up alternatives. My heart quickens at the realisation that actually, I'm in charge now, and I need to at least look like I'm on top of things, even if I don't entirely feel it. My mind goes blank, Emma helps me out.

'We've tried notes, signing, blinking and Morse code,' she winks. 'I considered the medium of dance, but apparently it's not a universal language.'

'Right.' I only hear what she's said after the fact. My focus to stay on top of this mixed bag of emotions pretty much entirely swallows my sense of humour.

'There's no evidence to say she can't talk, nothing on her records. It could be a post-traumatic thing of course, from the accident. We just need to give her time. From what we can tell, there's no next of kin either.'

'Okay…' I look back through Susan's file again. Mr Barnes's hand-writing spiders across the pages. 'Of course, this would be a lot more useful if I could actually read it,' I mutter, turning the file this way and that in an attempt to decipher his words. I ignore the fact that my own penmanship is no better. 'Oh, ignore me. Sorry! Okay.' I snap the file shut. 'Have we lodged it with mental health?'

'No, actually,' she answers, and for a second I feel like maybe I do know what I'm doing.

'Okay, I'll sort that, no problem. Anything else?'

Emma scans the whiteboard and looks around the desk. 'I don't think so,' she says, still visibly searching her brain for remnants of handover she might have forgotten. There won't be any. She is admirably organised. Intimidatingly so – or maybe that's just me. 'Nope, that's it.' She places her hands on her hips. All done.

'Great, thanks.' I offer up a box of Celebrations with a small thank-you card from a patient stuck to the front. Sweet treats are an up- or downside to our job, depending on your point of view. Emma reaches into the half-empty box of chocolates and twists open a wrapper.

'So, how was it?' she asks through a part-chewed micro Mars bar, casually leaning against the desk. She studies the empty wrapper; it crackles as she folds it.

'How was what?' I bite the side of my mouth, trying to remember the various excuses I planned for the inevitable return-to-work question. A porter jokes with a patient as he pushes him down the corridor and their laughter draws my attention. I pretend to smile in the hope she'll drop the conversation.

'Your hol-i-day!' She spells the word out, then purses her lips, eyebrows raised.

Sigh. She knows that I know what she's asking. And I know that she knows I don't want to answer. She twists the empty chocolate wrapper, dropping it back in the box. I catch it out of the corner of my eye, along with her expression – daring me to react to the unspoken law of empty wrappers in the bin, not back in the box. There are few things worse than going to treat yourself mid-morning and finding nothing but empty wrappers.

'It was great, actually. Lovely.' I flash a quick smile in her direction, then, head down to hide the twitch in my right eye, I push the chocolates out of sight. 'Just what I needed,' I finish, hoping I sound light and breezy, as opposed to constricted and very much swallowing back the urge to cry. Again. My newly cut fringe escapes its loose clip. *A side bang is all the rage*, according to the hairdresser. I admit it comes in handy for hiding behind.

'Was it though?' asks Emma. She tries to catch my eye.

I pull my sleeves down to hide the lack of suntan. 'It was great,' I trill, smiling wider. I place suddenly sweaty hands on my hips and take a shallow breath. 'It was brilliant, in fact. Much better than I expected. I'd love to go back, explore more, you know?' I laugh, throwing some sort of weird coquettish innocence in her direction and she quite rightly looks at me like I am an idiot.

'Did it rain the whole time then?' she asks.

I should have gone for that fake tan in the back of my bathroom cupboard. I mean, who really comes back from a holiday abroad without some sort of colour? Emma stares at me. 'Look,' I sigh. 'It's fine. I'm fine. Honestly. Everything's…'

'Fine?' She holds my gaze.

'It was six weeks ago, Emma!' Actually, I could tell her it was six weeks, two days and three hours ago, but the detail's unimportant. 'I know you think I've thrown myself into work, that I'm losing sleep over it, but I promise you, I'm not.' I stifle an ill-timed yawn and try not to think about this morning's call from Lou, where she casually dropped into conversation the rumour that my ex-boyfriend has a new girlfriend. Adding in the word 'allegedly' didn't stop it hurting.

'This holiday' – the word catches in my throat – 'totally gave me perspective. Daniel wasn't happy, and maybe I wasn't either.'

Lou had taken great pains to inform me of the social media research that led to her allegation, then said she was going on a shopping spree in Leeds to make herself feel better about it all. She'd hung up before I could point out I was the one who needed to feel better about things and her revelation wasn't exactly helping. I'd all but held it together until I found his favourite shower gel casually taunting me in the bathroom. I stood with my face beneath the shower jet, letting the scalding water drown my tears. Five years, a joint bank account and a flat-share apparently meant nothing to him.

Emma coughs, pulling me out of my thoughts. A week's supply of concealer and too much kohl is really all that's between my red-rimmed eyes and her watchful gaze. 'Perspective, you say.'

She was there on the day his text came through. We were on our lunch break. She saw me choke on, then completely unravel into, my roast chicken salad. 'I'm totally over it,' I say, thinly.

She peers at me to see if I really mean what I say.

'Its fine,' I insist, arms now crossed, the corner of my smile twitching along with my eye. Please, God, don't let my chin wobble. 'His loss,' I finish, then hold my breath, hoping this will mean the discussion is over.

Though she clearly suspects something, it wouldn't help for Emma to know I actually spent the last ten days in my pyjamas – sleeping, eating, watching trashy telly and reading Jilly Cooper's back catalogue. No crime per se, we all love Rupert Campbell-Black, but it wasn't exactly the booked and paid-for holiday of a lifetime that I should have taken; the holiday I bailed on because the very thought of going alone made me want to eat my own face. The glossy magazines tell me I don't need a man to make me feel complete, and they're right, I know they are, but when you're cruising towards thirty as a newly single woman, because the love of your life got bored, it's tricky to just move on. Or start afresh. Or even feel remotely okay when you hear he's met someone new. I loved him.

I love him.

I look around the ward, my ward. Thank God for this, is all I can say. 'Go home, chuck,' I sigh. 'I'm back. I'm on it and you came to the end of your shift ages ago. Go. Sleep. Eat. Whatever.' I stop before adding *let me hide in my office until home time*.

'You know you don't have to do this alone, right?' she says, kindly.

'I know.' I smile and let her give me a big hug, suddenly realising how much a bit of human contact can go towards healing... and also weakening my resolve. I gently extricate myself from her tight hold. 'I've got a job to do, Emma, and crying is not an option.' I sniff it all back.

She checks my face to make sure it's okay to leave, then nods in approval. 'Right, I'm off.' She kisses me on the cheek, then heads off down the corridor. 'By the way,' she shouts, 'congratulations!' Her thumbs up are swiftly followed by a heel click towards the exit, à la Dick Van Dyke in *Mary Poppins*.

'Thank you.' I smile, glancing to my shoulder at the temporary stripe I now wear three days a week. Acting ward sister. This is the new focus. This could be the very making of me. It's seven years since I qualified, almost eight. They're putting a lot of responsibility in my hands. I have to ignore the feeling of complete inadequacy and prove to my boss, Gail, the powers that be, and perhaps myself, for that matter, that I am up to this.

I look around again, at the files, the notes on the board, the corridors with bays and patients and nurses, all under my responsibility. I try to blow out a nudge of fear at the reality before me. Accepting promotion, albeit temporary, is fine by phone. It was good timing. A challenge to distract myself with, I thought. Now, though, it feels different – here, on the ward. My ward. I swallow. 'See you tomorrow,' I whisper, but Emma's already gone.

I push back my shoulders and look down at the piles of paperwork around me. Susan's file is on the top.

I sigh, then shove a Jaffa Cake in my mouth.

Can I do this?

I can do this.

I have to.

Chapter Two

RHYS

It's hard to tell if the grim, bleary-eyed, bitter-tasting disappointment is fuelled by hangover or guilt. Whilst feeding uncooperative limbs into my jeans, I felt sick. The stumble back to my place like some carefree twenty-something on an unavoidable weekend walk of shame gave oxygen to the self-loathing. I'm thirty-nine, it's Tuesday, that was my brother's girlfriend.

Untangling myself from the sleepy hangover of her X-rated grasp, I'd closed my eyes, hoping that when I opened them again, it would be somebody else. Anybody but her. I'd held my breath, tiptoeing out of her room, stopping at the squeaky floorboard by her door, just in case she stirred. Like a dick. I had no idea what I was going to say if she woke, or what I should say now. I pinch at my aching forehead, barely able to remember the conversation that led us to this.

Should I send a text? Say sorry? Or thanks? Or perhaps that this shouldn't have happened and can I have my Calvins back? It was supposed to be a night to support each other. To remember him. To help each other deal with the pain of losing the person we loved. But now I hate him. And I hate me. And I hate what she and I did. However good it was.

Our David always knew I liked her.

Jesus.

I pull up to my first appointment, take my phone out of the cradle and type out the first morning-after text I've ever sent: 'Sorry I had to leave, loads on. Talk to you later. R'

I almost delete it, then nearly add a kiss, before eventually just hitting send.

Of course, this probably wouldn't have happened had Mum been in. I called her first, stopped by her house. I needed to talk. I needed… something. To go round and share stories about him, to sit in his room, to avoid being alone. I tried her phone again this morning, conflicted with guilt about Michelle and worry for the fact that I went to bed without saying goodnight to Mum. We always talk before bed now, since he died. She said it gives her comfort. It does the same for me. Until these last few weeks anyway, when suddenly she's started going absent without warning. Maybe I should be pleased she's finding a way to cope, but I'm not. I just feel alone. And selfish.

I tuck my phone into my top pocket and grab our David's tool bag – it's hot to the touch. Like contraband. Like Michelle. I scale the steps leading up to Mrs Johnson's 1960s semi in the leafy bit of Norton Lees. Before I get a chance to shake off my morning and knock on the side door, she's opened it. Despite the smile on her face, her crossed arms and watch check confirm I'm running late. I'm already on the back foot.

'I know, I know. I am sorry, Mrs J. The traffic was awful, I needed to pop down Heeley to pick up a few bits, the lads got me talking and—'

'You've always got an excuse, haven't you, Rhys Woods?' She purses her bright red lips, but I detect a tiny smile too. One of those you get from someone who finds it impossible to really be cross with you. 'You were the same as a kid. Do you remember when you lobbed that brick at our Paul's head and you made summat up about it being too heavy and falling in the wrong direction?' The sparkle in her eye undermines her crossed arms. 'And how many times must I say this? I think we've known each other long enough for you to call me Sylv!'

She steps back just enough for me to squeeze past her. Sweet yet musky perfume launches itself up my nostrils in the same way it did back in the early nineties when I'd snog Zoe Owen round the back of the bike shed before geography. What was it they all wore? White Musk from The Body Shop, I seem to remember. I bought it for her for Valentine's but she wouldn't accept it. She was someone else's girl-friend too. I've got form.

I head through the lounge and into her kitchen. 'I'm eternally sorry for Paul's stitches,' I say. 'The brick was heavy. I was six!' I repeat the excuse I've always given for that particular childhood incident. 'Anyway, I couldn't possibly call you Sylv, Mrs J. You are a client, the wife of a man I dare not cross…' Mr Johnson was the local Boxing Club trainer. A bit like Paulie from the *Rocky* films, only bigger. And tougher. And not quite as lyrical with his advice. 'And you are my best friend's mother. It's not right. Now, can I make us both a cuppa before I set about your stopcock?'

My phone rings in my pocket. The initial relief at hearing it is quickly replaced with frustration when I remember I set Mum up with a new tone so I wouldn't miss her calls. It's not her tone. I can't answer if it's Michelle. Not in front of Mrs J.

'I'll make the tea, you answer that. It could be work. Or one of your ladies trying to track you down. A woman hates not knowing where her man is, Rhys!' She taps manicured nails, which match her lips, on the Italian-style marble-esque worktop. Towards the end, David hated coming here. I thought it would help, the flirting, the interaction, but he ran out of patience for it. Called her a sad old cougar – though not to her face, thankfully. He got nasty like that, towards the end. He was bitter. Michelle said the same last night, said though he was around, he'd 'gone' long before he finally…

'Sugar?' Mrs J asks, interrupting my regular daydream, the one in which I see my brother's face for the next to last time, when maybe I could have said or done something different. When the phrase 'pull yourself together' should never have left my mouth.

'No, thanks.' I shake off the thought. 'And for the record, I am nobody's man, Mrs J, except for my own. And I'm happy to keep it that way, thank you very much.'

'Ahh, girls must be breaking their hearts over you – that height, those tanned muscles. Do you still play rugby, Rhys?' The heat of something prickles up my neck. Embarrassment? Guilt? Annoyance? 'And those eyes! I'm not sure if you're asking for a bone or inviting me to bed!' she cackles, ignoring how inappropriate her banter is.

As last night's alcohol dissipates, so too does last night's bolshiness, the arrogance to flirt with someone I shouldn't. 'Mrs J!' I groan, moving out of reach. Flirting with a client is not necessarily unknown – I'm a thirty-nine-year-old single man – but I'm all out of it this morning.

'So, how many've you got on the go these days?' she grins, reaching into her cupboard, teetering on one foot as she ignores the mugs right in front of her and opts for china cups from the top shelf. 'Oops,' she giggles, pulling her top back down over her waist. I pretend I haven't noticed. 'My Paul says you've a whole line of 'em chasing after you, you lucky boy. Any of them marriage material? You'll have to settle down eventually, you know! Do us a favour, love, pass the rejects over? I wouldn't mind getting our Paul back out of the house and on with his life now. Kissing forty is no age to be at home with your parents.'

Her observation is a little unfair. My best mate's marriage broke down last year, and after a few weeks on my couch, he really had nowhere else to go, much to his frustration. I let the deconstruction of our love lives wash over me as she hands over a drink.

'And besides, I want to use his room for a nail salon. I've got ladies waiting for me to get my own place. Your Mum could come see me, you know. Give herself a little pampering.' Mrs J's tone changes, just like everyone's does when they ask after Mum now. 'How is she?' she asks, head cocked to one side.

'Okay. Mostly. You know… Mind you, I've not spoken to her since yesterday morning so your guess is as good as mine.' I heft the tool bag on my shoulder, irritated.

'Ahh, poor love.' She sips at her tea. 'It must have been such a shock,' she says gently, apparently not hearing the grief cliché klaxon. 'I said to Paul, I said I don't know how I'd cope if—'

'Yeah, no, I dunno,' I interrupt.

I blame the internet. It tells people to say something. To not ignore the difficult conversation when someone dies. But people stop reading at that point, glossing over the bits that suggest you avoid certain responses because those in the throes of grief might find it trite instead of caring.

'I suppose he must be at peace now,' she says, nodding gently, and I bite my tongue. That's the one that bugs me the most. He died angry and sad and rejected by the one person he needed most. Where's the peace in that?

'Give her my love when you speak to her, won't you?'

'Yup, will do.' Because that's the other thing people do: they consider how the parent might feel, but presume the sibling will step up and take charge of the situation. Become the nominated adult. They forget that at the same time my mother's son killed himself, I lost my brother.

'I'd better get on,' I say, looking around at nothing in particular just to avoid eye contact. I avoid talking about my brother at the best of times, never mind now, when his girlfriend's perfume lingers on my T-shirt. 'Do you need to run any water before I start?'

'No, love. I'm nipping out to the shops, I'll be back in half an hour or so. Will you still be here at lunchtime? I can pick up a tuna pasta salad from the Co-op if you like? Gotta look after that bod of yours, haven't we!'

'I've got a pack-up,' I lie. 'Cheese and salad cream cob.' I back out of the kitchen, retreating to the relative safety of their avocado bathroom.

Slinging my stuff down, I check my phone. No message. No number. So not Mum then. Where is she? Where was she last night when I swung by? Why, when I need her, is she suddenly so distant?

Chapter Three

KAT

I put my hair up in a clip, away from my face, wipe my eyes and fumble my glasses back on. I pick out a compact mirror from the drawer to check if I look okay, or if the glasses look as ridiculous as they feel. Maybe it's the office wobble I'm having, more than the glasses. These piles of meeting notes, reports, emails and the sudden, overwhelming level of responsibility is probably the thing that tipped me over the edge this time. It was definitely not the cryptic Facebook status Daniel just posted.

I still wish I'd put my contacts in this morning.

I adjust the glasses, my hair and my composure, then pick up Susan's file and head out to introduce myself.

'Knock, knock,' I say, peering around her faded, harlequin curtains before squeezing through a gap. 'Good morning, how are you feeling today?' I smooth out the fabric, joining the gaps to protect her privacy. I flick through her notes, comparing them to the chart on her bed. Susan faces the opposite direction. Her head is a mass of silver-grey hair that shines as if fine threads of platinum are running through it. It's cropped neatly into the nape of her neck. Tidy. Out of the way.

'I'm Kat, the ward sister,' I say, then feel like I've jumped the gun. 'Well, acting ward sister. Three days a week, starting today. All the other days I'm just a regular nurse.' Though her eyes remain closed, Susan slowly turns her face towards me. She doesn't look fifty-six, I suppose. Though I'm not sure what I expect fifty-six to look like. Certainly not plump and, through the bruising on her left side, fresh-faced. Almost youthful. No hard paper rounds here. 'I'm Kat seven days a week though,' I joke, then wish I hadn't as she tries to open her closed eyes, managing only one, the other closed and swollen. Perhaps that's why my attempt at humour goes unacknowledged. I don't suppose I'd be feeling all that perky under the circumstances either. I smile my well-practised bedside sympathy smile: head to one side, a gentle eye blink and a nod. It's a skill learned in week one of your training; unless, that is, you're a doctor.

'I've been on holiday, actually. Well, sort of… but don't tell anyone else that, eh.' I half smile but Susan doesn't respond. I step closer to try to read her face. 'This is my first day back. I expect all that loung-ing around will be a distant memory by six o clock tonight.' I leave a gap for her to comment. Just in case. 'Has everything been okay?' I say eventually. 'Since you came in, I mean. Are we looking after you?'

Nothing.

'Of course we have, we've got a great team here. How was break-fast?'

Still nothing.

I move the table that straddles her bed, noting the barely touched cereal in her bowl. 'Are you in any pain or discomfort at all?' I take her wrist, read her machine, scribble a note of pulse and oxygen, then rewrite them so they're legible. 'We can organise more pain relief if we need to. You just say if you…' I stumble over the clumsy suggestion. 'I mean…'

Hooking the clipboard back on the end of her bed, I rest against it and take a deep breath. Though her eyes are swollen, there's an intensity to her look. I search my mind for something to say, something that shows I'm the right person to be in charge of the ward. In charge of her care. 'Your consultant, Mr Barnes, will be on his rounds shortly. He'll no doubt go through it all with you then, but, well, all things considered, you may be with us for a few weeks yet.' She winces, moving her arm slightly. 'Careful,' I say, helping her to readjust. She's got tiny wrists, almost childlike. She's not frail, just petite. 'Your arm's going to be a fabulous patchwork of bruising,' I say. She looks down at it, then up to the ceiling.

There's a beat. And then a cough. The woman in the next bed practically exporting her spleen.

I lean in towards Susan. 'Coughing is the worst,' I say, parking myself in the visitor's chair beside her as the patient coughing in next door's bed picks up a gear. 'You alright there, Mrs Nielson?' I raise my voice so Mrs Neilson might hear, then go for a conspiratorial wink before I have the chance to stop myself. 'That cough is pretty bad,' I shout. 'Have a little drink, my love, I'll be with you in a minute.' There's a grunt of response before the cough starts again, all gravelly, gritty and raw. And repetitive. Definitely repetitive. I lean in closer to Susan, an instinctive sense of my old self showing up. The self that knows how to be a good nurse. The self who deserved this promotion. The self who can totally put life to one side while she does her job. 'We've tried all kinds to get rid of that cough. One of the volunteers even rubbed a menthol vapour on her feet. It's an old wives' tale that allegedly works on babies. Didn't make a blind bit of difference with Mrs Nielson, mind. But you know, desperate times and all that.'

Just as I think we're developing a bond, albeit over phlegm, Mrs Nielson coughs louder and Susan closes her eyes.

I try to come up with a new line of conversation. 'The tea trolley will be around soon,' I say. 'Can I get you one? Yorkshire, obviously.' Susan turns her head away from me, the mass of silver replacing the bruises. I move around her bed so I can see her face again. 'Then Connie, our lady with the library trolley, she's in later. Calls everyone "dear" despite not exactly being a spring chicken herself. It's mostly true crime and Mills & Boon.' I think about my bookshelf at home. Daniel always took the mick out of my books. 'I love a Mills & Boon,' I say. 'Grossly underrated.'

There's no trace of days-old make-up, like most recently admitted patients. No earrings; her lobes aren't even pierced. There's no ring, wedding or otherwise. No jewellery at all, save for a single, fine gold necklace with a tiny cross. Despite her silver hair and baby-soft skin, Susan is the very model of plain.

I open my mouth to speak, but the words are instantly replaced with a mouthful of fabric as Susan's curtain swishes open and Mark Barnes strides in. He stands, puffed up and important, as I try to recover my composure, detangling the curtain from my mouth, hair and stupid bloody glasses. There's a time we might have laughed about it, back when I saw the funny side to anything.

'Good morning, Susan. I'm your consultant, Mark Barnes. Please, though, just call me Mark.' I swear I hear a giggle out in the corridor. 'How's that leg, how are you and have you any words for us today?' The boom of his Mancunian voice shares her silence with the ward. I wonder how that makes her feel.

'Not yet,' I say firmly, tucking my errant fringe back in its clip. I give him my sternest stare but his lack of eye contact means it goes unnoticed. He moves to stand beside me, his head still buried in her file.

'Is there anyone you'd like us to call, Susan?' he asks.

I resist the opportunity for sarcasm. *Ooh, that's a good question. Did they teach you that in medical school?* Instead, I simply answer on her behalf. 'We haven't established anyone as yet.'

'Okay, well…' Mark drops his voice to an ineffective am-dram stage whisper. 'See if you can gain her trust.' He narrows his eyes and directs his pen at her. 'Try to find out what's going on. She needs a support network; this lack of communication is a concern.'

'Of course,' I say. 'I'm waiting to talk to someone on MH.' I use the code for mental health so as not to alarm Susan.

Mark nods, folding his arms across his chest to sum things up. I'm not sure if it's the impression he's aiming for, but he has the look of a peacock: all front and display. 'We've reset your leg, Susan. You were lucky there were no additional problems. No internal bleeding, no pins required. Obviously you're badly bruised and you need to take time and the help offered to get back on your feet, but you're alive. So, you know, that's a win.'

A win. Yes, I bet that is exactly how she feels. You can tell that by the look on her face…

'Steer clear of buses for a while.' He lifts his chin. It's freshly shaven and looks remarkably smooth up close. And then a hint of his aftershave hits me. Just a suggestion, but it's unmistakable. Bleu de Chanel. I bought it for Daniel last Christmas. He opened it and put it on as we sat beneath the tree. I can still feel his neck as I kissed it, taking in his new smell. We had nobody to visit that day. We lounged around the house, wrapped up in each other, chocolate and Prosecco. My heart aches. What changed?

'Obviously, we need to keep you in, Susan. Work through your rehabilitation,' Mark continues as I step away from him. 'Perhaps though, when you're ready, we can talk through the best way to get you discharged and back home.'

Susan stares at him, the eye she can open bunny-in-the-headlights wide. She's locked into his gaze as he waits for a response that doesn't come. He reaches for his penlight, leans in and flashes it in her eyes before I can intervene. Susan doesn't flinch, and even from my standpoint, I see her pupils dilate in perfectly functioning response. Her lid stays open for a while; striking hazel eyes with flecks of green, stare back at Mark.

Mark moves away, sidling back up next to me. Actually, he probably isn't sidling, I may be judging him unfairly given his lack of bedside manner and that aftershave. I resist breathing in.

'Do whatever you have to do, Kat. She really needs to talk to us at some point.' The artificial strip lights of my ward reflect in his eyes. We should turn them off. Save energy.

'Of course,' I say. I wait for him to say something, but he's just looking at me, at my hair and most probably the glasses. I push them back up my nose. 'Holidays suit you,' he eventually says. 'You look...' I bite my lip closed, hoping he can't finish the sentence he started, despite wondering what he's really thinking. 'Well, anyway.' He nods, smiles, then leaves as swiftly as he appeared. 'Mrs Nielson,' he shouts. 'If you keep coughing like that, you're going to pop a rib!' The squeak of his shoes on my lino signals his final, and frankly overdue, exit.

It's suddenly as quiet as any hospital ward ever gets – just a distant hum of nurse chatter from the desk and second-hand TV sounds that leak a combination of *The Jeremy Kyle Show* and *Cash in the Attic*. Even the coughing has momentarily stopped. I catch my breath, then turn back to face her. 'He's right, Susan,' I say, gently, needlessly tidying her impeccable bedding. 'You will need some support when you're ready to go home. If there is anyone we can call for you…' Susan closes her eyes, turns her head and practically sinks back into the bed. Camouflaged into her surroundings. I'm dismissed.

And that's when I realise there's a tiny part of me that's envious. She can switch off, turn her back on us all. What I'd give to do the same. Camouflage. Hide away from the extra responsibility, the smell of his aftershave, the reality that, whilst I wait for Daniel to collect the last of his things from our flat, he's out, he's moved on. He's not coming back.

Chapter Four

SUSAN

The rattle and squeak of a trolley edges into a dream where I'm lost in a forest with no way out. I'm searching, looking beneath bushes and around trees. I'm crying out and hearing only my own echo in response.

The smell of undistinguishable hospital food replaces the smell of damp pines and loneliness. I keep my eyes shut, even though I sense someone by my bed. A plate is put down, cutlery clatters beside it. The bed jolts slightly as my table is pulled closer, within reach.

'Here you go, love,' says a new voice. 'Enjoy.'

The footsteps leave. I try to unstick my eyes; my left stays dark, my right clears with each blink, bringing food into focus. A jacket potato, sliced in two. Yellowy butter melts off its flat surface, dropping down onto wilting salad. There's a chipped pot of grated cheese beside it. Nausea swells, as it did in the forest.

The nurse from before – was it Kat? – peers into my bay, eyeing up my plate as if checking my progress, like a mother whose child regularly rejects dinner. 'You hungry?' she asks, her tired face full of hope. She has a paper cup of tablets in her hand. 'Mmm, jacket potato and cheese,' she says unconvincingly, presumably in an attempt to sell it to me. 'And salad…' She rubs her stomach. 'I missed breakfast. Ended up snacking on chocolate when I got here, and trust me, Jaffa Cakes do not slow release energy till lunch time.' Her words are upbeat, but her spirit is not. 'Here, let me…' She reaches for my knife and fork, fluffing up the potato, sprinkling cheese in a dry little pile on the top.

'Drink?' she asks next, pouring a plastic cup of water from last night's jug. 'I just wondered if you'd had a chance to think of anyone we might call for you, Susan? No pressure. It's just visitors, they can help when you're…' She trails off, as if censoring herself. 'Visitors help,' she finishes. There's something in her eyes that I recognise. A distraction. A source of pain or heartache. You can just see it in some people.

I look down at the wilted salad on my plate.

'And we wouldn't want anyone to be worrying about you,' she adds.

If only somebody was worrying. If only someone had noticed I didn't get home, that I didn't close the curtains; that I haven't opened a window, watered the plants, or moved the car in months. I forgot to cancel the milk.

'You need to eat.' She pushes the plate closer to me, her voice gentle, caring. 'These tablets will make you feel sick if you don't line your stomach first.'

I pick up the fork, moving potato around the plate. The ache in my leg pulsates, the discomfort strangely reassuring. She watches and I find myself doing what I always have, what's expected, old habits that even this deep-rooted loathing can't kill off. Melting butter drops to my sheets and Kat reaches to brush it off for me. 'We can change those, if you like. Just say.' I part my lips just wide enough to take a small amount of food. Nausea returns but I chew through it, like a good girl. Fifty-six yet still unable to do as I please and see it through.

Kat picks at the papers and magazines on my side table. A Sheffield Star from three days ago sits beneath an old magazine covered in faces I don't recognise.

'I bet they're thrilled to have their bikini bodies cross-examined, don't you think?' she says, flicking through the pages. 'You bothered if I…' She hovers it over the bin, eventually dropping it in when I don't respond. I take another mouthful of lunch. The cold of the butter penetrates the heat of the potato. The cheese is an odd mix of strong and tasteless. Foreign on my palate. Combined, it clags and sticks in my throat. It constricts, but I keep eating.

Kat looks around, noticing my bag. The brown leather satchel gifted by Mother many years ago.

'Have we looked in here, Susan?' she asks. I think about the nurse who roughly opened, glanced through and buckled it back up the wrong way; too tight. 'Would you mind if I…' She reaches for it. Slowly. More carefully. 'In case they missed anything before?' It sits in her lap to begin with, just within my reach. I push food around my plate. 'Take those,' she says, nodding in the direction of the paper cup of medicine. I knock back the tablets, holding them on my tongue as I reach for the water. They leave a fine coating of bitterness behind.

'Well done.' She looks back down at my bag. 'Can I take a look inside?' she asks. I turn my attention back to the plate of food, charging my fork with more potato.

The buckles rattle as she undoes them. Mother used to say that buckle rattle announced my arrival. I wonder if Kat smells the thick aroma of well-worn leather. I loved that smell, it was home and safety and familiarity itself. I'm not sure if I still smell it, or just believe that I do, the memory strong and fresh.

'Gosh, you're organised,' she exclaims, picking through the compartments. 'Purse, pen, keys.' She announces each item as she places them on my starched white bed sheet. Inside the handbag, at the back, she finds the pocket with my leather-bound diary. Gold letters declare the year: 2016.

'Is this yours, Susan?' she asks.

I take another mouthful of food before pushing the plate away from me.

'Can I look?'

I close my eyes.

There's a crack from the spine of my diary. The sound of each page turned is amplified, it's deafening. His name lies within those pages. His number. If she finds it, if she calls, if he comes... Then there's a pause, a silence. My breath is shallow as I drift back towards the forest, searching desperately beneath fallen trunks of moss-covered trees, panic rising in my chest. I hear the words, 'Who is Rhys?' but I've gone, I've run away, I'm racing, searching through the woods; lost as much as I am found.

Chapter Five

RHYS

My phone rings just as I wedge an arm up Mrs J's U-bend. Managing to extract said arm, the front door opens and Mrs J returns. She shouts something about lunch up the stairs and, by the time I find my phone, shout back to Mrs J and swipe to answer the call, I've missed it. Bollocks. There's no number on the missed calls so I rest my phone on my thigh in case a voicemail comes through, looking down at the initials on David's bag whilst I wait. I had them stamped on the front, a gesture to prove I meant what I said about us going into business together – I'd train him up, we could be partners. He did okay, he knew enough, but his heart was never in it. I wonder if it would have been in anything? He never found his true vocation. We were opposites, he and I. Dark and light. Push and pull. Lost and found?

A voicemail alert brings relief. I loudspeaker it, searching my overalls and tool bag for a pen that works.

'Hello, this is Nurse Kat Davies at Sheffield Hospitals. We have a patient here with your telephone number in her diary. I wonder if you might be able to contact us so we can verify your relationship with her? My telephone number is…'

In the absence of paper, I try to write down the digits on my suddenly sweaty palm. My heart makes a bid for freedom via my ribcage and now I can't find my car keys. Why do I never put them in the same place? Why didn't Mum call me back this morning? Or reply to my texts? Why is the hospital calling? What's happened to her? I take the stairs three at a time.

'Have you seen my keys, Mrs J?'

'Done already?' she asks, surprised.

'No.' I spot them on the side, lurching to reach them and dropping them on the floor. 'Fuck it!'

'Is everything okay?'

'I don't know. Look, sorry, I'll come back, I've just, I've gotta go!' I hear Mrs J shout after me as I race out of her house and leap into my van, which starts on its fourth tickover. I need a new van. And I need the traffic not to be shit. And I need the east side of the city to be much closer to the hospital.

Shit.

It takes me twenty minutes to do the thirty-minute journey and I hope and pray that the recently defaced speed camera isn't working. The one-way system and multitude of bus lanes do not serve the person in a hurry very well. I'm out of breath as I make the run from giant car park to even bigger hospital. Every corridor looks identical. Each sign seemingly points in every direction but the one I want.

I turn back on myself and head to reception, jigging about at the desk, waiting for the queue of people to go down so I can ask which direction I should take.

'Woods,' I repeat, now at the front of the queue but drawing a blank from the officious woman on the desk.

'When was she brought in?' asks the lady, clicking at her computer and frowning.

'I don't know, I had a call half an hour ago.' I try to remember the nurse's name. 'Kat!' I say, banging my hand on the desk. 'Nurse Kat Davies.' The receptionist mutters something inaudible to herself. I tap the desk, impatiently.

'Ward four,' she says, unimpressed.

I dodge an elderly couple and a heavily pregnant woman as I jog over to the lifts, pushing all the buttons, watching the lights and floor numbers, waiting for one to arrive. When I get up to the ward, I sneak straight in behind a couple of cleaners and a woman in one of those open-backed nighties. I practically leapfrog the desk, startling a nurse making notes in bright green pen on a whiteboard. 'Nurse Davies?' I ask. 'Nurse Kat Davies?' Fuck. All this heavy breathing. 'She left a message for me, I think she has my mum here?' I'm scanning the rooms, hoping for a glimpse of something to tell me she's alright.

The nurse turns to face me; her badge tells me I've got the right person. 'You! You called me! I'm Rhys.' I take a deep breath, wondering when I got so unfit. 'Rhys Woods.'

'Oh, Mr Woods,' she says, surprised. She steps out from behind the desk, ushering me down the corridor. 'I wasn't expecting you to… I thought I'd…' She looks at her fob watch, pointing me in the direction of a Family Room, and my mouth runs dry. I can't help but pause before going in, stopped on the threshold. I've been here before. They all look the same. Smell the same, sort of clean but loaded with a heady mix of bad news and despair. The nurse, Kat, motions me in. I rub my chin, stubble scratching at the palm of my hand, taking one step, then another, finding myself in the middle of a room exactly like the one in which me and Mum were told David couldn't be saved.

We'd found him too late. It was not in his best interests for them to keep him alive.

Kat offers me a chair. I don't sit.

'Are you okay?' she asks. There's no mirror to check and see what she sees, but if my face looks anything like my chest feels… 'Please, take a seat,' she repeats. This time I do as I'm told. She crosses her ankles, rests her elbows on her knees and leans in. Dark brown hair drops forward and she pushes it back behind her ears. She has studs in, tiny gold ones like Mum's. 'Thanks for coming, Mr Woods. My name is Kat, I'm the ward sister.'

'Is she okay?' I demand, impatient with her pace, uncomfortable in this room. 'You rang me. You said you had a lady here. My mum? Is she okay? Please tell me she's okay, because I don't think I can do this again.' I stand back up, pacing the room, its four walls closing in.

'She's fine, it's fine, goodness, I'm so sorry, Mr Woods.' The words pour out of her. 'I didn't mean to alarm you.' The nurse blushes. 'I don't think it is your mum. There's really nothing to… Can I get you a drink?' She stands, trying to catch my eye. She takes off and adjusts her glasses, searching my face, reaching for my arm, squeezing it gently. Her hands are soft but certain, and there's something in her touch that calms me down. 'I don't believe this is your mother, Mr Woods. We don't believe she has any family, in fact. To be honest, it's complicated.'

I let out the biggest breath, rubbing my eyes and stretching out the stress in my arms. I feel like I've just had the worst kind of sugar rush. And then my mobile phone beeps:

'Sorry I missed your call, phone was on silent. Will be home in an hour or so. Call round when you get chance if you like. Mum x'

Fucking hell.

Breathe.

She's okay. She's okay.

I drop back into my chair but it still hits me like a truck: the room, the smells. The rush of ice-cold blood when you realise. Technicolor memories fight my relief that Mum's okay. That today won't end in that ultimate nightmare again: when you wake up one morning and your world is normal, everything seems fine, until the unexpected, the unspeakable, happens. And you go to bed that same day having lost a brother. The tick of a second that spins life 360 and though you're back in the same place, everything has changed. It's unlike anything I've ever experienced, before or since. It wrapped up with me standing in a family room, almost identical to this, wondering how to silence the sobs of a parent who'd lost a part of her, her child, her reason for getting up each day. The child she'd nurtured as a baby, as a teen, as a grown, complex man who never quite knew where he fit in life. I'd stood with her in my arms, crumbling as I tried to hold her up, without knowing if I'd ever understand my own, supremely physical pain. A pain that remains, tied up. Bubble wrapped.

I grit my teeth together as I push it all back down. I clear my throat. She's okay. Mum's okay. She needs to start answering me when I call her, but she's okay. Dropping back down into the chair, I slip my phone into the top pocket of my overalls, behind the logo I know is there: 'Woods Brothers Plumbing'. Brothers. 'Sorry! That was… Sorry,' I say, ruffling my hair to rub away the peak of stress. 'Sorry, okay. I'm fine,' I say, telling myself just as much as her.

'Perhaps we should start again.' Her voice is patient, understanding. She sits back down, beside me this time. Her knee touches mine until I shift position. My heart is returning to its normal pace. Her eyes, deep brown, study me; read my mood, maybe. 'My name is Kat. I am the acting ward sister here. I called you because we have a lady with us for whom we've been unable to identify a next of kin.' I nod, as if I understand. But I don't. 'The only information we could find among her things was your number. In the absence of anything else,' she says, scratching at something non-existent on her skirt, 'I thought it was worth a try.'

'Right...'

'To be honest, I wasn't expecting you to just turn up.' She shifts in her seat. She looks young. I imagined ward sisters to be all middle-aged and mumsy. 'I think I suggested you call us first?' She looks down at some papers, taking her hair out of a clip and scratching at the back of her head before twisting it tightly and pinning it back up.

She looks up at me, chewing the inside of her mouth. 'Mr Woods...'

'Rhys,' I correct.

'Okay, Rhys, can I ask if you know a Susan Smith?'

I rack my adrenalin-riddled brain. 'Hang on, let me think,' I answer. 'I meet a lot of people through my job. I'm a plumber. I mean... maybe I know her...' I pick through customers from recent weeks. 'Did she say she knows me?'

'Well, not exactly, no.' Kat switches the cross of her ankles, letting them rest right over left, at their narrowest point. She holds a file on her lap, her patient's name in capitals printed along the top. Susan Smith. The name does feel familiar. 'Susan isn't actually talking at all at the moment. Hence this all seeming... odd, I imagine.'

'She's not talking?' Susan Smith... There's a memory peeking through the fog. A quiet woman. Small. Whispered tone. But... 'I think I do know her, actually,' I say. The memory comes closer, the grey clouds parting and her face appearing. Her demeanour quiet, but intense. Sort of arresting.

'Your number is the only thing in her diary. We were sort of hoping you might know why that might be?'

'Is this a joke?' I ask, suddenly, jumping up to search the room for signs of a hidden camera. 'Is it Paul? Winding me up? Is he getting me back for that time I tried to set him up on a blind date with an old school teacher of ours? I'm about to be plastered all over MTV, aren't I? At least Beadle's dead, God rest his soul and all that.' I realise this can be the only explanation, though wish he'd found somewhere else to set me up. 'I must say, I didn't have Susan Smith down for joining in with this sort of thing though. Is she here?'

'You do know her then?' says Kat, and I detect her sense of relief.

'Well, I know her, yes. I mean, I don't *know her* know her, but I know her. If that makes sense?' I can hear for myself that it doesn't. 'I didn't realise Paul knew her though,' I add, confused.

Kat pinches at the bridge of her nose then gets up, straightening out her skirt over her knees. 'How would you describe your relationship?' she asks.

'Mine and Paul's?

'You and Susan.'

'Oh, not a prank then?' She shakes her head. 'Well, I don't know… Erm, close enough to make small talk, but I wouldn't rock up to borrow an angle grinder out of the blue,' I joke, then instantly wish I hadn't from the look on Kat's face. 'Sorry, it's these rooms, they… We did some work for her. My brother and I. Like I say, we're plumbers.' I stop, closing my eyes as my heart splinters. 'I'm a plumber. We were there quite a few times in the end, I guess you get chatting. When you spend hours in someone's airing cupboard, you sort of briefly become friends.'

'Right,' she says. 'Friends.'

'Well…' I've overstated it for want of a better way to describe it. 'What happened to her?'

Kat tips her head to one side, holding back her words as if trying to form the correct sentence. 'She had an accident,' she says simply.

'I remember addresses, houses, before people.' The image of Susan's semi-detached house is clear in my mind. Awful carpet, a sort of emerald-green paisley. 'Norton Park Way!' I exclaim, in some kind of eureka moment.

She looks down at the file to check. 'Yes.' She perches on the edge of a chair opposite. 'That's right.'

'Right.' I sit back in my seat. 'Well, yes, then, I do know her.' My eyes flick up to meet hers. Relief has spread across her face and a warning signal grows in my stomach. 'I mean, like I say, I don't know her all that well, but I know her. I started to think she made up jobs for us to do, actually. She always seemed to have something else she needed.'

'She was lonely?'

'She lived with her parents, so…'

'Yeah, it seems they both passed away, just recently. When did you last see her?'

'Oh. I see.' How do I explain that the detail has been erased by life's twisted turn of events, probably only a few days after I last saw her? 'Well, I guess this was last year, late summer, into the autumn. Then perhaps again, earlier this year.' I realise how certain I sound about timing and feel the need to explain. 'My brother—'

'Maybe he could help, your brother?' she says excitedly. 'Is he local? Could we call him?'

'Oh no, he's…' The words suffocate. 'He's not…' I hate the word. I hate saying it. It's as if the moment you say it out loud it becomes true. Which is ridiculous because it is true. But I can pretend otherwise if I don't say it. 'He's no longer with us,' I say quietly. 'He died in March.'

'Oh gosh, I'm so sorry. That's…' She looks around the room as if suddenly adding everything up and hitting the jackpot.

'He couldn't go on, you know?'

'Oh, I see.' That she instantly understands is something of a relief. 'Yes, we have reason to believe that's how Susan ended up here,' she says, quietly. I turn to face her and her hands shoots up, pinching her lips together. 'Oh, not that I should… That's probably not, I shouldn't have told you that.'

There's a pause, then a siren outside, arriving or leaving, I'm not sure which. I remember being in the ambulance, holding his hand as they raced from Mum's to here. He'd already gone but they just wouldn't call it, forcing him to breathe instead. I kept looking at his face, trying to work out why. Why he'd done it. What triggered the course of action that led him to give up. I kept reliving the months leading up to it. I still do. Searching for an answer.

'What makes someone do it?' I hear myself ask. 'What makes someone give up?' Kat shakes her head, but doesn't answer. 'I always think we should have seen it, seen what he was thinking before he…'

She stands and comes towards me, taking my hand to sandwich it between hers. 'Sometimes there's a reason. Something someone can't resolve. Sometimes those around them can make a difference,' she says, searching out eye contact, forcing me to look at her. 'But sometimes we can't. Susan is on her own. No family. No friends either, it seems. If, and I don't really know for certain, but *if* she intended to hurt herself, there'll be a reason. There always is, it's just not always ours to understand.'

I process her words, looking out of the window, recalling the atmosphere the last time I saw Susan. David's mood. They talked, no more than she and I though. I think back to those few short months when it was me and our David against the world. Or that was what I tried to tell him.

'I'll talk to her,' I say.

'It's fine, Rhys. There's no need. Really.'

I catch Kat's eye this time. Hold her attention. 'I'll talk to her. Maybe I can help,' I say. 'They seemed to get on. Maybe they had common ground. Maybe he told her things he didn't say to us. Maybe she told him things.' The more I speak, the more I realise this could be the very thing I need. A chance to understand. And if I understand, maybe I can work through my hurt, maybe I can help.

Kat shifts her weight, looking out of the porthole window in the door. The longer she takes to answer me, the more I realise I need to do this. Because maybe, just maybe, Susan holds the answer to David's end. I look around the room. The walls are covered with images of historic Sheffield: the cooling towers, the roundabout down by the markets, Sheffield's now legendary Hole in the Road. I remember Saturdays, getting off the bus with Mum and David. We'd go down that underpass to see the fish tank. You could see the tops of buses circle the hole, and we'd look up, feeling like ants in some kind of weird fish bowl. We'd get chips, then walk up to the now concreted fountain outside Orchard Square shopping centre. The three of us. I was the big brother. I was supposed to look after him.

'I'll talk to her,' I say.

Before Kat can say anything, I head out of the door, looking up and down the corridor in search of Susan.

'Rhys, wait.' Kat chases after me. 'I should probably…' She tries to get in front of me, and in so doing, leads me in the right direction. 'I just need to check with her,' she says, hurrying backwards to try to intercept me. The end bed, on the ward we've come into, is surrounded by curtains.

Chapter Six

KAT

'Everything okay, Kat?' one of the bank nurses asks me, noticing Rhys surge forward towards Susan's bay.

I'm out of control. I'm out of my depth. 'Sure, yeah, fine, thanks.'

Rhys moves past me. 'Susan?'

'You have a visitor,' I shout over him, trying to sound calm, whilst regaining control of the situation. 'Of course, if you're not up to it, I can always ask him to leave.' I search Susan's face for a response. A hint as to how his arrival makes her feel. Whilst there's nothing obvious, there is a hint of something as her eyes widen on first sight of him.

'Susan,' he says again, his voice less in control this time. The steel he had as he left the family room has dissolved. He studies her face, then down her body to her leg and around the room. She doesn't shift her gaze, which seems to compound his feeling of uncertainty. He smiles then throws a nervous wave. There's another beat before he stuffs his hands in his pockets like a naughty schoolboy, and the change in his demeanour knocks me off balance. Though in theory this is a little unorthodox, my gut tells me to let it play out just a little.

'It's Rhys.' Cough. 'Rhys Woods…' He looks to me, then back to Susan. 'Of course, you know that already, don't you. It's not your memory that's gone, is it? Ha! Or is it? Haha!' Susan stares. 'Um, sorry.' He looks to me. 'Sorry,' he mouths.

The pained expression on his face, combined with the stumble over his words, gives rise to the feeling I made the wrong call here – until I turn and see Susan move her head along the pillow to better face him. There's something in the look in her eyes; it's a picture I've not seen before, a familiarity. They stare at one another and the intensity suffocates me, if not them.

Eventually, he breaks the silence. 'This looks… bad?' he says, pointing to her face, then plastered leg, before hiding his hands again.

'Kat!' A nurse shoves her head around the curtain, pulling on my arm. 'Bed two's had a fall, quick, help!'

'What?' I jerk to follow her, then realise I'm about to leave Rhys and Susan alone.

'Kat!' the nurse shouts.

'Coming! Rhys, Susan, sorry.' I hover half in, half out – torn. He looks at me, but Susan stares at Rhys. 'Sorry,' I repeat, against my better judgement. 'I'll be back in a minute!'

Chapter Seven

RHYS

Nurse Kat has gone. With a sudden, panicked waft of her hands, which I assume is supposed to encourage us to chat amongst ourselves, she's disappeared. Through the slightest gap in the curtain, I see her rush to the more important emergency and out of sight.

Shit.

'So, Susan,' I start, then realise I've prepared nothing to follow up with and my small talk is notoriously poor under pressure. I catch another flash of Kat hurrying past, before she's gone again. It draws my attention to the gap in the curtain and I take inspiration from that. 'Shall I close these?' I ask, pulling the fabric together, layering them one over the other to eliminate any gaps to the outside. Pleased I've reinstated her privacy, I then wonder if I really want to be cordoned off with her, or her with me, so push my hand back between the curtains, wiggling them apart a little. 'I'll leave it like that,' I say. 'Best of both worlds.'

Susan blinks from me to curtain, curtain to me.

This was a bad idea.

Maybe I should leave.

Her hazel eyes are fixed firmly on mine – one more so than the other, where bruising spreads from eye to cheek to jawline. I want to ask her if it hurts. She watches my every move: hands out of pockets, back in. A roll to the balls of my feet, then back to rest on my heels. I hug my arms in tight. She sees it all, just like Mum used to when she was suspicious of me in the garden, back in the days I'd sneak tomatoes from the shed. I make a tiny movement to the left, a change of weight, she follows it. They didn't teach this kind of situation at plumbing school. The art of mute customers was not a module between back boilers and shower installation. Nor was extricating yourself from a customer who may have the answers to all your questions, but not the voice to share them.

And yet, I'm still here.

I go to rest my arm on the contraption from which her leg hangs, but let my arm do a weird hover in mid-air as I think better of it. She watches that too. I opt for perching on the tip of her visitor's chair instead.

'I guess Kat will be back soon,' I say, nodding my head too many times. We sit in silence for a few seconds. The rescue mission continues outside with shouts, an alarm, lots of squeaks of shoes on lino and orders echoing down the corridor outside – occasionally punctuated by a cough from the bed next door. There's a window open; in a pause from the panic, a child shouts down below, a tantrum maybe. I don't know. I was never any good at kids. I pull at my T-shirt and blow my hair from my face. She's still watching me. I remember now, how she stood in the window upstairs, watching as we drove the van away from that last visit.

'Are you okay?' I ask, somewhat stupidly, really. 'I mean, I know this… but… are you…' She blinks. 'I don't generally find I'm called out to customers in situations like these.'

She blinks again.

I think back to the first few times we went to her house.

'Do you remember I tried to persuade you not to bother with all the extra work?' I sit forward. 'All those visits from us. You didn't really need the new boiler, did you?' I lean back slightly in the chair and it squeaks. 'Were you…' I somehow can't bring myself to finish the sentence. If she was lonely – because that's what I assumed at the time, and, I guess, it's what I assume now – is it even my business to know? Is that what drove her to do whatever they think she may have done? Was David lonely too? He had me, he had Mum. A text alert sounds on my phone and I check it. It's from Michelle. He had Michelle.

I swallow. A sense of guilt catches in the back of my throat. I turn my phone off, vowing to look at the message later. Maybe.

'I have a problem with faces…' I say, not really sure where I'm going. 'Terrible. I could probably describe the majority of my client's bathroom suites. Faces though, not a chance.' Susan stares. A gentle and welcome breeze disturbs the curtains. It cools my face and draws away eye contact. I look to her leg, trussed up and plastered. 'Never seen this before,' I say, nodding at the traction. 'Thought it was only ever like this on the telly. You know, Holby or summat.' She looks down at her leg too now, and we're united in a newfound focus. And then a bubble of something ignites a snigger, unwelcome under the circumstances, yet I can't dampen it. The snigger turns to a guffaw, and to my shame, I'm forced to expand on the reason for my inappropriate behaviour considering this ridiculous situation.

'Did you ever see that sketch?' I giggle, feeling worse between the laughter. 'Peter Cook and Dudley Moore. In the leg division, you are deficient,' I say, pointing. 'Sorry.' I try to swallow it all back, but

Susan cocks her head to one side and I could swear she wants to know more. 'He goes to this audition, for Tarzan.' I rub my eyes. 'He bounces in, like literally, he's bouncing.' For reasons known only to the god of all things wrong with this moment, I get up to demonstrate, hopping on one leg in front of her. Susan's head moves slightly in unison with my hopping, which, frankly, doesn't help me put a lid on this. 'The director, Cook, tells him he is deficient. In the leg department. He says Tarzan is traditionally played by a man with two legs, and that with just one, Moore is at a disadvantage.'

God, I wish I wasn't laughing.

'But that he does have the edge on anyone without legs at all,' I shriek, then completely lose it, my laughter no doubt leaking through the curtains and across the ward. But when I gather the strength to open my eyes, Susan's resolutely straight face deflates my hop and I grind to a very slow stop.

'Sorry. Yes. Erm… It was very funny,' I say, resting my hands on my hips, the humour in my story fading fast. 'You probably had to watch it for yourself.' I clear the life-size frog in my throat. 'Mum always says I'm useless in a crisis.' I stuff my hands back in my pocket. 'I got the giggles at our David's funeral, you know.' Susan's eyes flip up to meet mine. Perhaps I should have mentioned this more gently? My tone softens at the memory, stemming the flow of sadness. 'We were heading down Hutcliffe Wood Road. Me, Mum and our David's girlfriend.' I stuff my phone deeper into my pocket. 'I remembered some stupid thing we'd done as kids, when we got into trouble, back in the days when life hadn't pissed on both our bonfires, you know?' Susan swallows. 'He killed himself,' I offer, more bluntly than I think I intended. I shock myself with the words. 'In March,' I add. 'Not long after we last saw you.'

I bite at my cheeks; my heart rate quickens.

If I knew her better, properly, I'd pull her face towards me and search out a response to what I've just said. I'd ask her how that makes her feel. I'd ask her if she just tried to do the same. I'd ask her why.

But there's a breath of air across my face and I don't.

I look around her bed. A change of mood is needed. 'Do you want anything?' I ask. 'A drink? Your cup's here, and some water. Shall I...?'

Susan reaches out for her cup, eyes pinned on mine.

'Here.' I pour, pass, then watch as she sips, grimaces and returns it straight away. 'What? What's up?' I sniff, then take a sip myself. Stagnant water coats my throat, and I fight back a cough as I swallow. 'Jesus, how long's this been here? You can't drink that. Just a minute.' I escape her bedside, pulling the curtains behind me. My legs feel weak; my lungs empty of air. I take a deep breath to renew my strength before heading off in search of water.

Kat is in the corridor, deep in conversation with one of her colleagues. 'Sorry to interrupt. Erm, Susan, she needs a drink.'

'She what?' she says, distractedly.

'Susan. She wants a drink.' I signal in her direction; the water slaps in the jug and I just manage to steady it before any spills. 'This water, it's a bit...' I pull a face. 'Rank. Where would I get fresh?'

Kat looks confused. 'Did she actually *ask* you for a drink? Did Susan *speak*?'

'Well, no, but...'

Kat awaits further explanation. 'You left us alone, so I was just trying to make small talk. I offered her a drink. She had some, but this water's been there too long,' I say, raising my eyebrows accusingly.

'Right, well, great, that's... The water cooler is in the kitchen.'

'Thanks.'

'I'll be back with you both in a moment.' She turns back to her colleague, giving instructions for the patient who took a tumble.

'Sorry,' I say, practically doffing a non-existent cap as I catch her eye again. 'Where's the kitchen?'

'It's just there.' I follow Kat's very slow line of sight to the closed door right beside us. Unmissable letters on a sign make up the word 'KITCHEN'.

'Oh yeah,' I say, pointing. 'Kitchen.'

I push through the heavy door, letting it swing shut behind me. There's an open window at the end of the room. I lean over the worktop to hang my head out of it and wonder how long I could hide here for. And then maybe escape. Shin down the drainpipe. I glance down the seven or eight floors to the ground… Maybe not.

Turning on the tap, water cascades over my fingers until the temperature is cool enough to drink. I replace my fingers with the jug, watching it swill and fill up to the top. I wonder when her parents died. How she felt, suddenly on her own, how she feels. Has she adjusted? Can you ever? Maybe I'm overthinking it. It *must* have been loneliness. In that house with her ageing parents, what life could she have had? She'd said once it was her duty to stay at home, to care for them. Why? Now that her 'duty' was finished, was her life worth ending when effectively it had just begun?

When Dad left, it was me, Mum and our David. The three of us. When I moved out, it was sort of inevitable David would stay. An unspoken agreement. He was younger than me; he didn't feel the urge to cut the apron strings like I had. Even when he got together with Michelle, he made no move to leave. He just seemed better at home. Secure. It's funny – now I think back, I remember seeing him chat to Susan. He'd shown her a photo, something on his phone, and she'd quietly laughed. I remember now, in that moment, thinking that maybe he'd turned a corner. That maybe it was okay he stayed at home. That Susan was okay, however quiet she seemed. But if she did try to end things, she couldn't have been happy. And neither could he.

What drives someone to opt out like that?

I splash brain-freezingly cold water across my face, armour up and fight the wandering thoughts away. Jug full, I head back to Susan. We couldn't help David in the end. But that doesn't mean it's always a lost cause, does it?

Chapter Eight

SUSAN

'Pass us your cup,' he says, his arm outstretched. The water ripples just slightly in the jug. He hands the cup back, gingerly, over full. Water spills as I take it, so desperate am I not to touch him.

'Sorry,' he says, his voice more certain than before he disappeared. 'The shakes and overfill, bad combo.' He quickly brushes my sheet then wipes and dries his hand on his overalls. I let out a long-held breath to take a sip.

Ice cold trickles from mouth, to tonsils, to throat and then belly. The cold makes me shiver but I drink and drain the lot, holding it up for more. I feel wet around the edges of my mouth; Rhys wipes his own as if he has the ice-water moustache.

'Thirsty!' He grins, showing me a tiny sign of the boy he might once have been. 'Here.'

He pours less this time, passing it back as he reaches to place the jug on my table. I hold the cup in my hands, focusing on the contents until I sip, stop and he takes it from me. 'There.' He puts it by the jug, reorganising what little is on my table. I want to reach out and tell him to stop, because, suddenly, his presence is overwhelming. But I can't, I can't tell him anything. Well, I could. But I won't. If I start talking, I make all of this real. I give them a chance to change my mind.

'Great, these, aren't they? These patient stations.' He taps, checking the wood just like he did at my house: the edge of the kitchen worktop when I made him and David a drink; the door to the boiler cupboard as he diagnosed the problem. The roof of his van as he bid me a final farewell, telling me his brother would be about if I needed anything else. He was a broken soul too, his brother. David. I recognised it straight away. It's like an invisible badge of honour that only another broken soul can see, or feel. I'm not sure what it was. I didn't realise just how broken, or even why, but I could see something. I thought I saw it in Rhys, too, but he's not like his brother. They aren't the same. Why would they be?

Rhys is still looking at the wooden box beside me, swinging it around on its castors to get a better view. 'There could be everything you need at your disposal with these things.' He pulls at the stiff doors to reveal empty shelves, except for a box of tissues beside the spare pack of hygiene gloves, or so the cleaner told me when she offered to unpack my bags. He reaches in and pushes them to the back, his arm lost inside the vast emptiness of a cupboard that should store my belongings. The essentials for my stay.

'Where's your bag? I'll unpack for you before I go.'

Don't go, I want to say. My emotions fight each other over what I want, what I feel, what I need.

I blink.

'Your bag?' he repeats, and I stare at him. Does he wonder why he is here? Does he look at me and think anything? Or feel anything? Or suspect anything? Or is it all just a weird coincidence to him? And which version of the events do I prefer?

'What?' he says. 'What is it?' He wipes the back of his hand across his mouth. 'Have I got something on my face? Is it ketchup? I nailed a bacon cob this morning and haven't checked in the mirror.' He reaches back in the cupboard for some tissue. 'Where is it? Point to it.' He leans in a little, I can smell him. Not aftershave, or deodorant. Just him. His smell. He wipes his face. 'That's me all over, that is,' he says, checking his face in his phone. What a knob.' He looks up sharply. 'Oh, language, apologies.' He colours, just as he did the day he swore after dropping a spanner on his knee, the time we sat and talked. David had gone for supplies; it was just me and him.

The curtains around my bed fly open, instantly breaking the spell.

'I am so sorry about that, Rhys, Susan.' Kat's cheeks are ruddy and flustered. She falls in beside Rhys, reaching down to me. I follow her hand; her nails short and tidy, her hand resting on mine. 'Are you okay?' she asks.

Rhys looks to me, then answers on our behalf. 'We're fine… I think. Is the patient?' he asks her.

'I think so,' she starts. 'She will be.' She shakes her head, seemingly ridding herself of any uncertainty. 'Yes, it's fine. All fine.' She smiles, back in charge.

'Are you okay?' he asks, noticing what I had seen too, that she doesn't look okay, no matter how she sounds. He reaches out to her as she did me and I wonder what it might be like, to know someone who cares like that – other than the person getting paid to. To know someone who thinks like that; who reaches out when you look like you need it. A familiar sting bites at my eyes and I close them, searching skyward for the strength to move past the pain.

'Honestly, it's fine. Just a momentary panic. We're a bit short-staffed, that's all.' Her cheeks grow ruddier. 'I can manage,' she says, as an afterthought. I'm not sure who she's trying to persuade.

'Of course.' He peers at her, then nods. 'I was just offering to help Susan get organised. Unpack a bag into her cupboard or something.' He looks around. 'Is there one?'

'She didn't come in with anything, apart from her handbag, I'm afraid. I was rather hoping we'd find someone who could help bring a few things in for her. Hence calling you, you know, just in case.'

'Of course.'

'I wasn't expecting you to just be her plumber.'

'No.'

Just the plumber.

I lift my arm, reaching it up towards him, and in the split second it takes him to respond I realise what I'm doing and snatch it back, thrusting it beneath the covers.

Just the plumber.

I search out creases on the bed, focus on my leg, the toes that point out from my cast. I focus on them as my eyes glaze and everything shifts out of focus. Kat says something to Rhys, nodding for him to follow her. He smiles at me, then disappears through the curtain.

'It's probably best if you go,' she whispers. 'She'll grow tired quickly. Don't worry, you don't have to come back if you don't want to. I mean, she clearly responds to you, I've not seen her engage with anyone before, but, well, I understand if you don't feel able.'

'I'd like to help,' he says quickly, his voice breaking. 'If you think I can, that is.'

'She does seem to want you around.'

There's a pause. I don't breathe.

'Right. Okay then. Well, I'll be back.' I hear him step to move away, then stop, his boots squeaking on the floor. 'Just… keep her water fresh. You know?' There's a second's beat before he moves again.

I count his footsteps: twelve before I can hear them no longer. There's a cough from the next bed. Kat sticks her head back around my curtains. 'Try and get some rest, Susan,' she says. 'I'll come and see you in a while.'

I wonder, if I close my eyes tightly enough, if I'll be able to hold the image of his face until next time.

Chapter Nine

KAT

I retreat to my office, shutting the door firmly behind me; an accepted sign for 'Do Not Disturb'. I groan as I plonk down into my chair, wondering at what point I'll feel I've got this. Wondering if everyone feels like this, like a fraud, like at some point someone more capable will realise I'm not equipped to do 'grown-up' effectively, never mind do so with employment responsibility. I stretch my arms out, nudging my computer, which whirs into action and shows Daniel's Facebook page. It fans the pain I'm trying to ignore. Now isn't the time to be looking at this.

I minimise the screen, then grab my pad to start making a list of jobs to do. Rhys's telephone number is at the top and I sit back to think about his visit, and how Susan looked when he stood by her. How do you describe someone for whom fear and need mix with every breath they take? She was certainly more engaged than the times I'd talked to her on my own. Less dismissive. He wasn't so obviously surplus to her requirements, and yet she was constrained somehow – at least when I was around too – as if she was pinning her mouth and heart closed. The water though, the reaching out to him, something happened. There's something there. Perhaps he is the person to help her. He certainly read what she needed.

My office door flies open. 'Kat! Just the woman.'

Mark stands tall and proud in the doorway, apparently oblivious to the fact that door shut equals knock first. It irks me, but probably only because he made me jump, which always pisses me off. Daniel would do it on purpose, just for shits and giggles. Jump up at me whilst I daydreamed out the window, washing the pots. Hide in the wardrobe when I crept into bed early in the morning after a night shift. Then he'd laugh at me when I would visibly jump, forcing me to punch him on the arm as a result. Mark is still standing in my doorway: feet apart, arms stretched above him. He uses the door frame to steady his weight, and the fleeting vision of frame coming away from door, followed by him face-planting on my office floor, is just about amusing enough to temper my wrath at his barging in.

'I'm on my way out now,' he says, patting his bag as if to prove it. 'But I just wanted to check on Susan Smith before I left. Has there been any progress? Is she talking yet? Someone mentioned a visitor?'

'Yes. He's gone now though.' I leaf through the folder I've just picked out. If I don't engage, he won't come closer. I won't smell him, and therefore Daniel. But like a man with too much confidence, and little understanding of subtle body language, he steps over the threshold. He is now officially in my office. I supress a tut.

'Who was it?' he asks. 'The visitor. Were they helpful? How are they connected? Did she speak to them?'

I flip the folder shut and place it in my in tray for later. 'They don't really know each other that well, to be honest. It was a number in her diary. Turned out to be her plumber.' Mark raises his eyebrows. 'I know, you'd think it shouldn't work, but it did. Somehow, he was helping. I was concerned she was getting tired so encouraged him to leave, but he may be useful, yes.' I say this as if it's a decision I came to ages ago and not one that has just come to me now that Mark's in front of me, hanging on to my every word.

'Right,' he nods. 'Well done, you.'

'Thanks.'

'Plumber though…' he says, thinking. He gives me a wicked look as he leans on the spare chair by my desk. 'Maybe it's a euphemism.' He raises his eyebrows lasciviously. 'Maybe plumber means—'

'I hardly think so, do you?' I interrupt, giving him the kind of look Mrs Shepherd used to give Lou and I in sixth-form assembly, as we giggled over Pete Earnshaw.

'Fair enough,' he smirks. 'As you say, if he's helping. That's great, well done. Brilliant.'

He looks around my desk, eventually picking up a photo of Lou and me from back when we did the all-night charity fundraising walk. I'd quite like to extract it from his hands. And change it for one where I'm not wearing a Madonna bra. And wig. And hot pants that channel *that* John Paul Gaultier outfit. Somewhere on my desk is one of those pens that you tip upside down and the girl loses her bikini. A classic tat gift from someone's holiday. If only I could dig it out and hand it over. Create a diversion, then encourage him to leave me alone so I can make some notes about Susan and Rhys.

'Let the Mental Health team know about the development. They're advising fluoxetine. There's a prescription on the system for her. Can you get it processed, please?'

'Course, what are they thinking?' I search the system as he talks.

'It could be a selective mutism thing. Post-traumatic maybe. The anti-depressant is one treatment for it. Here, I brought you this book about it.' He rummages in his bag, pulling it out along with car keys, tangled headphones and a handkerchief. I didn't have him down as the handkerchief type. 'Present from my grandma!' he says, picking it up and stuffing it back in his bag as he passes the book over. 'There are other approaches, but it's basically about eliminating any stress and increasing all the things that make her comfortable and relaxed.'

I think about her face when she first saw Rhys; a glimmer of something in an otherwise empty soul. I flick through the pages.

'Have a look, familiarise yourself with the symptoms and treatment.'

Still flicking through the pages, I wait for him to leave but he hovers, looking around as if searching for something else to discuss.

'Right!' he says eventually. He turns suddenly and leaves, a Zorro cape short of a swish. Uncertain what just happened, I let my head fall to my hands, cracking my face on my glasses. I pull them off and fling them on the desk, wishing I still had spare contacts in my bag.

'Oh,' he says, sticking his head back around the door. 'I keep meaning to ask…' He looks over his shoulder then steps back over the threshold. I'm forced to put the glasses back on – and vow to go back to those lenses. 'What time are you off tonight?' He drops his voice a little, but not quite enough, considering what he's about to say. 'I wondered if you might like to come out for a curry?'

His words hang in the air between us, suspended by his hopeful eyes and my deep-seated panic. He's holding my gaze properly for the first time, pretty much, since we met. I pull out my fringe from behind my frames, suddenly feeling a little bit warm. My lack of immediate response seems to fluster his usual confidence. 'You'd have to tell me the best place, I'm still finding my way around.' There's a chink in his bravado.

Shit! Does he… Is this… Oh God, is he asking me out?

'Ah, sorry. I can't…' I scour my dazed brain for a reason. A legitimate reason for not joining him for a curry. 'I've got a few jobs to do around the house, actually. Popping to the big B&Q on the way home, have you been? Queens Road. It's massive!' I mime the size with my hands then wish I hadn't. 'Nurse by day, not-particularly-handy handyman by night…' I say, inflecting up at the end of the sentence, which makes me die a little bit inside. I reach for my neck, which for some reason burns to the touch. I pull up my collar, hoping it hides the hives I feel forming in giant telltale splodges across my chest. Do I normally do this when asked out on a date? In my late teens I threw myself into university, letting off steam at Sheffield Uni's infamous Pyjama Jumps down town. Dates were few and far between. Thankfully. Mostly it was nights out on raspberry alcopops and the odd fumble in our Student Union. When I started work, I was focused on that, until Daniel came along and charmed me one night at the Leadmill, watching some live band. In fact, I don't even think he asked me out on an official date. We just sort of… got together. And we stayed together for five years. So I've no idea how to react to being asked out on a date.

'Thanks, though. For asking,' I say, gawkily.

'Right,' he says. 'Course, sure. No problem.'

Oh God. Have I just made a massive assumption? He's new to the area. He has no friends. What if it was just for curry… Oh, that's embarrassing. 'Maybe another time?' I half offer, wondering how long it will take to move on from this most awkward of awkward moments.

'No, no. It's fine. I get it.' He folds his arms, pushing his chest out slightly and clearly searching for the Mr Just-Call-Me-Mark Barnes confidence again. 'To be honest, I'm off tomorrow anyway. If the weather stays this good I might just head down the Wig and Pen with a paper and sink a few pints. Medicinal of course.'

'Sorry!' I say, and the look he gives me is one I've not seen before. Warm. Gentle even. Like someone capable of caring. I'm taken aback, but before I can say anything else he spins on his heel and leaves, again. I hold my breath in case he comes back, but get nothing other than a waft of his aftershave and the feeling I've just made a mistake, though I don't really know why.

There is some chatter outside before the nurses erupt into giggles and someone wolf whistles in the direction of my door. 'Say nothing!' I shout, and they collapse into giggles again.

I can hear my best friend Lou's voice in my head: *Get back on the horse, Kat. Any horse. Don't be picky. Just get on it and ride away those blues.* Except I'm not ready. There's a ping of an email from my computer, and I click to open it, grateful for some distraction. It's from Lou. An update to her Pinterest board with new pictures of bridesmaid dresses and honeymoon locations. Because that's all I need right now – a wedding, to remind me just how lonely I really feel.

Chapter Ten

RHYS

I push open the door to my childhood home, a two-bed, terraced house on the outskirts of Sheffield.

'Mum, are you in?' I shout, taking my boots off and putting them neatly away, as Mum insists all visitors do. It's familiar. It's safe. I moved out nearly ten years ago, but it never felt like I left. Maybe because David was still here, maybe because she didn't bother redecorating my room, despite doing up the rest of the place. When Dad left, this was our happy place. It was our home. The three of us against the world. I run my hand against the wall. Maybe I should move back in for a while.

'Mum?'

The synthetic odour of pine bleach drifts down the stairs; she's cleaning again. She loves to clean. More so since David died. If it were possible for a house to cartoon sparkle, this one would. Diamond glints would emanate from skirting boards, dado rails and shelf tops. Mum's is the only one in the row to have immaculate nets at the window, clipped front gardens and perfectly cleaned windows washed the old-fashioned way: vinegar and the local gazette.

'Hello, love,' she shouts down. 'I'm doing the bathroom. Put the kettle on, I'm proper gasping.'

'You're gonna bleach that new pattern off – I'm not tiling it again!'

I head into the kitchen and fill the kettle, peering out of the window. When I was growing up, I had no idea we lived on the breadline, or that times were in any way tough. My redundant steelworker Dad met a woman on the picket line. Left us without really looking back. For ages we struggled. Hand to mouth, Mum would say. This house was rented off the council for years, till the Thatcher era when, like so many others, Mum was encouraged to buy it. She pushed and worked and borrowed and grafted to keep it in good order, just to give us our own place. Something done without Dad. In spite of him, even. As soon as I could contribute, I did. Bits of cash here and there to help out. My paper-round wages. My bar tips from glass collecting when I turned thirteen. She'd stuff it in the breadbin, only using it when she was desperate. I still do give her cash; she still won't spend it. Maybe she would if I lived here, and at least then she couldn't go AWOL. And I probably wouldn't end up in places I shouldn't.

'Alright love?' She flings fur-trimmed marigolds under the sink, before washing her hands and applying Lily of the Valley hand cream. 'How's work?' she asks with a peck on my cheek.

'Alright. Busy.' I kiss her back, my hand hanging on to the kettle as it boils.

'You're looking peaky.' She reaches for my forehead then eyes me suspiciously, taking a sniff. 'Or is it drink? Have you been out on a bender? Because if you have, I don't approve. You won't get nowhere in life without a bit of hard graft!' She wags her finger at me.

'I went to work!' I say, hands up in submission. 'I haven't sacked the day off to go drinking since I was twenty-two and ended up jamming with the Mexican pipe buskers outside City Hall. I think I've still got one of their ponchos. And, yes, I know, hard graft.'

She softens. 'The biscuits are in the cupboard. Right at the back, on the top shelf. If I hide 'em, I forget they're there and won't eat 'em all. Never mattered when our David was here, he'd finish 'em before I got a look in. He loved a Garibaldi.' She goes to the fridge to bring out a jug of milk she's decanted from the bigger bottle. I've never understood why she does this. 'So what's with your face then, son?'

I go into the lounge; our David's chair is out of place and Mum bustles in after me, shifting it back in its spot. 'Must have forgotten to – well, anyway, do you want the pouffe?' She doesn't wait for my answer, sticking the old leather footstool under my feet. That was David's too. Something he picked up from a flea sale. Mum had complained it probably literally did have fleas, but he refused to chuck it out. Of course, as well as the fleas, it's now riddled with sentimental value. The chair and the pouffe and our bedrooms: all that remain unchanged in a house newly done up with floral wallpaper, velour curtains, statement feathers and too many fake flowers. 'I only have myself to please,' she'd reasoned as we wandered around Atkinson's fabric section, searching for the perfect curtains.

She tidies magazines up, placing them in a rack. 'Come on, spit it out. What's up?'

'It's nowt, Mum. Nothing.' She raises her eyebrows in disbelief. 'Honestly!' I insist. My phone rings, so I reach straight to my pocket for it in the hopes of a moment's distraction. It's Michelle. I cancel the call quickly before flicking the phone on silent and shoving it deep into my pocket.

'Ignoring calls! That could have been work. You are definitely not right. Come on, out with it,' Mum demands.

'Oh, I don't know. It's nothing major, not really. It's just weird. A day I wasn't expecting. Well, a morning really. And you know, it sets you thinking.' I try not to get maudlin about stuff, life is too short, but sometimes, something nags.

'Go on,' she sighs. 'And this better not start with you complaining I didn't call you back either. I got your text. Grown women don't have to check in with their grown-up children.' She stares at the crumbs my biscuit just made, and like the boy I'll always be to her, I pick them up and eat them, saving the newly vacuumed floor. 'Have you been on the shake 'n' vac again Mum?' I don't need her answer, the smell of it hangs heavy in the air: vanilla. 'With that, bleach and hand cream, it's like an impeccably clean tart's handbag around here,' I tease.

'Stop changing the bloody subject and tell me about it,' she snips.

'Okay. So, I went to Mrs Johnson's—'

Sharp intake of breath. 'Has she been flirting again? I swear that woman's obsessed. It's since she moved up to that house, you know. She weren't like that when she lived next door. It's as if living in a semi up the posh end of town has turned her into a nympho or something. She's gone crazy with the power.' Mum all but utches up her chest. 'I just don't get her anymore.' She shakes her head in dismay.

'I don't care to think about Paul's mum and her appetite for sex, thank you very much,' I shudder. 'No, I was doing something with her U-bend and—'

'Was it clean?'

'Was what clean?'

'Her U-bend. I heard she has a cleaner now! Very la-di-da.'

'Mum!'

It's this gossiping and curtain twitching that reminds me why I moved out in the first place. I hated it then, and I still do now. I think it's a distraction, a displacement even, and it's the only reason she still has nets. Bright, white lace to hide behind as she noses on everyone else's business. 'So, my phone goes,' I explain. 'But I didn't get to it in time. Anyway, there's a message left on my voicemail, a nurse, telling me they'd got some woman in hospital with them.'

Another sharp intake of breath from Mum suggests she is beginning to enjoy the prospect of a drama. 'Go on,' she encourages.

'Obviously, since we haven't spoken since yesterday afternoon, I assumed it was you. I panicked and legged it over there—'

'I hope you drove carefully, Rhys Desmond Woods.' I hate it when she uses my full name. 'There's no use killing yourself just to get to me. It's no secret your van is a death trap.'

'Well, it wasn't you, was it?'

'No, course it wasn't.' She coughs. 'I've been here all day.'

'Didn't know that though, did I, Mum?' I throw her a look, then dodge the clip around my ear as she moves to straighten out the side table. 'All I knew was they had a woman in hospital and I hadn't been able to get hold of you all night again. Can't you at least text me when you go to bed? Or get up? Or both?'

'I'll do nothing of the sort.' She sits back down, arms and legs crossed, with her elbow resting on the side of her chair that has begun to wear.

'You used to.'

'That was then, things change,' she says.

'Well. Anyway, it wasn't you.' I rub my face with my hand, still trying to download and compute the events – not to mention the subsequent stoked emotions, flames from burning embers. 'Somehow, I ended up sat with this woman for half an hour before I was asked to leave.' I take a sip of tea. 'Her drinking water was stagnant.

I know they're understaffed, but really? It's a good job I checked it for her.'

'Who was it then?'

Mum can smell a story at twenty paces and it'll be down the bingo hall before the day's out. But I'm interested to know if she can shed any light, if Susan is more than just a customer to me. To the family. 'Susan Smith.' She trips through her mental Rolodex of names, clearly desperate to find 'Smith, Susan'. Gossip is always better if people know the protagonist. 'I knew a Susan Brown once,' she says. 'Awful woman. Flame-red hair. Total hussy.'

'Yeah, it's not her.'

'And a Susan Killigrew too. Do you remember her? Your dad had a soft spot for her – not that she was the only one, mind, but we won't go there. Him and Killigrew were childhood sweethearts. Nice woman. Ran the paper shop for a while, stopped doing it when she had her fourth. Last I heard, she'd gone up Scotland.' I don't remember her, not that Mum was waiting to see. 'Susan Smith though... I don't know a Susan Smith.' She's disappointed. And so am I.

'No, I thought not.'

Mum grimaces at her tea and takes it back into the kitchen, presumably for more milk. 'Do you think it's weird she only had my number with her?' I shout through.

'You never know when you might need a plumber, love.' Mum comes back, drinking her tea, this time without the grimace. 'Presumably you asked her?'

'She doesn't talk.'

'She's dumb?'

'I don't think you can say that anymore, Mum.'

'I'll say what I like, I don't mean owt by it.'

'Yeah, still though. I don't…'

'Look, whatever, Rhys, finish that Garibaldi then I can put the tin away. Not your problem anymore, eh, love.' She winks, presumably thinking she has put an end to the conversation. Whipping my cup and the biscuit tin away, she kicks the pouffe back to the wall. 'Now, enough talk about strangers and solitude. I wanted to talk to you.'

'What?'

'Well, you know how… The thing is… You see…' I sit back, watching as Mum gets up and busies around the lounge. 'You're not going to believe it,' she says, laughing. Then she stops, looks out of the window and peers at the back garden. 'The postman's been stealing money out of birthday cards.' She turns to face me. 'And…' She sits back down. 'Doreen down the road's 'ad a new hip and apparently she can dance again.' I look up at her, confused. 'It's amazing!' she says, clapping her hands with glee.

'Good… Lovely…' I'm not sure what response she's actually after.

'They thought she was going to have to move into sheltered accommodation, for help and support and that, but not now! Isn't that brilliant!'

I'm in agreement that this is brilliant, but not sure what it really means to me. Or her. Or Susan, laid up in that hospital bed all on her own.

'The hospital bed swamped her you know, Mum. She looked tiny.' I've said it out loud before I realise.

'She's not your responsibility, love.'

'No, but—'

'But nothing, love. Don't get drawn in. You've enough to think about with work and life and stuff…' She pauses. 'We both have.'

'They don't think her accident was an accident,' I say, looking into my cup at the bubbles in my tea.

'Oh. I see,' says Mum, putting her cup down. We sit silently for a second. I know she's thinking the same as me. Anything like this takes you straight back to the moment you find the person you love... like that. 'You know you can't rescue people, Rhys. Don't you?' Her voice is small, wrapped in hurt. I nod, because it's easier that way. We've always had to agree to differ on this point. 'She isn't yours to save any more than our David was,' she adds. I rub my eyes, refusing to give in to how I feel.

She picks up a cushion, smoothing down the feathers and stretching out the corners. 'You alright, Mum?' I ask. I can always tell when she's got more to say; she seems to perch on the end of her words. Usually a gentle nudge does the trick. 'What's up?'

'Nothing's up. I just... We all have our own stuff going on.'

'Like what?' I ask, studying her face as she reaches for another cushion. 'I don't know, Rhys, just stuff, gosh, stuff.' There's a pause. A stilt in our chat. 'I'm more than the sum total of mother and divorced housewife, you know!'

'Course you are, I know that, Mum.' I look around the lounge, the pictures of flowers and words of wisdom on the walls. The picture of me and our David. 'I wondered if I should move back in, you know.' She looks up sharply. 'Just for a bit maybe, I feel like... I need you. And maybe you need me?' I ask, hopefully.

'You don't need me, love. You need life. And besides, I'm fine. There's plenty around to keep an eye on me.'

'Like who?' I say, incredulous. 'We both know them lot down the bingo would sell their mothers given half a chance.'

Mum checks her watch, and glances towards the front door. 'I have... people who care,' she says. She gets up and moves a few pots about on the mantelpiece. 'I've got stuff to do, love. Get yourself off.

We can talk about this another time. Let's not rush into anything. And don't go worrying about this Susan woman either. Like I say, not your responsibility. Here's your keys. Call me tomorrow, okay?'

'Okay, alright. I'll ring you later,' I say, but Mum gives me the look, then bundles me out of her house. 'And what's changed?' I say, remembering what she said, but she's already closed the door.

I climb in the car, pulling out my workbook from the glove box, flicking back through the pages, today, yesterday, last week, last month. It's all my handwriting to begin with, then I get to March and it becomes a mixture of mine and David's. I go back as far as last November and see an entry: 'Susan Smith. Outside pipe. Norton Park Way.' Next to her phone number is a tick to show it had been sorted. I fling the book on the passenger seat and drive home, detouring down Norton Park Way.

As I drive down the road, it becomes more familiar. I remember next door had a brand-new van on the drive. A VW T5. I'd said to David how I wanted one, that maybe we should get a loan out, get the van all liveried up with our names. He'd not been fussed. I slow down by her house. The T5 is still parked next door. Susan's own little brown fiesta is parked on the driveway. Tiny trickles of memory begin to filter through – and I'm on her landing. Explaining that we've done the outside tap and that she doesn't really need a new boiler too. Trying to dissuade her from spending money she doesn't need to spend. She was insistent though. She said that if I didn't do it she would get someone else. She was quiet, but firm. It was an odd mix. David had shrugged, as if to say, *if that's what she wants.* She mentioned names of people she could call and I knew they'd overcharge her, take advantage. We agreed to come back and do some basic maintenance. Sort out a few bits and bobs. I said that if I was wrong and she needed to replace the boiler within twelve months, I'd give her a discount. By the third visit, she persuaded us to come back again and fit the new boiler. That was another couple of days' work.

All in all, I must have spent five or six days working in her house, and David spent another two. In fact, I was there so long, and talked so much, I joked about paying her for therapy. How had she seemed when I left her house that last time? Were there signs? Like the ones I now know we missed with our David? But I barely knew her, and I don't suppose I'd have noticed even if there were. She was quiet, but I wouldn't say sad. I guess there was something I can't quite put my finger on – something different about her. Chatting to customers goes with the territory. But somehow, this had been different.

Chapter Eleven

KAT

The second thing I do when I get home is hurl myself onto the sofa. The first thing, obviously, was to put my pyjamas on. I don't care if it's only 6.30 p.m. and still a heady twenty-six degrees outside – I am so very over today.

I've now lived on my own for the full six weeks (two days, et cetera) since Daniel left. And whilst I am trying to adjust to this whole living-on-my-own thing, because there is a certain luxury in being able to wee with the toilet door angled perfectly to continue watching *Scott & Bailey* through the mirror, there are also times I wish I wasn't alone. Not necessarily that Daniel was still here, not if he doesn't want to be, I suppose, but just that I wasn't alone. Maybe that I had a flatmate. Or someone who understands how I like my steak – medium-rare with jacket potato and my bodyweight in Roquefort – or who appreciates that opening the Pinot is a priority. Perhaps someone who enjoys washing the pots. I can almost hear them taunting me – the pots, that is, not my imaginary flatmate. They're all dried-in stir-fry and crusted milk. What did I do before he moved in? When this place was mine and mine alone. When I was solely responsible for its upkeep. For the pots. What happened to make me so rubbish as a singleton?

I reach for my bag, which rests against the last box of Daniel's shit that he still hasn't collected. Stuff he didn't bother packing when he cleared the rest of the flat out. When he walked out with the iPad and the Bose speakers and too many phone chargers. When he took the cushions he hated and the bedding I bought. I don't know why I bothered packing up the photos and pictures and the clay pot he made when he was six. We only ever used it for the car keys, which are something else he took: the keys to our brand new Ford Focus, Freddie. Still, I guess he also picks up the bill and massive loss in value since driving it off the forecourt. Karma.

He clearly doesn't care about the sentimental value of any of this stuff, but why does he think I want his school 'treasures'? They're a reminder of the kind of slightly crap pottery our children would have brought back… Well, had I ever had a chance to persuade him to have them. He'd always been adamant he didn't want them. Had too much he wanted to do, no time for kids. *They're a bleed on your bank balance*, he always said. I thought he'd come around to them one day, maybe I was wrong. Besides, why should I have to take this box of mementoes to him? He forgot it, he should come fetch it. Then maybe we could talk. Work out what happened. Start again?

Unless he really does have a new girlfriend.

Or I find the strength to believe what part of me thinks: that I deserve more than someone who doesn't really care, even if for years I thought he did. Even if for years, I forgave him his quirks, like the fact he found public displays of affection abhorrent. I accepted that. It didn't matter. Because I loved him.

I can feel a hiccup-cry coming on. I'm overtired.

Or maybe I'm just beginning to realise that it really *is* over.

How could he fall out of love so quickly? So completely. Am I that unlovable? I yawn, then growl out loud. I can't keep doing this – I can't. I'll never move on, I'll never sort myself out. And what's the alternative? Spending the rest of my days pining for him? I switch the telly on to chase away my thoughts, to drown out the silence of being here alone. I channel hop until I find a rerun of *Friends*, the one with Joey and Janice's day of fun.

I pick out my notebook from my bag; Rhys's mobile number stands out on the top of the page. That's something I hadn't foreseen in my future when I set off for work this morning: the arrival of an overheated plumber who would crumble in my family room. He was pretty shaken up, which panicked me to begin with – I really didn't want to start my first day as ward sister by making a rookie error – but there's no denying he came into his own with Susan. Mark's book backs up the theory that Rhys could be helpful to her. I guess, if he's up for helping, there's no real harm. If I'm going to get Susan to talk, she needs to feel supported and nurtured. She needs comfort and security. If Rhys brings that, we need to make the most of it. Of him.

I aimlessly doodle as I process the pros and cons to this course of action. Ten minutes pass and I look down to see a pad full of detailed, scribbled squares, malformed 3D boxes and a million shaded triangles. The ring of my mobile phone jolts me back to now and I fumble to answer. 'Hello?'

There's a sniffle on the end of the line, and a tiny voice says, 'Kat?'

It's my brilliant, if slightly melodramatic – read: high maintenance – best friend, Lou. 'You frightened the crap out of me then. I was just…' The sniffles ramp up a gear so I change tack. 'Hey, Lou-Lou!

What's up?' Experience tells me to rearrange myself and get comfy, Lou's sobs suggest this call will be a long one.

'It's him.' Sob. Sniff. 'He is a shit and the wedding is off!'

'Again?' I say, because I've lost count of how many times she has called this wedding off. It's almost as if she's doing it for effect.

'Yes. But I mean it this time.' Nose blow. 'You won't believe what he said to me.'

'What, Lou? What did he say?' I lean my head back, eyes closed.

'He told me we can't afford to go on honeymoon to Jamaica and we should either scale the wedding back or go on honeymoon next year. I mean, who even does that? Who takes their honeymoon a year after their wedding? And if I am good enough to marry, why am I not good enough to save up for and take on a five-star retreat to Jamaica?'

The deep sigh I release goes unnoticed by Lou. Every deep sigh I've ever released since our friendship started in 1998 has gone unnoticed by Lou. 'I suppose you could ask yourself the same question, chuck.'

'What? What do you mean?'

'I mean, if he's good enough to marry, why is he not good enough to wait for the honeymoon for?'

'You're not being fair, Kat. He said he'd take me somewhere nice but to leave it with him. I mean, this is my wedding, I'm only ever going to do this once and I want it ALL to be perfect. Don't I deserve that?'

'Of course you do, Lou, but if the budget won't stretch and Daddy won't pay up, it's a no go.'

'Daddy will pay, but Will won't let him.'

'It is Will's wedding too, you know.' I open my eyes and study the slice of sunlight cast across the ceiling from my part-closed kitchen door. 'Look, don't write him off. Any man who can put up with you deserves a chuffin' medal, therefore Will doesn't deserve grief over the fact he can't furnish you with your every wish. Life isn't like that.' Not that Lou would know – Mummy and Daddy aren't short of a bob or two.

'A medal? Do you think I'm hard work to live with? Do you think he has to put up with me?' she whines.

A cloud passes over, fuzzing the slice of sunlight. 'You have your moments.'

There is a reason I have never flat-shared with my best friend of forever and a day. I happen to know that not only is Will planning to take Lou to Jamaica on honeymoon, but he has booked a three-week, all-inclusive, five-star hotel at £500 per night. Unbeknown to her, he is preparing a ceremony where they can renew their vows in private – despite the fact they will only just have got married – and he has organised a special dress for her to wear for the occasion, because he knows she will love the whole thing. He shared this secret on a night out down West Street.

'Look, Lou. Don't be a princess about it all. You two are perfect for each other, and he will only ever do the absolute best he can do for you. If it means waiting for the right time, then wait. He'll make it worthwhile, I promise.'

'Do you think so?' she sniffs.

'I wouldn't have said it if I didn't.' I pick at, and pull out, a feather from the sofa that's been sticking into my leg. It's long and white, and floats gently to the floor as I drop it.

'Aww, you are right, you know. We are perfect for each other, aren't we.'

'You are.'

'Bless him, I really love Will.'

'You do, Lou. Thankfully he loves you too.'

'Yeah. He does. Aww.'

I can picture the doe-eyed look she'll now be sporting. If she had a cord on her receiver, she'd be twiddling it in 1950s pin-up fashion, looking down at a pewter-framed photo of her future husband, the only man who's ever loved her for who she is: a right royal pain in the arse, with a heart of solid gold.

'So, Nurse Kathryn of Sisterhood,' she says, her mood instantly lifted. 'How has your day been? Any hunky doctors joined the team, anyone you could strike up a friendship with? Or even a fuck buddy – surely you need one of those? They can heal over, Kat!'

And just like that, the drama is over.

'They cannot heal over, Lou. That is a medical impossibility. Besides, it wasn't that long ago.' Which is part of the problem. I never saw it coming. We had sex the night before he dumped me – surely that's not the sign of a broken relationship? 'I don't need a man, Lou, I have told you this before.' I have told her that. And amongst the pain, I do believe it. Maybe I should get it made into a fridge magnet. A reminder each time I top up my wine, whilst microwaving a meal for one.

'I know you don't *need* a man, chuck, we can see you are an independent woman of independent means, and we largely admire you for it.'

'Largely?'

'Yeah, well, you know. Sometimes you might do well to soften up a bit. You can be a bit… what's the phrase… buttoned up. That's it. You can, though, you know.'

'Buttoned up? Where've you heard that phrase? Do you even know what it means?'

'It was on *Call the Midwife*, and of course I do.' I notice she doesn't explain, but life's too short to push her.

'Look, you know what I mean. You need to get out. Live life. See people. Do you even remember the last time you went on a date?'

I shudder at the thought of it, a thought I've buried deep amongst the student debauchery. It was a couple of months before I got together with Daniel. So roughly five years ago. An ex-colleague set me up with her brother's flatmate. He wanted to show me his reptile collection, and though he assured me this was not a euphemism, it turned out it very much was.

'You know I have a recurring dream about a python, Lou.'

'Oh yeah,' she says, remembering. Lou is the only person who knows about that date. 'It wasn't one of your better dates, was it? You could at least have had some fun on the holiday that never was.' Lou is also the only person to know the truth about my bailing out on that one. 'You said you were going to shag your way around the archipelagos.'

'I know.' I think I probably did say that. I like the word archipelago. In fact I was only going to Lesbos.

'And a road closure is not a good reason to miss check-in,' she says disapprovingly.

'I nearly missed check-in.'

'Nearly. But you didn't.'

'No.'

Both of us hold out to see who will break the silence first. I have a good track record in forcing her hand. It's about the only thing I can do in our relationship, but this time, I break first. 'Look, cut me some slack. I am on the edge of a tightly controlled, emotional cliff-top right now.'

'Ahh, babe. I know. Look, never mind. It happens. Will has a couple of single ushers. Maybe there will be someone at the wedding you could hook up with!'

'So it's back on then!'

'It was never *really* off. As if I'd not marry my Will.'

'As if indeed.'

'Oh, hang on, babe, I've got to go. Will's back from work and after shouting at him on our last phone call I think I'd better slap some lippy on and show him how sorry I am. Love you, bye, bye, bye.' She hangs up.

'Love you, bye.' I say into the ensuing silence. I'm left with an image of Lou's own particular style of sex-crobatics, burned onto my retina from the time I accidentally walked in on them both on a weekend away in Robin Hood's Bay. Every time she talks about sex, I'm back in their room.

I try to shake it off, looking around the flat. Having not made it to B&Q, all the little jobs seemed to stand out. It's been long enough; I really should get this place sorted. *I* bought this flat. *My* name is on the deeds. But until he moved in, I guess it wasn't a home. Just a place to crash and burn. Nothing's changed in here since the day I came home to find he'd moved out after sending the text. It was like someone had thumped me in the gut with a removal van. He had taken almost everything, except for my grandma's dining table and a threadbare rug I'd bought on a whim. When I'd first brought it back, he'd sneered, then placed it beneath the dining table, refusing to have it in the lounge. I should have seen it coming then; things could never work out with a man who couldn't put up with a rug. 'Bollocks,' I say, the frustration lost in my empty flat. Then I get up, and pull and push the dining table enough to release my rug from its hiding place.

'It's vintage, not threadbare,' I mutter, holding up the table with my shoulder and pulling it out. I drag it into the middle of the lounge, yanking it straight and standing back to admire it. The waft of air as I drop it fans the feather back up in the air. I catch it, placing it on the side. My lounge. The last box of his stuff taunts me from the corner, so I shift it to the front door. If he won't come and get it, I'll take it to him. I ignore the chin wobble and the stinging eyes, and instead I nod, folding my arms as a final act of Fuck You. Then I wipe salty tears from my cheeks and make myself Coco Pops and Pinot, like any good woman in control of her own destiny should.

Maybe Lou's right. Maybe I should get out there. See people. Maybe it will help. Maybe I should have gone on that date with Mark, or whatever it was. Or Rhys – he's attractive. Maybe he's single. Not that that is any more appropriate than dating a consultant.

Maybe I should download Tinder…

Maybe not.

My pad sits to my left, Rhys's mobile number surrounded by the badly drawn procrastination. Too late to call? Or text, maybe? Slightly scared by my train of thought, I rip the page from the pad, screw it up and throw it in the rough direction of the bin, missing. Work. That's what I'll concentrate on. Work. And Susan. I get up and head into the bathroom. I stare at the reflection. The glasses. The hair. I google Nana Mouskouri, vowing to go back to my contacts from tomorrow.

Gripping my fringe back makes me look more like I did before the crisis kicked in. Maybe I'll drop that box up to Daniel's mum's. Just in case…

Chapter Twelve

RHYS

It seemed like a good idea at the time. Pick up some flowers and a few bits and bobs. Take them over to the hospital to show Susan that someone cares. That she isn't alone. Use the opportunity to sit for a while and chat, see if maybe I can get her to open up.

Except, as each floor number shines bright in the lift, a niggle forms in the back of my head. As the doors open I begin to acknowledge that this isn't entirely an act of altruism. Or whatever that word is. I walk towards the ward. I'm being selfish. I felt compelled to come, like I needed to see her again, but this is less about doing something nice and more about satisfying something deep inside of me that says *don't walk away*.

A nurse holds open the door on her way out. I pause, considering what Mum said. Susan's not my responsibility. You can't save those who don't want to be saved. But before I can turn around to leave, she is wheeled back through the ward and she sees me standing there, flowers in hand. Being helped back into bed, she shifts her body, trying to sit up as I walk towards her. There's a look on her face, a knowing look, and whatever my motives for being here, it actually feels like it's right. Besides, maybe you *can* save people.

'Good morning,' I say, aware the nerves are dissolving. The questions I have are quieter, more muted.

'Hi,' says the nurse tending to her.

'I brought Susan a few bits and bobs.' I offer up the bag of stuff by way of justification.

'Are you up to visitors, Susan?' she asks. I'm almost certain the corners of Susan's mouth hint at a smile. Or perhaps I just want them to.

'Okay. Lovely.' The nurse turns to me. 'Just, go steady. She tires very quickly at the moment.'

'Of course.' I nod and take a seat beside her. She's had her hair washed. Fine silver strands fall across the bruising, which is beginning to morph from red and purple to orange and yellow. 'Your face looks autumnal,' I joke. She moves her hand up to gently touch her cheek, pushing the hair away. 'You're looking great,' I try to reassure her. 'I hope you don't mind me dropping by again. I was passing on my way to a job and thought you could do with a few things, assuming you haven't had any other visitors who've beaten me to it.' I look around for signs that I'm not required, aware of an odd relief when I see nothing. 'So, how are you today? Have you been practising your dance moves for when you get out?'

I reach into the bag for the flowers. 'Carnations,' I say. 'My granddad used to grow them in his back garden; I thought you might like them.' She reaches to pick them up, rubbing her fingers over sugar-pink, ruffled petals. 'I've never bought flowers for anyone before,' I say. 'Not even my old mum. In fact, handing these over is like a statement of commitment in itself, isn't it? Before I know it we'll be married with dogs and you'll knit us matching jumpers.' I stop short of suggesting names for our children. Little bit weird.

Susan looks down at the bag.

'Grapes, do you like grapes? I know, it's a bit stereotypical, grapes for the sick and all that. But you know… no pips. Here.' I stuff a couple in my mouth, before attempting to say, 'Try one.'

She reaches towards the bag, dipping in for a handful. My shoulders drop and I lean back in the chair as she takes the rest of the brown paper bag, letting it rest in her lap. 'I popped down the market first thing – these are as fresh as you like. None of your supermarket shit.' She looks at me. 'Sorry.'

I reach down into the carrier bag for the not-quite-ready-to-eat bananas, placing them on her table along with squishy peaches. 'These need eating today,' I say. 'They were on offer, to be fair.' I roll the sides of another paper bag down to fashion a bowl, and try to balance all the fruit within it. As a peach topples, I realise I've supplied her with a small grocer's worth. 'You could pass some around, I suppose.' She hands back the grapes and I add them to the pile, eating the ones that won't sit. 'Now, tell me,' I say, scrunching the empty carrier into my pocket. 'How did you sleep?'

There's a flicker of something across her face, an involuntary answer to my question, perhaps. I wait for a second, just in case. She swallows.

'Juice?' I reach for the orange juice I bought her. 'It's got bits,' I say, shaking it, then twisting the cap to pour her a glass.

'Rhys!'

Kat's voice makes me jump and I spill some of the juice.

'Sorry, here.' She plucks out tissues from Susan's supply and wipes at my leg before opting to take the juice bottle and letting me mop myself up. 'Sorry, I didn't mean to…' She looks at Susan. 'He's back!'

'Well spotted.' I laugh – then cough, then stuff the sodden juice tissue in my pocket. 'I just, I was aware Susan didn't… I wanted to help and…' Somewhat pathetically, I point at the fruit and say, 'I brought grapes.'

'Lovely…' Kat looks from me to Susan to the fruit and then back to Susan, who I'm relieved is showing no obvious signs of distress, before looking back to me. The juice from the tissue is now seeping through my pocket. I give in and retrieve it, letting it flop into the bin.

'Lovely,' she repeats.

'It's nothing.'

'I'm sure Susan doesn't see it that way.' Susan picks out another grape. 'Well, it's lovely to see you again, but I have a few checks I need to do, I'm afraid. Could give us some privacy for a moment?'

'Sure, of course. Look, I need to get to an appointment now anyway, perhaps I can swing by later. Will you still be here?' I'm looking at Susan.

'She'll still be here,' says Kat, glancing quickly at the contraption Susan's leg is trussed up in, largely committing her to her bed for the foreseeable.

'Ha! Course. Well, not ha… but you know.' I reach into the mock fruit bowl for one of the peaches. 'You don't mind, do you? For work.' I flick it in the air, letting it ricochet off my arm, almost dropping it instead of catching it slickly in my hand, like they do on the telly. Idiot. 'You want one?' I ask Susan, throwing her one to catch, which she does. 'Great. I'll see you later then. Good.' I point at them both, stepping backwards away from the bed as Kat raises her eyebrows. Susan slurps at her peach and I'm reminded of the time I used to visit my nanan when she was in the home. It was never for very long, just passing through, really, but Mum always said how much of a difference it made to Nan's day. How it lifted her spirits. Yet somehow, this time, it's my spirits that are lifted.

Chapter Thirteen

KAT

I rest my head against the sandwich machine. Money in, eeny meeny miny mo-ing between chicken salad and a BLT. Emma's arm reaches across and presses for the BLT. 'I hear you were invited on a hot date last night.'

I step back as she pulls open the vending drawer, motioning for me to collect my lunch before opting for the same herself. She pauses, shoves more money in, then retrieves a bag of prawn cocktail crisps like a giddy kid with a school trip pack-up. 'Well?' she says, winking repeatedly as she waits for me to catch up.

'Wow. That didn't take long to find its way around. Also, prawn cocktail, really?' I grimace. The chocolate machine tempts me into a mid-afternoon pick-me-up. 'Actually, I was invited for curry, which may or may not have been a date, but was, in either case, as awkward and awful as you might imagine. I'm barely over the trauma.'

'He isn't that bad, you know,' she chides. 'You're single. He's single. I don't know what your problem is.'

'My problem, dear friend, is…' I try to work out what the problem actually is, opting for, 'He wears the same aftershave as Daniel.' It's not the strongest of problems, but it's a problem all the same. We push through the ward doors, squeezing splodges of sanitiser and simultaneously hand rubbing like we're hatching a dastardly plan.

'He has higher-than-average looks and seems to be a nice bloke too. You're being short-sighted if you ask me!'

'I didn't ask you,' I grumble.

'Speaking of which, where has the foxy face gear gone? Have you just spent hundreds on new glasses to return to the safety of contacts?'

'They weren't hundreds. And I should never have been talked into them. They weren't me.'

'They could have been,' says Emma, sitting down opposite my desk. She looks at me with a face that suggests she knows me better than I know myself and I ruffle my fringe back down as if to prove a point. Emma takes a bite of her sandwich, looking smugger than someone with mayo on their cheek ever should. She leans across, dropping bacon from her sandwich on my desk. 'Have you seen his arse, though?'

'Emma!'

'I know, I know,' she says through a mouthful of BLT. 'Inappropriate klaxon. It's just, things have been a bit slow round these parts of late!'

I ignore the parts to which Emma is gesturing. 'If you're so interested, why don't YOU hop on that bandwagon, as it very much were?'

'What bandwagon?' says Mark, suddenly standing in my office. Because of course – of course! – the bandwagon would arrive at the very moment we're talking about it. My chest tightens at having almost been caught out. Emma, her face hidden from his view, goes wide-eyed and cocks her head, giving me the sign for has-it-just-got-hot-in-here, she's all wafting nurse uniform and blown-out fringe.

'Nothing,' I say. 'No bandwagons. Now, what can I do for you?'

He eyes us both suspiciously. 'I just wanted to let you know that the mental health team are coming in tomorrow for a meeting about Susan. I'd like you to attend it with me.'

'I won't be in until 1 p.m. tomorrow. I have an appointment in the morning. A bridesmaid dress fitting actually.' He raises his eyebrows. 'I can try and change it?' I offer, not daring to imagine Lou's response if he says yes.

'No, no, it's fine. The afternoon is better anyway. I'll make it 4 p.m.'

'Of course, absolutely.' I pick up my pen and scribble the details in my diary.

Mark looks between me and Emma, his mouth open as if to say more, then stops. 'Great, thanks. See you tomorrow.'

'Yep. See you tomorrow, 4 p.m. sharp,' I reply, flipping my diary shut in an unnecessarily efficient fashion. 'Have a good day,' I finish, failing to lessen the pomp.

'You too.'

He hovers, then exits, leaving Emma to whistle out loud. 'Well, you could literally cut *that* with a knife!'

'Cut what?' I ask.

'The sexual tension.' She says it in the kind of way your mum would. Not really wanting to say the word sex out loud but not quite mouthing it either. 'Surely you felt it!'

'Oh, for fuck's sake, get a grip, woman. Also, why have YOU gone pink?'

'I haven't,' she says. 'And fancy that, a manager swearing.'

'I'm allowed. And also piss off.'

'Power mad, that's your problem.' She bins her empty sandwich box. 'Anyway, if you want to pretend you don't want conjugals with the hot doc, let's move on. What's happening with Susan?'

I bite my tongue to save any further response. 'Pretty much the same, though Rhys came back.'

'Did he?'

'Yeah, with half of Interflora and a year's supply of fruit, it seems.'

'Wow. Nice. Or creepy?'

'Mmm, not sure.' I pick at my food, thinking.

'What?'

'I don't know, there's something… strange.'

'Strange how?'

'I don't know.' I place my sandwich down, suddenly not terribly hungry. 'Sweet, I think, but… it's weird. I walked in this morning and they were like bookends, all mirrored body language. I keep wondering if the plumber story is just that, a story. It's as if they really *know* each other.'

Emma finishes her crisps then reaches for my chocolate, opening it up and breaking herself a piece off. 'Get your own,' I say, stealing it back and pretending I wasn't just about to hide it in the drawer for later. It's fine. I can share. 'And if it is a story, why? To what end? I think I'll let it unfold a bit. He threw her a peach, you know.' Emma looks at me blankly. 'She caught it,' I say, as if that explains everything.

'Oh, well. That's that then. Road to recovery right there.'

'Sarcasm equals lowest form of wit!'

'Pot and kettle springs to mind.'

'My point is, Susan responds to Rhys in a way she doesn't to us. She engages with him, through actions if not words. She listens to him. I don't think she pays attention to a word I'm saying.' Emma mock yawns. 'Yes, you're hilarious.'

'I know I am. Look, if his visits help then it's worth it, isn't it?'

'Yeah. I guess.'

'See what happens then, as you say. Besides, what harm can he do?' She gets up to leave. 'Oh, and Kat?'

'Yeah?'

'Hot consultants can sometimes provide efficient distraction from social media stalking.'

I snap my head up to look at my computer screen, which has woken up, showing Daniel's Facebook page again.

'Old Chinese proverb. Or something.'

She winks, launches the rest of her lunch rubbish in the bin and leaves me to hover my mouse over the log-out button. God, I miss him. I can't help it. I just... I miss having someone to share my day with. To offload the stress of this new responsibility. Would I tell him about all of this – Susan, Rhys? Maybe not details, but principles. And by talking, I'd work through new ideas. I pinch at my nose, my other hand still resting on my mouse. I also miss his arms, his hands kneading away knots in my shoulders, tension in my neck.

I look again at the photo I'd been gazing at earlier. I took it when we were out for a meal to celebrate our fifth anniversary. Then I notice something, something I hadn't seen before, despite all the times I've looked at it. Daniel's eyes were focused on something behind me. Or was it someone? My stomach drops slightly as new realisations dawn. This photo, his distant gaze – when did I begin to ignore that? When did I accept his distraction? When did it become the norm?

And though it's obvious, that even as we toasted our relationship he wasn't quite present, it still hurts. I still hurt. And I don't think I want to anymore.

Chapter Fourteen

RHYS

'I'm back, as promised, and I brought you something,' I say to Susan, offering up the flowery notebook it took me forty-five minutes to decide on. Most of that time was actually spent trying to work out if this was even a good idea, I suppose because part of me now accepts this isn't about her. This is one hundred per cent about me, trying to get close to someone who can answer the questions I've now worked out how to articulate. What prompts someone to opt out? What makes someone give up? Why can't those who love you make you feel it's worthwhile keeping on? Why can't you see what's good in life? Is it selfish or strong to want to end things? How do you stop it happening? In the end, I just shut my eyes and picked one off the shelf. The design was irrelevant; the potential contents were not. I lift it a little higher, urging her to reach out. 'It was this or one that looked like an old-fashioned book. Or something with owls. Anyway, I hope you like it.'

She doesn't take it. 'I thought you could draw or something. I don't even know if you can draw. Can you?' I open it up, click the matching pen and scribble a terrible pig. I look at it for a second then add the word 'Oink' in a speech bubble above its head, just for added clarification. 'I'm better with pipes,' I say, passing it to her. 'If you can't draw, maybe you could write in it. Poetry? A short story?' she looks blankly at the pad. 'A shopping list, maybe? I could pop out and get some bits and pieces for you.'

I rub my hand through my hair. Susan shifts to look at me. It's the first time since I arrived today that we've actually met each other's eye.

'Susan.' A guy in a white coat, with both stethoscope and ego, approaches her bed. 'Oh, you have a visitor.' He checks his watch and I look at my own: 3.30 p.m.

'I'm Rhys.' I stand, offering my hand for him to shake.

'Rhys, yes. I didn't recognise you without the chainmail.' I stare and he stiffens. 'And the white horse?'

'Excuse me?'

'Knight. In shining armour. I've heard all about your visits.'

There's a beat. A pause as we eye each other up. Or maybe that's just me eyeing up him, trying to work out if he's friend or foe. To me or Susan. Not that it matters. 'Oh, I see.'

'Sister Davies told me everything.' He rolls the sleeves on his arms, wiping his brow. 'I'm Susan's consultant, Mark. Hi.' He finally shakes my still outstretched hand.

'Shall I go?' I ask her. Though she doesn't answer, she does slowly reach for pad and pen. Perhaps I'll stay.

I watch him check Susan's traction and listen as he chats through the next phase of her care. She no more responds to him than she has any of us. When he leaves, she puts the pad down and reaches for her handbag.

'So as I was saying,' I venture. 'I just thought I'd bring the notebook in and you can use the book for whatever. No pressure. I've got a Sheffield *Star* too. It was that or the *Daily Mail*, so, you know.'

Her fingers nimbly unbuckle her bag and she reaches in, pulling out a key. It's a simple, silver Yale that hangs from a thin strip of pink ribbon. She holds it out and it swings from her finger.

'What's this?' I ask, not taking it from her.

She reaches for my hand. It's the first time we've touched. Her hands are cool and soft – creamy, like good quality bond paper. Like Nanan's; she'd take my hand and pat it each and every visit. Susan places the key in my palm, moving her fingers to take hold of mine, curling them over.

As she does, Kat appears. 'Hi, Rhys. Mr Barnes said you were back.' She's smiling at me as she reaches for Susan's notes. Susan pulls her hand back to the bed, my fingers unfold and her key sits in plain view on the palm of my hand. 'What's that?' Kat asks.

'A key.' I wonder if the sudden heavy beat of my heart in my chest is guilt or an unexpected coronary. I guess I could be in worse places.

Kat looks at the key. 'What's it for?'

'I'm not sure.' I look to Susan. 'I think it might be to her house. Is it?' I ask. 'Is this a key to your house?'

Susan blinks.

'Oh, I don't think...' Kat reaches out, snatching it from me. 'I don't think that's a good idea,' she says, shooting me a look that suggests I've just been busted for manipulating a patient. My inner injustice alarm sounds but I bite my tongue, for Susan's sake. Kat gives the key back to Susan, who duly drops it back in her handbag, leaving the bag on her lap. 'We can provide anything you need, Susan. If there are things you need from home, I'm sure I can arrange someone from here to collect them for you.'

Susan looks down at her hands, neatly placed upon her bag.

'I'm sure Rhys is very busy,' she says, and I bristle at the suggestion she is taking this choice away from both Susan and myself. 'Do you have a minute, Rhys?' Kat asks briskly. Her face is steely and closed. Even passing through detectors in airports, I feel like a criminal, so despite the fact I'm irritated by her judgement, I suspect I look as guilty as hell.

Chapter Fifteen

KAT

Furious, I pull him to one side, my arms crossed. 'Whilst we do appreciate your help with Susan, I don't think it's in any way appropriate for you to take her house key, do you?'

He stares at me, his mouth falling open.

'Well, do you?' I push with whispered accusation, checking up and down the corridor, craning to make sure there's no one hovering in my office. I feel as if I've let this situation unravel. Have I? Is this my fault? 'What were you thinking?' I demand under my breath.

'Excuse me, Sister.' His voice is low and firm. He stops, swallows, then begins again, this time a little quieter. 'I wasn't thinking anything, actually.' I signal for him to stop talking as someone walks past and he waits until they're out of sight. 'Susan gave me the key. Okay? She handed it to me.'

'Why would she do that, she barely knows you,' I scoff.

'I'm as surprised as you are. I didn't get chance to ask her!'

I eye him up, trying to read between lines. He looks ruffled. Irritation has replaced his charm, but then I guess it would if you were caught out doing something you knew was inappropriate. 'She *gave* me the key, Kat,' he repeats.

A nurse appears beside us. 'Do you have next month's rota yet, Kat?'

'Erm, yes, I'll, erm, print it and drop it on the desk later. What time are you in till?'

'I'm going now, actually.'

'Ah, okay. Give me a second.' I paint on a smile, waiting for her to leave.

Rhys looks me dead in the eye. 'I asked her if she wanted me to pick anything up from the shops. I brought her a notebook – I thought it might help. I was trying to encourage her to write something down.'

'We've already tried the notebook option. She rejected it,' I tell him officiously.

'I didn't know that, did I? And it can't harm to keep trying, can it?'

I cross my arms, waiting for him to continue.

'She went into her bag, she gave me the key. I didn't get a chance to react at all before you'd walked in and made all the assumptions,' he spits. His arms are folded tight across his chest. 'I'm just trying to help,' he finishes, his cheeks flexing.

A cleaner pushes a mop and bucket past us. Rhys and I fake-smile in unison, before looking back at each other, smiles instantly erased. 'I see.'

His indignation makes me wonder if it's possible I've overreacted. He holds his ground and I begin to feel I've misjudged him. I think maybe I should backpedal slightly. 'Look, just to be clear, I can't encourage you to visit her home. It wouldn't be appropriate, okay? We can sort what she needs. Promise me you'll leave it at that.'

He looks at me, his face hard and cross. 'Scout's honour,' he says.

I get the feeling he's still pissed off with me. And I also get the feeling he's justified.

'Are we done? Can I go say goodbye to her, or do you need to escort me to and from her bedside now?'

The nurse after her rota returns. 'Sorry,' she says. 'I just – I have to go and—'

'Don't worry. I'm coming.' I turn to Rhys. 'No games,' I say, as if this final warning ensures I stay in control of my ward, my patients, my career. He looks at me, rolls his eyes and heads back to Susan.

Chapter Sixteen

SUSAN

I've heard the hushed tones, but I can't make out their words. If he leaves, without coming back, then that's the end. I've ruined it. Now he'll never know, and I will never rest. I hold my breath when they finish and relief washes over me when I see his face again.

'Well, that could have gone better,' he says, hands on hips, his fingers drumming. 'Why, Susan?' he asks, as if genuinely expecting a response. I suppose now might be a good time to give him the courtesy of an answer, but instead, I reach back for the key.

'I've been told it's not okay. I think they're concerned about the fact we don't know each other that well. Fair enough, but I just got right 'done' out there.' He points beyond my bed and, heart racing, I reach for his hand. Ignoring the rush of pain I again feel at his touch, I push the key into his grasp, then quickly reach for the pen to write my instruction.

'Book of fairy tales, bedside table.'

I rip out the note and pass it to him.

He reads it, then looks in the direction of Kat's office. 'I'm not sure…' he says, letting out a deep sigh. 'Maybe I can ask someone from here to collect it. Maybe Kat?' But before he finishes I've written another note: 'YOU. PLEASE.' I turn the notebook to face him, and reach up to push his hand, complete with key, back towards his body, ignoring the rip in my soul as we touch. I look him straight in the eye. I need that book. I wipe a tear, but not before he's noticed.

'Are you sure?' he asks, nodding slowly. I blink. 'Okay.' He folds the note, pushing it into his pocket along with the key. 'Okay.' He sighs, nods again, then leaves, glancing over his shoulder before disappearing from view.

I push away the notebook, sink back into the bed and stare out of the window. His visits. His care. His face. Without the book, I cannot do this.

Chapter Seventeen

KAT

Lou sits on the worktop, her hands stuffed under her thighs as she swings her legs and chats me through mood boards whilst I cook. 'What do you think of these for the table?' she asks, her thoughts darting between wedding and gossip. 'One on each place setting.'

'Nice. Ish.'

'Maybe you were right and he did ask Susan for the key.' She unpins the now rejected wedding favour photo, throwing it in the bin. 'Oh, and flowers. I love these, don't you?' She points at a hessian-wrapped bunch of freesias and my grandma's perfume springs to mind. 'Maybe he's a manipulating mastermind. Or a burglar. She just handed over easy access.' She frowns at the picture, eventually ripping it off too. 'Is the glitter a bit much on these?'

I glance over her shoulder. 'Roses are beautiful without added bling,' I suggest.

'Her house insurance will be null and void,' she says, glaring as she moves the picture of the glitter-dipped roses to the top of the board.

'You didn't see his face, Lou. I accused him of manipulation and he was like an injured bird – but with an attitude. Hurt and pissed off, you know?' Lou raises her eyebrows. 'He doesn't look like a burglar,' I add.

'No, he wouldn't, would he? Since they got rid of swag bags and monochrome branding, it's been notoriously difficult to identify them. Sharpen up, Kat!' She rolls her eyes at me, leaning across to nick a mushroom from the pan. 'And, for the record, you can never have too much glitter at a wedding.'

'Maybe Will could do me a quick character check? Run his name through their computers or something? Coppers have access to that stuff, he'd know if he was dodgy, right?'

'Well, I can ask him, Kat, but he tends not to do that anymore. Not since we found out Mum's gardener had a record for nicking one of *those* magazine's off the top shelf when he was twelve and I happened to mention I knew about it. Will said I couldn't be trusted.'

I do remember the incident. Not the gardener lifting the magazine, but the moment Lou mentioned it. The look on his face as she accused him of all kinds of perversion. 'Poor guy, never seen anyone leapfrog a box tree,' I say. 'He was puce!'

'Well, we can't have just anyone trimming Mum's bush, can we?' Lou cackles at her own joke, and I can't help but join in. 'So what is he like then?' she asks, sneaking in the question while I'm off guard. 'Rhys I'm-not-a-burglar-but-might-be-a-little-bit-weird the plumber.'

'Lou!'

'What? Give me a description, then I'll know what to tell the police when you suddenly disappear and they need a prime suspect.'

'For God's sake!' I dish out the food into our waiting bowls, chipped from clumsy efforts at washing up. 'Mind, it's a bit sharp,' I say, twisting the broken side away from her.

'You need a dishwasher,' she says. 'Or a lap boy to do the dirty work.' I turn my back, heading for the lounge. 'Go on then – descriptions. Paint me a picture,' she shouts after me.

'Well…' I sigh, thinking. 'He's quite tall. Maybe six foot two? And he has medium brown hair, sort of floppy.'

'How floppy? Aidan Turner Poldark floppy, or Zayn Malik the early years?'

'Erm… Aidan Turner, maybe? But it isn't curly. And he doesn't carry a scythe. He's got Poldark stubble though, enough to pass as sexy, not lazy. And good arms, yes. He has great arms – plumber, you see. Manual labour. Keeps them fit, doesn't it.' I sip at my wine whilst I think what else. 'His eyes are a sort of hazel brown with greeny flecks? If you look closely.'

'If you look closely?'

'Well, you know. They're sort of inviting… A little bit naughty. But he doesn't look like Aidan, he just…' I trail off. Lou is staring at me; bowl down on the table, arms folded. Through the Botox I can almost tell her eyebrows are raised.

'What?!' I say.

'Explicit description,' she says.

'You asked.'

'I did. Yeah. I did.'

'What?!'

'Nothing, Kat. Nothing at all. As it happens, you'll be relieved to know that pending nuptials bring with them new levels of maturity. See, I'm mature. I'm saying nothing.' She stops and I think I've got away with it. Not that there is anything to get away with. 'Except this…' Lou dances around my lounge. 'You fancy the plumber, you fancy the plumber.' She throws down a perfect running man and I'm as jealous as I am annoyed.

'I do not!'

'You wanna do rude things to him. You fancy the plumber.'

She's bogling now. 'Lou, I don't!' Her accusations ruffle my feathers.

'Have you got up close enough to smell him? What does he smell like? Did it drive you crazy with desire? Like Mitch in Year 9? Kuoros.'

'Sometimes you are a knob,' I say, stirring food around my bowl, trying to let her teasing wash over me because I know that's all it is, and I know I don't fancy him. If I did, or if I fancied anyone, for that matter, moving on from Daniel might be easier. 'Now pass me the wine.'

She runs back into the kitchen for it and hurries back with it wedged into the crook of her arm. She juggles bottle, bowl and glass, topping me up as she settles in beside me. We fall into comfortable silence as my mind wanders a little. Maybe I should fancy him? Can you make yourself find someone attractive? He's a good-looking bloke, it's true. But I have no urge to role play *Poldark* with him. I don't think he's really my type. If I even have a type. Jesus, I can't even spot it myself these days. I've been institutionalised by Daniel. Bound to fancy him and him only. Or men that look like him. Or remind me of him. Or smell like him… No, not that. All of which is harder to do when your best friend keeps telling you he was a shit.

'Okay, so you don't fancy the plumber.'

'I don't,' I say, relieved.

'Fine. Understood. Whatevs. But what about the doctor, the one who asked you out?'

'The consultant, you mean. Mark.' I shovel a mountain of noodles in my mouth whilst I search again for a reason I turned him down. If there was anything *to* turn down.

Lou recoils at the sight of food around my face. 'Attractive,' she says, as I wipe juice from my chin. 'So not the plumber and not the consultant. Jeez, you are high maintenance!'

'Me!' I almost choke on my dinner.

'Will's best man might be about to dump his girlfriend. You two would be perfect together!'

'I thought his girlfriend was your friend!'

'Not really. She's a miserable cow. Do you know, the last time we went out for dinner she spent the whole time complaining the wine wasn't good enough? At Nonna's! As if. And she said the food was cold.'

'Maybe it was.'

'It was gazpacho.'

I guffaw.

'You want high maintenance, she's got it in spades. High mainte-nance stupidity in a fake Herve body con.'

'Wow, Lou, don't hold back! Still, if he can go out with someone like that, I'm not sure he's really the man for me, you know? And as I keep telling you—'

'I know. You don't need or want one. You're fine on your own. Cool, whatever. I just think it'd be nice for you, that's all.'

I finish my dinner to a backdrop of *Coronation Street*. Lou updates me on the storyline, because apparently Deirdre was freed almost twenty years ago and I am out of touch. I nod in agreement as if I a) understand and b) care.

'What's that?' She asks, nodding towards the room elephant that is Daniel's last box of shit.

I glance at it dismissively. 'Some bits and bobs he who shall not be named left behind. I texted him but didn't hear back.' Lou nods at the same old story. 'So I've decided,' I say, deciding on the spot. 'I'm going to take it to him.'

'You are?' she says, stunned. She flicks her eyes forward, avoiding confrontation like you would a bear. Or a gorilla. Or someone with a really short fuse on all matters ex-boyfriend.

'Yes,' I say, refusing to expand. I've not entirely thought this through. But I do know that I am taking back control. I'm going to show him that he can't just walk out and leave me without properly clearing up the mess. I'm going to just check whether he does or does not in fact have a new girlfriend so I can move on, or not, once and for all.

Lou clears her throat. 'I guess there's no room for a plumber whilst an ex is knocking about.'

'I don't need room for a plumber, Lou.'

'So you say.' She looks at the box, nods in part approval and part, I suspect, recognition of my ulterior motive. She gets up with a groan, collects her mood boards and motions me to get up. 'Look, I'm going. Got to swing by Daddy's on the way home and ask him for extra cash for the horse-drawn carriage.' She gives me a kiss. 'Daniel is a loser who has inhaled quite enough of your life. It's about time you cut loose.'

'I'm cutting.' I snip the air as she heads out the door.

'And I'm getting roses tipped with glitter,' she shouts. 'See you tomorrow – eleven thirty, outside Debenhams!'

Back on the sofa, I wrap up in the sounds of my flat: next door's telly plays the *EastEnders* theme tune; the guy upstairs pads around his room; a distant siren races from somewhere by the ice rink in the direction of Manor Top, and a police helicopter shortly follows. Through leaves on the trees, summer rain breaks. A welcome interruption to the stifling heat, the pressure. And in that second, something inside me breaks too. My own self-bound ties unpick, beginning to set me free. I grab my keys and bag, hulk the box onto my hip and let the front door swing shut behind me.

Chapter Eighteen

RHYS

Through overworked windscreen wipers, I see Mum's face peering through the nets. I wonder how much of her neighbours' lives she's spotted, logged and noted for future sharing, all under the guise of waiting for me to arrive. People arriving home from work, kids back late from school, drenched from the unseasonal weather. I tease her by throwing an elaborate wave and she instantly slinks away from the kitchen window. By the time I've wrenched the handbrake up, she's at the front door, waiting.

'Finally,' she says, ushering me in. She checks up the road, then moves past me as I kick my shoes off then tidily rearrange them. Following her, I just catch her moving the pouffe away from David's chair. It's not like her to leave it out. Something's up.

'I made you a sandwich for lunch. You might as well eat it now, unless it'll spoil your tea? You out tonight?' I shake my head. 'Well, it'll put you on for a bit then.' She points for me to sit down, then passes me a lap tray complete with a cheese sandwich and can of Coke, all served with a smile. Something's definitely up.

'You're chirpy, considering I'm late!'

'Oh, it's no bother. It's fine,' she coughs. 'What crisps do you want? Ready salted, prawn cocktail or I've probably got some beef at the bottom of the bag.' She roots around, her head getting progressively closer to entering the supermarket own-brand multi bag.

'Ready salted, please.'

She throws me a pack. 'So, thanks for popping round, love. You okay? You look tired. Are you tired? Is it work? Maybe you should have a holiday. When did you last go away?'

'I'm alright,' I say, hands up to stop her fussing. 'It's nothing a good pint and a sleep won't sort.' I take a large bite of the sandwich and mumble, 'Open them patio doors, will you? It's boiling in here.'

'What, and let all the neighbours hear our business? No, thank you. Besides, it's raining. My carpet'll get soaked. Go on, spill it.' She looks at her watch, perched on the edge of her chair, and I'm reminded she summoned me this time.

'Spill what?'

'Whatever's driving you to drink! Is it woman trouble?'

I think about Michelle, and for the first time in days I don't immediately push her back out of my mind. All this Susan stuff has given me a handy distraction from that particular shitstorm. 'Yeah,' I agree, for ease. 'I'm beating 'em off with the shittiest of sticks.' I lick salad cream from the side of my hand. 'If you must know, it's woman singular, actually.'

'Ooh, who? Have you finally got a girlfriend and you haven't told me? It's about bloody time!'

'No, Mum! No… not that. No, it's Susan.'

'Susan who?'

'Smith,' I say, as if that should clear up the confusion. The look on Mum's face suggests otherwise. 'The woman at the hospital.'

'The one you thought was me? Whatever for!'

'Oh, I don't know, Mum. To be kind. To help, maybe? She's on her own. I was being nice.' Mum thins her lips. I'm unsure if it's because of what I've just told her, or the fact I've just put my empty plate on the floor. I remedy problem two by taking it through to the kitchen, raising my voice so she can still hear me. 'Our David liked her. I thought it would be a good thing to do.' I step back into the lounge. 'And, well… there's something about her.'

Mum looks at me, her head cocked to one side in a mixture of confusion and dismay.

'What?' I ask.

'Nothing, son. Nothing at all.'

'What?' I sigh, fully aware that nothing at all means exactly the opposite.

'Nothing, honestly. It's not my business, you're a grown man. You can do what you like…' she adjusts her tabard. 'I just think it's a bit…'

'Spit it out, Mum.'

'It's no surprise you want to help someone apparently in her position, what with David doing…' She swallows the words we don't speak to each other. 'What with our David, I get why you'd want to help someone who tried the same thing but…'

'It's not that,' I say, aware I can't pull the wool over her eyes. I get up, ignoring the weather, and open the doors to her garden. Mum purses her lips tighter; a look of disapproval well practised over years of parenting two boys.

'I couldn't just leave her, could I?' I say, but Mum's expression doesn't change. 'What if it *had* been you? What if I wasn't around either and you were on your own?' She narrows her eyes, I rub my face. 'Wouldn't you want someone to give a shit?'

'You are around, so it's a non-question. And don't we pay our stamp for the NHS to give a shit?'

'They do, that's why they called me.' Next door's dog barks and someone, somewhere, mimics it.

'Why did they call you? Did you find that out?'

'I told you, she had my number in her bag. It was the only number they could find. They took a chance, and you know what? I'm glad they did.'

'Right,' she said. 'That tells me then.' She lifts her tabard over her head, folding it up and placing it down beside her.

'Didn't you want something?' I ask, locking eyes with her to force a change of subject. Our silence is perforated by the sound of a neighbour arguing. Anger, shrieks and swearing leak out of an open window, each word finding its way to us through the open patio door.

'See,' says Mum, to prove her earlier point about open doors and privacy. She gets up to close them. Scutinising the carpet for evidence of rain damage.

'So, what is it?' I ask.

'Well, I don't know if I want to discuss it now, to be honest.'

I groan, irritated by the sudden arrival of her stubborn side. 'Maybe I should just go then, eh.'

Mum turns to face the telly, neither agreeing nor disagreeing with my suggestion. She's been watching reruns of *60 Minute Makeover*, another episode is about to start and she doesn't turn it off. 'Come on, out with it,' I say.

'Maybe there's nothing to come out with.'

'Mum, Claire Sweeney's on your TV screen and the words "smug" and "jazz hands" haven't left your mouth. Something must be up.'

She sighs and shuffles back to her seat, perching once more on the edge. 'Well, I'm not exactly sure this is the best time, but since we're here…' She clasps her hands on her knee. 'I've met someone.' Her hands unclasp and fly up to hold her mouth, but the words still have time to fire across the room, punch me in the stomach, then linger like the giant, gloopy bombshell that they are. 'A man.' She clarifies, as if it were needed. 'I met him down the bingo. We've been friends for a while now.' Her voice is tinny, her words are tiny drops of sharp reality, pricking at my consciousness. 'Rhys,' she says almost standing, presumably to reach out to me, but I'm grateful she ultimately stays put. 'This isn't how I meant it to… I can't…'

It's supposed to be me and her.

'I'm not good on my own,' she whispers.

We agreed. We all agreed when Dad left. And then she and I made another pact when David died. No extras. Lockdown. Just me and her. 'I know you might think—'

'You can't know anything, Mum,' I whisper, my hands clenched into fists on my knees. She commits to standing up this time, hovering as she approaches, opting to stare out of the back door instead.

'Would've been sweet peas once,' she says, nodding towards the bindweed climbing her trellis. 'And tomatoes.' With her words comes the smell: a heavy, furry aroma of home-grown, plump fruit on the vine. A smell set free each time she opened the greenhouse in the blistering heat. 'I've just not been bothered this year.'

Her words pick at a button of guilt in the pit of my belly. 'I've missed having company. I always did, but I made a promise to you both. Christ, I worked so hard to get you in the first place, I wasn't about to let you down by going back on my word, but yes, I've missed companionship.'

'You've got me.'

'Rhys...'

'Well, you have!'

'You're not here. And I know what you're going to say, but moving in with me isn't the answer.'

'Is that why you've been so hard to get hold of recently?' I ask, but she doesn't answer. She doesn't need to.

'I wasn't searching for it,' she says.

'When?' I ask. She pauses, moving back to her chair. 'When?' I repeat.

'A few months ago.'

I get an inkling, a taste of something more. 'How many months ago?' I ask.

'David knew,' she says quietly.

I get up this time, running my hands over my head as I scan back through the months, searching for a starting point, some critical moment when I missed her mood changing, missed a hint. As David's life was being rejected by one parent, another was moving on with hers. Was that what tipped him over the edge? Was she giddy? Were there signs? It's hard to say. I wasn't looking for anything. Why would I? It was just the three of us!

'I go to his, usually,' she starts, quietly.

I wouldn't have noticed before, when David was about. I didn't come around that many evenings anyway. And David wouldn't have noticed either. He'd have just thought she was going down the bingo. Or he'd have been at Michelle's. But since he died, there've been times she's encouraged me to leave because she's going out, but doesn't want a lift. And there are all the times she hasn't answered her phone. The times I can't get hold of her to say goodnight or don't get a response when I text her in the morning. Like Monday. All those times she had something on and she didn't dare admit it.

'What did David think?'

'Rhys, don't do this.'

'What? Don't do what?'

'Don't blame me. Don't make me feel that this contributed. You know how bad he was, you know what those last few months were like.'

And I do. I know because I sat with him in our van, listening to him get angry about his life. About the state of it. About every nitty detail that he was picking apart. I was the one he punched when the hurt got too much and he didn't know where else to vent. I was the one who hid my own truth, my own pain and challenges, because his seemed bigger. I was the one who tried to get him back on track, give him a job, encourage him to talk to me, to Michelle. Anything to get him through it. I was the one who saw how much hurt searching for a past left behind could cause. And I was the one who knew exactly how he felt.

'He's been a real support. Through all of this,' she said. 'I can talk to him. I can cry with him.'

'Does he come here?' I ask.

'Sometimes,' she says, quietly. I look down at our David's chair, occasionally out of place, the pouffe she kicked away when I arrived today. I bite my cheek. 'He's very respectful, Rhys. Doesn't try to take over.'

'That's good of him.'

'He wouldn't dream of just wandering in, and…' She stops, letting her eyes fall to David's chair. She picks at the thinning fabric of the upholstery. It's David's chair.

I wonder how often he's sat here.

'I need you to be happy for me, Rhys. I'm allowed to be happy.' She coughs a little, sniffs and searches the ceiling. 'Losing your brother broke my heart, and nothing will ever fix that. Nothing. But that doesn't mean I've stopped living.'

Her eyes are full of tears, but she's holding back. She's fighting her corner and being brave and strong like she's always been.

'Rhys...'

But I can't take it. I head into the hall, pulling my boots on, stumbling into the radiator as I lose my balance.

'Please, Rhys,' she shouts through from the lounge. I open the front door, holding on to the handle in case I can summon the strength to say something, anything in response. To go back to her. To stop being a spoiled brat. But as I slam it behind me, running to the car, I realise I've summoned nothing – except the feeling that I've just monumentally let her down.

I pause. I should retrace my steps and apologise for even suggesting this had anything to do with David's final choices. But I find myself turning the key in the ignition and speeding away, digging into my pocket for Susan's key instead. At least somebody needs me.

Chapter Nineteen

KAT

I peer through windows smeared with thick rain. I fight a quiver in my hand as it prematurely hovers over the bell; I don't want to ding it till I'm ready, until it's my stop. Until I'm certain I'm doing the right thing.

Maybe I should ride on by; go full circle, back home.

Pull yourself together. Take control. Breathe.

Fat raindrops bounce off the pavement. The combination of biblical weather and passenger body heat fogs up the bus. Someone wipes a window semi-clean and I lower my head to peek through it. I seek out the shops before the pub: the chemist, the Co-op. My stop.

I'm beaten to the bell and the sound of it hot-pokers my nerves. A few people stand, moving carefully forward as the bus navigates traffic, slowing down, steering left. Those of us getting off take up the wait by the back doors on our double decker. A linen-suited passenger loses his balance as we draw to a stop, knocking into a girl in summer dress and sandals; she mutters under her breath but smiles, despite herself. Another girl looks out the window and down at her ice-white dress, before clutching her handbag in front of her in the hope of some kind of protection, from both the elements and those seeking a quick and easy thrill.

I wait, encouraging others to get off before me until someone finally lets me get off ahead of them. Here I am. Meadowhead. Not far from where I grew up, but far enough from where I now live. Daniel's stomping ground. When we first got together, he'd pick me up, drop his car back at his mum and dad's, and then we'd walk here. We'd have a couple of drinks in the pub, a game of pool if the table was free, then wander back. I look over to the empty garage behind the shops and a memory comes back to me vividly. I swear I can feel his touch, the weight of his body as he pushed me against the door. I'd been unable to breathe; I needed him. We needed each other. I remember we ran back to his place that night, knowing full well his mum and dad were out late. The bittersweet taste of that memory is fast replaced by the memory of the first time we split up. That happened here too – pretty much this exact spot. By then I had my flat in town, but he was still living at his parents'. I watched him walk away, back to their house on Little Norton Lane. He never looked back. I bite my cheeks, remembering how I did the same back then, desperate not to call out his name. Two days later he called me. He came around. He told me he'd been an idiot and we agreed he should move in. We were convinced that living together would fix things. We were stupid. We were wrong. We were drunk on the idea of frequent trips to Ikea and a joint Netflix account.

I'm stapled to the spot, my feet as heavy as my heart, and this box of his stuff. Water drips off the spokes on my brolly and I move it to one side for a moment. Rain falls on my face, then a break in the clouds brings warmth, dryness. It's like an omen. A precursor to my breaking free.

One way or another, by the end of this evening, I will have come out of this nightmare for good.

I walk, head held high, the three streets to his parents' house. My heart is in my mouth but I'm going to do this. He can have his box back. I can ask him what really happened. Then I can move on. I turn into their drive. His car's not there. I pause, relieved and disappointed in equal measure. Relieved because I'm not feeling nearly as in control as I want to be, and disappointed because surely this means I have to come back again. I crunch up the newly gravelled path and the rain starts again, in earnest this time. Their ginger tomcat weaves through my legs, meowing. He's sodden, like that cat at the end of *Breakfast at Tiffany's*, though I suspect I don't much resemble Audrey Hepburn; more's the pity. I knock on the door, placing the box on the top step, and wait. Through frosted glass, I see Daniel's mum approaching, closing their kitchen door behind her. The cat legs it through the flap in the garage door at the same time as she opens their front one. 'Oh! Kat! Hello, love. What a nice surprise.' She wipes floury hands on her apron, then pulls me in by the shoulders so she can kiss each cheek, looking over my shoulder as she does so.

'Hi, Pam, cooking again?' I say, annoyed with myself for stating the obvious.

'Scones. Or do we say "scons"?' She mimes the quote marks in mid-air. 'Who cares! Yes, I am.' She looks up at the gloomy sky. 'Are you... coming in?'

'No, thanks.'

'Oh, okay, love. Fine.' She looks back up the road again.

'I was just...' I point to the box I've lugged from home to tram to bus to here. 'The last of his stuff. He was supposed to collect it.'

She bends down to pick it up and we clash heads slightly as I do the same. 'Sorry,' we both say.

'I didn't realise there was anything left…' She holds the box to her chest, looking at me with pity and sadness. 'Are you okay?' she asks.

'Yeah, fine,' I say with gusto, because lying is better than standing on your ex-boyfriend's mum's doorstep and swearing. 'You?'

'Yes, love. I'm fine. We're fine. Colin will be sorry he missed you.'

I nod, wondering if I should ask her. It's probably not the done thing, really. *Did your son dump me because he was shagging someone else?* I need to know though. I need to be clear. I need to—

A car turns the corner and swings onto the drive; full-beam head-lamps make the rain look like glitter. As the driver kills the lights I see it's Daniel. Then the passenger door opens and an Amazonian beauty with mile-long legs gets out. And not like I'd get out of a car, clumsy and grappling for my handbag and phone. No, this one does it like a model, swinging her feet around to place them firmly on the ground, her heels pushing her up even taller than I first imagined. Her hair, not remotely affected by the weather, bounces on her shoulders as she shakes herself free of the car. It's like she stands within her own, perfect, weather system.

Fuck.

I hold on to my closed brolly. I feel even less Audrey Hepburn and more drowned rat or cat. Or Kat. I swallow hard, determined not to cry. 'Hi,' I say, then bite down hard on my bottom lip. 'You forgot…' I point to the box his mum is holding. She looks at me with pity in her eyes, which almost finishes me off. The beauty takes a few balletic steps over to the porch, kissing Daniel's mum on the cheek. 'Oh my God, Pam, tell me you're doing scones. I *love* your scones,' she oozes, and I think, *No! I do. I love her scones. You've probably never even eaten a scone.* She stands beside Pam, looking beautiful and skinny and very much at home.

I nod to myself. I get it. Finally, now, I get it.

'Good to see you,' I say to Pam. I smile at the beauty, nod in Daniel's rough direction, then huddle my coat around me, walking away as quickly as my comparatively short-arsed legs will carry me.

Around the corner and out of earshot, I look up to the sky and hiccup a cry as I walk. I let the rain fall onto my face, grateful it disguises my tears. Then I stop for a moment to gather my strength, but start to walk again before the evening's events completely overwhelm me. And there it is. The realisation that not only have I wasted five years of my life, but also the last six weeks. Six weeks when I should have been getting over that piece of shit and his unattainably gorgeous new girlfriend. It doesn't even matter if there was crossover, if she did see me off. The fact is – it's over.

I wipe away the tears, streaking mascara across my face and the back of my hand. I wipe it clean down my trouser leg, thinking that *she* probably doesn't let her mascara run. Or if she did, she'd never wipe it down her leg. It's no wonder he dumped me. I'm a hot mess. And not in a good way.

A van pulls into my side of the road, speeding through a puddle. I manage to dodge the spray of water that comes up and over the path. Not that it matters, I can't look any worse. The van stops sharply, just up ahead. The driver cuts the engine, jumps out and slams the door.

'Don't mind me, will you!' I shout, as he cuts across my path, seeking shelter beneath the arched porch entrance of the closest house.

'Sorry!' he shouts, fumbling with a set of keys.

'Rhys?' I ask. *This is all I need.*

'Kat?'

I look up at the sky, trying to work out at what point the universe thought it appropriate to not only furnish me with a shitty ex-boyfriend but, upon realising that was the case and crumbling into a filmic mess, throw me into a tricky work-related situation where I am supposed to be the epitome of control.

'Are you okay?' he asks.

'Me, yeah, fine.' I wipe my face again, and my nose. Just in case. He looks up and down the road, then back to me.

'Are you?' I ask, suddenly aware that he looks like he's been crying too. 'Is everything okay, Rhys?' Concern for him replaces my own self-consciousness. I move down the path towards him. He pushes wet hair back off his face and wipes his eyes.

'I'm fine,' he says. 'Never better.'

I think about Daniel and the beauty. I think about Daniel's mum and the look of pity on her face. I think about Lou and her teasing about the plumber. And I look at the plumber, who is clearly no more fine than I am. I sigh. 'Nothing a good drink wouldn't sort? I must admit intravenous gin would definitely help me right now.'

Rhys looks at me, squinting through the rain, nodding in agreement.

'Look, I should…' He signals up to the house.

'Course, nice place,' I say gesturing up to the house as he collects three unopened milk bottles from the top step. 'I always imagined living in one of these one day.' Or rather, I scoured the internet on a regular basis looking for a forever home, without realising Daniel didn't really want one.

'It's not mine…' His words trail off but I've already turned away. I need to get home. I need to get out of these clothes. I need to hide in the bath with a copy of *Bridget Jones* and my own deep-seated feeling of failure.

'It's Susan's house,' he says, quietly. So quietly, in fact, I almost miss it. I turn back to face him. 'This is Susan's house,' he repeats.

I look up at the clean, cream-painted wooden windows; the rose bush that climbs the red brick of the 1950s house. Blousy pink petals strain beneath the weight of the weather. There's that collection of milk from the doorstep.

'You took the key,' I whisper.

'She gave me the key,' he corrects.

'Does it make a difference?'

'Of course it does.'

I look up and down the road, then back up to the house, before turning to Rhys. 'Did she say what she wants?'

'A book.'

'That's it? You're getting dragged into her life like this for a book?'

'If it helps her, yes,' he says firmly, folding his arms tight. We stand in silence for a moment before he turns his back. 'She asked me to collect it. That's what I'm here to do. Stay or go; it's up to you. But I'm doing this to help her.'

'It's not ideal, Rhys. It's not protocol.'

'Fine, go then.'

I pause, trying to work out what to do. A gentle breeze whips up the smell of wet grass and hot, damp soil.

'How do you know what she wants? Did she ask you?'

He steps back down the path towards me, pulling out a crumpled piece of paper from his pocket. Susan's handwriting, recognisable from her barely used diary, forms the only words on the paper: 'Book of fairy tales. Bedside table.'

'I'm here to help her. That's all. I'll get what she wants, then I'll go.' Rhys walks up to the house. 'It's up to you if you come in too.'

Chapter Twenty

RHYS

I hear her footsteps as she chooses to follow me towards the house. I turn to look whilst trying to push, twist and unlock the door. She's looking around, checking her watch. Her face has changed; the caring Kat who stood by Susan's bed has disappeared, and in her place there's a stern figure. She looks harsh, pissed off, but she also looks vulnerable. Her cheeks have a trace of black, smudged make-up down them. 'I'm coming in too,' she says.

'Fine,' I say, finally pushing the door open over letters and newspapers and junk mail. I place the milk bottles down, and pull the key back from the Yale, stuffing it inside my jeans pocket.

It's the smell I notice first, sort of musty. There's a base note of something – furniture polish, maybe. It clings to my nostrils. It's not dirty, or dusty, I don't think. Just old. Clean, but old, like my nanan's house. I don't remember it smelling like this before. Stairs lead upstairs on my right, the hallway stretches narrowly before me and there's a door to my left. I search for clues to her mindset before she left the house the other day – a note, perhaps. But there's nothing except a feeling of innate hollowness to her home. I don't move.

Kat clears her throat, shifting to see over my shoulder. Slowly, she takes a step to stand alongside me. She doesn't say anything. The vintage carpet, busy with emerald-green paisley, swirls beneath my feet. Kat moves the green-striped curtains away from the front door, reaching down to collect an armful of post. She cradles it in her arms, looking for somewhere to tidy it before piling it all neatly on the mahogany phone table to her right.

'Where did she say the book was?' she asks.

'Bedside table.' We both look up the stairs.

'Maybe you should…' I say flatly, gesturing towards the stairs. I want her to say no, because I want to check the room for myself, but I won't have her assume I'm here for anything other than the book. Kat takes an uncertain step forward, making my heart skip. Then she pauses, her foot resting on the bottom step. She looks over her shoulder – not at me, just in my general direction. I follow.

Upstairs, the door is open to the box room at the front of Susan's house. It's empty except for the bed and bedside table – no book, so this can't be her room. It doesn't look like anyone's been in here for years. I shake my head, stepping back slightly as Kat moves to let me pass. Her breath is shallow; her arms are wrapped around her. I go to the only other room with a door open, at the back of the house, beside her airing cupboard. I can almost see her, standing beside me as I worked; I can almost smell the soup she was cooking for her parents' lunch. The memory is oddly vivid.

Inside the room, a bed is made, beige sheets tightly tucked into the mattress. On the table beside it, there's a book.

'Look,' Kat points. 'Is that it?'

I step across the room, the floorboards creaking under my feet. Gold italic writing weaves across the front of the book. *The Brothers*

Grimm: The Complete Fairy Tales. I nod, lifting it from the table. It's heavy. The fabric cover is slightly rough to my touch.

'Fuck.' Kat falls against the wall, letting out a breath so long it's like she's been holding it since we entered the house. She rubs at her face, looking pale and worn out. The earlier trace of mascara has now been wiped clear.

'Are you okay?' I step towards her, my arm out in case she falls.

She pushes herself back off the wall, brushing herself down, recovering her composure. 'I'm fine,' she says. 'I'm fine.' I follow her gaze as she surveys the room. 'I can't believe anyone could live like this.'

'Like what?'

'Like… she wasn't really here. It's as if she didn't want to disturb the house.'

She's right. That's exactly it. 'It's a bit of a time warp, isn't it?' I run my hand down a white and brown wardrobe that surrounds the bed. 'Welcome to 1976, we hope you'll be very happy here.' Kat tries to laugh, but it's constricted. 'Come on,' I say. 'We've got the book.' But I don't move, because although I know we have what Susan needs, I'm not sure I have what I need.

It's not that I expected to find it written on the wall, but I thought there'd be something. An indicator as to why someone would take their own life. Or try to. Not just Susan, but anyone. I was hoping for answers. I look around. I sniff the air. Is there something we've missed? Something I can go back to Susan and ask her about?

Kat half smiles at me, then takes the lead. I feel a thaw in her mood, a moment of breakthrough. Perhaps I've been unfair. Since the incident with the key, my ego has been bruised. I've been defensive. But this situation is bigger than me. Maybe it's bigger than both of us, and maybe she's seen that.

At the foot of the stairs, Kat stops. 'I might just check the kitchen.' She glances up the hallway 'She's going to be with us for a while. Maybe we should clear it of perishables, you know? Cheese or bread or something. That milk'll go off. Can you write a note to cancel any more? Since we're here.'

'And you think I'm the snooper!' I say, my voice not quite as light as I'd hoped. She shoots me a look. We're not totally out of the woods. 'Okay, fair enough. This way.' I lead her down the corridor, pushing the door open to the kitchen, feeling around on the wall for the switch. It flickers a few times before eventually kicking into life, bringing with it the sound of a gentle electric buzz. The room feels different to when David and I were here. The pots with teabags and sugar have gone from the side. The sink is clear of washing-up liquid and the yellow marigolds she put on as she cleaned up.

'Can you see if there are any bin bags anywhere? Under the sink, maybe? We could empty her bin for her.' Kat opens the fridge. 'Oh…'

'What is it?'

She crouches down, looking right into it. 'There's nothing in it,' she says.

I move around the breakfast bar, as if I really need to check for myself. 'Nothing?' I reach my hand in.

'Nothing. Not a thing. It's on, and it's cold, but there's no sign of it ever having had food in.' She reaches in, wiping the shelf. Our hands brush as I take mine out. She stands and sniffs her palm. 'Clean. Lemony.' She frowns. 'Who has an empty fridge like this?' Her face morphs from confusion to concern, which grows as she begins opening cupboards. Each one empty. 'There's nothing.' She opens door after door. 'Not a thing. I mean, we all have out-of-date tins in our cupboards, don't we! Look, Rhys. Look around you.' She stands upright again, hands on hips. 'This,' she says. 'This, here. It's not how people live.'

'You haven't seen my house,' I say, trying to joke, even though I'm beginning to understand what she's suggesting.

'Immaculate house without obvious signs of inhabitants is one thing – I mean, not *my* thing, but I've seen in those magazines, it can be a thing. But empty cupboards? Empty fridge?'

'Maybe she was going on holiday?' I say, trying out the lie.

'What, so she cleared the entire kitchen of all contents? How many holidays do you go on and do that?'

'I don't know when I last went on holiday.' I reach for a cupboard, again to check for myself, revealing more bare shelves. We look around at a kitchen that reflects the rest of the house in all its dated but immaculate glory. Maybe glory is the wrong word. This place is more sterile, and less loved. Her old white enamel cooker is free of stains or marks. Her melamine kitchen worktops are clear of anything whatsoever. Glass sliding shelves are the only thing to contain something: beige and brown crockery, stacked up neatly from large to small.

'It's like a show home or something,' I say, running my finger along the sparkling drainer.

Kat looks around her. 'It's sad...' she says quietly, moving towards the archway leading to the dining room. 'It's desperately, desperately sad.'

And I realise she's right. Sad. Sadness. There's layers of it, embedded in the walls, between paint and paper and the past. I don't know how I didn't notice when I was working here, because now it's unmistakeable.

Kat puts a hand to her chest. 'Oh, Susan.'

'What?'

She presses her fingers to her mouth, stopping herself from talking. She looks around again, until she can contain herself no longer. 'There was always the suggestion her accident was not exactly accidental, you know? But this? I wasn't expecting this.' I must look confused, because she continues. 'This is on a whole new level. It's not someone leaving because they're tired of life and can't see another way out. This is planned, detailed, manipulated to manufacture an easy get-out for all concerned. She's eliminated herself from the house. She's rubbed out any memory of her presence. Apart from that book, she's all but invisible here.' Kat pushes open the door from dining room to lounge and I follow. There's a carriage clock on the mantelpiece. Its pendulum swings the seconds clockwise, then anti; a mirror reflects our faces. On noticing each other, we look away. 'How broken is someone who'd do this?' she whispers.

How broken are any of us, I think. And that's when I have to close my eyes. Fighting away the memory of walking into David's room. The scene flashes before me, despite how deep I've tried to bury it. I scrunch my eyes tight shut; I snuff it out. I force the heel of my hand into my eyes to bring stars, not his face, into vision. Every last breath leaves my body, just as it did then, just as it almost had for David, and I drop into the chair. It's too close for comfort. It's too much.

'Rhys?' Kat moves towards me, bobbing down on the ground, resting her hand on my knees. I look down at Susan's book, running my fingers over the letters. Fairy tales. Morals to a story. Happy endings. I lift the cover, flicking through pages as thin as tracing paper. A newspaper cutting drops to the floor. It's brownish, almost tea-stained with age. Kat picks it up. She makes a sound, just the smallest sound, as she reads what it says. 'Oh no…' she whispers.

Chapter Twenty-One

KAT

'What?' he asks. 'What is it?'

I read the headline over and over: 'POLICE SEEK MOTHER OF BABY FOUND AT ST JAMES' CHURCH, NORTON.'There's a fuzzy black and white photo below, of a tiny, swaddled, screaming baby. I flip it over and read the final paragraphs of a film review for *Rocky*. There's a picture of a fresh-faced Sylvester Stallone. I turn it back to look at the baby again before realising Rhys is staring at me, waiting. I try folding the cutting to stuff it in my pocket; protect the privacy of the story. Her story? Before I can, Rhys has taken it from me. He reads the headline, holding the paper. His eyes skim across the words several times as his teeth grit and his jawline tightens. Then he just stares blankly at the paper, maybe past it.

'Wow,' he says. His voice is low and unfamiliar. He shakes his head. 'How could she…'

'We don't know what this is, Rhys,' I try. 'It might just be—'

'What?' he spits. 'You think this is a coincidence?'

'Yes, it could be. It might not be anything to do with her whatsoever. You don't know where this book came from, or how long she's had it. Just because…' I'm not sure what to say. I'm not sure what

I mean. Of course, it might not be anything to do with Susan, but I know exactly what he's thinking. Why else would it be here, if it wasn't part of her story?

'She was adamant I get the book. Why might that be if she didn't have something within it she wanted to hide,' he snarls, looking back at the paper. His unfamiliar mood is intimidating. I'm in a room with an angry stranger and nobody knows I'm here. I stand, taking a step back, not certain how frightened of him I should be. My palms are sweaty.

'Come on.' He jumps up, thrusting the book and paper cutting into my stomach. I flinch, but try not to show that it hurts. He stares, eyes wild, and I dig deep to maintain contact, gritting my teeth and fighting my confusion. I am frightened, after all. I maintain control, composure. But I don't know him, this man with a face of stone. He pushes past me to leave.

'Rhys...' My racing pulse pushes the fear to my heart, leaving me with a sense of coldness, of dizziness. I chase after him, sick and confused, not sure what's going on. He doesn't look like the man I've welcomed to my ward. He doesn't even look like the man who stood on the doorstep of this house not ten minutes ago. He was distracted then, he wasn't right, but he wasn't this. He wasn't... angry? Out of control? Or frightened by something? He stands by the front door, one hand on the lock, the other bracing himself against the wall. Despite my heart rate, and a voice inside my head that warns me against it, I reach out a shaking hand to touch his shoulder. He seems to respond as I move it down his back. His breath is heavy, and his body radiates heat as I lean in closer, but it's as if he relaxes a little. As if he needs my touch. Is this a delayed response to the house? Is it the book, the clipping? Is this to do with his brother? Whatever it is, he's not okay. I have to help.

'Rhys, talk to me. What's the matter?' He shakes his head, turning to look at me. His breath is hot on my face. As well as the anger, I detect something like fear. Or neediness. I can't tell which. His eyes focus on mine and there's a hung moment, a pause, a second when I can see pain, something he's hiding.

He hits his fist against the door. 'Fucking hell.' He pulls it open with force, a rush of air hits me full pelt in the face. He hurries down the drive to his van. I use my coat to cover the book against the rain, pulling the front door shut behind me. 'Get in,' he shouts. 'I'll drive you to the bus stop.'

Do I want to get in a van with him? In a confined space? 'Don't worry,' I shout back. 'I'll walk.' I look up at the heavy black clouds. 'It's only a shower.'

'Get in!' he insists, his fingers tapping on the top of his van. There's a strange tone in his voice, some sort of vulnerability. I can't just leave him in this state. If we go back far enough, it's my fault he's here in the first place! I run down the path, jumping into the passenger seat as he climbs in. He slams his door shut and the force makes the glove box drop open. He swears, brushing my leg as he reaches across to push it shut. He doesn't bother with his seat belt as he tries to start the engine, swearing again as it misfires. I nervously try to buckle up, though my shaking hands make me hash the simple task. He takes the seat belt off me, forcing it into the clip. I clasp Susan's book tightly on my knee, wishing I could check if the paper cutting was still trapped within it. He revs the engine to get it going, then lurches out into the road, the speed forcing me back into my seat.

'I'll drop you outside Mitchell's,' he grunts over the sound of an overworked first gear. We jerk from crossroad to crossroad on the backstreets away from Susan's house; navigating speed bumps that make the van's suspension thud.

'Be careful, Rhys,' I plead, holding on tight to the edge of my seat.

He swings the car out onto the dual carriageway at Meadowhead, joining a queue of traffic that leads up to the roundabout. 'Come on,' he shouts, banging his hand on the steering wheel. 'Why is there always so much fucking traffic around here at this time?'

I don't respond. I expect there isn't a right answer. I want to reach out, to calm him. I've never seen someone look so young and so old at the same time, so confused and angry and hurt. And that's when I realise, without doubt, that I'm not in danger. But he might be. In danger of himself. In danger of allowing whatever this situation has triggered to push the self-destruct button we all have. My heart still races, adrenaline still courses, giving me the sense that I'm outside my body, looking on, but if I don't try to help, well... I don't want to think about it.

'I'm not sure what happened back there. I don't know what this is about, Rhys,' I clasp my hands together, finding strength from within myself. 'If you need to talk, I can listen. Or I can find someone. You don't need to—' He quickly changes lanes, almost knocking a cyclist from her bike. 'Careful!' I panic, reaching out to steady myself on the dashboard, checking back to make sure she's okay. 'Slow down, please.'

'I didn't realise what time it was,' he says. 'I've got to be some-where.' He bites at the inside of his cheek. He's straining to see past the cars in line ahead of him. 'You know what really gets me?' His eyes are pinned forward. 'People who think they can manipulate me. Take advantage.'

'I didn't, I wasn't—'

'Not you.'

'Oh.' I think back to the tiny woman in the bed who can't talk. Or won't talk. 'I don't think it's that simple.'

'Get out the fucking way,' he shouts again, this time at someone hogging the space between two lanes. I'm on alert, leaning forward to make sure I can see out of the side mirror and into his blind spot. The car jerks and shifts as he moves up the line, squeezing us through a tiny gap.

'It seems pretty simple to me.' He leans to see past the bollard; he's next onto the roundabout. 'We don't know her, do we?'

'You do.'

'I do?' He takes his eyes off the road to look in my direction for the first time since we left the house. He shakes his head. 'I did a few jobs for her. That's it. Our David had more in common with her than I did. And even then they weren't exactly best mates.'

'She had your number.'

'Yeah, and why? That's what gets my fucking shit. I signed up to help her, make sure she didn't get fleeced by some cowboy, and the next thing I know I'm in her house, finding evidence to suggest your mute patient isn't as innocent and needy as she first appears.'

'We don't know that, Rhys.'

He throws me a look then pulls out behind a bus, changing lanes on the roundabout to sneak in ahead of it and fly around the island. On the other side, he pulls into the lay-by in front of the wine shop. A new restaurant pushes the smell of cooked garlic into the evening air. The bus – my bus – pulls in behind him, and I have to shield my eyes from the flashing lights reflected in the wing mirror. 'The bus,' he says flatly, pointing behind him to make me hurry up.

Before I've fully closed the door, he's pulled off and away, zipping through the lanes and down the hill, out of sight. The bus rolls up to me, the doors steam dump, then open. I pay, swing from rail to rail until I fall into a seat at the back of the bus. What the hell just happened?

Chapter Twenty-Two

RHYS

The lights at the bottom of Woodseats turn red for the pedestrian crossing and I slam my brakes on. Coming to a standstill gives me a moment to think, to breathe. I need a drink. I need several drinks. This can't be happening. I refuse to believe it, much less even think it.

I throw the van across two spaces in The Big Tree pub car park. Flicking the engine off, I sit, locking my arms against the steering wheel to force my back into the seat. My head pounds, my throat stings. My mind is full of images of newspaper cuttings, our David, Susan's house. Kat, standing at the bus stop in the pissing rain. This wasn't the answer I wanted to find. I was looking for insight, a guide, some hint at what drives a person to end their life, not evidence that Susan gave up because she couldn't face the truth about how selfish she'd been. How she'd left a child for dead. A child that, if lucky enough to be given a second chance, might one day try to find out who he is. What his story is. A child for whom the truth might be a push over an emotional clifftop. Tumbling, spiralling, until he hits a rock bottom that nobody sees, his emotions catapulting out of control.

Or a child who might never learn how to live with the truth. A child who might give up.

Susan doesn't deserve my sympathy now that I know the pain she's caused. She doesn't deserve my time. She doesn't deserve to… I stop myself from finishing what my subconscious has started. Survival is not mine to give or take away.

I pick out my phone to call Mum. Like the night I ended up in Michelle's bed, I need to offload. I need maternal words of wisdom to calm me down. But as she picks up, I recall this evening's revelation at her house, and bile rises in my throat as the reality of just how alone I am sinks in. I cancel the call before she knows it's me. I wonder if *he's* there. This new man. This person she can turn to instead of me. Sat in our David's chair with his feet up, a cuppa, and a total disregard for how things are meant to be. We said it was just us. Who do I have now?

I growl into the steering wheel then launch myself out of the van. A group of girls sit at one of the benches beneath the big, fairy-lit tree after which the pub is named. They huddle from the rain beneath a pub umbrella, smoking fags and messing around. Pushing each other, screeching and generally being stupid. Or having fun. Either or. The grown-up in me knows that I should probably avoid the pub and go straight home. Sleep off the stress so I can deal with this all tomorrow in a better state of mind. The child in me smells hops and the chance for mental obliteration. I fold. One of the girls whistles and shouts at me as I lock up the van. 'Come on Woods Brothers Plumbing, give us a smile.'

I scowl, head down, not in the mood for games. 'Your loss!' she shouts at my retreating back.

The bar isn't busy, just a few of the regulars dotted about and a small group of guys at the bar, no doubt chatting shit. It's hot, too hot. I look around for best mate Paul, he's usually here on a Thursday. There's no one serving at the bar when I get there. I reach into my pocket for wallet and change whilst I wait.

When I look up again, Michelle is stood at the pumps. Fuck. I don't need this. I really don't need this.

'What are you doing here?' I ask.

'I need the money,' she answers. 'I was going to tell you, but since you're avoiding me…' We stare at each other, both uncertain what to say or do. I kick myself for not doing the right thing in going straight home. Had I done that, I could have avoided this confrontation a little longer. Now's not the time, yet the sight of her does, in some way, soften the edge of my nerves. If only I could tell her what's going on. If only I could lie in her arms and ease the pain.

But I can't.

'Look,' we say at the same time. 'Sorry,' we both add.

'You first,' she says, pushing flame-red hair back from her face. Her trademark, heavily made-up eyes are wide and expectant and not as cross as I'd imagined they might be. I'd expected a torrent of abuse; I'd expected a shit storm. I think I'd expected all the things I felt I deserved.

'We are both to blame,' she says instead, cautious not to be overheard. 'It's no more your fault than mine. It's just one of those things…'

Well, maybe it was for her, maybe it was for me, but it doesn't feel like it. And it didn't feel like it then, which might explain why I feel so unsteady now as she reaches for my hand. I wish I could pull her in close to me. I need her.

'It was shit,' I say. 'It was a shitty thing to do. But you're right, we are both to blame. I guess I can't forgive myself as easily as you seem to have done.'

She looks stunned, like I've sucker punched her, and I wish I could take the words back because that isn't how I wanted to make her feel

– but instead I make a point of holding eye contact, owning up to my mistakes. Being a man about it. She runs her tongue across her teeth then opens her mouth to speak, but nothing comes out. She just nods, takes her hand back and reaches for a glass instead. 'Pint?' she asks, coldly.

I nod. 'And one for Paul, if he's here?' I pick out coins from my loose change on the bar. Counting out the cost of two pints. She slams the drinks down on the bar and I reach up to catch froth that escapes down the side of the glass. The bitter taste catches my tongue and I crave the dullness I'll feel after a few more.

Michelle picks up the change from the side, counting it out. I wait, pretending it's to make sure she's got enough when really it's because I want to take this all back. When all the change has gone into the till, she turns to look at me, leaning across the bar. 'I loved your brother, Rhys. And I am devastated he is no longer here.' She pauses a second but she's not done. 'I am devastated about what we did. How we repaid his memory. How dare we be so selfish? But you know something? Grief wraps you up in a film that blurs your vision. It suffocates and confuses you. You make bad calls, you do stupid stuff. You lost a brother, I get it. I lost my boyfriend. Yes, things had been hard towards the end, and I don't know what our future would have held had he not…' I pick up my drinks to leave but she grabs hold of my arm. 'Don't you think for one second that you've got the monopoly on grief, Rhys Woods. Don't you fucking dare.'

I grit my teeth, desperate to apologise, desperate for her not to be angry with me. Desperate to tell her about Susan and what we found. But instead I walk away. It's better for us both if she hates me.

I wander across to the corner of the pub where me and Paul usually sit. Red, gold and green lights chase each other around the slot machine. Paul stands before it, pushing money in, nudging the pictures, peering beneath the window to try and work out what's coming next. 'That's a mug's game,' I say, putting his pint down beside the glass he's almost finished.

'Nah, mate, Steve's just put fifteen quid in, it's defo gonna pay up. I'm on to a winner. Cheers.' He knocks back the last of his drink before picking up the fresh pint and clinking glasses with me. 'She was asking after you when I got here.' He nods in Michelle's direction. 'Is she okay? She looked pretty cut up on Sunday afternoon.'

'She's fine. I guess. I don't know really.'

Paul studies me. 'Didn't you walk her home?'

'No, just…' I shrug. Shake my head. Bury my face in my pint. Paul knows me too well – he'd detect the lie. 'She's fine,' I finish.

'Right…' he says. 'Okay then.' He takes another drink. What brings you out on a school night anyway? You do know you're supposed to be back at Mum's tomorrow, right?'

'Am I? Shit, I'm so high on the ride of life, I must have missed that.' I drain half my pint, looking over at the bar.

'What's up?' He pulls a stool up to the table. 'You wanna talk about it?' I shake my head. 'Mate, I've not seen you like this for a while.'

'Like fucking what?'

He raises his eyebrows. 'Oh, I don't know, sailing dangerously close to picking a fight with your best mate, maybe?'

'I'm fine. There's nothing to talk about,' I grunt, then add, 'Nothing I wanna talk about anyway.' Michelle catches me looking at her and turns away. Maybe I *should* talk to her. Maybe we can clear this up and move on. Maybe what happened is understandable.

I let out a deep groan, the sound coming out before I've realised I'm doing it. It's long and exhausted and Paul looks at me as if to say *told you so.* 'I've just had a shit week, that's all. I need some distraction.'

Paul nods to a girl he's been on-off shagging for months as a suggestion.

'Not that sort of distraction.' I shake my head.

'I saw your mum the other day,' says Paul.

'Oh yeah?' I've picked up the remote and I'm flicking through the channels on the TV suspended in the corner of the pub.

'She was down town, coming out of the all you can eat. She was with some—'

'I don't want to talk about that either.' I get up, draining the last of my beer.

'Talk about what?'

'I mean it,' I warn.

'Okay then.' He pauses. 'I was just going to say that she looked happy. Which, all things considered, is nice.'

My leg twitches. 'Yeah, well...'

'She's entitled to a life,' he says and a switch flicks. The switch that means I am now definitely up for a fight.

'What? Have you two spoken or something? Because that's the sort of shit she's been coming out with,' I hiss. 'Whose side are you on?'

'I am on your side, mate. I always have been, apart from when you're acting like a dick – then it's a bit harder. And no, we haven't spoken. But maybe if we had this mood of yours might make more sense. Jesus, mate, stand down!'

'There's nothing to make sense of. I'm fine.'

'Clearly.'

I reach down to hold my leg still, and my foot starts twitching instead. 'It's... nothing.'

'So you say.'

I push him out of the way to throw a coin in the machine, tapping the top as it spins and I wait. There's a celebratory toot on the machine and several coins fall into the bottom. Paul looks at me before scooping up my winnings. 'You leaving the van here?' he asks. I nod and he heads off to buy us another round.

Five pints and two chasers later, Paul staggers off, patting my back and muttering something about tomorrow being better or another day, I'm not sure – he was slurring, I wasn't listening. I stare into a void for a minute before Michelle shouts time and I push myself up, out of my chair. I hover by the bar, watching as she clears glasses off the side and into the dishwasher. This was how it started the other night, except she was on this side of the bar, with me. The last of her friends had left. She was circling whisky around a tumbler. I nudged her, gave her a big hug. She pulled up a stool for me to stay and talk. She told me how she felt bad because she'd run out of ways to help him. That she'd been thinking about their future, before it all happened, about if they even had one. She got upset. I told her she shouldn't feel bad. It wasn't her fault. That you can never save someone who doesn't want to be saved. I basically repeated Mum's line, even though I don't believe it. I probably wanted something to happen.

Michelle looks around to check what needs doing next and our eyes meet. I grit my teeth to fight back each and every emotion. I'm saved when she turns her back again and walks away. I stare after her. I wonder when it was I fell in love? I wonder how long it will be before I get over it. Over her. Over all of this.

Through the pub window I see the kebab shop, which makes my belly rumble. I sway out of the pub and over the road. Losing my balance on the step, I fall into the counter. 'Mixed with garlic sauce,'

I slur, throwing a crumpled tenner from my back pocket out for payment before scrolling through my phone whilst I wait. Someone has tagged Michelle in a photo from some house party years ago. She's laughing, smiling, she's happy. She doesn't deserve my attitude and yet I have no choice but to give it to her in spades. She's out of bounds. And she needs to stay that way. I growl into the counter top, shoving my phone into my back pocket.

'It doesn't have to be this way,' says a voice. I look up to see Michelle leaning against the kebab shop door. She gives me a gentle smile, one that makes me feel like she knows me inside and out, and moves to stand beside me. It reminds me of what I like about her. She's better than me. She's more grown up. She forgives herself, maybe even me. She's incredible. My kebab is plonked down on the side.

'This is stupid, Rhys. I don't want to be angry with you. You're too important to me.' I want to reach out and brush the hair that falls across her eyes, out of the way, so I can see the piercing blue that seems to reach something in me I cannot reach alone. 'You want a lift?' she asks. 'No chat, no… anything. Just a lift.'

Picking my food up occupies my hands. It stops me reaching out to pull her close. 'I'll walk,' I say. 'Clear my head.'

She nods and half smiles. 'You know, he'd want us to be friends,' she says, and I laugh to myself. 'I want us to be friends,' she adds. There's a strength in her eyes, though undermined by sadness. She doesn't understand what this is to me, what *she* is to me. Nor must she.

I lift my arm, wrapping it around her shoulders to bring her close. She smells fresh, of coconut and warmth. His Michelle. 'We are friends,' I say into her hair, kissing the top of her head, desperate not to breathe in any more of her smell. 'We are friends.' I give her a final squeeze then walk away, not trusting myself to stay strong if I look back.

Ten minutes later, I push open the door to my flat. The windows looking out onto the street are open, the curtains Mum made half sucked out, dripping summer rain on the floorboards. I dump keys, phone and kebab on the coffee table our David made. He should have done that for a living, crafted. Plumbing was never really his game. Woodwork though, chipping – he did it so rarely and yet the results were so beautiful. I place my hand on the top, beside the keys. The wood is soft. I can almost feel his energy. The table was shaved, shaped and sanded by his own hand, a gift for my thirtieth. He'd been almost embarrassed to give it to me, neither Mum nor I having had any idea that he was capable of such craftsmanship. Did he know how much I loved it? Did I ever tell him?

Puddles of water collect in dips and knots in the floor, but I don't care enough to clean it up. I drop into my chair instead, picking at my food, a sick feeling now replacing the hunger. I know what Mum would say, if she saw me now: *What a waste, look at the state of this flat, pull yourself together, son.*

I check my phone just in case she has sent me a message, like sometimes she does. *Night. Love you.* Anything. Because she needs me as much as I need her.

But there's nothing.

Through the open window, the familiar soundtrack leaks in: buses, the odd shout as someone walks home, sirens. In my bedroom, I wrap up in the muggy warmth of my sheets, feeling the weight of my body as I sink into the mattress. My head hurts from the beer and the chasers, and the strength it took to walk away from Michelle. A strength I don't know how long I can maintain…

Chapter Twenty-Three

KAT

After a fitful night's sleep, I've been wrapped up in a blanket on my sofa for the last hour, wondering what to do about Rhys. Susan, I can deal with. She's on my ward, she's not going anywhere, I can take my time. But Rhys? I can't see him coming back any time soon, and yet I can't help feeling he might need help. Someone to talk to. Whatever's going on, he's got issues.

He's also still got Susan's key.

Maybe I should organise for the locks to be changed. Would he go back? He was so… what? Confused? Angry? Frightened? I still can't quite work it out. I see the crumpled-up piece of notebook paper behind the bin and thank the universe that I couldn't be bothered to pick it up the other night. I'll call him, ask him to meet me and get the key back. If he agrees, I'll know we're okay. If not, I guess I'll call in the locksmith.

I unfurl the paper, tapping his number into my phone. It rings three times before he answers.

'Yeah?' He sounds as though I've woken him, all foggy and tired.

'Did I wake you?' I ask. 'Sorry.'

'Who's this?' he answers, his voice strained, as if he's stretching out sleep.

'It's Kat…' I twist my blanket around my fingers, pulling it up until I see the chipped polish on my toes. 'You okay?' I ask, tentatively.

'Just about,' he says, sounding bleary, distracted. Sounding anything but okay.

'I realised you still have her key. I thought I should get it back.'

'Stop me returning and ransacking the place?'

'I wasn't suggesting that,' I say quickly.

'Course not.' He doesn't sound convinced. 'Look, I've got appointments all day. I can't just swing by and drop it off.'

'It's fine, I can meet you. Where suits?' I need to pin him down. If I can see him, I can check his eyes, see if he really is okay.

He lets out a heavy breath. 'I dunno, I've got to pick up some bits first. I'll meet you at the train station in thirty minutes. Okay? If not, you'll have to wait. Like I said, I'm busy.'

'Okay, no problem.' I get up and jog into my bedroom, pulling out a clean uniform to throw on. I can meet Rhys, go to the dress fitting, then get to work by one if I'm lucky. 'Train station. Swing into the short stay, I'll be waiting.'

Susan will get her key back, and I'll make sure I've covered all bases with Rhys.

It takes me ten minutes to finish getting ready, run out the door and jump on a tram down to the station. I wait amongst the commuters as people rush past me in all directions on their way to work, meetings, to catch trains up and down the country.

Rhys pulls into the car park and up beside me, winding his window down as he pulls up the handbrake. He thrusts the key out towards me. 'There. One key. Okay?'

'Thanks,' I say. He nods, eyes forward, but doesn't go anywhere. 'Rhys, I've been worried about you,' I say. 'Last night, you... You left in such a rush, Rhys. You seemed so... Is everything okay?'

'Sure, never better. Life is dandy.'

'Rhys.'

He looks at me for the first time since he pulled up. His eyes are red-rimmed. His stubble is thicker. He looks terrible and I feel wholly and entirely responsible. 'Do I owe you an apology?' I ask.

'For what?'

'Calling you. Encouraging you to visit Susan. Letting you go into her house.'

'You didn't *let* me do anything,' he says. 'I was there to help her. I just didn't expect it to turn out the way it did.'

'No. No. Me neither.'

He rubs at his chin. 'Look, I'm sorry if I freaked you out. I can't really explain, it's just...'

'Yes?'

'It's complicated.'

'What is?' I ask, but Rhys doesn't answer and I'm not really sure where to go next. He lets out a long and laboured sigh that starts and finishes with a groan. 'Look, I should go. You don't owe me an apology. I'll be fine.'

He goes to put his car in gear and I panic. 'Rhys...' He looks at me and I see how vulnerable he really is. I jog around the front of the car and climb into the passenger seat before he can move away.

'What are you doing?' he demands.

'I'm not entirely sure,' I answer, truthfully. 'But I feel that you need my help and as we wouldn't even be here if it wasn't for me, I can't just ignore that. You have two choices: park up and talk, or drive and talk. But you need to tell me at least some of what's going on so I can work out how to fix this mess for you.'

Rhys looks at me, incredulous. 'You think you can fix this!' He laughs unkindly. 'You think you can jump into my car, demand I talk, and I'll offload my darkest secrets to you for you to wave a magic wand and make everything better? You're a nurse, Kat. Not my fairy godmother!'

I stare at him, my stomach dropping to my toes.

'Okay then, here, have this. I was adopted.' The penny begins to drop. 'Both me and David were. You remember David, the brother who killed himself a few months ago. Of course you do, I've told you that much already.' He stops talking, but his breath is heavy and I'm beginning to realise what went off back at Susan's house.

'I'm sorry, Rhys, I don't know what to say.'

'Really? But you told me you were going to help.' He stares. 'Apparently it took ages, the process Mum and Dad went through. They fought for me and our David. Mum always said they really wanted to be parents, but I've often wondered about Dad – if he just went along for the ride. He didn't stick around in the end.'

'Ah,' I say. As if I now understand everything.

'Oh, that's not it, though. No. Dad went off with some woman. Mum always made apologies for him. He was made redundant when the steelworks closed. She said he didn't deal with it very well, said he made a mistake, but she never tried to get him back so she couldn't have forgiven him. He stopped bothering with us pretty quickly. She'd try to set stuff up, visits and so on. I remember, one time, he was supposed to take us to see a film. *National Lampoon's Christmas Vacation* with Chevy Chase. He didn't bother turning up.' He laughs to himself, but not in humour. 'Dad just stopped turning up for everything in the end. He got a new family. Children of his own, apparently. Real ones.' Rhys lets out a deep breath. 'So we were dropped. Left. Abandoned.'

He labours that final point and I wonder how he must have felt, knowing the pain of parental rejection. How that affects each day. How that might make you feel to learn you were trying to help a person who has rejected a child. 'I guess that must have been—'

'Hard?' He rolls his eyes. 'Wow, why don't you just ask me how it made me feel and be done with it!'

I'm out of my depth and he can sense it. But I'm here, sitting in his van and trying to present a solution. I can't exactly bail now. 'Look, I'm sorry. I didn't mean to sound so trite.'

We sit in silence, both staring out of the windscreen. My heart is racing and I'm desperately trying to work out what to say next.

'Do you think suicide is selfish?' he asks without warning.

I hold my breath for a moment, my chest feeling the pressure. 'I don't think anything is ever black and white,' I answer, carefully.

'Leaving people behind though, people who might need you. What sort of person does that?'

'Someone who doesn't feel they have any other choice? Can't see another way out.' I close my eyes, searching for the strength to get this conversation right. Assuming it's even possible to do so. 'I think sometimes they believe those around them would be better off when they're gone.'

'How could anyone believe that?'

'I don't know. But I think in that moment they do. That's their reason.'

'And what about Susan?' he asks, his voice colder now. 'What might her reason have been?'

'Who knows, Rhys. We can't second-guess these things. We can't assume we've any insight into people's choices. Whether we agree, whether we respect her choice or not, it wasn't our decision to make.'

'What do you mean?' His voice is softening, as though the energy that fuelled his anger is running out.

'I suppose I mean it's all allowed. Forgiveness is everything.'

'How very noble of you.'

'It's not about nobility, is it, Rhys?' I shift in my seat to face him. 'It's about not letting other people's lives dictate our own.' My words reverberate back and I think about the look on Daniel's face when he saw me last night on his mum's doorstep. As if five years meant nothing to him. There was no remorse, no embarrassment, no hint that he needed to protect me from getting hurt. Maybe that's because he didn't care either way. Maybe he never did.

Rhys turns to face me now. 'Other people's lives do dictate ours, though, don't they? Or they affect them, at least. Of course they do. We respond to the things they say and do, we all feed off one another. We all breathe the same oxygen, we're all wired the same way. If your brother kills himself, how do you ever get over that?'

'Maybe you don't.'

I look down at my bag for the first time since leaving my flat. Susan's book and paper cutting safe inside.

'I understand that this is hard for you, Rhys, but we don't know anything about Susan, about her life. That article might not even be about her.'

'Who else would it be? What if her child tries to find her but can't because she's given up on life? That child's been doubly rejected.'

His anger returns. His face colours red.

'Susan's not dead though, is she,' I say. 'She survived. And maybe we're making a difference. Maybe you are. It wasn't her time, and now she has a second chance. And maybe that's because of you.' I swallow, aware of the poignancy of my words. 'Maybe she has a chance to make a different choice. And maybe, one day, that will be rewarded…'

'Mum always says love makes everything better. That it can fix even the most broken.'

'And what do you think?'

'I think my brother couldn't see it for looking.'

'What was he looking for?'

'His birth mother. His flesh and blood. He assumed it would fix everything inside that he felt was broken.'

'But it didn't?'

'We buried him,' he says, simply.

I look down at my fingers, my knuckles white because I've held them so tight. 'Does she know?' I ask.

'Who?'

'Your birth mother,' I say, treading carefully. 'About David, I mean. Maybe if she knew what he'd done, it might be the push she needs to do things differently – with you, I mean. As awful as it sounds, maybe there is a way to find something good from all of this. Maybe that would help you too? Maybe then, you can have a relationship with her even though—'

'She's nothing to me.'

'Not now, but she's your birth mother.'

'Not mine. Our David was younger than me. We had different parents.'

'Oh. I just assumed.'

'Yeah, well. You know what they say about assumption. Maybe that's why we were so different. Nature versus nurture or something. Anyway, getting in touch with David's birth mother isn't going to do me any good.'

The city's clock chimes 10 a.m. and Rhys checks his watch then swears. 'I have to go. Tell Susan I'm busy, that I can't come by. I can't do this, Kat, I thought I could, I thought I could help, but I'm not strong enough. It's too hard. Tell her...' There's a beat, a moment in which I sense he's trying to work out what he wants me to say. 'Tell her I'm sorry.'

He looks me in the eye, waiting for me to get out of the van. I gather my bag and catch him looking down, knowing full well what's inside. 'If you need to talk to someone...'

'I think I've said enough.'

'Not to me, I mean someone who can help. Just, let me know, okay? It's the least I can do.' I open the door and get out as he starts up the engine. Just as he did last night, Rhys pulls away and disappears within seconds.

I slide down into a bench beside the waterfall, reaching into my bag for the book. I let the pages fall naturally open and read. 'Then the children went home together, and were heartily delighted, and if they are not dead, they are living still.'

Chapter Twenty-Four

RHYS

Heat warms my face where a shaft of light bleeds August sun through the van window. The heavy pound of my hangover has taken hold since talking to Kat. I dig around for tablets, chucking several empty blister packs into the footwell before finding a single aspirin to throw back, coughing as it sticks in my dry throat.

I've got a day of jobs. Stuff to pick up for work. A living to earn. And yet I can't move from the side street I pulled up in when I knew I'd be out of Kat's view. My head hurts, my heart hurts, my whole body aches. What do I do? Where do I go from here? Should I call Mum? Michelle? Should I do anything about Susan? I want to run, I want to put time and distance between myself and all of this, but my gut, my instinct, says the story isn't over yet. I can't take it on. It's too big. It's just too much. I feel like I'm drowning.

A text message comes through to my phone. It's from Mum: 'We need to talk. I am here till lunchtime. Come over.' There's no kiss, no signs of a thawing mood from her, which pisses me off. What if I can't just drop everything and go over to see her? Then I remember the start of this week, when I thought I was about to lose her. When the idea I'd be officially alone in the world, was worryingly close to reality. Just me. On my own. No backup. No support. Alone.

Like Susan…

I flick through my workbook. There are a few appointments, including the return to Mrs J. It's nothing I can't cancel. I dutifully respond: 'I'll be there in twenty.'

Twenty minutes later, I park up outside our family home. Should I knock? Should I go straight in? I err on the side of instinct, opting for a combination of the two. The smell of grilled bacon greets me the second I open the door.

'Morning,' she says, not quite as effusively as normal.

There's a stickiness in the air. Bacon or no, I'm definitely not in the clear. My observation of her mood is proven with the cheek I am offered to kiss. No warm embraces this morning. No jokes and banter. Just a cheek. I give her a peck, as is expected; her skin is soft and plump. It makes me want to say sorry and have her wrap me up in a cuddle like I'm a kid again. Instead, I reach for the cup of tea that sits next to her own steaming china cup.

'How are you today?' she asks.

'I'm alright, yeah.' I resist telling her about my hangover or my chat with Kat. 'How are you?' We've never fallen out. Cross words occasionally, but not even those since we lost David. Because there's an unspoken law – you never know what might happen. I need her.

'Smells like you went out last night?' she says, sniffing in my direction before handing me a massive bacon roll and the ketchup fresh from the fridge. She gives me one of those looks like only your mother can. Accusatory with added knowing. I follow her into the lounge. 'Watch the crumbs,' she instructs me, and there's something reassuring in the normality of her request.

'Yeah, I...' I pause, wondering if I should tell her about Susan. About her house and what we found. Any other time, I would have shared stuff like this. I've always told her everything, yet this week seems to be unravelling all of that. I don't know if I'm ready to tell her anything, yet I probably need to now more than ever. 'I had a couple in the Tree, saw Paul for a bit.' Mum nods but doesn't look at me. 'Not a big session though,' I add, like a teenager hiding details of a night down the park with a bottle of Bacardi and twenty fags. 'Did you go out?' I ask, not sure I really want the answer. I take a bite of bacon sandwich; it tastes like home.

'Yes. For a bit. I popped round to see Derek after you left.'

Having not got as far as establishing names, I can only assume Derek is who I think he is. I bite back the need to check. 'He made me a cup of tea, listened whilst I let off steam, then I got the bus back.'

I nod, wondering what she said to him, what he said in return. Wondering what he thinks of me and feeling annoyed I even care. I shove the last of my bacon sandwich into my mouth as an excuse not to talk, wiping away the ketchup caught on my top lip. Salty bacon mixed with the sweet tomato fends off my thick head. Mum's long-service carriage clock, an award from her years at Marks & Spencer, ticks over our silence. I focus my attention on its spinning pendulum. Clockwise then anti. It's like the one at Susan's.

'This needs to stop,' Mum announces. 'You're not my keeper, Rhys, and, whilst I don't want us to fall out, Derek and I agree that you were out of order.'

Derek sounds like a cock.

'As he said, I am entitled to a relationship. It's not healthy to pretend you and your brother were enough for me for the rest of my life. I am a woman who needs companionship, not just well-meaning sons.' There's a beat. 'Son.' It's like a punch in my stomach each time she corrects herself. Does it do the same to her?

Mum hugs her tea, her hands interlocked around the warmth. She's gazing out of the window. I go to say something but she holds up her hand to stop me, so I wait for her to muster the strength to say what's on her mind.

'Sometimes,' she says eventually, her voice small and distant. 'I wake up in the morning and, for the briefest second, I'm in the life we had before.' She smiles, gently. 'David is asleep in his bedroom, or at the very least on his way back from Michelle's.'

I look away at the mention of her name.

Mum turns to face me. 'And then I remember. And it's like I've lost him all over again. The pain is as deep, Rhys. Deeper than words can say.' Her smile fades as her eyes fill. The tears wobble then topple down her cheek. 'And I cry. I cry for how I failed him. How I lost him. How I, his own mother, couldn't make it better for him. And my God, son, you have no idea how much that hurts. You can never understand what that's like. Even if you go on to have your own children, Rhys, you won't get it. And I am glad of that.' She takes a breath. 'Because I wouldn't wish this on anyone.' She reaches to her chest, pulling at the pain before retrieving a tissue from her sleeve and finally wiping her tears.

Normally I'd get up and give her a cuddle, but there's something fixing me to our David's chair. Mum looks tired, but she also looks determined. I want to say something, but nothing feels right.

'If Derek helps in some small way, if he gives me back some motivation in life, some happiness, well, I think I deserve it. If losing a child has taught me anything, it is to live for today. Appreciate every second. To love and be loved, Rhys, you know my feelings on that. Love might not have saved David, but maybe it *can* save me.'

A cold spread of fear bubbles inside me. She's about to announce she loves this Derek and I'm not ready for that; I'm really not ready. I'm not ready for any of this, for life moving on. I'm not ready to leave him behind.

Not that my show with Michelle backs that up.

Mum looks down at her uneaten breakfast and places it on the floor. 'I am trying to respect your feelings, Rhys. And I won't force my life on you. But as Derek says—' I look up sharply at the repetition of his name. She swallows, not finishing her sentence this time, reading my response and perhaps being the bigger of us both. Instead, she nods once to mark the end of what feels like a well-rehearsed monologue.

I look at her, trying to judge whether to say what I want to say, to hold my tongue, or to get up and leave. We are at an impasse. A stalemate. I'm trying to fight my inner child, the one who feels like he's losing his grip. And I'm failing.

Chapter Twenty-Five

KAT

Lou saw my mood as soon as we met up in town. I'd been waiting for her outside Debenhams, and was planning on suggesting breakfast somewhere nice before the fitting. She took one look at my face – all pale skin and bags beneath the eyes – before dragging me into Mc-Donald's for a Breakfast Wrap whilst she tried to pummel information out of me that I wasn't ready to give.

And then it was time for the fitting, and my life went from abandoned babies to pending weddings in less than an hour.

I reach for the designer bottled water and top up my champagne glass. Though it's carbonated, the bubbles don't fizz like the Moët in Lou's, though her second glass is now empty. She's obscured from view by a golden shot silk changing curtain. I can hear her giggling with the dress fitter, having declared she would show me her dress before I got sight of mine. It's barely half past ten. Opulence surrounds us.

I wait, mind full, wondering how to explain to my boss, Gail, that I came to be in Susan's house last night. Wondering about Rhys and all he said to me this morning. Thinking about Daniel. Revisiting our years together, the holidays, the trips to his parents' house on a Sunday, the times we talked about getting married. This might have been me trying on dresses whilst sipping champagne. Except we didn't talk about it, not really. It was something I would occasionally bring up, to be fast muttered about and then moved on from.

There's a fizz of excitement around me and I tell myself to suck it up. I need to put these things aside and remember that this is my best friend's big day. I need to be enthusiastic. This is her big dress. Or maybe it's a small one – who knows what she settled on in the end. Because that's the thing about Lou, you can never second-guess her.

Maybe I *should* talk to her about things. Sometimes she shares a wisdom I forget she actually has. What would she say about the last twenty-four hours? It's all replaying constantly in my head. It's no small relief that she's about to come out of the changing room.

'Oh my God, Kat. I can't believe how beautiful this is or how lucky I am or how amazing this is going to be. This lace is…' She trails off as the curtain opens and she glides out to stand on a box before the mirror. Apparently the box is important for height. Despite the interruption of odd formalities like this, my breath catches in my throat as she carefully steps up onto it, reflected like a fairy-tale princess in the giant, gilt-edged mirror. All thoughts of last night, of Rhys and Susan, disappear, as Lou and I blink back great big, girly tears at the sight of her. I've been so consumed by my own worries that I completely underestimated the impact of her ivory, silk and lace-clad glory.

'You look…' I can't quite find the words.

'I know.' She beams, twisting to look at each angle of her reflection. She's holding her arms out, fiddling with her fingers, unsure quite what do to with them. Eventually, she rests her hands on her hips, and her body visibly relaxes into the dress. She softens, and her head lifts tall and proud. 'I can't believe I'm getting married,' she whispers.

'I know…'

She sniffs. I sip at my water. We giggle.

The assistant checks how the dress is fitting. Deftly nipping, tucking and shortening as Lou obediently complies with her instructions. 'If you just turn slightly this way, we'll pin this a little more so we can make the final alterations. Nearly done.'

Lou sneaks a cheeky grin at me. 'You're next,' she says, clapping her hands together.

'This is all a long way off for me,' I cough. 'Jesus.' I ignore the tiny pang I feel at the thought.

'No, I don't mean this,' she motions to the dress with a look that says *highly unlikely* on her face. I try not to take it personally. 'I mean your bridesmaid dress.'

'Ah… yes.' The sight of hers had briefly eliminated the fear about mine. A knot of terror returns, tighter than before. Peach taffeta has been mentioned. I found a photo of such an eighties crime on Pinterest, adding it to her mood board as a joke. She didn't take it off. I could literally be wearing anything.

I check my watch again.

'You have plenty of time. It's ready, isn't it, Jenny?'

Jenny, the assistant, nods, then shouts to her colleague. 'Can you get the bridesmaid dress out for Miss Davies, please, Fiona?'

'I have to get going by twelve o'clock at the latest, okay, Lou? My shift starts at one and I've got a few bits to sort out beforehand. There's a lot on at the moment.'

'I know, I know. It'll be fine. What could be more important than a dress fitting, anyway?'

I don't think I can bring myself to try and explain exactly what is so important. My bag, with Susan's book inside it, taunts me like a big ugly bag of inappropriateness. I need to give it to Susan. Then I need to decide whether to talk to Susan about her house, and about the cutting, or my boss, Gail, first. Or maybe I could talk with Mark first. He's her consultant. He might have an idea about how to manage the situation. Though maybe I should give Susan time to think about the cutting, to respond. I could offer to help her find the baby… if it even is hers. Though, after Rhys' reaction this morning, I'm not sure families are my thing. I could put her in touch with someone though. Help from a distance. Which would have been the case had Rhys not been so hell bent on going to Susan's house for this book. I pull the bag tightly into me.

'What's in that?' asks Lou. It's as if mind reading is real and she is proficient in the art. 'You've not let it out of your grasp all morning. I've told you before, it's bloody ugly. Did you have to bring it here?' She lowers her voice to a whisper. 'This is a designer boutique, darling. That bag is straight off of Castle Market!'

'What was wrong with Castle Market?' I say.

'They closed it down, Kat. No more information required.' She purses her lips.

'Whatever. It's some stuff I've picked up for a patient. I just don't want to lose it, that's all.'

'Lose it! How? No one's lifting that monstrosity. And don't you have people to do that sort of thing for you, now that you're the boss? Doesn't the patient?'

'I'm not really the boss, Lou,' I say. 'And if only. At least it might have saved us from opening multiple cans of the proverbial worms.'

'What are you on about? And who is "us"?'

I've clearly, and frankly rather foolishly, said too much. Lou is all but sniffing out the story, like an ivory-clad truffle pig. 'Rhys,' I say, and she cocks her head in a silent question. 'The plumber?' I add, though I know it's accepted information and she is pretending to be this naive.

'Ohh, the plumber. Yes. Rhys. Right.'

'Lou…' I warn.

'The plumber you absolutely do not fancy.'

'Correct.'

'Whatsoever.'

'Exactly. And now is so not the time.'

'If you say so,' she says. For a second I think she's going to let it go, then she throws her hands in the air and looks at me like she did in sixth form when I tried to deny I had shagged Dean Waters. The news of my copulation with the school's squarest boy was made worse by the fact it was my first time. She didn't let it go for several years thereafter. 'I'm not here to judge you, Kat. I mean, I will judge you, obviously – BFF prerogative – but that shouldn't make a difference to you.'

'It doesn't make a difference to me, because I don't fancy the plumber. Not that it would make a difference if I did. This is all bigger than a crush that I don't have on some bloke from work – not least the fact that Susan is way more complex than I first imagined.' I throw a stupidly large-scale piece of information into the ring in an attempt to deflect. It's a poorly executed sleight of hand.

'Tell. Me. Everything.'

Regrettable.

The assistant saves me. 'You need to take this dress off now, please,' she says, guiding Lou back into the changing room. My relief at her being swept away is tempered by the arrival of my own dress.

'Hold that thought,' she shouts at me through the curtain. 'I want all of the details just as soon as I am de-frocked and we have taken a moment to bask in the deliciousness of your dress. You are going to love it.'

Grateful for the conversation stopper, I try to peer through the white bag that contains my wedding heaven or wedding hell, depending on the mood she was in when she chose it. I don't think it's peach. Or taffeta. But I can't see anything after a blindfold has been placed over my eyes and I'm standing in the changing room, part naked and slightly vulnerable, being dressed in secret. There should be rules against this kind of thing. Three minutes and forty-five seconds later – roughly – I step out to a sharp intake of breath from Lou and stand before the mirror. As the assistant unties the ribbon shielding my view, I see my reflection. A dress of rich, slate grey wraps me up in Grecian style. A matching flower corsage sits perfectly on my waist, and the halter neck skims my shoulders. Yards and yards of fabric hang in straight folds, and every time I move, it moves with me. For the second time this morning my throat tightens, as I realise I've never felt so beautiful or girly in all of my life. 'It's not…'

'Peach?' Lou says, reaching for the complimentary Kleenex and dabbing her eye.

'It's so…'

'Perfect,' she says. Then comes to stand beside me, talking to me through the mirror. 'Look at you, being all pretty and stuff.' She reaches for my hair, taking a clip out of her own and loosely pinning mine up. 'And look, you can have your hair up like this, if you like. With just a hint of make-up and a splash of perfume. I'll buy you some. You will be the most beautiful bridesmaid I could ever ask for.' She takes my hand and kisses it. 'Kat, I couldn't ask for a better person to stand by my side on my wedding day. I really hope you like it.' I look at my reflection, my eyes heavy and tired. And from nowhere, tears spill. Great, fat, unavoidable tears that are difficult to hide from your best friend. 'Hey, babe. What's the matter? Do you hate it?' She looks to the assistant, digging out more Kleenex to wipe my face. 'Oh my God, she hates it. She hates it.' Then she stage whispers behind my back, 'Get it off her, get it off.'

'No,' I cough. 'No. It's not the dress. It's beautiful, Lou, thank you. I love it.' I let her dab my tears. 'And I love you. And I can't wait to be there on your special day.' I sigh. 'It isn't the dress at all.' I take the tissue box now helpfully offered by the assistant, who is, no doubt, more than capable of handling blubbing wedding parties. 'I don't know why I'm crying.' I look to the floor, well aware that I *do* know why and that if I catch Lou's eye she will work out why too, and I don't want to explain myself. I try to resist as she pulls my face up to hers.

'What's so bad that you're crying in your bridesmaid dress, Kat? Because if you cry on that fabric, it will probably disintegrate.'

I take a deep breath, then tell Lou all about finding Rhys at Susan's house, about the book, about the lonely emptiness of her home. I describe the sudden, unexpected reaction from Rhys and our talk this morning. I tell her about my fear of having a patient who needs such specific care, and my lack of belief that I can give it. I tell her that I'm so wrapped up in my own confusion about Daniel, about work, about everything, that I feel incapable of making the right decisions about any of the things in my life right now.

Lou stays remarkably quiet throughout it all, which goes to show how seriously she is taking it. She doesn't once surreptitiously update her Facebook profile or tweet about anything I'm saying.

'So what are you going to do?' she asks. I shrug, overwhelmed, confused and exhausted. 'I've never seen you like this,' she says. 'You always know what you're doing and how to fix things. You always have! What's happened to change that? Why are you so... lost?'

'I'm not lost, Lou. I'm just busy, and hurting, and confused.'

The assistant appears, hovering by me as a new gaggle of girls arrive for their appointment. Lou squeezes my hand and I squeeze back, but something about the look on her face tells me she thinks it's more than my being busy, hurt or confused. 'I need to get to work,' I say, hopping off the step.

When I get out of the changing room, my uniform back in place and the weight of responsibility placed firmly back on the stripes on my arm, Lou is waiting for me, my bag in her hand. 'Here's your bag of trouble.'

I take it from her, checking the contents. 'Thanks.'

'How come you were there, anyway?' she asks, as we go back out into the non-air-conditioned sunshine.

'I was taking Daniel's stuff to his mum's.'

'Wow, really?' she asks, steering me away from the shop doorway.

'Yup.' I pull the bag onto my shoulder, as someone passes by knocking into it, jerking my arm back.

'Was he there?' she asks tentatively, helping me put it back on before squeezing my arm in silent support.

'Yup.'

'And?'

'And so was some Amazonian beauty with impeccable hair and legs I'd kill for.'

'Oh.' She drops her head, looking at her feet. 'I told you he was a loser.'

'I know. I know you did.'

'Maybe now you could go on that date with that consultant bloke.'

And she's back in the room. 'Yes, Lou. That's just what I need in my life right now – more confusion.'

'You need distraction. You need to move on with your life. You need… a shag!'

'Oh God, that's the last thing on my mind right now!' I groan.

Lou pulls me close, squeezes me tight, then plants a glossy kiss on my cheek. 'Don't diss it till you've tried it!' She winks at me. 'Now, go on, oh bridesmaid of mine, get yourself to work. Those patients need you! That patient. And the consultant!' I watch as she totters away. 'And you need you too!' she shouts, disappearing around a corner, leaving me to catch the bus.

Chapter Twenty-Six

RHYS

Our David's chair cuddles me, and my head drops back into its warmth. I let out a yawn and Mum sighs. We take the pause to look at each other. My mum, the one woman I could always count on. The one who understands me and forgives me. The one who picked me up physically when I went head over handlebars at age six. The one who picked me up emotionally when I failed every last GCSE I took. What does she think when she looks at me?

'There's more to this, isn't there.' She states it as fact, rather than posing the question. 'This isn't about Derek, or David, even. What's going on, Rhys?'

We reach the crossroads. Left: I tell her the truth. From Michelle to Susan, via the book of fairy tales and my panic about how the hell I deal with a world I can't control. Right: I tell her a lie to smooth things over, leaving me to get on with things on my own. Which, at the very least, protects her from more evidence I'm a royal disappointment.

'Rhys?'

'I tried to help that woman at the hospital. The one I thought was you.'

'Whatever for, Rhys?'

I think for a moment, realising I can't completely go left. 'Because she has nobody. Because she's alone in the world and I couldn't get her out of my head. The nurses said I was helping, and you know what, that felt good. It felt good to think that I could make a difference to someone.'

'But you make a difference to me, Rhys.'

'Still? But you've got Derek now, you don't need me.' I hear myself and I don't like it. I try harder to dig for the truth. To excavate beneath the spoiled-child exterior. 'I thought, perhaps, I'd learn to understand.'

'Understand what, Rhys?'

I cross my arms.

'Rhys?' she pushes.

'I thought if I helped her, I'd understand what makes someone want to kill themselves,' I answer quietly. 'I've said it before to you, Mum, but I don't think you understand how important this is. How much I need to know. I thought I could help her and, in so doing, lay a ghost to rest. She ended up in hospital because she tried to end her life. I might not have been able to save David, but perhaps I could have saved her.'

'Oh, Rhys.' She pulls the pouffe up towards me, sitting with her hands on my knees. 'Love.' She reaches up to stroke my face. 'People can't be saved if they don't want to be, we've talked about this.' Her touch pushes me back into the chair; the clock ticks out the seconds. 'When you say "could have"… is that what this is about? Has she…?' She can't bring herself to finish the sentence and I quickly shake my head, but resist explaining further. How do I tell her why I've had to stop? Why suddenly the woman I wanted to help has become the woman I can't stand to even think about? After a pause, Mum sucks at her teeth, before gingerly asking, 'Have you tried talking to Michelle?'

I bite my lip, hard. The metal taste of my blood bites back.

'Maybe she could help? Maybe you can help each other? Is she okay? Have you seen her? Why don't you two get together?'

'What do you mean get together?'

'I mean talk to each other. You want to find someone to help who might be able to help you, why not Michelle? At least she knew our David. And she knows you. She understands our family. Maybe she can help you and you her? How is she, do you know? I tried calling her this week and she didn't pick up. Maybe she's—'

'Michelle's fine.' I get up, moving across to the fireplace, away from Mum's glare. I shift the clock and a china dog about on the shelf. 'I saw her the other day, Mum, she's fine. Well, not *fine* fine, but she's okay. She's getting there. She's…'

Mum gets up to stand beside me, laying a hand gently on my arm, like mums do when they want to drive home a point without making you defensive. 'I just think you need to talk to people other than just me, love. Michelle is the obvious choice – she knows what you're going through. Maybe if you had someone else to talk to, you'd stop focusing on this Susan woman. I don't think it's healthy, Rhys.'

'I should get to work.' I turn, not quite able to catch Mum's eye.

'Yes, you should.' She pulls at my arms, seeking out the eye contact that I'd do anything to avoid. 'You did a kind thing,' she says, my hands clasped in hers. 'You didn't have to go back to her, you didn't have to get involved. You've done your bit, now let her find her own way through. You have enough to deal with.' She leads me through to the hallway, passing me my boots. I rest my shoulder against the front door, my hair covering my eyes. Mum brushes off imaginary dust from my shoulder, then says, 'Life is gone in a flash, Rhys. We know that better than many.' I open the front door, only half looking at her. 'Don't waste yours fighting fights you'll never win. With me or anyone.'

I smile a half-smile, which she duly returns.

'Maybe some time you could meet him,' she says. 'Derek, I mean…'

I nod, hoping my poker face hides the fact it's the last thing I want to do.

Chapter Twenty-Seven

KAT

I run down the wide-cobbled street of Norfolk Row to the overcrowded line of bus stops. People push, brush and knock me as they catch buses, or jump off them and rush into town. My bag, complete with Susan's book, swings and clips my shin several times before I move it up to my chest, tucked in tight. She isn't expecting me to bring it. Will she wonder if I've seen the cutting? Does she even realise it's in there? Will any of this bring back her voice, or do we risk pushing her further out of reach?

As I climb on the bus, the heat is stifling. The smell is thick with the heady scent of passengers. Is that what's making me feel sick? There's a free seat up at the back and I huddle into it, using the journey to plan various imaginary conversations in my head. I start with Susan, explaining why I'm the one to bring her the book, not Rhys. I'll say he has a lot on, that he's snowed under with work or something. That he'll try and see her later in the week. Maybe I shouldn't say that. I don't think we'll see him again. Then there's the conversation with my boss, Gail. How do I explain what has happened? How do I make sure she knows I made each choice in good faith, with good intentions? That I realise now they might not have been the right choices, but they were the best I could make with the information I had. How do I do that without getting my probation cut short? I don't want to lose this promotion. I want her to see she was right to take the risk with me. Will she still believe it when she knows about the events of the last few days? Maybe that's what's making me feel sick.

I can't lose this job.

I close my eyes, taking a second to breathe in through the nose and out through the mouth, anything to get rid of the butterflies. Opening them again, I watch the city go by as the bus weaves through the streets. Sheffield Theatres, Ponds Forge, office blocks and the Police Station. Passengers get on and off and I move the bag from the seat beside me to my lap, making way for someone to sit down. The weight of it rests heavily on my knees. It's a beautiful book. What does it mean to Susan? Or does she just want it because of the newspaper cutting?

The bus pulls up to my stop. I pull myself together and jump off, running up the tree-lined hill towards the main entrance.

I drum my fingers against the bag and flick through a rack of flyers for distraction as I wait for the lift. I swipe my way into the ward and head straight to Susan's bed.

As I approach her, she pushes an empty lunch plate away. 'Good morning, Susan. Or is it afternoon?' I look up to the clock: it's twelve thirty. 'How are you today? The bruising's a lot better. Was lunch okay?' I move her table out of the way, checking her water. 'Your book is in here, Susan. The one you asked Rhys for?' I hold it out for her to take, but she just looks at it with a flicker of confusion in her eyes. 'And your house key is here too. Shall I?' I place the book in reach, on her bed, picking up her handbag to check if she wants the key back in there. Nerves rattling, I leave them both on the side in the end.

Susan stares at the book, still not moving. I reach over and pass it to her. Her chest rises and falls as her eyes fix firmly on my outstretched arms, the deep red book. The butterflies flit back, up and around in my belly. I place it back on her table again but this time, slowly, she reaches out a soft hand, laying it on the top. She doesn't move to take it, or open it, but leaves her hand still, fingers covering the title. Eventually she looks up and beyond me, searching for anyone else. For Rhys.

'He sends his love,' I say, instinctively. Susan's eyes shift to mine, piercing my confidence in my rehearsed speech. The butterflies shift to great moths that leap from stomach to throat. 'He's quite… Well, he's busy. He said to say…' An intensity grows on her face. She's more engaged in my words than I've seen her before. Is that why they run dry? Susan no longer looks like an injured bird in the bed – she looks focused, almost determined. She opens her mouth and my heart stops. I hold my breath, waiting to hear her voice. There's a beat, and she closes it again, dropping her eyes back down to the book. And as quickly as I caught a glance of her, she is gone.

'Maybe he'll come by in a few days,' I say, because I think that's what she wants to hear. I don't sound all that convincing to my own ears. I swallow. The weight of her changing energy has buckled my confidence once and for all. 'He says he's sorry,' I add, fussing about. She reaches her hand out and stops me from patting the bed down. I pull up sharply. 'Sorry.' I smooth down my uniform instead. The trees rustle outside the window. 'Can you hear that?' I ask. 'The trees. Listen… They sound like the sea.' Susan lets her hand fall back onto the bed. I pause, letting the rustle bring back memories of family holidays in Cornwall. Happiness and ice cream. No responsibilities.

'Susan.' I speak carefully, words forming before I have the chance to consider their meaning. 'I was with Rhys, when he collected the book.

I just happened to be passing and thought it would be better for you both if I was with him. I hope that's okay.' She's staring at the book. 'The thing is, Susan…' I reach out to her, laying my hand on hers, which is still atop the book. 'I'm really quite worried about you. About your state of mind.' She lets her eyes wander from my hand to my shoulder, not making eye contact, but somehow making it clear she's listening. 'Your house, it felt… Well, it felt as if—' Susan looks to me now, pushes the book away from reach and turns her face towards the window. This is a no-go area. Out of bounds. But I can't just leave it.

'I'd like to help you, Susan.'

She closes her eyes, making her rejection of my offer known. After hovering a second, the absence of anything else to say crushes my confidence. I respect her decision and leave.

Heading into my office, I push the door closed behind me, resting against it for a second to process what just happened. How I can explain it, rationalise it, how I can make head or tail of the whole situation so Gail and I can piece together the evidence to fix this mess. To fix Susan. Because I see now that I can't do this alone. And perhaps I don't have to.

My finger falters as I dial Gail's number. Since becoming my line manager, she's been fairly unavailable. I wait for the ring, checking over my story, the reason for my call, the reason I went to a patient's house without following protocol first, the reasons I have cause for concern about my patient and my proposals on the ways we can deal with this. Mental health isn't my area, I'm out of my depth, but I can't walk away from the responsibility now placed on my shoulders. Her voicemail kicks in with a clipped invite to leave a message.

'Gail, hi, it's Kat. I…' I swallow to regain control. This is not the time to show nerves. 'I wondered if we could have a chat. About Susan Smith. I'll be at my desk all day, it's quite urgent. Thank you.'

I hang up, pressing the handset into the receiver so it definitely cuts the call. I go back out to the nurses' station, filing papers and tidying the desk up. I take a look through the opening to Susan's room. Her curtains are open and I can see she's moved herself up to sit. She reaches for the deep red of her book and I freeze, desperate not to miss a thing. I watch – my shoulders high and tight – as Susan lifts the book to her face, smells it. She runs her hands down its front. She lets her fingers trace the title, and I can feel it too. Its golden italics. The twist of its letters. Susan's breathing gets heavier, her chest gives a dramatic rise and fall. Mine does the same. She lifts the book, placing it on her knees, and my view is momentarily obscured by a porter pushing a patient past me. When she's back in view, Susan is taking a deep breath, then slowly opening the book. Thin, flimsy pages buckle and fall as she flicks through it, eventually letting it lie flat, naturally open. At the clipping? She stares at the page – or is it the photo in the story? Maybe both? Then she lifts the cutting, studying it. As I watch, I can see the baby's face that she sees. I can recite each word from the story. Do I feel what she feels? Queasiness. Helplessness. Deep, deep sadness. If that is her baby, she can't only be feeling that.

Susan places the clipping firmly back in the book, closes it tight and drops back out of view, the book clamped to her chest. Whether or not Rhys and I did the right thing by fetching this book, it's impossible to tell. And if not, how do you even begin to ask about such a story as that cutting, and what her role in it might be?

'Did Gail find you?' one of the nurses asks. I flip around at the sound of her voice.

'Pardon?'

'Gail. She was here earlier looking for you, asked if you could call her as soon as possible.' The phone in my office rings out and my heart stops. 'Bets on that's her,' says the nurse, and I swallow back a little fear. I jog back towards my office, before turning to ask, 'Did she seem…' But the nurse has gone.

I pick up my phone. 'Hello?'

'Kat, Gail.'

'Oh, hi, Gail. Thanks for—'

'Look, no time now but I just wanted to say I got your message about Susan and we need to talk anyway. I've got to go and see someone then I'll be with you – 3 p.m. Please make sure you're free to see me.'

'Yup, okay. Three. See you th—' But she's hung up. I write the appointment in my diary, my hands visibly shaking.

There's a sharp knock at my door and Mark pokes his head around. 'Hey – oh, you okay?'

'Sure, why?' I flick my diary closed and look up, trying to appear light of mood.

'You look a bit… stressed,' he says, stepping towards my desk. 'Can I get you anything? A drink? Something to eat? Chocolate?' He grins at his final suggestion, like he's just offered the solution to life's greatest challenge. 'There must be biscuits on the desk?' He gestures outside of my office.

'No, no, I'm fine, thanks.' I raise my hand to stop him. He looks at me, as if trying to work out his next move in a game of chess. I let out a groan and my head drops to my desk. 'Why is this job so hard?'

He laughs gently. 'The easy stuff generally isn't so worthwhile, in my humble experience,' he says, pulling up a chair to sit down.

'Humble?' I raise my head just enough to peer at him through my fringe, but his injured-bird expression suggests I've crossed a line we've not yet reached.

'What's the problem?' he asks, deftly moving us on. He leans back in the chair, taking on his officious doctor persona. He's a steepled finger away from therapist territory. If he had a beard, he'd be stroking it now. He'd suit a beard.

'It's Susan,' I say, and he leans forward. 'Long story, but I ended up at her house last night and it seems our fears about her accident were right. She had all but moved out of her house, erased herself from the very fabric of it. She certainly didn't appear to have any intention of returning. We picked up a book for her—'

'We?'

'Rhys and I.' Mark looks confused. 'Also a long story, but, basically, on his last visit she gave him a house key and asked for a book.'

'Asked?'

'Wrote a note.'

He nods his head, processing the information. 'Okay, so what are you thinking?'

'I don't know. This isn't my area. How do you deal with something like that without being confrontational and pushing her over the edge? The whole thing is unravelling out of my grasp.' I rub my forehead, wishing I hadn't said that last bit. Wishing I could take it back and present the picture of a ward sister in total control of her patient's care.

'I'm sure you have it all in hand, really. Have you filed a report on your visit?'

I hadn't even thought of that.

'Look, complicated patients always test our confidence, but I've only ever heard brilliant things about you, Kat. You will be dealing with it just fine, I am certain.' He smiles, his eyes sparkling, and I feel myself colour a little. 'You've got this,' he says.

'Gail's coming round shortly. I'll have to fill her in and see what she wants to do about things.'

'Tell her we've discussed it. Write me that report on the situation, explain how you got to be at Susan's, what you found and her responses throughout. Let's try and get it over to the mental health team before this afternoon's meeting. Can you manage that?'

I nod. 'I'll do my best.'

'They can advise us on the next course of action from their point of view. She's not going anywhere for now. We have time to help her. Don't worry.' He gets up to leave. 'Is Rhys still visiting? Has he been helping?'

'Ah, that's where it gets slightly more complicated,' I say. 'We found a newspaper cutting in the book, something about an abandoned baby. We don't know what her connection is to it but it touched a raw nerve with Rhys. He took the implication of her home and the paper cutting quite badly. He's got his own issues at the moment. I fear we might not see him again.'

'Oh, that is a shame. Is he okay?'

'I'm not sure…'

'Okay, that's one to keep an eye on too then. Call him, try to re-engage him if you can. Make sure he knows what services are available to him if getting involved with this whole Susan thing has triggered anything. We have a duty of care to Rhys now too.' Mark heads for the door. 'And don't worry!'

'Thanks.' I stand up, checking my watch. 'Did you want something?' I ask, remembering that he came to see me.

'Me? No, no… I can't remember. I'll come back if I do.' He smiles, tips me a gentlemanly salute, then disappears.

Chapter Twenty-Eight

SUSAN

How long do I wait? How long should I stay in case he does come back? In case the twitch in Kat's eye, the tightly folded arms and the quiver in her voice weren't giveaways to a lie at all, but prove nothing more than quirks of body language. That Rhys does plan to return, because he hasn't pieced together a truth I cannot explain away.

How long do I wait?

And if I do wait, as I have for a lifetime, and he does return, where do we go from here? Where do I begin? How can I ever begin to tell him why and how he came into my life? Would he even believe me? How much does he already know? How can I fix the mistakes that I've made?

I asked for the book to begin the process of putting wrongs right. But it feels as if its weight has pulled me down, dragging me beneath the murky waters of my lies. If there's a bitter taste in his mouth, perhaps I should do as I planned, put an end to my pain and guilt, and cause no more in others. Perhaps it would be easiest for us all if I simply walked away. I've barely been here in the first place.

But they have a right to know, don't they?

Chapter Twenty-Nine

KAT

I've been checking my watch every five minutes – an hour and a half really drags when your belly's swaddled with the weight of responsibility and nervous decisions. The report is typed as per Mark's suggestion, every last piece of detail I can think of included. I've reached for the phone several times to call Rhys, but each time something has stopped me. I'm not certain it's in his best interests. I'm not certain it's in Susan's either.

Three minutes to three. I stand and walk the perimeter of my room, stretching out knots in my back and arms. Gail is known for many things, punctuality being right up there with sharpness and a lack of suffering fools. Have I been a fool? My eyes are glued to the sweep of the clock's second hand as it moves in silent foreboding around the face. The hands tick onto three o'clock exactly and the ward door opens with a whoosh. I hear her before she arrives; a few orders in one direction – 'Emma, can you just check the kitchen, looks like someone forgot to sort the pots.' Then the continued, familiar clomp, clomp, slide of her gait. I can imagine Emma scowling at Gail's back before scurrying to do a job that isn't really her responsibility. Nobody says no to Gail.

'Kat.' She halts at my door like a sergeant major and I gulp. Is it visible? Can she smell my fear?

'Gail, I'm so sorry to…' I waft my arms around like an idiot. 'Thanks for coming.' I try to show her to the spare seat then wonder if I should be showing her to the seat she once occupied behind my desk. Her desk. I don't know. 'The thing is—'

'Sorry, hang on, Kat. Me first.' She strides in, hands up. Three steps and a slide, and she's at my desk. I sidle my way around to my side, the office door taunting me with just how open she's left it. Wide open. Impossible to hide anything.

'It is with an element of surprise,' she begins, bold and confident, 'because I must say, of all the things, I did not see this particular situation coming…' She sniffs, her nose in the air, arms crossed. My stomach drops to my feet. 'It seems that your temporary promotion as acting ward sister has come to an end.'

My legs buckle beneath me and I reach for my chair. Someone's beaten me to it. Who could it be? Only Mark and Lou know what's gone off. Emma knows a little but she wouldn't, would she? Has Susan found her voice? I lower my head, taking a pen to fiddle with, realising it's the inappropriate one I'd wanted to distract Mark with. Typical that I'd find it now. Gail's still talking, something about people's unforeseen attitudes and decisions. Careers on the line. I slide the pen beneath some paperwork and reach for another. I can't look at her. I don't know where to start or how to explain, or really, where I went wrong. I was just trying to do my best. How is that bad?

'You don't really need the detail, but suffice to say, she won't be coming back,' Gail finishes.

'Pardon?'

'Congratulations.' Gail stretches her hand out to shake mine. 'You're the new ward sister. Penny's decided to go private.'

I stare at her, long enough for her to wave her hand in my direction until I take hers and shake it. 'She's not coming back, Kat.' She smiles, and wanders over to the bookcase, looking at familiar titles she will have seen and read before. She lifts out the one Mark lent me, nodding approvingly. 'You're the second youngest to get this promotion in the last five years…' We both know she was the first. 'I get glowing reports from staff and patients when doing any kind of appraisal process on you, always have. Mr Barnes talks incredibly highly of you.' I blush almost as deeply as when he complimented me earlier. 'And you are obviously a confident and assured manager, though you may need to pay attention to the detail on some aspects. We don't have the luxury of staff numbers of old.' She's talking about the kitchen. I know she is. 'So, there you are.' She turns to face me, looking very pleased with herself. 'Congratulations.'

I'm stunned. This is not how I thought our conversation was going to go. I don't even know if I want this anymore. The responsibility… it's too much. I think.

'Now, this is a big challenge, it's about more than just patient care at this level. It's about management, strategy, understanding the bigger picture. Some patients are straightforward, some cases easy, but sometimes…'

I adjust the collar on my dress. Oh, how I know about the 'sometimes' right now.

'But I have faith in you, you'll do brilliantly.'

My mouth hangs open, I'm searching for the words to explain why this may be premature. Why I can't accept.

'Well done.'

'I'm not sure I'm ready,' I try.

'Nonsense, of course you are. Now, we can talk about some of the details next week. I need to get off. It's Jonny's school sports day and I've been limbering up for the mums' run. Sheena Daly has grossly underestimated my speed and I plan on putting her firmly back in her Lycra-clad box. I'm on annual leave now until a week on Thursday. Let's have coffee when I get back and talk about what's next. Okay? Great. Well done.' She smiles, about turns and marches out, leaving the words of my promotion hanging in my office. I hear her bark some more orders through the ward as I run after her.

'I can't accept,' I shout. She stops dead and turns to face me. 'I can't accept,' I repeat. 'Not until...' I cough, swallow, then gesture towards my office. 'I need to talk with you first. Can we? Please.' Gail's face is a mix of ice and thunder and total disbelief. 'If you could just...' I motion again for her to come into my office. The office. She looks at her watch. Poor Jonny and his sports day – though I can't help thinking I'm giving Sheena Daly a lucky escape.

Gail steps back inside, letting me close the door behind her. 'Take a seat,' I offer.

'I'm going to be late,' she snaps, sitting.

'I know, I'm sorry, but this is important.' She clasps her hands around her knee and waits for me to begin. And so I do. I tell her about Susan and the number. Rhys and the visits. The key. The book. The clipping. Her house. I tell her about trying to help, trying to do the right thing. Being in the wrong place at the right time or maybe, fortuitously, the right place at the right time. I can see from the look on her face that my rambling isn't helping.

'You're supposed to follow protocol with regards to patients like Susan. You can't just go wandering into her home.'

'I know, I understand that. But I had no choice, Rhys was going in anyway. And had I not, we'd never have this additional information that might just help us fix her, Gail.' I stand now, suddenly confident that whatever protocol dictates, I *did* do the right thing and I *can* help. I can make a difference.

Gail stares at me, then at her watch. She looks around the office, then stands, moving to the window, folding her arms. Saying nothing.

'I've talked it through with Mr Barnes, Gail. He asked me to write a full report.' I pull the screen around for her to see. 'It's all here. My findings, the detail, and my thoughts on what we might be able to do. He has asked me to submit it to the mental health team before a meeting we have, so we can organise a strategic course of action. Gail, I know this isn't ideal, but you were right, some patients are different. They require more care. Capacity doesn't always afford us that time, but on this occasion, we're fortunate to be able to take positive action.' I feel almost as surprised as Gail looks by my sudden confidence in the matter. Everyone else seems to believe I can do this – perhaps it's time I believed it too.

Gail stands. 'Send me the report as well. Make sure I have every single piece of detail. In the event that Susan, or any family we've so far been unable to find, suggests there is an issue with your actions, I need to ensure I have all the facts to defend you.' She turns and heads for the door. 'Kat…'

I hold my breath.

'This is a highly complex situation. Be careful. Track every single thing you do. I have to leave or I'll be late.' I nod. She nods in return then leaves, giving me no real indication of what she's really thinking.

I fall back into my chair, letting out a long-held breath. I stare at the screen, my report staring back at me. I delete the word 'acting' from my job title at the end of the paper, clicking save. Ward Sister Kat Davies. That's me.

Reading my words back, the gravity of this situation presses me back into the chair. I might feel a shade of confidence in my decisions, but it doesn't take away from the facts: I have a patient who, it appears, wished to kill herself. I have a patient who is quite possibly the mother of an abandoned child. And I have an innocent visitor embroiled in it all, throwing up a whole host of new concerns. I check my fob watch; there's half an hour before the meeting.

Before I get a chance to send the report to Gail, Emma comes squealing into my office like one of those screechy balloons let loose to flip around the room. She pulls the arms of my chair towards her and leans in to squeeze me too tight. 'This is brilliant, you are brilliant, I am so proud of you!' she says, squeezing me tight again before standing back to read my face. 'Ahh, look at you, all grown up and important. We need to celebrate! A night out! Leave this with me, I am on it like a car bonnet,' she says, apparently missing the small print all over my face.

'Emma, I can't. I've got to sort—'

'Nonsense, you HAVE to celebrate promotions. God, I am so proud of you. You've done an amazing job! I was saying that to—'

'Emma, please, really.' I raise my voice. 'I've got quite a bit on my plate now.'

'What's the matter?'

'Susan! Rhys!' I stare back at my screen, rapping my keyboard with a pen. 'It's just a bit overwhelming. All of this, you know?'

'Don't you be silly.' She takes hold of my hands. 'Kat, I have admired you since we first met in college, since that first day when you pulled me in close when you saw I needed it. You instinctively know what a patient needs and you always find a way to deliver it, over and above general medical care. You can lead a team. You can inspire others. You inspire me with your determination every single day. And I know,' she says, interrupting me as I try to stop her again, 'I know this has been a rough couple of months and I know the life you planned is not the one that you seem to be heading towards, but the one I can see panning out is so much brighter. Your career is going to flourish, and you have the chance to meet someone when you're ready, someone who appreciates how brilliant you are and who lets you be you.' She takes a breath. 'I never told you before because your life is none of my business, but I always felt Daniel wanted to keep you in a world *he* felt comfortable in, no matter if it was the right one for you. Nobody can do that to you now, you're free.' She pulls me in for another hug and her words spin around my mind. 'You're gonna nail this, Sister Kat,' she whispers into my ear. 'And I'm right behind you every step of the way.' I blink up at her, not sure what to say. 'I'll text you when and where as soon as I've got it sorted,' she says. 'We're going to celebrate!' She goes for the door and then pauses. I look through some papers, desperate to bury how overwhelmed I feel within the sheets of files and reports. 'Oh, I nearly forgot, Mark called. He's sending Susan down for physio while you have your meeting. One of the porters will be up for her in a minute.' She skips out of the office, whooping.

I open up my emails, clicking send on the report to Mark, Gail and the Mental Health team. Job one: done. I dig out Rhys's number to call him, but it goes straight through to voicemail. 'Rhys, hi, it's Kat. I wanted to check how you were doing, see if there's anything

I can do to help – with anything. I passed the book over, Susan has been reading it.' I pause, wondering if Mark is right about getting him back in again. 'If you felt able, I'm sure she'd like to see you again. Or if you need to talk, just ask.' I hang up. Close my eyes. Ruffle a bit of life into my hair before heading out for our meeting.

I've got this.

I have. Hopefully.

Chapter Thirty

RHYS

Day one of hiding was mostly spent in my bed, feeling sorry for myself. Day two, I drove out to Ladybower Dam and walked through the forest, head down, the shade from the trees keeping me cool. Day three, today, I had planned to return to work, not least because I need the money. I've already ignored messages from Paul, Kat and Mum; the missed calls stacked up and guilt got the better of me. Mum instructed me to meet her on neutral territory. So I'm here, at the Botanical Gardens. Trying to be a better son, a better human being.

She's waiting on a bench, her face towards the sunshine. 'Morning, Mum.' Her eyes slowly open and I lean in to give her a kiss. She reaches for my arms, letting me pull her up. I get a brief glimpse into a future where I'm the grown-up and she needs me. I don't like it. We stand awkwardly, not quite hugging, but not fully detached from one another. What I'd do to have her give me one of those mum hugs. The ones where you just know everything's going to be okay. Instead, she squeezes my forearm, before reaching back to collect her handbag. I miss her.

'I thought it would be nice for us to take a walk. Appreciate our surroundings,' she says. I nod, glancing at the gardens and pavilion.

Ornamental grass blows in a warm breeze and there's a heady scent in the air, maybe lavender. 'I love this place,' she says, breathy and rejuvenated compared to Friday. 'Despite the fact your dad and I used to visit, back when we were courting. We'd take a walk around then head over to Ecclesall Road for lunch.' She smiles a distant smile. It's not often she mentions Dad, and certainly not to replay a fond memory. A mark of her state of mind? 'Funny how life changes,' she sighs, a sadness crossing her face. It's timed with a passing cloud that cuts out the sunshine, and the sudden shade reflects our mood. 'Sometimes I wonder how I might have done things differently,' she finishes.

'Don't we all.'

Like when I told our David not to be frightened of finding his birth mother. That adopted children did it all the time, that it might be the very making of him. That I was going to do the same and it was all going to be worth it.

'I'd change a lot of things,' I say, desperately deflecting. 'The ouzo-fuelled welcome meeting on that eighteen-to-thirty holiday with Paul, for one thing.' Mum rolls her eyes. 'You might give me that look, Mum, but going on the pull when you're shitting through the eye of a needle is troublesome at best.'

'Rhys!'

'Sorry.'

I'm not sure we're in a place for banter yet. We walk on in silence, which is probably for the best. Mum occasionally runs her hand through the leaves, or bends down to smell summer-coloured petals of flowers I can't name. A toddler runs through the winding gravel paths, playing hide-and-seek with her parents. She giggles and screeches with delight each time she gets caught, tickled then hugged by both her mum and dad. Was it ever like that before Dad left? I can't remember. It so often feels as if life before Dad left belonged to someone else.

'I've been thinking,' starts Mum.

'Dangerous.' I nudge her arm but it's met with a sharp look. 'Sorry. Go on.'

'I think…' She stops in her tracks, takes a deep breath, then says, 'I think it's time you tried to find your birth mother.' She walks on as soon as she's said it, taking hold of some herbs and letting the scent rub onto the palm of her hand.

'No,' I say. This isn't up for discussion. I resist the urge to walk away, but do pick up the pace, passing her as she bends to read a plaque on a bench. I didn't come here to be hijacked on this subject. I thought she was trying to make friends again.

'Rhys, don't discount it. And slow down.' She pulls my arm to bring me back alongside her. 'I've just been watching you, since David… And this week in particular, I don't know what's happened to you. I thought you were coping, but then all this stuff with that Susan woman comes up, this sudden obsession with a stranger. You're avoiding your own issues.' I shoot her a look. Since when did she become the psychotherapist? 'And when I tried to talk to you about Derek—'

'What? What about that exactly?'

'Well, you have to admit you didn't take it well.'

'Do you blame me?' I stop beneath a birch tree. The sun filters through the leaves and shadows like lace dance across the path. 'We made a pact, Mum. We need each other. I didn't realise that pact was only valid while *you* needed it.' The words sting her, I can tell by the look on her face. And I'm sorry, but not sorry. And that makes me even sorrier.

'That's not fair, Rhys,' she says, her voice low and firm. 'Of course we need each other, and I will always be here for you, but I have to find a way to make my life the best it can be. For your brother's memory, if nothing else. And this is one way to do that, to try and find happiness in amongst the gloom.' She stares at me. 'You need that too.'

I hold her eye for a moment before walking on. She follows.

'I think you need to find your own life, your own story, Rhys. Your birth mother is part of that. She is part of you, and you her, and these missing elements of your life are the things that make it difficult to forge a pathway. A future of your own.'

'What are you talking about? I'm fine. Grieving, yes, but that's normal, isn't it? I feel like I let him down, Mum. I feel like I pushed him towards something that finally broke him. If it wasn't for me—'

'That's not true and you know it, Rhys.' She pulls my arm, swinging me around to look at her. 'Why would you torture yourself that way?' There are tears in her eyes as she reaches up to touch my face. I grit my teeth together, fighting back my emotions. 'David made his own choices, Rhys. Just as you should.' She pauses, letting her hand fall back down to her side. 'I just think your choice should include your birth mother.'

I stare up to the sky. A bird catches a thermal, rising high then swooping down low to the ground. I follow its arc, desperate to avoid the ache that swamps my body. This is the biggest hurt I've ever felt; grit sticks in my throat when I so much as think about any of it.

About the truth Mum doesn't know.

'Rhys?' she reaches out to me.

'Did you ever try to find out about her?' I ask, dropping down onto a bench beside us, eyes dead ahead.

Mum sits and fidgets beside me. 'No,' she eventually answers, her voice quiet. Is she embarrassed? I nod, slowly, and it's not long until she feels compelled to expand. 'I didn't want to know anything. I didn't want to find information that led me to assume anything. I didn't want to judge. I wanted to nurture you. I wanted to make decisions in the best interests of my child. I didn't want to find I'd second-guessed those decisions on the basis that I had your backstory. It was a long time ago, Rhys. I thought I was doing the right thing.'

I take in her words, mulling them over. I'm not sure I get it. Why wouldn't she want to know everything about me? Every last detail about her son.

'Your Dad, he wasn't interested either. Encouraged me to leave it.' She laughs to herself, a low, cynical laugh. 'That was enough to vindicate me.'

Do I tell her this answer seems weak? The choice of a coward. A word I never thought I'd use for Mum. How would she feel if she knew I was disappointed in her? Is it even fair that I feel that way? What do I know of the position she was in back then? What do I know about anything?

Except I know what she never bothered to find out.

'I thought, maybe one day, you could find out about it for yourself. If you ever needed to, or wanted to. And I support that one hundred per cent. I can see now it might have helped, and God, Rhys, I am so sorry if my choice was wrong. I truly am.' She reaches out to squeeze my knee. 'I will help you in any way I can, if you want to find her.'

I fold my arms. 'It looks like we'll never find her.' I've said it before I can stop myself.

'What?'

I flex my jawline, steeling myself before opening the wound. 'There's no record of her existence.' My voice is quieter this time, not quite so forceful, my resolve worn away. I can see, from the corner of my eye, that Mum's mouth is open, eyes wide. Confusion etched across her face.

'No record? How do you know?' She stares at me as if I'm a stranger, someone with a story she knows nothing about. 'I thought we talked about everything, Rhys, I didn't think we had secrets. How can you know this and not have told me?' But then she drops her eyes, realising that perhaps this isn't about a truth I haven't shared, but a reality I've buried. And perhaps also that she has kept truths from me too. Perhaps we're more alike than we realise. 'How do you know?' she asks.

I lean forward, burying my head in my hands. I want to run away. I don't want to do this. I don't want to talk about this – about anything.

'Can you tell me about it?' she asks, gently.

I shift uncomfortably beside her this time. My turn to feel awkward in my skin. Everything itches; bile rises from the pit of my belly. 'I can think of better things to talk about,' I say, staring at my feet. Flippancy kicks in to replace hurt. 'Global warming? Donald Trump? Chips served in tiny buckets on a piece of lake-stone slate, I mean whose idea was that? I blame Jamie Oliver,' I finish, running out of momentum.

'Rhys.'

The shoelace on my trainer is coming undone. I bend down to tie it then rest my elbows on my knees. I search for the best version of this story for her. The least painful. The one where I don't tell her that if she'd bothered to find out about my past, she could have protected me in my future. Because that's how the small boy inside me feels: like this is her fault. It was a feeling I could forget when we were distracted with our David. A feeling that now I can't push away. I know it's unfair and yet... Mum's looking at me. Waiting for more.

'When David contacted the agency, he had an appointment, didn't he?'

'Yes, you took him. He didn't want me to go.'

'Right.' I bite the inside of my cheek and Mum reaches a hand out, placing it on my back. The warmth from her hand reaches through to my heart. 'When he went in for his appointment, I don't know, something just… I thought maybe I'd like to know too. Maybe it would help him if we both went on this journey together.'

'You'd never been interested before.'

I shake my head. 'I know.' I take a minute to think about that. About why I'd never wanted to know. Cowardice on my part, this time. 'So I went in too. I asked for my file. It was all very straightforward, easier than I'd expected. I don't know, maybe part of me only asked because I didn't anticipate it being that easy. Perhaps I thought they'd ask me to come back and I could pretend I didn't have time or something. I forget now what was really going through my mind because there it was. Within seconds. My life in paperwork, easily picked out of a metal filing cabinet marked 1976.'

I feel as hollow as the day I read my papers. I feel that sense of expectation, immediately crushed by devastation. It's deep in my gut. That it returns with such clarity all but knocks me over.

'My file. My name. My date of birth.' I take a deep breath. 'The word "abandoned" beside it in capital letters, red pen. Pretty perfunctory really, considering.'

Mum lets a breath, a small cry, escape. It's that sound I've wanted to avoid. A sound that links to sadness. To guilt. To responsibility. And yet it's a sound that I'm relieved she makes, because in some way it makes her feel a tiny part of the pain I felt when I read those papers.

And then I feel bad for wishing that upon her.

My throat aches as I fight the need to cry. I will not. 'So there you go. That's that. End of story.' No sooner have I confessed the details than I wrap them back up and, like always, package it all away. I bury deep the need to get up, to shout, to lash out at her, at the world, at anyone or anything, in the hopes it might eradicate my feelings. Instead, I slowly raise my head to the sky, fighting with every bone in my body the animal instincts I feel.

She reaches inside her bag to pull out a tissue, not quite able to extract it from one of those plastic packets of ten, three ply. I take the packet from her. 'I've told you before about these, Mum, they're a nightmare. Useless in an emergency.' My brightness is false under the circumstances but I'm not conceding. I pull out a tissue, flick to unfold it and pass it to her. 'Handy chuffing Andies. Handy, my arse.'

Mum stares. 'How can you be so flippant, Rhys. How can you… When you've just…' I get up from the bench as she wipes her eyes, blows her nose then stuffs the tissue up her cardigan sleeve. How can I not be like this? To be anything else hurts like fuck. To be anything else makes me question everything I am. Everything I believe myself to be.

To be anything else makes me question Susan.

When Kat told me what the newspaper cutting said, my heart flirted with the idea, but my head pushed it aside as ridiculous, as wishful thinking. Despite my anger at her for doing that to a baby, if it *was* me, if I *was* that baby, then that meant a chance for a happy ending, and despite all my cynicism in life, I have dared to dream that might be in my future.

Stupid really.

Like those things happen.

The family from before walk past us. The toddler is now in a pram, eating an ice cream, the majority of which is around her face. She has

tiny, green sunglasses on that make her face look like a squished alien.
The parents smile proudly. Mum and I try to smile back.

'I can't believe it. I can't... and you never said anything. You must
have been so...' She reaches out to touch me again, her hand resting
on my knee. I take it in mine, choking on the weight of the moment. 'I guess that explains a lot,' she says eventually. 'I mean, how
you've been dealing with things.' She looks straight into my eyes.
'Why didn't you tell me?'

I let out a protracted groan. 'I don't know. I guess I was trying to
be strong for David. At the meeting, they told him his mum wasn't
interested, that his contact was likely to be met with silence. The look
on his face when he came out of that office, Mum, it all hurt so much,
I just...' I can feel myself going and I can't allow it. 'He needed us,
didn't he? It had been his moment and I strolled in and made it my
moment too. Maybe that's why...' I hold back. 'I parked it. Filed it
under "move on".'

'But you don't have to move on. You're allowed to hurt, Rhys.'

'I don't want to,' I say, thinly. 'I can't. It's...' I run out of words.

'Too much?'

I nod, once.

'Oh, Rhys, what did we do to deserve all this? Eh?' She blows her
nose. 'Some people sail through life, don't they, why can't that be us?'

'What would you do with your time if there wasn't any gossip to
formulate for the bingo?' I say. She shoots me a look that makes it
plain I'm off target, and once again, I feel it. 'Isn't hardship the thing
that makes us?' I say, trying to fix the moment.

Reaching back up her sleeve, Mum pulls out the now disintegrated
tissue. She throws it in the bin beside us, as if a dysfunctional hanky

is the straw to break the camel's back. 'I think I'd like a break from it now,' she says, voice wobbling.

We sit quietly, apart from the occasional sniff from Mum. Each time one of us thinks we've found something to say, we stop, closing our mouths, preferring the silence. The clouds pass, letting the August sun beat down on the back of my neck. I feel it prickle in the heat.

Eventually, Mum asks, 'How is that woman?'

'What woman?' I pretend, gritting my teeth.

'Susan? When did you last go?' She wipes her face, and stands, offering her hand to pull me up this time.

'I haven't seen her. Not since last Thursday.' I hook Mum's arm through mine, staring straight ahead as we walk on. 'I went to her house, with Kat, her nurse. Susan asked me to collect something. Well, she wrote a note. She asked for a book. I thought I should help her, in the absence of anyone else. I imagined you, being on your own. And I couldn't stop thinking about our David and the fact she had tried to do the same. I wondered if the house, the book, might offer up more answers than I was getting in my visits.' Mum squeezes my hand. 'Well, anyway, it all got complicated. We found...' Mum hangs off my trailing words, and I realise I can't say out loud that which I can't yet face. 'There weren't any answers. Except that she'd just decided to end things. No big reveal.' I start walking faster, Mum unlocks her arm from me in an effort to keep up without being pulled over in my haste.

I start shaking my head, bubbles of frustration popping in my belly. Because this conversation is making me think about everything I've tried to ignore these last few days, especially the possibility that Susan and I might be connected in any way. I don't know if I'm ready to find out. Happy endings are rarely that. I'm not living in a Disney movie. Singing birds do not surround me as I walk.

We arrive back at the pavilion where we started. I grit my teeth, clean out of things to say other than, 'I should go. Jobs to do.' Mum nods, sadly. 'I'd drop you off somewhere but…' I can't work out a reason why not, except that I need to be away from everyone and everything.

'It's fine, love,' she says. 'I'm… I'm meeting Derek anyway.'

'Right.' I fold my arms, pulling myself in tight at the sound of his name.

'I'd love you to meet him,' she says, gently.

'Like I say, jobs to do.'

'Of course.' She looks at her watch. 'Gosh. It's two o'clock already.'

I look down at my watch, aware that it's now visiting time.

'I feel like we're leaving this unfinished, Rhys.'

'We are, Mum. I was abandoned. My story will always be unfinished.' I say it matter-of-factly. I give her a fleeting kiss on the cheek; she smells of Silvikrin and talcum powder. I fight the need to linger, turning towards the car park and my van.

She stands and waves as I pull away, and I can't escape fast enough. Both from her and from all the things I've said. I want to reach inside my belly and remove them one by one, never to be uttered or heard or remembered again. For the second time in a week, I'm driving across Sheffield like an idiot incapable of keeping control of his emotions. I don't even know who I am anymore. Or why I'm about to pull back into the car park at the Northern General. Except that maybe there *is* a ghost to lay to rest here, just not the one I thought.

Chapter Thirty-One

RHYS

A nurse I vaguely recognise nods to me as I make my way to the ward. I feel sick. My stomach flips. What am I doing back here? What am I going to say, and am I really ready for her answer?

As I approach Susan's ward, I'm stopped in my tracks as I see her hobbling down the centre of her room towards her bed. My feet are rooted to the spot; at first I neither want to stay nor leave, but the longer I watch her, the more I'm compelled to let her know I'm here, that she's not alone and she can do this. Each step is aided by crutches, effort and pain etched on her face, and I want to take it away. I want to make it better somehow.

'Wow,' I exclaim, bounding over. 'You're up on your feet, that's amazing!' She stares up at me, eyes wide, mouth open, studying my features as if to check it's really me. I move to the empty side of her bed, relieving her of one crutch as she sits down to climb in, eyes still firmly pinned on me. I pass the crutch to the nurse on the other side and she wedges it with the other, easily within Susan's reach. 'I can't believe it, Susan. How are you? You look…' She looks different. The bruising is now a faded yellow across her cheek, with a more natural pink beneath it, no doubt from the newfound strength to walk.

Susan still searches my face. As if, despite knowing me, she can't quite place who I am, or is confused as to why I'm visiting, and for a second I share the feeling. Why am I here if not to ask the question? Except that now I am here, I can't. Because what if the answer is no?

'Hello,' says the nurse. 'Are you here to visit Susan?'

And now I'm uncertain, as if I crossed a line she chalked without my knowing. 'Yes… If that's okay with you, Susan?'

She swallows. Then reaches for her empty cup, passing it to me, like the first time I came. It's a sign. A signal for me to stay. 'I'm Rhys,' I tell the nurse, taking Susan's cup and duly filling it.

'Of course you are.' She smiles. 'You're just how Kat described you. Go steady with our patient, please. Don't stay too long – the physio she's been having is quite intensive, she'll be tired.'

'Of course.'

The nurse leaves and I pull up a chair. Susan stares at me, and the child in me wants to offer an explanation. 'I'm sorry I haven't been around for a few days,' I begin, leaning my hand on the patient table and tapping it slightly. 'Did Kat tell you I had stuff on? I asked her to. It's great to see you doing so well.' Our eyes meet and I can just about make out the tiny pinpricks of her pupils as they retract each time she blinks. The curtains around her bed are open. The juice I brought is almost empty. The book is on the table at the bottom of her bed.

The book.

'Kat told me you were doing well.'

Susan looks towards the book, then back to me.

'Has it… helped?' I ask, reaching out to pick it up, but she gets to it before me. The pages fall open to the start of a new story and she begins to read, I think.

Uncomfortable silence is interrupted only by the turn of each page, the sound magnified in my frazzled brain as if she's ripping it right beside my ear. Noises in the ward seem louder. Exaggerated. I feel small and out of place. I fidget, picking at my fingers, biting the cuticle on my thumb. I find a speck of paint to scratch off my jeans. She continues reading and the silence forces me back into her home, and the reason she's here.

'You didn't plan to go home, did you?' I say suddenly. Susan lets go of a page she was about to turn, resting the palm of her hand on the book. Eyes down.

'Your house. It was like you were gone, Susan.' I pause. 'Maybe like you'd never been there in the first place.' She closes her eyes and I wait a beat. When she reopens them, she starts reading again. But this time each page turns faster, as if she isn't reading at all, just flicking through the book as distraction. Scanning it. Is the cutting still trapped within the pages? 'Why would you do that?' I ask. 'What could have happened in life to make you do that?' I stop short of making a suggestion.

The suggestion.

Is she my mother? Would I recognise her if she was? Is? How would I ask, how would she answer? Does she even know herself?

This is stupid. I shouldn't be here. I've walked away from this before and I should do so again. I have a mother – I don't need another. Especially not one that didn't want me, whether that was Susan or not. And yet, I feel there is something I need to say.

I lean closer to her, the chair creaking as I do so.

'I've been here before, Susan,' I say, my voice low. 'With someone lost. Someone who couldn't see the point in carrying on. And I couldn't stop him. I couldn't make a difference.'

She looks to my hand, now resting on the edge of her bed.

'I can't let that happen again,' I say, quietly but insistently. I feel suddenly, overwhelmingly, as if her survival depends on me. And if she doesn't survive, I might never know the truth.

I wait. I watch. I study her face: the shape of her nose, her eyes, her tiny mouth. I trace an imaginary line from my hands to hers. Are we alike? I feel my mouth run dry. The absence of any response from her pushes me back into the chair, my legs stretched out beneath her bed. I groan, rubbing my face, my forehead tight with confusion. My phone beeps and I sigh, then groan as I read the message.

'My mum,' I explain. 'She wants to—' I cut myself short, but Susan moves position, turning her body just enough to be able to face me. It's the most I've got from her since I arrived today. I take a deep breath. 'She's met someone. She has a new fella.' Susan closes the book. 'I'm not ready. I don't like it. It hurts, somehow,' I say quietly. 'She's amazing, my mum, like truly amazing. I love her, and she raised me, but it's complicated because she's not...' I look up, just in case Susan responds, though I'm not sure I really want her to. Not yet. 'Well, anyway, I love her, but...' Susan drops her eyes to my phone, watching as I flick the message up and down on the screen, trying to work out how to respond. 'I saw her this afternoon.' I read her message again, using it as a distraction from having to look at Susan, confused by my own confusion.

If Susan was... is... then I should just say something. I could just ask.

If I am her son, couldn't that be the thing to save her?

Wouldn't it?

But what if it pushed her further?

What if I was to blame, again, for someone opting out of life?

'She wants to know if I fancy dinner with them. This evening.' I fling my phone on her bed. 'I'm not ready. I'm not in the mood. I just don't want to.' I look up at Susan. 'And now I sound like a spoiled brat, right?'

Susan picks up my phone. She types, then, handling my phone like it's made of glass, passes it to me. 'I would love to meet him. When and where? I'll be there. X.' She hasn't sent it. It's a draft. And I don't agree. I don't like it. And yet, as Susan holds my gaze, I press send. The sound of a tiny swoosh signals it has left my inbox, and Susan nods. Then she reaches to the back of her book and takes out a crisp white envelope. In her handwriting, it is clearly and cleanly marked: 'Mr James Grey'. There's an address on it, somewhere in the Lake District. Ambleside. She has perfectly placed the first-class stamp in the corner. A precision I don't share. I turn it over in my hand. 'Who is this?' I ask, holding it out to her. She pushes it back to my chest, then leans back in her bed, holding the book. She takes a final look in my direction before closing her eyes again. Within seconds, her breathing softens. I watch her, realising that the woman beneath the bruises and plaster is emerging and she's not how I remembered her. Before, she was somehow hidden. I can't figure out what I can see now, or whether I was blind to it before. Or even how it makes me feel. She lets out a breath of sleep. Her eyes flicker and her hands relax, letting go of the book. I take it from her, placing it carefully on the side, and look again at the envelope.

'Is this to be sent, Susan?' I say out loud to her tiny, sleeping frame. 'And who's James?'

'Best post it, eh, love,' interrupts a patient over the way, seemingly having watched our whole encounter. 'I saw her put a stamp on it earlier. She must want it gone. Do her a favour, and let her get some rest, that's what they said, love.'

'Post it?' I check.

'Why else would she write it?'

'I guess so. Will you tell her I have it? That I'll post it tomorrow if I don't hear different, okay?'

'Aye,' she says. 'Will do.'

I pass Kat's office by the nurses' station as I leave. The door is closed and I pause for a second, wondering whether to knock and see her. But she might not even be in, and I don't know what I'd say anyway. How do I explain why I'm back, or what I might be thinking? The sick feeling returns. She knows things I don't talk about. A stranger who's drawn out secrets without lies. I've had a reprieve. What more could she unpick if I saw her? I can't do this at anyone's pace but my own. I hurry out of the door as another message comes through: Mum's instructions to meet her and Derek at a wine bar by the Chinese. I fold Susan's letter into my back pocket and disappear before Kat finds me here.

Chapter Thirty-Two

KAT

'Lou, I can't talk now. I'm at work.'

'Okay, what time do you finish? Will's best mate split up with his girlfriend and I am trying to organise a get together.'

I tap my pen on the table, my chest tightening. 'Really, Lou. This couldn't wait? You couldn't have just texted me the details?'

'Well, of course I could have, but then how would I give you a full list of what to wear, what to say and how to act on our double date?'

'Lou, I don't need a list.' Or a double date, but I resist dropping that in.

'That's what you think. Last time we went for cocktails you arrived with dry-shampooed hair. I mean, really, Kat? For cocktails?' I guiltily run my hand over my hair. It's possible I'm overly reliant on it, though how she guessed I don't know. 'Anyway,' she carries on. 'What's up with you?'

'Nothing, I'm just really busy. Sorry. It's the new job. There's a lot more to think about and I'm only just getting to grips with it. I don't want to make any mistakes, you know.'

'I get that. I mean, we're all busy.' I resist pointing out she's currently a lady of leisure, funded by the Bank of Mum and Dad. 'Look,

Will's best mate is also the best man. It's customary for you to know each other before the day. You'll be walking back down the aisle beside him, you know. It might be nice for you two to at least have met. I just—'

'Okay, sort it, Lou. But not for tonight, I'm already out.'

'Again! On a Monday! Who with this time?' Lou makes it sound like my social life usually revolves around hers. She may have a point.

'I'm off tomorrow. And it's just a little promotion celebration with work. Nothing massive. A few drinks and some bowling.'

'Eww, those shoes though…'

I'm with her on that one. I scribble out a mistake I've made in a patient file. 'Look, I have to go. Any other day, okay. Just text me when and where.'

'Okay.' I detect a slight sulk in her response. 'And you promise you'll wash your hair?'

'I promise. Guide's honour.'

'We were in the Guides together, Kat. I remember your honours…'

'Button it. Love you, bye.' I hang up, letting my head drop to the desk immediately afterwards. Emma sticks her head around the door. 'You ready? Got to be there in two hours. What you wearing?'

'Honestly, Emma, I've no idea,' I mumble into my desk. She waits until I've forced myself to lift my head up and look at her. 'Look, I've got reports to write, this paper about Susan after Friday's meeting and, at some point, I really do need to wash my hair.

'Dry shampoo!' suggests Emma.

'Look.' I point to my bag, also on my desk. 'I'm just finishing this, then I'm out the door.'

I make another mistake on the paperwork before giving up, putting it all in my in tray and reaching for my bag. I put some papers on the nurses' station, pinch a chocolate from a new box that has appeared and pop through to see Susan. 'I'm on my way out for the night, Susan. How was physio? Are you feeling okay?'

'I should say she's alright! That nice looking chap came in to see her,' says Gloria over the way.

'What nice chap?' I ask.

'The plumber. The only nice chap there's been around here – with the exception of the porter who normally works on a weekend, the consultant with a crush on you, and that lovely young cleaner who can't speak a word of English but has a bum as tight as—'

'Gloria!' I interrupt. 'Mr Barnes does not have a crush on me,' I add quickly, prickling pink.

'Whatever you say…' Gloria raises her arms in innocence, totally in contrast with the obvious smutty thoughts she's been entertaining whilst holed up in her bed.

'I didn't realise he'd been in,' I say, hefting my bag to my other shoulder and stuffing my hands in my uniform pockets. 'Nice though – that he came back, I mean. He said he was busy…' Susan looks directly at me and I bet she can see that I know something. I'd bet the remainder of my life savings. All £4.66 of it. 'Well, I'm glad that's sorted then. Well done. Lovely. Okay.' I move my bag again, neither side proving comfortable. I rub my neck, massaging a tightness that seems to have grown worse in the last few minutes.

'I'd better go. I've got a night out. Bowling. Celebrating my—' I stop myself. 'Yes, well…'

Susan looks over at her book.

'You want this?' I ask, passing it to her. I haven't seen the clipping since I brought it in. I resist the urge to open the book and find it. She takes it from me. 'I'm not in tomorrow,' I say. 'See you Wednesday?' I pause a second, waiting to see if she'll open the book whilst I'm here. She doesn't move. 'I'm off then. Bye, Gloria. Behave.'

'Not bloody likely. Our Maria brought me her laptop so I could download that series with Tom Hiddleston. *The Night Manager?* I see glamour and his bottom in my future. You fancy it, Susan?'

I shake my head in dismay and leave them to it.

Chapter Thirty-Three

KAT

The tram pulls up at Centertainment and a faceless announcer calls out our arrival, followed by the next destination. Most of my carriage gets off at the same time, spilling onto the side in a messy group that splits in different directions. I reluctantly move to get off; reluctant because I am knackered, emotionally wrung out, and really in need of a night on my own to gather my thoughts on life. Last week's strength has slowly dissolved with the news of Rhys's return visit and I'm not quite sure why. Perhaps because I didn't know. Perhaps because I didn't get to see him, and check he was okay. Perhaps because the meeting with Mental Health made it clear I had to monitor the situation closely. How can I monitor it if I don't know what's going on?

I get caught up in the crowd, falling in behind a young couple heading in the direction of the cinema. Her hand is forced into his back pocket, like teens in lust are wont to do. Experience reminds me it's also the most uncomfortable and cumbersome way to walk. I remember those days. Then I remember they were a long time ago and I'm running too late to be wistful. I check my watch – ten minutes late, to be exact. Most of which I can blame on staring vacantly at my wardrobe in hope of inspiration for a bowling-but-would-prefer-to-stay-at-home kind of outfit.

The rest of them will be booted and ready to bowl by now. As I make my way through wafts of Burger King, Nando's and petrol fumes from the car park, I pass a group of lads outside the bowling alley waiting for one of their own to join them. The abuse they hurl as they see him arrive is thrown right across my path. 'Sorry, love, that wasn't meant for you. I'm sure you're not a massive dickhead!' one of them says. 'Nah, she's not a massive dickhead – she's well fit though!' says another, stuffing his hands into his jeans and thrusting. It's enough to turn me back around for home, but Emma sees me through the glass doors and waves. No going back now.

The sound of the heavy balls hurtling down alleys is only just audible over Jessie J, Ariana Grande and Nicki Minaj, each singing something loud and screechy. Despite wishing I was at home in my pyjamas, I find nervous tension moves me to the beat as I queue for shoes. The group of lads I passed are now queuing behind me, talking about my arse. I stuff my hands in my back pocket, then remove them, not sure which draws more attention. I search for backup in the form of Emma, but she's moved on and is already at an alley, chatting to Mark. He leans into her, whispering something in her ear, the music forcing a certain proximity. She throws her head back in raucous laughter and I'm reminded of how far from being that sort of girl I really am. The sort who enjoys the rituals of a mating dance, who can hold her own when being catcalled by lads barely through their GCSEs.

'KAT!' shouts Emma, fighting to be heard over the din. She's dancing to the music, drinking some kind of alcopop through a straw. Her usual uniform has been replaced by skinny jeans, a white shirt and a huge grin on her face.

'Evening!' I shout, painting on a more upbeat mood. 'You look swit-swoo.'

She flings her arms around me and kisses the side of my face. 'You are so late!' she shouts over the music, right into my ear, frowning before slapping the side of my arm and demonstrating that not only am I late, but I'm woefully behind on alcohol consumed. 'So, we've got ourselves signed up,' she continues, pausing briefly to dance to the start of a new song. 'You and Mark are on one team, me and Chris are on the other.' I look around for Chris, one of the radiologists from work, waving as I spot him. And then I realise there's no one else here. Our work night out looks suspiciously like a double date.

'Where's everyone else?' I ask Emma sternly. 'Emma, I'm really not in the mood for this. Now isn't a—'

'I asked around,' she says, leaning into me, 'but nobody else could make it. I did wonder about cancelling, doing it another night, but it seemed a shame not to come out anyway. They all send their love though, and their congratulations.' She beams at me. 'And besides, Chris could make it and… Chris is lovely.' She grins in his direction, to his total obliviousness.

I feel a hand on the small of my back and turn to face Mark, who offers me a cold bottle of Budweiser and a grin that does go some way to melting my ice. 'Nice to see you,' he says. 'Out of uniform, that is.'

I pull up at the V of the lime-green vest top I'd opted for, feeling suddenly very underdressed in several senses of the word. 'Yes. Nice to see you too,' I say, taking the drink. 'I was expecting a few more of us than this!' I sip the lager, grateful for the bubbles and a sudden hit of cool air from the vents above me.

'Were you?' He sounds surprised, 'I thought it was only ever us four. I was looking forward to getting to know you a bit better.'

I shoot a look towards Emma, who, judging by the coquettish look she has on her face as Chris hands her first a pink then a pale turquoise bowling ball, is pretending she knows nothing about ten pin bowling. I happen to know this is a fabrication and it's tempting to call her out as payback for luring me into a double date. I was there when she unexpectedly beat the returning champion in our student bowling league. I couldn't speak for days after, so hard had I cheered her on. I peer from Emma to Chris, then to Mark, taking another swig of my lager. The fuzz of alcohol begins in the tip of my head and I decide there's nothing for it but to throw myself into the evening. I knock back another slug.

'Congratulations on the official promotion,' says Mark. I look away, taking another drink. He leans back in; the heat of his breath on my neck sends an odd tingle up my spine. There's the faintest smell of his aftershave too, thankfully different to Daniel's this time. I let myself breathe it in. 'Well deserved,' he says, chinking my bottle. His proximity feels oddly comfortable so I move away slightly, both from him and his aftershave, nodding and drinking instead. No good comes from dropping my guard. He studies me for a second and it makes me feel odd but I can't quite put my finger on why. 'So it's me and you against Chris and Emma then?' he says.

'You any good?' I ask, happy with the change of conversation.

He shrugs.

'Okay, well.' I finish the bottle off, picking up another, enjoying the gradual detachment from my feelings. 'I should warn you that what I lack in bowling talent I make up for in an unnecessarily competitive nature. I'm afraid I won't be able to help myself from trying to win, despite it being unlikely. I apologise now if I get aggressive.' Emma gives me the cue that it's my turn. I hand Mark my bottle, pick up a ball, saunter down the approach to throw it with gusto, then watch it veer straight into the gutter. 'Bollocks!' I say, sulkily taking back my drink. Mark gives me a wry grin.

Emma takes her time to choose a ball and listens to Chris for advice before sashaying down and preparing to launch her first shot.

'She's an expert, right?' Mark guesses, his arm touching mine. He's warm, but also gentle somehow. He's more relaxed out of work than in. I think about conversations with Susan where he's been focused, in consultant mode. That lack of bedside manner seems unlikely from the relaxed man standing next to me now. As does the uncertainty he's shown in my office at times. Here, he seems like a man who knows his destiny. He seems in control. An unexpected shyness falls upon me. A nervousness. It's easier now to see what people have been saying about him. He's not unattractive... I shift balance on my feet so we're no longer touching. He looks at me and smiles, his eyebrow very slightly raised.

Emma launches her first ball down the alley, kicking her leg out like a real life ten-pin bowler, effortlessly scoring a strike. Chris jumps up and runs to lift her for celebration, clearly thinking he is top of all the teachers. I roll my eyes at Mark, who just grins.

'So, how's Susan after her physio?' he asks.

'Stop!' I put my hands up. 'Shop talk is off limits.' He looks at me as if to ask why. 'Susan has been the most intense and challenging patient of my career. Between that, my personal life and my temporary then permanent promotion, I have been pushed and shoved all over the emotional place. I'm now working on imbibing sufficient beer not to care about any of it.'

'Really,' he says, doubtfully.

'Well, okay, enough to stop obsessing over it for a few hours. So let's keep it that way.' I take another large swig.

'Okay…' he says slowly. He narrows his eyes slightly, sizing me up. There's an odd shift, a sensation in my belly. 'No work talk,' he agrees eventually.

'Mark!' shouts Emma. 'You're up.' She clicks her fingers in the direction of the bowling alley. I drop into the bench seat and watch him.

He's wearing dark blue jeans. Not skinnies – because he's not a teenager with scant regard for procreation – but straight cut, just skimming his thighs. His light blue Oxford shirt is buttoned up to the top, cuffs rolled almost to the elbows, and it matches the light blue of his hideous bowling shoes. It's not the outfit I expected of him. Though I'm not sure what I expected, really, I'd not given it any thought before. He throws the ball down, scoring a perfectly accept-able half strike.

I reach for my lager, turning my nose up slightly on discovering it has quickly reached room temperature. 'Alright?' asks Mark, walking back towards me.

'Mmm,' I say. He stays beside me a second before moving over to talk to Chris. He throws his head back, laughing at something Chris has said. I wonder what the joke is, and whether he really is different outside of work or if I've been so wrapped up in my own stuff that I've formed an unfair opinion of him.

He turns to face me before I get the chance to look away. 'You're up,' he mouths. Emma is dancing her way back to Chris, another strike played. Chris looks bemused, but – by my reckoning – quite taken with her. I let out a sigh, feeling out of place, then get up to take my shot.

'I'm going to the bar, I'll get you a colder drink in,' he shouts over to me. 'But if you miss this one, it's your round next.'

I lift and feel the weight of the bowling ball in hand, focusing my eyes on the pins. Arm back, swing, release. And, following the line down the centre of the lane, amazingly, my ball takes out all the pins. I turn, arms aloft in victory, to see... Daniel.

Chapter Thirty-Four

KAT

My arms drop slowly, taking with them my all too briefly lifted spirits. 'Daniel…' He looks around, then back to me, looking me up and down as if I shouldn't be here. Or as if he doesn't want to see me. Or perhaps both, just to make me feel even more insignificant.

'Well done,' he says, nodding at the large X on the screen behind me. 'You weren't much good at stuff like this when we were together.' He says it with that sneer he always had when making a joke at my expense, and yet it's also a sneer that makes him look his hottest, like he's pushing me, challenging me to react, which was always when sparks flew at their most intense. He looks over his shoulder, then back to me.

'Thanks,' I say, surreptitiously pulling my jeans up to give a better silhouette. He always hated my muffin top. For the second time tonight I feel awkward in my clothes, in my skin, just awkward in general. Maybe I *should* have gone for that PVC shift dress he bought me last Christmas. I rejected it on the basis it was too short to bowl in. And also PVC. It might have been better for bumping into your ex and wishing you looked smoking hot though. Not that it should matter.

Mark comes back with two bottles, stopping when he realises I'm talking to someone. I smile to encourage him to join us, not really wanting to be totally alone. I take a swig from the bottle he passes me, glad that he hasn't put his arm around me, but sort of wishing for the very briefest of moments that he had. That I could look like I was with someone, like I was happy. Not that it should matter. Again.

'This is Mark,' I say, intentionally not expanding.

'Hi,' says Mark, his arm outstretched. Daniel shakes his hand, eye-balling Mark, and I know, because I know Daniel, that he's doing so in the hope of an explanation as to who he is. I cross my fingers Mark won't give it. There's a hung moment as the three of us stand there, just looking at each other. Mark glances at me, apparently misreading the situation.

'I'll leave you to it,' he says, and I wish I could scream, *No! Don't go!*

I watch him walk away before turning my attention back to Daniel with a roll of my eyes that I'm not entirely sure contributes anything useful to this situation. 'Sorry, I didn't mean to interrupt,' Daniel says, watching Mark. 'Is he...? None of my... Well, anyway, it's great to see you. I should...' He signals to move on but I manage to catch him first. Suddenly, I have questions. 'How's...?' I ask, realising I don't even know the Amazonion beauty's name. Perhaps I'll find that out before I ask how they met. Or when.

'Natasha? Yeah, she's good.' He looks over his shoulder again. 'She's...' He points in the direction of a small group of friends and I see her standing there, the tallest amongst them all. The woman with legs up to her armpits and glossy, flowing hair. She's laughing, chatting – and stunning. And that's when I notice what I hadn't seen before. Whilst it's by no means imminent, she is definitely caressing a delicately swollen belly.

'She's pregnant?' I hear myself as if outside of my body.

Daniel shifts on the spot. Once upon a time he had swagger and gloat; now, before me, he looks as if the life is draining from him rather like sand in an hourglass. I turn, slowly, to look him in the eye, and say it again. 'She's pregnant.' It's a statement this time.

'Yeah.' Daniel swallows, his face pale. 'She's pregnant.'

I begin nodding. Assessing the scene. My eyebrows rise higher as I continue to stare. Then the reality of what this means begins to sink in, and despite every part of me wanting not to care, wanting to be glad this proves he's an absolute shit, despite me wanting to walk away and never see him again, despite me beginning to feel like I was over him, my heart is slowly breaking. Everything I thought I understood of our relationship for the last five years becomes a lie and I'm standing in the middle of a bowling alley, my recently ex-boyfriend in front of me and his undoubtedly pregnant girlfriend walking towards me with a smile across her face. I fight against the overwhelming urge to properly, properly cry.

'Congratulations,' I spit, then hiccup, hoping that if I look up at the ceiling I can flick the tears back inside my face. 'Marriage next then,' I say, meaning it as a bitter joke but getting the immediate impression from his half nod that not only has he gone back on his decision to never have children, but that marriage is suddenly an attractive proposition. I suppose anything's attractive with a woman just a toga short of a goddess on your arm. 'Right. Sure. Of course. Well, that's…'

'Thanks.'

'Sure. Couldn't be happier for you.'

'Thanks.'

I'm not sure if we are asking and answering each other's statements with any accuracy. Or in the right order. Half sentences and pained expressions and, on my part at the very least, a desire for the universe to swallow me whole to end this nightmare. Maybe it's not that much different to the years we were together. Natasha instinctively interlocks French-manicured fingers into his. I torture myself by trying to seek out an engagement ring and judge him on the size of it.

'Hi,' she says, bold as brass. Not that I know how bold brass really is. 'Kat, isn't it?' He smiles sheepishly at me. 'The cab's here, baby,' she says to him. Then she moves a hand to the small of her back, which somehow pushes out her baby-full stomach even more. 'Sorry, Kat, lovely to see you again. Hey, we should get...' She half motions the end of the ill-thought-out suggestion of us meeting up for coffee, or dinner, or perhaps to do a handover. Outgoing updating incoming on Daniel's strengths and weaknesses. I wonder if he's ever asked her to go to that 'special' wine bar down Attercliffe? She stops herself, smiling patronisingly, before waddling away with I'm-pregnant-don't-you-know determination. She might as well have pissed up his leg, such was her need to prove their association. Well, she can have him. And very soon, I'm sure my heart will agree.

Daniel opens and closes his mouth a few times before realising he's better off just leaving. He slopes off and any restraint I was clinging on to fades. Emma has appeared behind me. She takes my arm and leads me to sit down.

Mark looks on, from a distance, no doubt uncertain what to do for the best. I wish he could telepathically read my request for him to come back beside me, if only to momentarily make Daniel think further about what he thought he saw when he almost asked who Mark was. I drain my bottle of its contents, looking around for another. In the absence of any, Mark appears by my side, albeit late, passing me his bottle with a sympathetic smile.

'He's a shit, Kat. He always was, you just could never see it. I know this hurts, I know it has since he left, but honestly, hun, you are so much better off without him.'

Mark and Chris back off. The lights drop for Nineties at Nine and the boys take shots on mine and Emma's behalf. I sit stunned, wondering which Spice Girls track they're going to play and really hoping it isn't 'Mama' because I am not doing a great job of holding it together as it is. Emma holds my hand whilst trying to stop herself from jigging along. I should have listened to my gut and stayed at home.

'I think I might go,' I say.

'Pardon?' shouts Emma.

I lean into her ear. 'I said I think I might go home.'

'Nooo! You can't! Don't let him ruin your night!'

I begin to tell her he hasn't, but she can't hear and I'm done shouting. Chris is trying not to look over at Emma, but it's clear he's quite taken. They really don't need me all maudlin in the background. I give her a kiss and a big hug and tell her I'll be fine. She gives me puppy-dog eyes but knows she won't change my mind.

Standing by the counter, waiting to get my shoes back, I feel vulnerable. I'm not sure if it's the situation or the lack of footwear in a public place. I look down and wiggle my toes as a larger pair of feet appears, in socks with the word 'Monday' down the side.

'I thought I'd check you were okay,' the voice says, and I look up to see Mark handing over his bowling shoes.

'You've got the days of the week on your socks.' It's not really a question so much as a statement, an observation. A way to deflect from how hard I'm working at holding myself together.

'Present from my mum,' he says. 'They're oddly addictive. I had a pair of Thursdays on yesterday and everything went to pot!' He makes me smile, I'll give him that. 'You want a drink somewhere? You want food? Or do you just want to go home and wallow in your pyjamas?' It's almost like he knows me. 'Because I can go along with any of those.'

'Do your pyjamas have the days of the week on too?' I ask, taking my shoes from the attendant.

'Would it make a difference to your answer if they did?'

I give him a look, stepping into my shoes.

'So that was the ex then?' Mark asks, tying up the laces on a pair of tan brogues.

'Hmm?'

'The bloke with a face I'd like to punch.'

'I'm a lover, not a fighter Mark,' I say. 'Though maybe if you had punched him, I might feel better.'

'To be honest, I'm no fighter either. I'd probably miss, or break a bone in my hand.' He holds open the door for me as we walk out. The summer evening is easing into a pink, blue and grey dusk; a few stars emerge as I look, out of place in a sky not yet dark. 'Pretty,' I say, straining my neck to look up and beyond the brick and metal of the cinema, bowling alley and fast food restaurants.

'Yes,' he says, quietly, and when I look back, he's not staring at the stars but at me. With a look on his face that confuses the hurt in my soul.

'It was my ex,' I explain. 'He cheated on me. He is not worth my time or my tears. My head knows this, but...'

'Hearts sometimes need to do a bit of catching up,' he says, pulling me in for a side squeeze. He smells all warm and sweet and not entirely unpleasant. I realise he's smelling my hair. 'Come on,' he says, pulling back and putting a barrier between us, despite offering me his arm. 'Let me take you home, okay? At least then I can head into town, drink too much and pick up some woman without wondering if you made it home or not.'

'Wow, you really know how to romance a girl,'

'You didn't look like you wanted romancing.' He smiles.

'I was talking about whoever you pick up tonight.'

'Oh.' He laughs to himself. 'To be honest, I'll probably just pick up a bottle of wine and head home. Watch some telly. Read a book. Sleep.'

He flags a cab down and opens the door for me to get in. I buckle up as he sits in the pull-down chair in front of me. His feet stretch out to the side of mine; each time we go over a bump our legs touch. 'Sheffield's pretty at night,' he says, looking at the waterfall as we pull up at the traffic lights. 'Look how the water reflects the dusk.' We stare in silence before he breaks it with, 'I like it here.' He nods, looking at me with an intensity that makes my belly flip a little. Nerves? Are those butterflies once again lodging in my stomach? And if so, what the hell are they doing there? 'It's a place I can see myself staying for a while.' I bite my lip. His comment is pointed, but I'm too upset to try and navigate it, or my feelings around it.

The cab takes a left towards my flat. Cars line the road and a few streetlights lead the way. 'Thanks for seeing me home.' I reach into my bag for my door keys.

'You're welcome, Ward Sister Davies. Congratulations again. With the exception of your ex-boyfriend's arrival, I had a good night.'

Part of me wants to say *me too*. A bigger part stops me.

As I shut the cab door, Mark moves to sit where I had been and leans forward to give the cabby an instruction. I wave, turn, and let myself into the darkness of my empty flat.

And now I don't have to pretend this doesn't hurt anymore.

Chapter Thirty-Five

RHYS

So, this is it. The big reveal. The introduction. How many more ways can I try and dress up the horror that is meeting my mum's new... Well, anyway. Having tried to drown out my inner monologue, the one screaming at me not to do this, I showered, dressed and came out to meet her. Them. When I arrived at the wine bar, Mum came up and hugged me so tight I thought she might faint from the effort. She asked me if I was okay, after what we'd talked about. I wanted to turn the clock back, take away the new thing she had to worry about. My birth mother. I wish I'd never told her.

Derek ordered Prosecco and three glasses. Mum apologised as she led me over, said it was fine if I wasn't in the mood to drink it. I drank it in any case. To say we enjoyed the fizz and chat is an oversell, but we tried and Mum seemed happy we were finally all there together.

Now we are in the restaurant, watching intently as our waiter deftly shreds the duck he's just brought to the table, his face hard in concentration as he preps and presents our crispy starter. Derek and I have exhausted safe discussion topics about the weather and the state of the Sheffield ring road, and tension is pushing its way into our happy little threesome now. Mum, all the while, is trying to manage it.

'We love the Zing Vaa, don't we, Derek,' she says, nerves present in the wobble of her hand as she fills glasses with bottled tap water.

'Yeah,' I say. 'Me too.'

I bite my tongue so as not to remind her that me and David used to come here every few weeks for an early tea after work. I try to forget about the times Michelle joined us. How we'd all sit and chat and laugh and, for the sake of my brother, I'd ensure any feelings I had for her were buried. 'I remember the first time I tasted Chinese,' I say, layering cucumber on top of duck and plum sauce. 'Mum's cooking is great—'

'Ooh, it is,' Derek interrupts. 'Hearty.'

My eyes flick up to him, then her, wondering how often she's made him these home-cooked, hearty meals. I carry on. 'Yes, but there was something in the sweetness of that first lemon chicken I ever had. It awakened taste buds my thirteen-year-old mouth didn't know I had.' The thought of its sticky-sweet deliciousness makes the back of my tongue clack, in a good way. Derek nods. Mum smiles, proudly. I occupy my mouth with a duck roll.

We carry on eating in awkward silence. Derek starts fumbling over cutlery, and then he and I simultaneously notice Mum's wine glass is empty and our hands clash as we reach for the bottle. He concedes, which would be fine, except Mum's put her hand over the top to stop me filling her glass. 'I'll get tipsy,' she says, her elbow dropping off the side of the table.

A gentle, oriental soundtrack is just audible over the sound of the other diners' conversation. A table of businessmen are being obnoxious to our left, a young couple are eating chicken and chips to my right.

'So, how's the plumbing world?' asks Derek eventually, assembling his third pancake. I try not to count how many are left, to make sure we all get our fair share. It doesn't matter. It doesn't matter.

'Yeah, good. Busy. Mostly.'

'Sign of a good workman if you're busy, well done,' he says, and I see Mum glance at him with a look of appreciation.

'I've always been very proud of what he achieved, haven't I, Rhys?'

'I think so, yeah.' A bit of plum sauce dribbles down my chin and drops onto the pocket of my new white shirt. 'Ah, fuck it,' I say, then look up sharply at Derek, who is offering me a napkin.

'Vinegar or lemon juice,' he says.

'Pardon?'

'To get that out. Vinegar or lemon juice. Soon as you get home or you've no chance. It can stain like a right'un, that stuff, I've been there.'

'Cheers,' I say, not sure I have either vinegar or lemon juice at home but sort of impressed he has any clue how to approach such a thing.

'Perks of living on yer own, see. You learn the hard way. My wife, she died about fifteen years ago. Cancer. She was brilliant at getting stains out. When she passed, it took me years to work out how she did it. In fact, it weren't till I fathomed out the internet that I had any idea how to do owt around the house. I'm a right messy bugger. Made me realise how much she did. God rest her.'

'Sorry about your wife,' I say. 'That must have been…'

'Well,' he interrupts. 'Losing anyone is hard. You know that too.'

'Yeah,' I say.

I wonder for a second what David would think: of this situation, us out for dinner. Would he have liked Derek? Had he noticed a change in Mum? Is that how he found out? It's hard to imagine. He didn't generally notice subtleties. Michelle always said she loved what made him a square peg in a round hole, despite it being the same thing that made him blind to her new haircut, or an anniversary, or when she needed a cuddle, not her own space. 'Hard is definitely one word for it,' I say.

We fall back into silence, and no sooner have we finished the starter than our plates are whipped away from us with quiet efficiency. The restaurant's matriarch oversees the process as our main course is delivered to our table, hot and sizzling on the marble lazy Susan.

'So what do you want to know?' Derek's question breaks the silence – that and the banging of china against china as he spoons egg fried rice into a bowl decorated with burgundy willow trees. Mum watches us, chewing on noodles and her usual Kung Po Chicken.

'About what?' I ask.

'About Me. My life. My intentions—'

'Derek!' Mum practically chokes on a prawn ball. She reaches for her wine before remembering she'd rejected a top-up.

'What? The lad's sat there wondering what I'm all about. And who can blame him. I'm just being upfront.' He beats me to the top-up this time, filling her glass with the lukewarm house white.

She takes a sip. 'You don't have to be upfront, Derek. Rhys can wonder all he likes. This is not going to turn into the Spanish Inquisition.'

'You're right,' he says. 'We're on the wrong continent for one thing.' He motions to our Chinese-themed surroundings and I break into a smile.

'It's okay,' I say. 'It's none of my business, Derek.'

'True. It's not. But I like your mum. And I think she likes me. And whilst we are in no hurry, I do enjoy spending time in her company and I happen to be aware that you are not entirely comfortable with this. See, I'm not in the habit of backing away from the opportunity to make sure someone has the facts before they judge.'

I stare at him, not sure if I admire his Yorkshire bravado or if I'm pissed off with the confrontation. But he isn't being confrontational.

He's not stood before me pruning peacock feathers and puffing up his chest, but he's not afraid to tackle the elephant in the room.

'I was married at eighteen to my childhood sweetheart, Marilyn,' he begins. 'We met at a dance in town. She was from a wealthy family and I was poor. Her bit of rough, she used to say.' I grimace, and occupy myself by dipping into Mum's dish to try her food. 'We were very happily married for thirty-two years. Two children: Jane and Peter. I've four grandchildren: Amy, Clare, Jonathan and Matilda. I live up Greenhill, by the shops. I bought a flat there when Marilyn passed because the kids had left home and I didn't fancy staying in our family house on me own. I was a manager down the steelworks. Pushed paper mostly, though I don't mind getting me hands mucky. I like walking, music, reading, crosswords… and I like your mum.' I notice her smile at this; she looks younger. 'I think you do a great job of looking after her.' He reaches out and pats her hand, letting it rest there for a moment before going back to his food. 'And I feel sorry for your loss. Life can be shit.' He takes a sip of his drink. 'So that's me,' he says with finality, loading his bowl up with his second round and looking at me expectantly.

'Right,' I say. 'Well, that pretty much clears that up then.'

We look at each other for a moment. I search for how I feel. Torn. Because I like him. He seems straight, uncomplicated. And he looks at Mum like she's a precious jewel. And though I can see she feels uncertain about that, I can also see she likes it. And maybe needs it. It's not as weird as I thought it would be. It doesn't feel wrong. But all that in itself is somehow contradictory. I try to find something to say in return, but there must be too long a gap because Mum fills it first.

'Goodness, I don't think I could eat another thing.' She pushes her bowl away, leaning back with her hands on her belly.

'Me too, love. I'm stuffed.' Derek pushes his chair away from the table, dropping his napkin to the side. 'Excuse me a minute,' he says, squeezing her shoulder before disappearing in the direction of the toilet.

Mum watches him retreat before turning her attention back to me. 'How are you feeling?' she asks.

'I'm okay, Mum,' I say, picking at what remains of the food in front of us. 'He's nice,' I mumble into a prawn cracker.

'I know,' she agrees. 'But I meant about what we discussed earlier. I keep thinking about how long you've kept that to yourself, and why you felt you couldn't talk to me.' She takes a deep breath, reaching for my hand. 'I'm so sorry if you felt I was too wrapped up in David to hear you.' There's a tear in her eye, a gentle wobble in her chin, and the guilt swallows me whole. 'You should never feel that I'm not here for you, Rhys. You're my boy and there is nothing more important.' She sits back a second, regaining some composure.

'Mum—'

'You don't have to say anything, love. Just know I am here for you, no matter what else is going off.' She motions to Derek's place just as he makes his way back through the restaurant. 'Hello, love.' She smiles at him as he takes his seat back beside her.

She reaches out and rests her hand on his knee. He picks up her hand and kisses it, then puts it back on the table, half nodding towards me. I appreciate that he doesn't reject her, but that he doesn't expose me to any more of their affection than I really need on our first meeting. And I realise that though she hasn't told me that she loves him, it's obvious that's what she really wants me to know.

So the three that became two is now a three again, and I need to work out how to make the adjustment, for her sake.

Chapter Thirty-Six

SUSAN

We can store a memory away, but it never truly dies. We can ignore its existence, we can hide from the emotions it provokes, but it will return when the soil of life is overturned. For too many years I tried to hide, and for as many years the truth refused to die. I simply buried it again, daily.

That these memories have now returned to play out in my mind with such crystal clarity reminds me of what I always knew: I will never escape the choice I made when the suffocating tidal wave of pain became the sting, then a gulp, then a cry. Confusion lay before me. A thing I knew, yet did not, became true.

The pain drew me inside of myself that day. When guttural pushing became a sharp intake of breath, I saw the briefest picture of what life could become, and I was too afraid to face it. It was a split-second choice, maybe not even that long. I was as much inside of my soul as out, looking down on myself from above. And so I found a way to live: inside, above and hidden, all at the same time.

My duty is done. The debts owed were repaid when I laid my parents to rest. I kept my shame. They escaped the secret. It's clear to me now that I'm surplus.

I faltered, here. I almost believed in the care she gave me. I almost believed in him. But the reality is that I'm not the person any of them need. I don't have the strength to face this. They are better off without me, and that is the only truth I can face.

I reach for the book of fairy tales, to do for the last time what I have done almost every night since that first: I read a bedtime story for the child I left behind. Tomorrow, I will leave.

Chapter Thirty-Seven

KAT

Stretching tension out of my arms and back as I walk through the gate from the flats in to the park, I look up to the clouds and pull my coat around me tightly. My phone rings again. His tone. Daniel. That's the third time this morning. I pull my phone out of my pocket and, after waiting a few seconds, relent. A part of me is intrigued by his uncharacteristic insistence.

'Daniel.'

'Kat, are you okay? I've called a few times.'

'I know.'

'Oh. Right.' It's reassuring to hear him cough, as though squirming, down the line. 'So, good to see you last night.'

'Was it?' I ask, stopping in my tracks. A runner jogs past me, her ponytail swinging with each step she takes.

'Well, yes. I mean, I know... It was good to see you out, I mean.' He coughs again, his voice breaking as he tries to pick up the conversation, regain some control like he always used to. And that's when I realise my devastation is slowly being replaced with disgust. 'Was it... a date?' he mumbles.

'Would it matter if it was?'

'Well, I just…'

I shake my head, searching the sky for divine intervention as the last five years of my life suddenly drop in to place.

'How far along is she, Daniel?'

'It's complicated,' he answers.

'Complicated! How complicated a question is that? Unless you aren't the father!' As I say it, I suddenly wonder if I'm right. Have I made the mother of incorrect assumptions? Is this the moment I learn the truth and we can begin to work past it?

'No, it is mine, it's just…'

Of course it is. For a second, he almost had me again. I almost gave in. The realisation of the hold he has over me propels me to pick up the pace. Head down. Refusing to let these tears escape, because he doesn't deserve them. 'I have to go,' I say.

'Kat, I'm sorry, I… You…' There's a voice in the background that stops him. I hear her ask him who's on the phone. She sounds like I did every time his phone rang: suspicious. He gives her some flannel about a work call, just like he always did with me, and I pull the phone away from my ear, take a deep breath and hang up.

I've been a victim of his lies and shameless self-interest all this time and I didn't see it. A victim of time passing, time I could have spent with someone else. Time I could perhaps have just spent alone. Working. Living. Learning who I am and what I really want out of life, over and above work. Did he ever love me? Is he even capable of that? And what the hell was this call about?

Five years.

Wasted.

I'm not sure if it's the call, the weather, the trees or the lack of sleep, but the air feels heavy. I feel heavy. How do I get over this?

You'd think it'd be easy, knowing what I do now. My brain knows it's time to move on, and my heart does too, I think, but how? How long does it take? When will I stop feeling as though my insides are being squeezed and my heart is dead? How dare he take hold of me so tightly that when he lets go I tumble so wildly out of control? How dare he do that, and how dare I let him.

I walk faster. I have to work out how to stop this. I have to work out how to reclaim my life, myself. Who even am I? What defines me? I've spent five years living as his girlfriend. Okay, I was Nurse Kat too, but who was I outside of work? I'm almost thirty. Aren't I supposed to know these answers by now?

I flick my hood up, hiding in the anonymity it provides. The runner from before runs back down, her eyes focused dead ahead. Maybe exercise would help me.

When did I become the kind of woman whose life's happiness revolves around someone else? When did I give that gift away?

It's time to take it back. I deserve more.

I deserve better.

My phone rings in my hand and I swipe it open with force. 'Stop it! Stop calling me. Leave me alone. You don't deserve me and I want nothing more to do with you!' I shout.

'Kat, it's me.'

'Emma? Sorry, I—'

'It's fine. Look, we have a problem.' She sounds strained, worse than I feel.

'You okay? Where are you? Is everything alright with Chris?' I instantly feel guilty that I've spent the hours since I saw her drowning in a vat of self-pity and never once checked if she got home okay.

'I'm fine – well, no, I'm not, but I'm at work. Kat, it's Susan.' I stop, partway up the hill to the park. 'She's gone.'

'What? What do you mean?' I push my hood back from my face.

'I mean she's disappeared. I've just got in. Rona went through the handover, then I went to check on everyone, and she wasn't in her bed. I didn't think anything of it until I came back round a bit later. She still wasn't there. Gloria said she'd not been there all morning. I checked the bathroom and nothing.' There's a beat. 'Kat, I think Susan's gone.'

I turn, starting to walk down the hill, before picking up the pace and beginning to run back down the hill, to the gate. 'How can she be? I don't understand.' My legs are heavy and clumsy, unfamiliar with my pace. I let the gate swing shut behind me as I fumble for my keys.

'I don't know, Kat. But she has gone. Handbag, crutches, gone.'

Holding my breath, I push into my building, taking the stairs two at a time. Ice forms in my chest as disjointed pictures piece together. 'How could we have let her...?' I begin, but stop myself, we don't need me to finish that sentence. Blame isn't going to help us find her. 'Look, I'll be there as soon as I can. Don't panic, Emma. We'll find her,' I say, trying to reassure her, picking up my bag and heading straight back out of my flat. 'I'm on my way.'

'I'm so sorry, Kat. Your day off as well.' There are tears in Emma's tone and a voice in the background. 'Okay, thanks for letting me know,' Emma says, away from the phone.

'What?'

'Gail's on her way in too. They just caught her before she left for the airport.'

'Right.' I swallow hard. 'Good. Great. Well done, we need her… Okay, I'll be there as soon as I can.' I run up the road just as a bus is about to pull away. 'STOP!' I yell, running across the road in front of it.

The driver slams her brakes on, opening up the doors. 'Jesus, I could have knocked you over! Where's the bloody fire?' She shakes her head at me as I apologise, holding my pass to the machine and taking a seat.

The bus bumbles into town, joining a queue of rush-hour traffic just by the ice rink. The guy in front of me groans. I tap the rail on the back of his seat, trying to check off a mental list of things we need to do in this situation. I dial the ward; Emma picks up straight away. 'Emma, get someone on CCTV, check if we can see which door she left from and which direction she headed. Get all internal and external footage. I'm sure we can find her that way, she can't have gone far…' I suddenly realise the very public nature of this private conversation. 'We'll find her, Emma, I promise.' I hang up, realising I've made a promise I can't be certain to keep.

The bus grinds to a standstill. Three lanes of heavy traffic are stationary. Drivers in cars are straining to see what the hold-up is. One gets out of his car for a better look. He catches sight of me on the bus and shrugs his shoulders, then lights up a fag and smokes as he waits.

Someone behind me dings the bell and gets off. I just manage to dodge my head out of the way of their bag as they swing it over their shoulder. A couple more passengers get off the bus. I consider doing the same but the reality of this situation has started to fully sink in, and I sink too, my spine pressed into my seat. What have we done? Or what haven't we done?

I shake off the moment's self-pity and look at my phone. What can I do, what can I do whilst I'm waiting? Rhys! He was getting through to her. He came back. Maybe she called him. I flick through my recent calls to find his number. I tap and wait, peering out of the windows for a break in the jam. As it rings out, a few more people get off the bus, which is enough encouragement for me to do the same. I jump into the gridlocked city-centre road as he picks up.

'Kat, hi. Erm... how are you?' A driver honks his horn as I nip through the traffic that has started crawling along the road. 'Where are you?' he asks. 'It sounds like downtown New York!'

'I'm outside the train station. I'm trying to get into work, but the traffic is awful and oh, fucking hell—' The traffic starts moving just as I make it to the path down the side of the station. 'Back on the bus or run for a tram?' I ask Rhys.

'Tram if I was you, sounds awful!'

'It is. Right, tram.' I start running, my bag banging on the back of my legs as I go. 'Look, Rhys, have you heard from Susan? Is she with you?' I cross my fingers, hoping.

'With me? No. Why would she be?'

'No.' Shit. 'Okay, don't worry. Look, I'll call you later. I have to go.'

'Kat, why would Susan be with me? What's going on?'

'It doesn't matter. It's nothing. Look, I've got to go,' I say, climbing the steps to the tram stop just in time to see one pulling away. 'Fucking hell.'

'Kat, are you okay?'

'No. Rhys. No, I'm not okay. I am very far from being okay.'

'What's happened? What's happened to Susan?'

I fall into a blue metal chair and my bag slaps onto the floor. 'Susan has gone,' I say, using my hand to cover my mouth. 'This morning.'

'What do you mean, "gone"?'

'I mean gone. She has gone. She is not on the ward.'

'Gone where?'

'I don't know where, Rhys. If I knew that, I wouldn't be calling you, would I!?' I take a short breath, trying to pull myself together. 'She's gone, Rhys. Taken herself off without telling us, gone. Disappeared into the night, gone. Not on my ward where she should be, gone. Are there any more types of gone you'd like?'

'No, no, no! She can't!' he shouts.

'She has.'

'Why? Why would she do that? Why now?'

'I don't know, Rhys. I don't know. But she has and we can't find her and not only am I frustrated but I'm... I'm terrified.'

'What can I do?'

'Nothing. Not really. Just let me know if you hear from her. Okay? Please, straight away.'

'I'm going to her house. See if she's there. Maybe she—'

'No! No, don't, Rhys.' His response is more dramatic than I expected. So now I'm panicked about Susan and concerned about Rhys. 'Look, I'm going to have to call the police and register a missing person anyway. It's fine, Rhys, they'll get in touch if they need to talk to you.' I'm not sure he's listening.

'Where are you now?' he asks.

'Park flats. The tram's coming, I'll be in work in about half an hour.'

'I'll come and fetch you, we can both go to Susan's. The police could take ages, Kat! What if she's...' He stops himself.

'No, I need to get to work. Help the team. I have to do this by the book, Rhys.'

'The book. Right.'

'Don't worry. We'll find her,' I say, once again making statements I
have no control over. The tram pulls up and I step on, leaning against
the cool of the yellow metal grab rail. 'I'll call you later, if you like,'
I say.

'Please! If you hear anything. I need to know, okay?' He hangs up
as the tram moves off and I wonder what has changed for him. What
has shifted to make him go from angry to distant to suddenly needing
to find Susan almost as much as I do?

If I don't find her, my career is surely over. And then what will I
do? I bite back the tears that are fighting to escape. Keep it together,
Kat. This is not about you. Don't give in to any of it. You're more than
that. You're better.

Chapter Thirty-Eight

RHYS

I sling on last night's clothes, grabbing my keys and wallet as I head out the door, letting it slam shut behind me. Unusually, the van seems to appreciate the urgency this morning, starting on the first tickover.

I cut up through the backstreets from Woodseats to Norton and follow the road past the water tower to Susan's. I take the speed bumps too fast, my suspension banging and groaning. Pulling up at her house, I unclick my seat belt, opening my door before the engine shuts down. Then a thought crosses my mind, stopping me cold. The reality of what this might mean stabs me in the gut. What if she's here, but she's not? What if she came back to finally end things? What if everything Kat and I have tried to do has made no difference whatsoever? What if it made it worse?

What if I'm not enough to keep her alive?

Nausea swells.

Everything about her house looks the same. It's still and empty-looking, just as we left it last week. The next-door neighbour's door opens suddenly, and my heart splits for a second. He lifts the boot to his T5, throwing bags in, taking something out and dropping it into his own hallway. He locks his front door.

'Hey,' I say, jumping out of my van. 'Sorry to bother you, but have you seen Susan?' I jog towards him, legs like jelly. I'm breathless with nervous energy.

The neighbour opens his van door, standing behind it as he leans to put his keys in the ignition, and shakes his head. 'No. Not for weeks, actually.' He looks at me, then to the van. 'Did she book you?'

'No, no. I'm her... friend.'

I hope he doesn't notice the pause before I categorise myself. Is friend how she'd describe me? Would he believe anything else? Do I? Whatever, he seems convinced and steps out from behind the van door. 'We've been worried, actually,' he says. 'Me and the missus. I mean, Susan keeps herself to herself, we all know that, but, well, normally we see her come and go. Less so since her parents...' He trails off, looking at me with suspicion. 'A friend?' he checks.

'A friend,' I say, the word sticking in my throat this time, trying to feign nonchalance to hide the reality of my emotions, my uncertainty, confusion and fear. 'I've been worried too,' I say, looking at my watch then to her house, anything to break eye contact with him.

The neighbour nods, then looks at his own watch. 'I'll be late for work. Tell her to shout if we can do anything,' he offers, climbing into his car, but not before taking another good look at my van.

'I will, cheers. Oh, traffic – it's mental, stacked up if you're off into town.'

'Really?'

'Yeah, avoid Woodseats and Queens Road if you can. Not sure what's happened.'

'Right, cheers.'

He gets into his van, turning left out of the drive with a hesitant thumbs up in my direction. I wait until I can't hear his car anymore then unlatch the gate to Susan's drive. With each step, my heart beats faster until I reach her door. I rub my chest to try and massage the panic into submission. 'Come on,' I say, then focus, knock and wait.

Nothing.

I try again, knocking louder and trying the bell too. It rings somewhere in the house, distant and broken. Like me. Like her.

Still nothing. This was easier when I had a key.

I look around at mid-morning suburbia. There's no movement. No cars, no sounds of commuter traffic.

Think. Think.

When I was a kid, Mum used to hide a key to our house in the back garden. I check for evidence of any more neighbours, or the postman, before moving around the side of her house and into the back garden. I look around the overgrown flowerbeds, plants heavy on earthy soil. I find nothing. Then I spot an overgrown Fatsia in the corner, its large lime-green leaves swollen and hanging low over a drystone wall between patio and lawn. Lifting the leaves, I peer under: bingo. A muddy jar nestles in the undergrowth. I pull it from the grasp of the weeds. A single key on a familiar, albeit dirty, pink ribbon slides and rattles inside. The scent of blooming roses hangs heavy in the air as I strain at the screw top and free the key. I look between it and the back door. Maybe I should wait. Kat did say she'd call the police.

And then I remember Susan's face when she first saw me. And the touch of her hand as she reached out to me. The notes. The connection. The newspaper clipping and my adoption file. The chance that if I leave it, by the time they get here it'll be too late. And then I'll never know the truth.

I've been too late before.

I fit the key into the lock, wrestling with it until it opens. Taking a deep breath, I push the door. A draught excluder sweeps across the floor, catching on folded newspaper acting as a doormat. I close the door again and turn to face the stillness of her kitchen: again, nothing's changed. Everything in her house appears to be just as we left it. As *she* left it. I move from kitchen to dining room and through to the lounge, careful not to leave my mark or make a mess. Careful to check each piece of her home, to try and work out if it might have moved. I pull at the lounge door and it clicks open, just as it did when we first came here. I look back over my shoulder, seeing nothing but a shaft of light with dancing dust. 'Susan?' I say gently, at the bottom of the stairs. 'Are you okay? Are you here?' I don't want to frighten her, if she is. 'Susan?' There's no sound, no movement, no response. I head upstairs, my heartbeat quickening, each breath more difficult than the last. My throat is sore from nerves. The stairs squeak as I get to the top and I hold on to the banister to steady myself. I stand by her bedroom door.

I've never been a man to pray. I've only ever asked for divine help once before – to no avail. And yet I find myself looking to the ceiling. If there is such a thing as God, as some higher power who can intervene, let them be listening to me now. Let me find her. Let her be here, in mind as in body. Let this be okay.

I twist the handle and push the door open, my eyes closed, my head bowed. I feel like glass, instantly breakable.

But there's nothing. Her room is empty.

Relief almost drowns me. I let out an audible breath, stuffing my hands in my pockets and leaning against the door frame. In my pockets, my hands meet cool paper. I pull it out. The envelope from yesterday. There was no call to stop me posting this. No reason given as to why I should not. I study it, front and back. I hold it up to the window to see if I can see what's inside. I step closer to the light for a better look, turning it over and reading the name and address on the front.

I pick out my phone and dial Kat.

'Rhys?'

'Tell them not to waste time, she's not here.'

'What?'

'I came round, I couldn't just sit and wait. She's not here so tell them not to waste time trying.'

'Okay. Okay. But Rhys, you know you shouldn't have—'

'I had to.'

'Rhys…' I hear her talking in the background. 'Rhys, I've got to go.'

'What? What is it?'

'I'll call you if we hear anything.'

She hangs up and I look at the letter. I should have told her. I should take it to her. Or I could cut out the middleman and take it straight to its recipient.

Mr James Grey. An address in the Lakes… Maybe that's where Susan is headed. I don't think about it anymore. I hurry down the stairs, lock up her house, replace the key in the jar and the jar in the garden. Then I run back to my car and make for the Lakes.

Chapter Thirty-Nine

RHYS

Foot pressed down, I drive. Past Mum's, eyes pinned forward, into Derbyshire; heading north.

Summer tourists slowly drive the twists up and over the hills and I have to stop myself taking risks to overtake. I'm no more benefit to her dead than she is to me. Derwent Dam glistens in the morning sun. The trees gradually give way to stretches of road, which eventually wind round towards Manchester in all its grey and blustery glory. The envelope rests on the passenger seat. Every now and then I reach out to it, making sure it's still there. Keeping it safe.

Some two and a half hours later, the landscape shifts as I pull off the motorway. Mountains rise from the horizon, some with tips sharp against the summer sky, others, further away, disappearing in a haze. I pick up the signs for Windermere, eventually catching sight of its steel-grey water up ahead. I roll down the window, taking in air much cleaner than home.

A sudden rush of fear, or guilt, or possibly both, descends like icy water through my chest. This isn't a game. This is real life. Her life. Maybe mine. If she has found her way up here, what do I say to her? Is it time to come right out and say what I think? Is it even possible?

She can't have been that young when she left this baby. Not really. Sixteen, maybe seventeen. Old enough to know better, surely? Maybe it's all in my head. A fantasy.

The letter should be with Kat. Or the police. It shouldn't be on its way to a man I've never met, whether it's addressed to him or not.

What was I thinking?

A lay-by appears by the side of the road and I swing into it, pulling up sharp, the lake sprawling out before me. The enormity of my stupidity dawns on me. I've hidden from this for the last year, since David and I read our adoption files. I've sat beside Susan in the hospital and not said a word. What makes me think I'd do it now if she were here? And what makes me think that this James Grey knows where she is, or where she might be? Do I really want to find her? I mean sure, I want her to be found, but by me?

I escape the van, suffocated by its heat. I fight for breath in the cool air by the water, bracing myself against the drystone wall. Cars speed along the road, forcing a rush of hot air against my back. I'm five minutes away from this address - I look at my watch - and I'm a good three hours from home.

A light breeze ripples the water, dancing up, down and across the lake. The surface sparkles as though it's flecked with tiny diamonds and a boat is propelled by a breeze caught in its voluminous sail. The people on it wave in my direction, but I turn away, reaching back into my van for my phone. It rings as I pick it up.

'You are not going to believe what I have just seen, Rhys!' Mum is practically clucking down the phone line. This must be gossip.

'Mum, I—'

'You know the new postman, the one who replaced the guy who nicked birthday money from people's cards, that one? Well, I've just seen him come out of Doreen's house up the road, her granddaughter behind him all suspicious like.'

'What does suspicious look like, Mum?' I sigh, my body forced against the wall by the air from a passing lorry. I press my finger to my ear so I can still hear her. 'Oh, you know, Rhys, both tucking shirts in, glancing over shoulders as they run away.'

'Mum, sorry, can this—' I try to interrupt her but she's in full flow.

'If Doreen had any idea of what was going on, I swear to God she'd have a coronary. Her heart's bad as it is, she's on them tablets for it now, you know. And I'm sure her granddaughter's barely legal.'

'She's nineteen,' I say, remembering the night Paul made absolutely sure before taking her home.

'How do you know?'

'It doesn't matter. Look, Mum, I can't talk, I need to make a phone call.'

'Oh, sorry, love, are you on a job? It's just I couldn't believe my eyes, I had to tell someone.'

'Okay, look. I'll call you back.'

'Okay, okay. Go on then. And I just wanted to say thank you, too. I know last night was hard, but thank you for coming out with us. It meant a lot to me. Derek and I had a lovely time.'

Derek and I. Derek and I.

'Me too, Mum.' I hope I sound more enthusiastic than I feel.

A tourist-filled steam cruiser lets out a long, low horn sound. 'Where are you?' she asks.

'I'm... in the Lakes,' I say quietly.

'The Lakes!' she shrieks. 'What are you doing up there? You never said! Are you okay, Rhys? You sound a bit... What's happened?' Her voice shifts from indignation to concern.

'It was a last-minute decision,' I say, climbing back into my van. 'Basically, Susan went missing overnight. She'd given me something to post, but for some reason, when I heard she'd gone I…' I rest my forehead against the steering wheel. 'Shit, Mum, I've made a right mess of this.'

'Oh, Rhys,' Mum says. I picture her resting against the sink, turning her back on the net curtains as a real problem unfolds.

'I need to call the hospital. Let them know what I've done.' I look over at the letter.

'Okay, love. Okay. Don't worry, it'll be fine. They'll find her, they will…' Mum sounds less convinced than I'd like. 'It'll all work out.' She and I both know that isn't always the case. 'I'll hang up then,' she says, reluctantly. 'Keep me posted.'

The line goes dead. I dig deep for the backbone to put this right, then dial Kat. It goes straight to voicemail. 'Kat, it's Rhys. I've been an idiot. I'm in the Lakes, about to hand deliver a letter Susan wrote and gave to me for posting. Call me as soon as possible?' I pause, then hang up. There's nothing more I can add to make this sound better.

I try searching my phone for the hospital number, but it isn't saved in my call list. I search the internet for Sheffield Hospitals, but there's no 3G by the lake. No connection at all. I sit in the car for a moment, dread and regret seeping from every sweating pore. I lift the letter, holding it up to the light again, turning it over to read the address. What was going through her mind when she wrote this? When she gave it to me? What is the point of it? Have we made any difference to her state of mind, or is this her final act? I don't know why, but there was something about the book, the way she held it… Whatever connection it gave her seemed strong. I thought she was going to be okay. I really did.

The book.

I dial Kat's number, and again it diverts to voicemail. 'Kat, check her book, check if she took it. Check the clipping too. She needed that book, remember? She needed it. Maybe if she has it we have time. Maybe this isn't…' I stop myself. I can't say whatever jumbled thoughts are in my mind. 'Call me,' I say, reluctantly hanging up again.

I look at the road beyond and behind. I check my watch and start the engine, pulling out of the lay-by and away. I've come this far…

Chapter Forty

RHYS

Traditional Lakestone buildings line either side of the narrow hill. At the top, I turn into Ambleside's mock suburbia: a tiny estate of identical houses nestled amongst the hills. I crawl the van along, seeking out house numbers in search of the right one. A man walking a Border terrier peers back, suspicious of the stranger in their midst. I pull up outside the right house. There's a black BMW on the drive and a caravan behind it. I check my phone for 3G signal: still nothing. I do a quick check for available Wi-Fi networks but they're all password-protected. I turn the volume on my phone right up, just in case I get a signal without realising and Kat calls back.

I cut the engine and birdsong replaces the rumble of the van. Someone nearby is cutting their grass and the sound alone makes me think I can smell it.

My mouth runs dry as I walk up the drive. What do I say? Where do I begin? Holding the letter in my mouth, I rub sweaty palms on my jeans. I take the letter back into my hands and knock on the porch door. There's a collection of family shoes, muddy wellington boots and a pink and black dog lead visible through the glass. A small, fluffy, yappy dog jumps up at the door and a girl in her late teens pulls it back by the collar only for it to escape again. 'Rio, get back,' she says, pushing it with her foot while opening the front door. I move down a step, making her suddenly tower above me.

'Yeah?' she asks, though doesn't appear to care what my answer might be.

'Hi, sorry to bother you, but I was looking for a Mr James Grey?' I check the letter in case I've got it wrong. But I've been glancing at it for the entire journey. I haven't got it wrong. The girl says nothing, but steps back, picks the dog up under her arm and heads inside. 'Dad, it's someone for you.' She goes down the corridor and into a room, taking a final, cursory glance in my direction before slamming the door shut. A man comes down the stairs to the front door. When he sees me, he pulls up short, suspicion slowing his last few steps. He stares at me.

'Hi... Sorry to interrupt you.'

He leans forward slightly, probably taking in my face and van for e-fit purposes. 'I...' He looks shaken, or accusatory perhaps. 'I don't buy from the door, I'm afraid.' He seems to trip a little over his words. 'There's a sign.'

His eyes are focused on mine as he points to a sticker in the window. He's about my height, similar build. But he has that air that fathers have, like proper grown-ups. I've often wondered if that arrives when the child is born – here's your baby and with it, a book on 'How to adult.' He peers at me again, shakes his head and steps back to close the door.

'Wait.' I put my hand out to stop him, resting a still sweaty palm on the glass panel of the door. 'I'm not selling anything.'

James pauses, looking at the glass as he pulls the door back open. I resist the urge to wipe it clean. 'I'm here about a friend of yours. Well,

I think she's a friend. Sorry, it's a bit… Are you James Grey?' The man narrows his eyes slightly, trying to work me out. 'Mr James Grey?'

'Yes.' He nods, slowly.

He folds his arms, resting against his front door. I hold out the letter, his name, in Susan's handwriting, facing up. He peers at it, but doesn't take it.

'It's a long story. And probably, now I'm stood here telling you, it's a little unbelievable too. But it has happened and that is why I'm here.' James looks at me as if a load of shit has just escaped my mouth and I have to accept it probably does appear that way. I try again. I try better. For her sake. 'There is a woman in a hospital in Sheffield. She won't talk but she wrote you this. I think. And, well, I say she's in hospital, but actually she disappeared. This morning. We're trying to find her.'

'Sheffield?' he asks, his arms still folded. I nod. The girl that answered the door has now come out of the room at the back of the house and is watching me fall over my words. The dog sniffs at my feet.

'Yes, sir. Sheffield.' I'm not sure that calling him sir was altogether necessary. I try to shuffle on the spot without standing on the dog.

'Dawn, go and put the kettle on, please. I'll be through in a minute.'

'But—'

'Thank you.'

His authority is sudden and clear. Dawn heads up the stairs, watching me over her shoulder. She mutters something to someone out of sight. All I hear is 'Dad' and 'door' and 'weirdo'. Under the circumstances, it's an astute assessment.

'So, what does this have to do with me?' asks James.

'Honestly? I don't know.' I cough to clear my tight throat. 'I don't know her that well. She was a customer.' I shift uncomfortably on the spot. 'I'm a plumber.' He doesn't need this detail but I don't know what else to say. *I think she may or may not be my mother, but I'm not entirely sure* probably wouldn't help my cause. And besides, I still don't know if I can say that aloud.

'She had my number in her diary when she was taken into hospital. In the absence of any next of kin, they called me...'

I stop talking when I see the look in his eye as I nervously relay the strange story. I can see why he looks at me that way. Three hours from home – one hundred and fifty miles – and I'm saying that visiting a mute patient I barely know is what we all get caught up in, from time to time. Sure. Why not. It's normal.

Except, it feels like it is.

Okay, maybe not normal. But it feels right, and no longer like something I'm just doing to get answers about David. It feels like there's more to it than that. Not that I've any clue how to explain that to the man before me, given that I can't explain it to myself. As much as I don't understand how she could have walked away from a child, whether I was that child or not, maybe I can relate to the broken soul within her. And not just because of our David, but because the broken soul is me.

I look to my feet, then to James, with a sense of emerging clarity. 'Have you ever met anyone, Mr Grey, and just felt this sense, from the very first time you locked eyes, that you were meant to be connected?'

James stares but doesn't answer.

'I'm not a religious man, Mr Grey, not particularly spiritual, but I've begun to wonder if sometimes people come into your life for a reason.' The words roll off my tongue, sentences formed before I really know what I'm going to say. My confidence is growing. 'Or sometimes people stay in your life longer than perhaps they should.' I think about Michelle. 'In truth, I should have passed this letter to the police the moment I heard she'd gone missing. Instead, I got in my van and came here. I don't know why, or what prompted it, but I'm kind of hoping fate has intervened. Because if not, I'm in big trouble.' I thrust the envelope towards him. 'A letter for you, Mr Grey. Hand delivered, on behalf of Susan Smith.'

James's persona of nominated grown-up pales, along with his face. He drops his eyes to the letter, taking it from me as he studies her writing. The lawnmower starts up again in the nearby garden. A phone rings out somewhere. But James just looks at the letter.

'I used to live in Sheffield,' he begins. 'Years back. I was a kid, really,' he says, his demeanour suddenly much less assured. There's something about it I recognise, a dint in his armour.

'Are you still in touch with anyone from there?' I ask hopefully.

'No,' he answers sharply, then looks up. 'We left pretty quickly. I lost touch with everyone. It wasn't like nowadays – we didn't have the internet or anything. When you moved, you moved.'

'Right.' I nod and pause, then decide to just go for it. 'So do you know her?' I know my purpose now. I have to make sure I've tried to get an answer for her, at the very least.

He stops turning over the letter and looks at me.

'Susan Smith,' I repeat. 'Did you know a girl called Susan Smith?'

He studies my face, as I try to study his. He looks older than I first thought. His hair is greying at the sides; hazel eyes hide behind metal-framed glasses.

'Are you okay down there, Jim?' calls a voice.

'Yes, love, fine. I'll be up in a minute.' He pulls the door firmly closed behind him as he moves down the steps. I make way until we're level. Eye to eye. That's when the next thing hits me: this man has a wife, a family, a job and a home. He has a dog that is still sniffing around my feet and a look that says Susan Smith is a lifetime ago and I've just made a grave error in judgement.

I lean against the side of his house, exhausted.

'Do you know something,' I say, dropping down till I'm crouching, my hand ruffling my hair. 'I came here convinced I was doing the right thing.' I laugh. 'I had a crisis in confidence by the lake, you know, almost turned back…' I lift my head towards the sky. 'And I would have done, had I had any phone signal to call the hospital. I should have listened to myself.' James steps back and sits down on the step, pulling the dog away from me and onto his lap.

'My brother died,' I explain. 'Six months ago. He…' I stop, ducking out of saying the truth out loud as usual. 'He died.' I look across at the letter in James's hands. The confidence of minutes ago, the clarity, it's all disintegrated, replaced by a cold wash of fear. The same wash of fear I felt when I woke up beside Michelle. The same wash of fear I felt when I left Mum after she told me about Derek. A trio of bad decisions.

I push myself back up again, preparing to leave. 'I thought this would solve it all, you know. That I'd deliver that letter, you'd read it, tell us where she was and we'd find her. All ready to embrace the elusive happy ever after. If it wasn't so painfully real, I'd laugh at my own stupidity.'

I kick at the ground. An army of ants skirt the edge of the concrete path, following each other across a crack and down the side of the path, out of sight. Do they question what they're doing, or just head onwards, blindly?

'Susan Smith was a long time ago.' He stands, handing me back the letter as he turns away. 'I'm sorry, I can't help. But I do hope you find her.' He drops the dog back inside the porch and closes the door behind him.

'Mr Grey,' I shout through the glass. 'James…' He pauses on the threshold of his inner door, his back towards me. 'Take it. She wrote it for you.'

I drop it through the letterbox, then turn and head back to my van.

Chapter Forty-One

KAT

I rush into my office. Gail is sitting in a spare chair, balancing a combination of laptop, notepad and phone between her knees and the coffee table.

'One of the patients believes Susan gave Rhys a letter to post,' I say, pulling myself tight into my desk and picking up the phone. 'I'm just going to call him now.'

'Great. The police are checking over the CCTV. They believe there is a sighting of Susan leaving at around five thirty this morning.'

'Where?' I dial Rhys' number.

'Out towards Barnsley Road. She could have picked up a bus, so they're on to the companies to check with drivers and check all CCTV they have. It will have been dark, not likely any local residents will have seen her, but I suppose you never know.'

'You'd remember a woman on crutches, right?'

'You would expect so,' agrees Gail. 'They're trying cab firms too.' She makes a note in her diary then scrolls through some papers in Susan's file whilst I wait for my call to connect to Rhys.

'Hello?'

'Rhys, it's Kat. Can you talk?' I pull clean paper from the back of my diary and poise my pen. 'There's no news yet but we've been talking to the patients, to see if there's anything we missed. Gloria, the woman in the bed opposite, says Susan gave you a letter to post?'

'That's right.'

'Do you still have it? Can you remember who it was for? Or their address maybe?' There is a pause on the other end of the line. 'Rhys?'

'Yeah, I'm here,' he says, sounding distracted, sounding tired.

'Do you still have the letter?'

'No,' he says. 'No, I don't, I...'

My heart sinks a little as his voice trails off. 'Okay, don't worry. Can you remember the address? Or a name? Anything at all?' I start writing down the basics he has. 'Do you know how to spell that?'

'F. I. S. H. E. R. B. E. C. K,' he spells. I open up my internet browser and search for the address in maps. 'Ambleside,' he adds. I write that down, holding it up for Gail to read too. She makes a note in her own pad. I flick back to my screen.

'Fisherbeck... Ambleside... Okay, I think I've got it. It's residential, right?'

'Yeah. Look, Kat—'

'And what did you say the name was? James...?'

'Grey. With an e. Look, Kat, I'm here.'

I stop writing. 'What?' Gail looks up at me. 'You're where, Rhys?'

'Ambleside,' he says. 'At James Grey's. I hand delivered the letter...' His voice trails off again and I drop my head into my hands.

'I don't understand... Why didn't you...' Gail has moved to stand beside me. I write a note on my pad for her to catch up on the detail, and her eyes widen as she reads it.

'I drove up here without thinking. When I realised I'd made a mistake… Look, it's complicated. And I couldn't get in touch with you, your phone just went through to voicemail.'

'I don't have it on in the hospital, Rhys!' I say, reaching into my bag to retrieve and switch on my mobile.

'I didn't know what else to do,' he says. 'I'm so sorry, Kat. I thought it might help, but… hang on.'

'What, Rhys? What is it?'

There's a voice in the background, speaking brief, undecipherable words. Rhys comes back on the line, breathless and urgent. 'Kat, James has asked me to go in and talk to him. I'll find out everything I can and call you straight back.'

'Rhys!' I shout, but he's hung up. 'Shit!' I throw my pen across the desk.

I try calling him back, his number now imprinted on my mind, but it just rings out then goes to his voicemail. My own phone kicks into life with a message alert. I throw that across the desk too. 'He took the letter,' I say to Gail. 'He's up in the Lakes now. At this man's house.' I refer to my pad. 'James Grey.' I scrunch my face up tightly then release in the hope that some clarity prevails, or that this headache might shift. I rub my temple, an ache pressing behind my eyes. I pull open my drawer in search of aspirin. The blister pack from hospital supplies stares back at me and I wonder if Gail sees it. I push the drawer closed.

'So who is this James Grey?' she asks, her eyes focused on my notes as if the answer lies within the scribble.

'No idea.' I drop back into my chair, all energy drained. 'Rhys said he'd call me back. I've no idea who he is or what the letter says, or why Rhys thought it appropriate to just go straight up there. What was he thinking?'

'The whole situation is a mess,' says Gail, more to herself than me. My heart sinks. She takes my notes and heads back to her temporary station in my office. 'Okay,' she sighs, her voice drained of hope. 'I'll take all this down for the police. I think there's an inspector in with Mark at the moment. There are patrol officers looking for her and a press release coming out shortly to make the public aware. We will find her, Kat. We will.' I hear her telling me what I've been saying to Rhys, to Emma. I've even said it to Gloria. In truth, the longer it goes on, the less likely we are to be right. She doesn't sound like she believes it any more than I do.

I swallow, hard.

The list of all the people involved in finding Susan puts an already real situation into full perspective. I no longer feel sick and frightened. I feel dread, deep in the pit of my stomach. Susan is missing. Susan. My patient. My responsibility. Shit.

'Let me know if you hear anything else, Kat. In the meantime, keep on top of your ward. We need to maintain normality for the rest of the patients. They mustn't sense any panic, okay?'

'Of course.' I fold my arms, feeling small and helpless. 'Jesus, what a mess, Gail. I'm so sorry…' I search for something appropriate to say. 'You should be on holiday,' I start, realising that's the last thing she'll want reminding of.

'I should,' she says, then lets out a sigh herself and forces a half-smile of support in my direction. 'There's nothing like getting thrown into the deep end, Kat.'

I nod, watching her fill her arms with papers and laptop and then leave. In the lone quiet of my office, tears I've been fighting back force their way through my resolve. My hope, my self-belief, everything I was trying to rebuild on shaky foundations is fading fast. I'm swamped by the scale of the problem. I'm blinded by the ache in my neck, my head. I pick out two tablets from the aspirin in my drawer, picking up my phone to listen to the new voicemail message as I knock the tablets back with the only drink I can find: cold tea. I gag. I listen and delete Rhys's first message, asking me to call him back, waiting for the second to kick in. Hospital lunch smells waft through my open door; it's business as usual out there.

The second message begins: 'Kat, check her book, check if she took it,' he says. I can hear the panic in Rhys's voice, the worry. I look down at her book, lying on my desk, and flick through for maybe the tenth or eleventh time just in case I've missed it.

But there's nothing. The clipping has definitely gone.

Chapter Forty-Two

RHYS

There's an uneasy quiet in his office, a tiny room at the front of the house. The muffled buzz of daytime telly seeps through the walls from the lounge next door. James's wife was ironing and complaining about their daughter when I walked through. Something about attitude and mess and how on earth can they get through to her? James didn't respond, just introduced me as a friend of a friend from Sheffield and asked her to bring us some drinks through. Old school. She asked him if he was okay, said he was looking peaky, but he told her not to fuss.

He's sitting at his desk now. Beneath books and papers, I can see mahogany and a green leather inset that matches his captain's chair. Dappled grey files line the walls, with names and dates marker-penned on. A printer sits beneath the window, stacked high with more papers and boxes. He pulls a small black chair over, motioning me to sit down.

'Sorry for the mess,' he says, nervously pushing a few papers about without actually moving anything out of the way. 'I know where everything is, even if nobody else does. It drives my wife crazy.' He wipes his face, scanning his desk as if searching for something. 'Can't say I blame her.'

She comes in with a tray and a pot of tea, two china cups on matching floral saucers beside a bowl full of sugar cubes, with tongs to serve. She looks around for somewhere to put it but James takes it from her, laying it on top of a pad. There's a tiny plate of biscuits too: a couple of custard creams and a bourbon. 'I didn't realise we were having visitors,' she says to me. 'I'd have gone to the shops, otherwise.' She motions to the biscuits as if they require an apology, and then looks to James, perhaps to check there's nothing else he needs before she leaves. 'Are you sure you're okay?' she asks, laying a hand on his shoulder.

'Yes, I'm fine,' he answers, leaning into her touch. She pulls back slightly as if to read his face. There's an apparent shorthand in their communication, filled with tenderness and longevity. I feel a pang of envy.

'I'll take the phone through,' she says, reaching behind him to lift it from the cradle on his desk. He holds on to her arm, letting his fingers run down till their hands touch as she leaves, pulling the door quietly to.

James stares at the closed door for a moment before shifting his gaze out of the window. One hand holds the chair he sits in, his knuckles paling so tight is his grip.

I go to speak. 'I owe you an—'

'You did the right thing,' he interrupts, quietly. He takes the letter out of his top pocket, dropping it on the desk. 'It's right that I have it.'

I nod and he mirrors me.

He reaches for the tea, his hand shaking as he pours. He didn't strike me as a nervous man when I first saw him on the doorstep. But as hot, brown tea spills onto the tray, pooling in the corner where it's not quite level, it's clear he's unsettled. I don't know if I should reach for a tissue from the box on my right to mop it up or stay in this chair until I'm asked a question. He moves the mug and the milk. I sit tight.

'Bear with me,' he says, smoothing Susan's envelope out before him. 'This is …' He shakes his head.

There's a photo on the wall: James and his wife on their wedding day. She's dressed in a knee-length shift dress, white for the wedding, but short for the seventies, maybe early eighties, I guess. Her hair is held back by a heavy white band, shoulder-length veil caught in the wind, and they're both smiling widely at the camera. He looks like a bygone footballer – all hair and moustache and disproportionate bell-bottoms. He looks happy.

He catches my line of sight, glancing at himself in the photo and then back to Susan's letter. 'This all happened a long time before I met my wife,' he says. 'Eight, nine years, maybe. Have you read this?' He motions towards the envelope.

'No, sir.'

He nods, but not really as if he understands. 'And how did you say you knew her again?'

'The hospital called me, when she had her accident.' The word sticks in my throat, I cough myself free again. 'She'd been a customer, but as I said outside, I just… I felt I needed to help. That it was important. I can't explain it really.'

He studies me, surveying my face, his eyes eventually settling on mine. 'She was wonderful,' he says. 'Compelling almost, you know?'

I suppose I do know.

He reaches to take a sip of his tea. He places his cup back down. 'She was quiet, to begin with. She grew up in a house where she was seen and not heard, you know?' I nod, though I can't really relate. 'We used to go for walks. Through gardens. To art galleries…' He smiles, and I want to ask what he remembers. 'Graves Park…'

I look to the ground as he pulls out the letter. When I look up, his jaw is tight, his eyes red-rimmed and disbelieving. Through the paper, I can see handwriting unlike that which I associate with her. It's less urgent. I can't decipher the words, but they flow like she has poured each one smoothly from heart to page. I want to reach out and take the letter from him, but he folds it closed, holding it tight.

Chapter Forty-Three

SUSAN

Dear James,

I don't know if this letter will make it. And, perhaps, that doesn't matter. Because if it does, what you will read may not be something you can do anything about. I don't know the path your life took when you left. But I felt that, this time, I needed to at least try to mend what I could, before I go.

So where do I begin?

Hello? How are you? I hope this finds you well? All such openings sound so trite in comparison to what I am about to tell you. In truth, it seems strange writing to you like this now. I did it often in those early days. I felt you were the only person to whom I could pour out my secrets. Each letter was written in darkness, burned in private. I had no intention of sending them. I suppose I just needed a way to unlock the things I couldn't say out loud. Pen to paper has always been easy for me.

I say that, but I've been staring at this paper for ten minutes. Perhaps it's not so easy nowadays. I suppose I don't know where to begin. Bear with me, James.

My life has been a fortunate one. Quieter than I imagined, than I dreamed, it would be. Than we dreamed. I remember our talks into the night, beneath our tree. You told me all the things you wanted to do. I hope you live in the hills. I hope numbers pay your bills.

I hope you're happy.

I didn't teach. In the end, it seemed like something other people did. Making a difference wasn't really for me. You made me believe I could be and do whatever I wanted, but when you left, the real me came out. I suppose that's what I mean by my life being quieter.

I don't blame you, by the way. I should say that here and now, for the avoidance of doubt. I know you had to leave. That it wasn't your choice. Choice wasn't ours to take back then, was it? Not really. Sometimes I've wondered if things could have been different, if we were young today.

I stayed at home. Mother and Father needed me to be around and I needed to do that for them. I felt I owed them that much. I took a job in the records office in Sheffield. I was unknown there. A paper-pusher. The invisibility of it saved me. It kept my secrets for me.

Father died last autumn, though he'd gone long before in all but body. Mother passed away this January. Hers was sudden, but peaceful. They are buried at St James's. And with them both gone, my job is done, the price of their protection duly paid. That sounds like I begrudge it. I do not.

All the while I protected them, I carried another burden, which I can no longer hide. The burden of the secret I kept from you. It is to my shame and my desperate sadness that I held this from you for so long. That it happened. That I allowed it to end up the way it did. I do not expect your forgiveness.

There is no easy way to say this, James, and I am sorry for what will undoubtedly follow this news, but you have to know that we have a child. The newspaper clipping I enclose is our son. Born in Graves Park beneath our tree, and left – in desperation – on the steps of St John's Church.

He was beautiful. Perfect. A tiny picture of us both.

He was everything I could not have, everything that could not be. How could I have returned home that night as a mother? Their reputation, my life, yours… all irrevocably changed by our act of weakness. We may not have been quite children, but we were not very much more. You'd gone, it was too late.

James, I have regretted my choice every day since. I lied, every day of my life, and I felt torture because of that. But I never had the strength or courage to change it. And now here we are. So many years have passed; such is the brevity of human life.

If this letter finds you, I hope, though do not expect, that you can forgive me. Even if I can't be here to accept it. For that too, I am sorry.

Should you choose to try and find him, tell him I am sorry. I couldn't even manage that. His name is Rhys Woods. From Sheffield. He's a plumber, and the kindest man I've ever had the pleasure to sit silently in a room with.

I only wish I'd been stronger.
With my love, forever yours, and his,
Susan. X

Chapter Forty-Four

RHYS

'And you've no idea what the letter says?' James asks again.

'She never said, and I didn't ask. I was distracted at the time. It's hard to explain.'

James nods, hands clasped, knuckles still white. There's distance in his eyes, as if he is visiting their past to try and work out why she'd contact him now.

'Does she hint where she may be? Does she say anything we need to consider?' I ask. 'I can call the police, tell them all about it.'

He looks down at the letter, folded tight in his hands. I can see him thinking, and I cross everything there's something in her words that we can go on. Disappointment swells as he shakes his head, seemingly out of words.

I try, a few times, opening my mouth to impart wisdom I don't have, thankfully stopping myself before I say something stupid.

The edge of the letter shakes just slightly, a ripple from the continued tremor of his own hand.

'Nobody should ever have to face something like that alone,' he says, quietly.

'Something like what?' I ask, my mouth running dry.

James shakes his head again.

'Like what?' I repeat.

'She always felt a weight of responsibility to them.'

'To who?'

'Her parents.'

I don't understand what he's saying. I screw my face up in question, but before I can ask, he speaks again.

'I always thought it was because she was an only child. She knew their care would ultimately come down to her and she seemed to wear it like a badge of destiny. We'd sit sometimes, and I'd ask her what she wanted to be. She'd talk of teaching and I'd tell her she could do it. Because she could have. When she was away from them, when she briefly escaped their expectation... she shone.' A sad smile falls across his face, his eyelids low and heavy. 'I don't think I ever truly understood how much their approval dictated her life. Like I said before, we were still young, and I guess we just didn't see things like we do now with age.' He flicks his eyes in my direction, taking the letter back. 'Or is that just romance?'

'I don't understand...'

'We remember things as we want them to be, don't we? Humans, we're known for projecting on others what we want them to see of us, whether that's good or bad. Maybe the memory I have of her is my own projection.'

I consider his words. Is that what this is for me too? Am I being a fool to think there's even the remotest chance that she's the woman who gave me life? Is this trip all just romance of one form or another?

'I remember it all though,' he goes on. 'The walks, the laughter, the cinema trips. The love. Maybe it all formed to protect the memory I had of the girl I left behind. Or maybe she wasn't that girl at all.'

He holds both hands around the letter. 'She can't have been,' he says simply. 'The girl I knew would have survived.'

'We don't know she hasn't,' I say, the fear we might lose her returning, deeper.

'Forgive me, but living and breathing doesn't mean she survived, just that she is alive. It's not the same thing. She hasn't led the life she wanted. The life she hoped for. We met at church. Her parents were God-fearing – not fanatically so, but they held their beliefs much stronger than our family and they required the same of Susan. It seems that requirement obscured all else.'

I think of the crucifix that she wears. How the chain rolls as she breathes, when she moves.

'She had questions, but rarely asked them. Certainly not of her parents, at least.' His voice has shifted, frustration ebbing into his tone. 'Can you imagine living a life in which every decision you took was based on your parents dogged view of the Will of God?'

'My Mum's never been religious. Unless you count the bingo? She's fairly evangelical down her local Mecca.' I shift when he doesn't respond to my ill-timed quip. 'You said you moved away?' I ask, bringing us back to his story.

'Yes. Almost overnight. For several months before that, Susan and I had been courting. Sounds old-fashioned, doesn't it, but that's what you did. The church approved certain levels of relationship and that was where we were at. They didn't realise how we talked. We kept it secret. Just for us. We named our children. Our dog. Our cottage.' He lets a brief smile cross his face. 'Just as we were about to explain our feelings for each other to the church, to her parents, my father lost everything and our status changed. A single bad business decision on his part and our handsome home in the leafy suburbs became a house share. Church handouts kept us fed and watered while our home was repossessed. Although we tried to carry on, I'd been sworn to secrecy about the whole thing. The church knew, and Susan's father knew, but he didn't approve of his daughter's relationship with the son of a failure. Leaving for a new life was our only choice.'

'Did you tell her anything?' I ask.

'I went to see her father, pleaded with him to let us stay in touch. I told him I loved her. That I wanted to finish college, move back to Sheffield and get a job. That I wanted to marry her. He disapproved of such sentimentality. He believed we weren't more than children, incapable of understanding love and all of its ramifications.'

I try to imagine such strong opposition.

'They were lost in a time warp. Locked in the 1950s.' He drops his head. 'I told him so. I was almost eighteen, for God's sake. Okay, I wasn't fully a man, but I wasn't a boy. I was angry. Frustrated. I was impetuous.'

He gets up, stepping to the back wall of his office. He moves some papers about, files away her letter, then comes back and sits down, resting his hands before him. He looks exhausted.

'I wonder how things might have been different had I stayed in Sheffield.'

When I arrived less than half an hour ago, James looked like a man in charge of his destiny. A man who knew life and his role within it. He was the man of this house. He was in charge. Now, James looks broken. He looks grey. Aged. His brow is scrunched and his eyes are weak.

'So, she's gone,' he says.

I nod. 'This morning.'

'But she gave you this before she left?'

'Yesterday. I was going to post it today. Then when I heard she'd gone and, I don't know, I went into autopilot. I just got in my car and drove. I don't know if I thought she might have come here, or if you might know where we should look. I've been stupid.'

He looks at me questioningly.

'I got as far as the lake and then I had this moment of clarity. I pulled over, realising I should have given the letter straight to the police. I shouldn't have taken the situation into my own hands. I just… I don't know. I don't know. All I did know was that I couldn't change it. I was almost here, and I just had to hope there'd be something within her letter that might help us find her.'

'And yet,' he says, 'there's nothing.'

'No,' I concede. 'It seems not.'

I drop my head back, my eyes closed. 'I'm so sorry, Mr Grey. James. I am so sorry, I just… I tried to do the right thing. But I didn't think. I wasn't thinking. I don't know what was so important for her to write to you, I'm just sorry I swanned in and dropped it on you like this. I've been focused on finding her for my own reasons, I guess I'm not entirely thinking straight.'

As I open my eyes, I see he is nodding. Agreeing with my words. Each nod seems to build an unspoken, invisible wall around the pain I've just brought him. 'I think you should go.' He stands, going back to reach for the letter from the shelf. He takes a key out of a red plastic pencil tidy, unlocking a drawer in the bottom of his desk to get another key. 'I'm sorry for your long journey, and that this has all been a waste of your time, but I think you should leave.' With each word, and each action, his body gets stronger, more upright. Uptight. His face changes, closing down. The demeanour of a man in charge returns. He reaches for a tin in a secret drawer within his desk. He unlocks it, puts the letter in and puts it away, reversing the process to hide the second key in the bottom drawer and the first key back in the pen tidy. 'I should get on with my life. I have a daughter, here in my house. A wife. We need each other.' He changes his mind, reaching for the pen-tidy key again, placing it instead in a briefcase beside him, which he moves to the side of his desk, away from view. Then he stands before me, looking to the ground, waiting for me to go.

I stand up, but can't leave without checking one last time. 'Have you any idea where she might be? Where she might have gone?' I ask. 'Is there anything you can think of? A favourite place? Or a friend we haven't thought about? I can see I've made a mistake coming here, and I understand, I apologise, but… please.'

'It was a very long time ago, Rhys. Sheffield's changed, Susan's changed… I wouldn't know where to begin.'

My shoulders drop, the full realisation of this wasted trip weighing them down. I dig around for my wallet, taking out a dog-eared business card and dropping it onto his desk. 'Just in case.'

He gestures towards the door, encouraging me to leave. We don't look at one another. 'Thank you for the tea,' I say to his wife as I pass back through the lounge. She watches me, confused. The dog sleeps in a shaft of light that falls across the carpet. Daytime television still plays out.

I walk out of the front door, turning to say goodbye, surprised to find him on the path behind me. 'We weren't kids, Rhys,' he says. 'It was love. First love, but true love. Do you understand?' His look is intense and I can do nothing else but shrug, pretending I do understand. 'They say your first is your most intense because you've never known it before. It suffocates.' He takes a sharp breath that stops his words, then heads back inside, closing the door between us. He watches as I get in the car, and watches as I pull away. I see him watching until I'm out of view, and I realise I understand, totally, the kind of love he talks about. And I understand how intense it becomes when that love is not rightfully yours. And whether I like it or not, I understand how he can walk away. What reason has he to stay?

Chapter Forty-Five

KAT

There's not much to look at out of my office window. Yet I stand with my arms crossed, tucking myself tight in, lost in the view of the concrete and impenetrable windows of the hospital block over the way. I walked the ward, checked on the team, made sure everyone was okay, then retreated back to my office, waiting for Rhys to call. I've tried him a couple of times but can't get through. There's the sound of a helicopter in the distance. Air ambulance or search team?

A knock on my office door makes me jump. 'Sorry, I didn't mean to startle you,' says Mark. 'Can I come in?' I signal to a chair by way of answer. He comes in but doesn't sit down. 'Are you okay?' he asks.

The calmness in his voice, the warmth and sudden arrival of a bedside manner I didn't know he had, combines and finds the weak spot in a wall I've been trying to rebuild. I turn, tears streaming down my face, arms still folded as I try and fail to hold myself in. 'What if she does it this time?' I sniff through the tears. 'What if we're too late?'

'Hey, hey!' He jogs towards me. 'Come here.' Mark pulls me into a tight hold, his arms wrapped around me, strong and firm. His head rests on top of mine. I feel the heat of his breath on my crown.

'They're doing everything they can, but we have no control, Kat. We can't do any more than we have.'

'But what if we made mistakes, Mark?' I say into his chest. 'What if I made mistakes and this all goes horribly, horribly wrong?'

'You weren't even here when she left, Kat.'

'No, but she's still my patient. This is still my ward,' I hiccup.

He squeezes me tight, then holds me out, looking into my eyes, brushing hair from my wet cheeks and tucking it behind my ear. I drop his gaze, feeling awkward and vulnerable. 'You are a brilliant nurse, Kat. Susan has made her own choice to leave. We know this is a complex situation, and you have done everything you can to help her.' He pulls me back in, and I'm relieved for a break in the intensity. 'You've gone above and beyond.'

'That's what I'm worried about. What if I made the wrong call somewhere?'

'You did everything you felt you should, every step of the way. That's all anyone can ask.'

Against everything inside telling me not to, I let my head relax into his touch, his strength all but holding me up. His certainty and confidence combined with empathy and warmth brings about a tiredness that swells over me. I let myself stay in his arms a little longer. 'Thank you,' I whisper, realising how good it is to feel I'm not alone.

'It's nothing,' he says, with another squeeze.

I lift my head up to look up at him. Mr Just-Call-Me-Mark Barnes. He smells different again today, no aftershave at all this time. He smiles gently as he studies my face. My heart quickens and for the briefest moment I wonder what it might be like to kiss him…

'I have to go,' he says, clearing his throat as he stands back. 'I just…' He strokes the back of his head, looking down at his feet. 'I just wanted to check you were okay,' he says, backing off to the door. 'Try not to worry, okay?' He closes the door behind him, looking through the glass one last time before leaving me alone and confused in my office. I have a patient on the missing list and I'm standing here considering what it might feel like to kiss a colleague. Frustration at my own stupidity replaces the tiredness and fear. 'For fuck's sake, Kat!' I shout out into the room, at the exact same moment my phone rings.

'Rhys?'

'Kat, yeah, it's me.'

The line comes and goes; his signal is breaking up. 'Where are you? Did you talk to him? What happened?' Emma peeks through my window now and I signal for her to come in. She pulls a chair up to my desk.

'I saw James, we've spoken,' he says.

'Did he say where we might find her? Did he know where she might be? Any clues at all?'

'No,' sighs Rhys. 'He couldn't help.'

'Great. Brilliant. So, we've got no letter and no help. Perfect.' Frustration has fully set in. 'So what's your next big move, Rhys? What's your next solution for my patient?' Emma reaches her hand out to mine, taking hold with a squeeze. I look up at her and she signals for me to take a breather. I nod. 'Sorry, Rhys.' I stretch out, then rest my forehead in the palm of my hand. 'I'm just... Sorry, that was unfair.'

'It's okay,' he says quietly.

I try again. 'Do you know what she wrote *in* the letter? Is there anything in there that the police could use?'

'No idea. He didn't share what she wrote and it didn't feel appropriate to ask if I could read it.' I put the phone on speaker so Emma can hear too. She starts making notes. 'The only thing he said was that she'd been afraid of her parents. That she didn't appear to have led the life she dreamed of and I guess that's why he couldn't offer any insight. He didn't seem to really know the woman she'd become.'

'Right. Can he talk to the police?' I ask. 'Can he fill them in on what he knows? Let them have the letter in case they read something he's missed?'

Rhys sighs. 'He says he doesn't want to get involved. That he can't. That it was a long time ago and he has a life now, a family.'

Emma shrugs with resignation. We've both seen situations in our career where people walk away from the things that upset family equilibrium. 'We have to pass the information over, Rhys,' I say. 'Even if he's not willing, you still have information that might help the police. More details with which to build a picture of her character, the choices she might make. It could make a difference.'

'I know,' he says. 'I know...'

'Shall I tell them?'

There's a pause, I assume for him to work out how much more he is prepared to take on here. 'I'll call them. I'll tell them all I can. I'll do it now,' he says resignedly.

'Okay, Rhys. Do you promise?'

'Of course.'

'I'll text you the number now.'

'Thanks.'

'Drive carefully,' I add.

'I will.'

He hangs up. As I text him the incident line for the case, Emma looks over the notes she's taken: 'Parents. James. Family.'

'It's nothing they don't already know,' she says, handing it to me.

'I guess not.'

'You look exhausted, Kat. What time do you finish?' she asks.

I look at my watch. 'I dunno, it's my day off, isn't it? I don't know if I should stay until we find her or go home and wait.'

'Well, I'm on till nine tonight now. I can keep my ear out and let you know of anything till then, at least? There's not much else you can do here, is there?'

I look around at my desk, the scribbled notes and messy files. My computer screen still shows the map I searched out James's address on. 'Probably not.'

'Go then. If the police and Gail don't need you either, just go home and try to rest.'

I let out a groan; my body clicks and aches as I stand. I try to stretch out the pain in my arms and my back. 'Okay,' I agree. 'You're probably right. We're not exactly pulling up trees here, are we?'

I gather my things together, and with a kiss on Emma's cheek, I head out of the office.

Chapter Forty-Six

KAT

I push open the door to my flat, ignoring the airless heat that hits me full in the face. I stand in the middle of my lounge with no idea what to do with myself. I go to the bathroom to wipe away the remnants of the make-up my salty tears didn't wash away. I ignore the pallid reflection looking back. I go to the lounge, sit at the head of my dining table and point the chair towards the window. Late-afternoon sun flickers through the trees onto the path leading up to Norfolk Park. A young girl pushes an empty buggy as her toddler runs on up ahead. A helicopter hovers nearby and the door to my block of flats slams shut as someone comes or goes.

And I feel faint. Like I'm not really in my skin. Like I'm somewhere above, observing the mess I'm hurtling through. The car crash. The total fuck-up. I rest my feet against the windowsill, pushing the chair back till it meets the dining table, and sit, suspended, caught between wall and table, not moving.

I think back over the last week or so: the first time I saw Rhys as he raced into the hospital in a panic. The sadness in his eyes when he talked about his brother, and the sense of purpose that replaced it all when he thought he could help Susan. How I saw a flash of life in

Susan when Rhys busied himself around her. How she would look at him. The note she wrote. The book. The news clipping and the overwhelming sadness that her entire life could be dictated by one choice. A choice she never quite forgave herself for. Her life not lived, but dedicated to the care of her parents. A life she is now desperate to leave behind because she can't see what place, what purpose, she has within it.

Is it a life I could have changed, if perhaps I'd done things differently?

I shift my legs, letting the chair drop back to the ground. I head into the kitchen, reaching to the top of my cupboards to pull out a packet of cigarettes I hid in there months ago. I lift the lid and sniff inside, tasting the memory of a first draw. I dig out a lighter from the back of the cupboard and kiss the flame with the end of the cigarette. Thick smoke hits and burns the back of my throat as I inhale, the initial buzz quickly replaced by a dizzy sickness. I run the tip under the tap, waiting for the fizz to fade. There's a knock at my door.

'Yep?' I say, opening it. Lou stomps straight in, carrying a wicker basket and bottle of Prosecco.

'Did you forget we were supposed to be going out for an afternoon picnic? We've been sat in Graves Park for the last two hours waiting for you.'

'Who has?' I ask, racking my brains for any memory of such an invite.

'Me, Will and his best man! I texted you like you told me to?'

I roll my eyes, not remembering a thing outside of work for the last few days.

She stands before me, hands on hips. 'I saved you some salmon, but it's probably gone off in the heat,' she says sulkily, slamming the basket on the kitchen counter. 'Where the fuck have you been?' She folds her arms and stares, waiting for an explanation, then sniffs the air. 'Have you been smoking? No bridesmaid of mine is a smoker. It stinks in here.' She opens the other kitchen window, faux coughing and looking at me in disgust. I lean against the kitchen side, groaning.

'What?' she says, accusingly. Then looks at me again, seeing past her own annoyance and through to the reality etched on my face. 'What's happened?'

I open my mouth to try and explain everything and nothing comes out but a sob and stream of consciousness that even I can't decipher. It starts with Susan and Rhys, but shifts to Daniel and Natasha and the baby bump from hell before moving back to the fact we've lost Susan and this afternoon's sudden urge to kiss Mark. When I finish she reaches for the box of cigarettes herself and lights one up, taking a drag and passing it to me. 'Blimey!' is all she can say.

We sit together for a moment, sharing the cigarette in silence. We both blow smoke in the general direction of the kitchen window.

'What am I going to do, Lou?'

'Go out and get wasted?' she jokes. I roll my eyes.

'When I went into nursing, I didn't really think about this sort of thing. I'm not even sure I thought about career progression.'

'From what I recall, you specifically opted to train as a nurse because they had the best nightlife during training.' She nudges me, trying to raise a smile.

'Feels like a lifetime ago,' I say, briefly lost in nostalgia. 'A life with few responsibilities and a bank account swollen with student loan.'

'Lots of fun.'

'Lots of boys.'

'LOTS of boys!' she teases.

'Until I met Daniel.'

Lou nods, offering me a final drag of the cigarette before throwing it out of the window.

'Did you know she was pregnant?' I ask. 'And, like, a lot more pregnant than the seven weeks or so we've been apart.'

Lou pouts, looking at her feet. 'I'd heard, but didn't know for definite.' She lets out a whistle. 'I didn't want to upset you if it wasn't true!'

'Oh, it's true alright.' I smile, sadly. 'She is most definitely, one hundred per cent up the duff with my ex-boyfriend's baby.' I sniff. 'Bet the bitch doesn't even get stretch marks.'

'At least you can chase after the plumber now. Or the consultant. Who has the best career prospects? Who are you going to see most? Whose services might you get the best benefit from in a professional sense?' She's desperately trying to lighten my mood, and I love her for it, but now really isn't the time. 'Okay, alright. I get it,' she says, checking her watch. 'Look, I have to go, we're meeting with the vicar tonight. Apparently they want to check our religious intentions. I have to pretend I'm a virgin and agree with the Holy Ghost or something.' She plants a kiss on my forehead. 'I love you. You're going to be fine. Have some rest.' I follow her to the door. 'Call me tomorrow, okay? Let me know you're fine. And avoid the salmon, just in case.'

I take a deep breath, wondering if things will resolve themselves that quickly. I can't help feeling that they won't.

Chapter Forty-Seven

RHYS

I push through the double doors to the pub, cracking my fingers and stretching out my neck and back after spending the majority of the day in my van. When I called the police, they asked me to drop into Woodseats Station to get the detail down in a more official way. I told them as much as I could and had begun to feel a glimmer of hope that they hadn't found Susan, thinking maybe she had taken herself away to think, to heal. Until the officer mentioned a suspected sighting of a body down by the canal. Divers were heading straight down.

Michelle is working behind the bar again. My initial relief at seeing her is quashed when I realise I can't reach out to her. I stand by the bar, watching as she finishes serving the customer before me. I want to place my arms around her and feel her hold me too. Almost as much, I wish we could at least be friends.

'Hey, you,' she says, moving to serve me next. 'You okay?' She automatically reaches for a pint glass, flipping the tap, her eyes pinned on me. She smiles, her eyes sparkling just slightly, like they always do. 'What's up?'

'I need that drink,' I say. 'And food. I've eaten nothing all day.'

'The chef called in sick. I can basically do you anything micro-waved, or crisps.'

I bury my head in my arms. 'Crisps, not Scampi Fries,' I mumble into the bar. A packet of something lands by my side, swiftly followed by the pint. 'You wanna talk about it?' she asks.

'No.' I sound as sullen as I feel. 'Not to you anyway.'

'Wow, thanks. Way to make a girl feel wanted.'

'I'm not supposed to be the one making you feel that way,' I say out of the corner of my mouth. 'That's part of the problem.' I sip at the beer then put it back down, suddenly not so thirsty.

'I thought we were friends,' she says, leaning into me. She smells sweet; her breath is hot on my arm. I close my eyes, digging deep for strength and resolve. 'Rhys?'

'We are, but we probably shouldn't be.' I stand tall. 'Michelle, it's not right. I can't do this. I can't be your friend because that isn't how I feel about you and it hasn't been how I've felt about you for a long time. Longer than I care to admit. And when he was here it was fine because I would never have done anything to hurt him. Or you. But now...' My voice breaks, and I take a second to pull myself back together. 'Now he's gone, I'm finding it hard to justify staying away.'

She drops her head, straightening out a beer mat as she takes a deep breath. When she looks back up to me, her eyes glisten and she's biting her bottom lip – now it's her turn to keep her emotions under wrap.

'Michelle, I have had the worst few weeks. Weeks that included me making a big mistake.' She looks away for a second, then back at me. 'Weeks in which I met a woman who is so broken, so inter-minably broken, and yet through my stubbornness, or delusion, or something, I don't know what, I thought she could help me. Then I thought I could help her. Perhaps even turn time back on itself. Get a better outcome this time.' Michelle shifts her head to one side. 'Find peace with David through saving her. Then it unravelled even further, to something I could never have anticipated. And somehow I've just spent all day driving up to the Lake District and back with the ridiculous notion that that was in all our best interests.' I pause to take a breath. 'And do you want to know what I learned? I learned that the only person's life I can sort out is my own. The only life I have any control over is the one I lead, through the choices I make and the relationships I keep.' I look down at her hands, reaching out to place my hand on hers. 'You are...' I try to find the right words to describe her. 'You are smart and funny and beautiful and I have never met anyone like you, who makes me feel like you do, and I probably never will again.' Her eyes are full with tears and I have to stop myself wiping them away as she blinks and they tumble down her face. I can feel the pain she feels but I have to do this anyway. 'But you are who you are, and that means I have to walk away.'

She gives a shallow nod. 'I know,' she whispers. 'I know.' She forces a smile, then pulls her hand from mine and disappears into the back room.

I stare at the space where she was just standing, the emptiness now loud and uncomfortable. I want to shout her back. Instead, I growl into the bar, because although I know I've done the right thing, it feels like the biggest mistake of my life. I knock back my pint, letting the bitterness wash away the soreness in the back of my throat. I replay the conversation with James, with the police, and each visit I've ever had with Susan, over and over in my mind. Trying to pick out anything I might have missed amongst my self-serving need to get involved.

And then I realise something. Something I didn't see because I've been consumed with finding Susan and working out if she really is who I think she is.

James.

Why would someone write a final letter to someone from their past if that person hadn't played a significant role in it?

If that person wasn't…

Shit! How did I miss that? Is James the father of Susan's baby? Is James…? I down the rest of my pint and grab my keys, wallet and phone to head back over to the police station. As I head out the door into the car park, my phone rings. 'Rhys, it's James. I'm in Sheffield, coming down Abbeydale Road. Where are you?'

Chapter Forty-Eight

KAT

I jump out of bed, flinging a hoody on over my pyjamas. I scrabble around for my contact lenses, and then opt for the rejected glasses in my haste. I catch sight of my face, once again unfamiliar in the frames. I throw my hair up and, collecting my keys and phone on the way past, run out of the door.

I jog up to the top of the road to wait for Rhys. I'd asked him to explain but he hung up. I consider calling work to see if there's any news but decide to wait until he gets here. I have a feeling there's something in this and I need to give it time.

I hop from foot to foot, peeling my hair from my face, wondering if the weather is too hot for my hoody, then not really caring in the big scheme of things. I check my watch, my eyes searching out every new car that turns the corner. A black BMW pulls up, the passenger window rolls down. 'Get in,' says Rhys.

'I was looking for your van,' I say, buckling up and leaning forward to try and see them both.

'This is James,' Rhys introduces the driver. I look through the rearview mirror at the man driving the car. His eyes flick to me as he says hello, but quickly return to focus on the road. Rhys turns around in his seat to face me. 'He's…' He stops and looks at James, studying his face as though he has a million questions, but none he can speak out loud. There's a strange atmosphere in the car, something unsaid. He looks back to me. 'James thinks he knows where Susan might be.' I stare at him. 'Down there,' he instructs him.

'These roads have changed,' says James.

'Just keep going along here, you'll pick the road back up in a minute, then it's straight past the recycling centre and then the water tower.' James nods his understanding. Rhys turns back to me. 'They used to meet up at a little brick shack in Graves Park.'

'Have you told the police?' I ask. 'Have they looked?'

'I just got in the car with James and we came straight for you. We can get there and we can find her, Kat. Then we can call the police when we know she's okay.'

'We can't do that, Rhys. That's not… We have to call them now.' I stare at them both, trying to work out the thought processes that led them to think this was okay. I pull my phone out of my pocket. 'I'm calling them,' I say, dialling the number. As the call connects, my battery dies. 'No, no, no, no…'

We swing into a car park. 'What?' asks Rhys.

'My phone, the battery died. Give me yours,' I demand.

'We're here now, come on, we can call them in a minute.' He leaps out of the car as I fumble with phone and keys and seat belt.

'Rhys,' I shout, running after him as he and James set off.

'He's right, let's try to find her first,' shouts James, blipping his car locked as I catch them up.

'Rhys, please, give me your phone, let me call them.'

'This way,' says James, breathless as he runs up the hill. It's almost nine o'clock; the sun has faded but there's still a pinkish light in the sky.

A helicopter scans the field and I wonder if they are looking for her here. I wonder if I am needlessly worrying because they've beaten us to it. James ducks around bushes and suddenly there before us is a graffiti-tagged, red-brick building previously hidden from view. I swallow. James, Rhys and I stand beside one another, looking at the building.

'Susan?' James calls out, tentatively. None of us move. There's no response to her name. No sounds at all. Glassless windows show an inside held in near darkness. It's Rhys who moves first, taking two steps towards the paint-peeling, wooden door before pulling up short. 'I can't do this,' he says. 'If she's in there, I can't see that. Not again.' He drops back and I take hold of his hand.

'I'll go,' says James. He doesn't move to begin with, but eventually, carefully, he takes steps towards the door. 'Susan?' he tries again, but I don't think any of us expect her to answer. He reaches to hold the wall, steadying himself as he navigates his way around litter and over-grown weeds by the doorway. He swallows as he looks to the sky, then pushes the door open. It catches on the uneven ground before flying open and banging on the inside wall, making us all jump. I hold my breath as he steps inside.

He's out of sight, just for a second, before we hear him shout out. 'Nothing.' He steps back out. 'She's not here.'

'Shit,' says Rhys. 'Shit!' he repeats, louder, lunging forward to kick the side of the building. 'Shit, shit, shit!' he shouts, turning around with his hands on his head.

'Rhys…' I reach out to take his arm. His eyes are wide with fear. 'Come on,' I say, pulling him away from the house. 'Come on…' I turn around to see James walking away. I shout after him. 'We really need to call the police now, let them know you're here. You might be able to help them. Do you have your phone?' But James carries on walking. I look to Rhys, whose eyes are still wild. I pull him along, taking his hand in mine. We follow James away from the little building and back down towards the car park. We approach a pathway and James comes to a standstill, looking across to an old oak tree.

'James?' I say, as he changes direction towards the tree. He crosses the field; a group of friends are packing away a game of rounders. They stand back to let us pass through their group. 'James?' I call again, but he doesn't respond. He just keeps walking towards the tree. Rhys and I follow at first, but I feel Rhys pulling me back, making me stop and wait as James carries on.

'He told me about this on the way over. It's their tree,' he whispers. 'Apparently it's significant.'

James walks slowly to the base of the tree. He reaches out, letting his hands rest on the trunk. I imagine how it feels: rough, cool. He walks around it, his hand touching the whole way, before eventually settling on the grass beneath it, his head in his hands. The air around us grows cooler; the drop in temperature heightens the smell of freshly cut grass. The smell of summer. I shiver.

'Should we go to him?' Rhys drops my hand and steps towards James. I wait, a few paces behind. He crouches down beside him, resting his hand on James's shoulder. I walk towards them, stopping just behind Rhys.

'I don't know why I thought she'd be here,' says James eventually. 'Stupid, really. All these years I've barely thought about her. Not really. And now this. Why did I think she'd be here? Like nothing had moved on.' He shakes his head.

'It was worth a try,' says Rhys kindly.

'I guess.'

I watch as Rhys studies James's face, before eventually he says, 'James, are you…' He stops himself as James looks up and their eyes lock. Rhys stands, swallowing the rest of the sentence as he holds out his arms for James to pull himself up, slowly, with the effort of a man carrying more than just age in his body.

'I know this isn't…' I pick out the wrong words as I try and take back control of the situation. This situation. My patient. 'Look,' I try again, though the two men don't respond. 'I know this is painful for you, and I understand why it's difficult, James, but I have a duty to ensure we keep the police informed about this. I could lose my job if I… We need to call the police.'

'Please don't,' whispers a voice behind me.

I hold my breath, not daring to look, staring at Rhys and James and waiting for their reaction. James looks first at me, then beyond me. He pales as he searches the face of the person behind me and I know, from the slow realisation that dawns for him, that it's Susan. Gently, disbelieving, he shakes his head. 'Please don't,' she repeats, her voice, tired and unfamiliar, breaking. His shoulders drop and it's almost as though he begins to recognise the face of a woman he hasn't seen for decades. Slowly, I turn.

'Susan.' I reach out to her but she doesn't move. She's lost in the vastness of the park, the dusk that has swallowed us all. She is quiet and tiny. Almost invisible. She's not looking at me. She stands, barely breathing, as James finds the strength to move towards her. Forty years have passed since they were last here in this park, and I can see him searching her face, looking for the girl he knew. Both look somehow younger, the people they once were now seeking each other out. I step back, and bump softly against Rhys. We stand, lightly touching, saying nothing.

'Oh, Susan,' says James. And Susan looks to the ground.

'I'm so sorry.' Her voice is barely loud enough to break above the sound of our collective breath. 'I'm so sorry, James,' she repeats, and as he steps towards her, she falls into his arms, the sound of forty years of pain escaping her tiny body. James rests his chin on her head, wrapping his arms around her and waiting for it to pass.

It's dark before we leave the park.

Chapter Forty-Nine

SUSAN

James guides me from his car towards the building in which Kat lives. His arm is gently secured around me, holding my weight as I take slow, clumsy, steps forward. Kat didn't want to come here. She was insistent we should go back to the ward. James took one look at my face and knew that wasn't what I needed. He always knew just what I needed. I could never hide how I really felt from him, even back then.

Kat tried to push him, but he insisted we go anywhere but the hospital, just for now. It was like a weight lifted from my shoulders when she reluctantly agreed.

'I should be taking you to the hospital, Susan,' says Kat again as she pauses by her front door. I shiver and James takes his coat off, draping it around my shoulders. He pulls me in close to keep me warm. My arm, still thrust into the crutches that keep me standing, rests against his chest. I can feel his heartbeat. Just as I did all those years ago. His smell is oddly familiar, despite the time that has changed and shaped us.

'Come in, come in,' says Kat, nervously. 'Rhys, can you flick that light on?' He looks around. 'There, by the kitchen door.'

The light kicks in, instantly chasing away the shadows from outside. Windows across one wall of her flat are now thick and black. Reflected in them, I watch Kat hurry around her home. Rhys hovers. I stand, beside James, unable, or unwilling, to break contact.

'Sit down,' says Kat, taking my hands. Her touch sends another shiver through me, and the spell is broken as I have to move away from James. She passes Rhys the crutches, taking my weight as I drop into the chair.

'How long were you out there for?' says Kat, rubbing warmth into my hands. She hands James his coat back, wrapping a thick picnic rug around me instead. It doesn't smell of James. I wish I still had the coat.

'I'll put the kettle on,' she says.

Rhys pulls out a chair by the table, knocking it as he does. A candlestick wobbles, then falls. 'Sorry.' He strains as he reaches down to retrieve it. With unsteady hands, he tries to place it back where it was. It's off-centre but he doesn't seem to notice. The confidence he showed at the hospital has now completely gone. There's something in his eyes. He knows... Should I take his presence here as a good sign?

He watches Kat busying herself in the kitchen, swearing under her breath as she knocks things too, overfills the kettle, drops spoons. 'Fucking hell,' she mutters, and I see her take a moment by the sink, resting her hands on the edge of the worktop then reaching into her pocket to pull out her phone, plugging it in to charge. Rhys, noticing, makes to move, but stops himself. Kat looks into the lounge and they catch sight of each other. I drop my eyes to my knees, to the rug.

James sits in the chair just across from me. I don't need to look at him to know the pain I am causing. The distress. That he is here... He hasn't changed. The boy I fell in love with, the one who thought the world's weight should rest on his shoulders, he hasn't changed.

'Sorry,' I hear myself say. 'Sorry.' I repeat the word, trying to clear the soreness in my throat. It aches each time I try to speak, but I must, now. I owe it to them all to explain. I just wish it didn't hurt so: my throat, my head, my heart. Keeping this all inside, choosing not to talk, that was somehow easier. If I didn't speak out loud, I didn't have to build relationships that might stop me from finishing what I had begun.

Except it didn't work. The more Rhys came to see me, the harder it all became. How could I do that to him, how could I just leave, after all he had done for me?

James leans forward, reaching for my hand, and I let him take it. He's on the edge of his chair, and he doesn't look at me, but he places his other hand on top of mine. His hands are soft. Warm. And I remember exactly how his touch felt all those years ago. It's the same, though now it feels like his affection isn't rightfully mine, no matter how much I want it. I can't say as much – or perhaps I don't want to – so we stay like that. Just touching.

Kat comes back into the room with drinks. She bends down before me, resting her elbow on the seat. 'Susan, I need to make some calls.' Her voice is low and uncertain. 'The police need to know we've found you. The hospital need to know you're safe.' She seems frightened and nervous, but somehow still in control, trying to do the right thing. 'And pain relief, you must be…' She looks down to my leg. Until now, I haven't felt a thing. Perhaps it's just the fact she's mentioned it, but now I can feel a thick, hot pain deep inside my leg. I nod again. 'If you don't want to go back to the ward, maybe you'd be more comfortable at home?' she suggests, and my heart constricts. 'We could try and implement a care plan. Perhaps I could take some time off and help to begin with?' She looks to Rhys, who fidgets. They both know what she's suggesting. A return to the place I rid myself of. 'Familiar surroundings might help?' she finishes.

James keeps opening his mouth to say something then closing it again. It's Rhys who speaks next.

'Why did you go?'

James glances up sharply and I see him shoot Rhys a warning look. He rubs my thumb with his. Kat stands up, looking around for something to sit on, opting to take up position on the sofa beside me.

'Sorry.' Rhys tries again. 'Sorry, it's just… I don't understand… I don't understand any of this.' His voice is flat. Proof again, perhaps, that he does know. He's piecing the evidence together. Did James show him the letter? 'I mean, after everything…'

'Rhys,' interrupts James, but I squeeze his hand to signal that it's okay. Rhys needs to say what he's thinking. We all do.

I take three breaths, as shallow and calm as I'm able. 'The letter,' I say. My voice cracks and breaks, as though all these weeks I've stayed silent have broken it. 'The letter for James.' I pause. James takes his hand back.

'The boy I fell in love with had principles.' I smile. 'Morals. He always did the right thing.' I look across to the boy, now a man, who hasn't changed. 'I knew if he was still the man I fell in love with, he would receive the letter and try to find me. But that wasn't what I wanted.' James leans back in the chair, his eyes uncertain, hurt even. He adjusts position, covering pain with a poker face of dignity. 'Writing a letter is one thing…' My voice breaks again, and I falter. 'There were things I needed to say. Truths I had to share.' The wave of strength helping me speak all this is broken by the reality that the secret I have kept is out. That the people in this room know my darkest hour and have every right to judge me. And yet, I owe them the truth. I am still here, in part, because of them.

Because of Rhys.

James gently shakes his head. The light catches a flash of wetness on his cheek. He takes out a folded handkerchief and wipes his face. Rhys shifts in his chair.

My strength subsides again, taking with it the resolve to supress all the pain I've fought so long to hide. James reaches for my hand, but I cannot take it this time.

Rhys stands, moving around the room until he stops beside James. And that is when I really see it. So clearly, it takes my breath away.

'The clipping,' says Kat. 'Was that you?' I give a shallow nod and hear Rhys make a sound. 'I can't imagine how frightened you must have been,' says Kat. 'Alone, giving birth, I can't even begin to…'

'I was terrified,' I say, quietly. 'I can still feel it, hear it, hear me, hear the baby as he made his first cry. I can smell the tree and the blood and the woods that I walked through to get home.' My confession whips me dry of breath and I have to take a moment to refuel. But refuel I do, because now it has to be shared.

'Every year, on the seventeenth of May, I've walked to that tree. I've walked up to the church. Then I've walked through the woods, back home. I've retraced the steps from that night and I've cried at how deep the secret was buried.'

Rhys looks up and Kat wipes a tear from her cheek. James whispers, 'Oh, Susan.'

'And every night, from that day to the night before I left the ward, I've read our baby a bedtime story, a fairy tale, saying the words into the night and hoping that somehow, some way, he might have heard them.'

'The book…' says Rhys, staring at me.

'The book,' I nod, knowing without doubt that he knows, but wondering when he'll share that fact with me. With James.

Chapter Fifty

KAT

She shifts in the chair, wincing at the pain. 'Are you okay?' I ask. 'You don't have to do this, you know. You should rest. I'm going to call work now and let everyone know. Okay, Susan?'

She nods, slowly.

Rhys gets up and walks back over to the dining table. His arms are crossed. 'Why me?' he asks, suddenly. I stop and turn, the landline in my hand, poised to call. His mood has shifted: he's agitated, the muscles in his jaw flex as he waits for Susan's response. 'Why did you have my number in your diary? Why did you keep calling me back last year? Why me?'

James stands. 'Rhys, I think—'

'It's okay,' interrupts Susan.

James shakes his head. 'Now isn't the time, Susan. You don't have to do this right now.'

Susan reaches out a hand to James this time, taking it briefly to reassure him before dropping it and resting her hands on her own lap. 'Rhys asked the question because he needs to hear me say it.' James looks to Rhys, and I can see there's something here that they each know. Something I'm not privy to. I lean against the wall and wait.

Susan takes a breath, turning her head to speak over her shoulder as Rhys stands behind her. 'What I didn't realise, the night I walked away, was that from that moment onwards, I'd be looking and wondering, daily. A baby in a pram, I would strain to check. A toddler, I'd watch, just in case, my heart suspended. I'd follow people, years later, who shared familiar eyes, or his jawline perhaps.' She nods towards James. 'I'd seek out anything that might hint at the possibility I'd found my child. But I never really knew, before. It always felt like a maybe, a possibility.'

Rhys's face is blank, frozen in the moment. He doesn't seem to be registering what she's saying, and yet she continues as though he does.

'When I started working at the records office, it wasn't long until I realised it meant I could find the file. I went, several times, to search papers from the weeks and months around when it happened. When I finally found it, I would stand as dusk fell and colleagues had left the office. I'd look at it in my hands, daring myself to open it up fully, to read it properly. I walked away several times before I finally sat down and processed each word.'

Rhys sits, staring into the distance and I think I begin to realise what she's saying.

'You would have been seven when I found out.'

Rhys swallows, his eyes glazing. Susan continues. My heart has stopped.

'I could see when you'd been adopted, and the name of the family who took you. You were real. A boy with a name, something that was never mine to bestow. The name of your mother and father were there. Your address. It was strange, I…'

Susan breaks off. She can't see Rhys try to blink away his sadness, but I do, and it takes every fibre of my being not to go to him, because now isn't the time; this isn't about me wading in to rescue anyone anymore. It's bigger than I could ever have imagined.

As Susan begins again, her voice weakens. She's tiring, fast. 'I suppose in some way, as much as the information I learned gave you life, it pushed you further away from me. The pain it caused, well, it's not something I could ever have foreseen.' Susan wipes away a stray tear. James watches, not moving. Rhys continues staring at the ground and I feel like I can't breathe. Or move. Or speak. As if by doing so, I'd break them all.

'I remember the first time I saw you,' she says. 'As a grown man. I was on my way into work – on the bus because my car was in for a service.'

Rhys has gone sheet white. The room feels cold, despite the warm temperature.

'You were in your van. You pulled up to the traffic lights beside the bus. The window above me was open and I could hear your music, it was so loud.' Her voice is pained. How would it feel to recall a memory like this? 'You were singing at the top of your voice and from the second I laid eyes on you, I couldn't believe it, I just…' Rhys looks up. 'It was different. You were different. And then I saw the name on your van. Woods Brothers. Below it, your name and contact details. My hands shook as I scribbled your number. I was terrified you'd be gone before I could take it all down. I got up as the bus started moving, walking down the aisle to try to keep up with you until you'd gone, out of sight, turning left down Abbey Lane.' She pauses and I still can't breathe. The room falls silent until she eventually says, 'I knew you were my son. I had no doubt.'

My mouth falls open, my eyes sting.

'I kept your number in my bag for weeks before finding the courage to actually speak to you,' she finishes, quietly.

Her smile has faded. Rhys isn't moving and James seems transfixed by her. Perhaps I should have left them to do this alone. I'm in the middle of a story that doesn't feel like mine. An intruder in their truth.

'Do you remember when you turned up at my house that first time and I invited you in? You put your hand out to shake mine and I turned my back? I just couldn't… I pointed you in the direction of the airing cupboard and let you head on up by yourself because, just as I had known at the lights, with you finally standing before me, I could tell.' She swallows, hard, then whispers, 'The line of your jaw, your nose, your eyes. It was as if James was standing in front of me again.'

James looks over to Rhys, his eyes wide. Is this new information? Or was it all in the letter?

Another tear makes its way down her cheek and she raises her hand to wipe it away, her movements slow and tired. 'I knew it was you.' There's another pause before she says, 'My son.'

James slowly stands.

Rhys still stares, not moving. Then his eyes search the ground before him. He clenches his jaw, looking directly at Susan first, then James, then back to Susan. Eventually, his voice flat, detached almost, he says, 'How could you?' and I realise how fine this line of truth has become. How dangerously close he is to unravelling. 'How could anyone just leave a child?' he says, his voice low and disgusted.

'Rhys,' says James. But Rhys isn't ready to be silenced.

Chapter Fifty-One

RHYS

I move away from them both, rubbing my hands through my hair, trying to process the information. It makes no sense at all, yet all the sense in the world. And it's not new. From the second I saw that clipping, I wondered, but couldn't believe it. Then again, when talking to Mum at the Botanical Gardens, I knew when I sat before her, that last visit on the ward. But I can't process it. I want to shout. I want to run. I want to leave. And yet, I want to tell her what this means. To me.

I perch on the windowsill in the farthest corner of the room. Away from them all but facing them.

'I spent years,' I begin quietly, not really sure what I'm going to say, 'knowing nothing of where I came from, not caring because I didn't need to. I had a mother who did everything she could for me and my brother, and I didn't need to know more – until he did. Our David. When he learned his own history, something that would eventually tip him over the edge, something that made him take his own life, I found my file and read what was inside and everything… crumbled. I was supposed to be there to help him. To give him support, and there I was, needing somebody for me. But there was no one.'

Kat looks at me with pity in her eyes, but I'm not done.

'How could someone do that?' I whisper. 'I could have died, out there on that step. I was helpless and yet still… you walked away.'

'Rhys,' interrupts James.

'It's okay,' says Susan.

'And yes, I was lucky, I was found. I was given another chance, but the truth came out and almost broke me. But I couldn't let it because our David needed me. Because his needs overtook mine. And maybe I let them, because that was easier than dealing with this.'

I think about all the times David tried to meet up with the woman who rejected him in favour of a lifestyle he didn't fit into, and the pain of losing him punches me in the gut all over again.

'And then he died. And that swamped everything further. I shelved it all because it was too much. It's too much for one person to take.'

Kat reaches her arm out, moving towards me. 'Rhys, I'm sure this is all…' But she can't finish what she has started. Does she sense I want nobody anywhere near me?

'And now, I stand here, in the flat of a woman I don't know, with two strangers who, it turns out, are my parents.' Susan makes a small sound, a cry perhaps. I can't see her face through my own tears. 'I can't even… I don't know.'

James tries again. 'Rhys,' he says, without moving.

'What!' I answer, anger and confusion spiking my tone. 'What? What do you want me to do? How should I take this information? How should I process it?' My legs give way. Kat rushes to me, helping me regain my balance, sitting me back down in the chair by the table. I can't focus on anything. New and confusing details begin to filter through: the date of birth I've never known; the look in James's eyes when he'd read the letter and called me in; the look as he asked me if I knew what was in the letter and I shook my head; the realisation I had, about who he must have been, and how he avoided that when in the car, racing to find her before she'd totally given up on us. On me. Only now does any of it make sense.

'Why?' I ask again. 'Why did you do it?'

'You don't have to answer this now, Susan,' says Kat. 'Perhaps we should take a break. I think you should go to the hospital. Get checked over.'

'I felt ashamed of every choice I made from the moment you were conceived until the day I left you behind,' answers Susan, interrupting Kat. 'I was weak, Rhys. I was selfish. And I was frightened.'

I grit my teeth as I fight a pain that grows and multiplies inside my heart. The pain of being left. The pain of this truth. And the pain that the woman who gave me life is so clearly hurting still.

I look over to James. His eyes are locked on mine, his face familiar. Susan's right, it's so obvious. The same jawline, as she said. We're the same build, too. He's a part of me. And I'm a part of him. Of them. It's like the mist has cleared and my whole self has arrived. Who I am. The point of me. My history, emerging from a fog. And I don't know how I feel about that.

Before I have time to work it out, James gets up, walking towards me. I fight the tiny part of me that wants to move away as he crouches down to get a better look, taking my face in his hands. I feel the warmth of a man I never thought I'd know.

'When you sat in my office, I wanted to tell you, but I didn't know where to start. I kept thinking you had a right to know, but where does one begin with something like that? I didn't even know if you knew you'd been adopted. I barely understood it all myself. I'm so sorry.' Tears stream down his face. 'I'm so sorry.' He pulls me into an embrace, like the ones I craved from Dad even before he left us, before I even knew that's what I needed, what I wanted. With James's touch, I feel barriers fall, their ruins gathering at my feet, replaced by a new strength, a strength I haven't felt before. I take hold of James's arms, so we can see one another, and there we stay, unwilling to break apart just yet. I am found.

It's Kat who eventually interrupts. 'I know this is huge. And I know you all have a lot to process, to talk about, but I'm sorry, I must call someone,' she says, her voice tight and small. She stands in the doorway to her kitchen, her face apologetic. 'I'm sorry – I just – I have to.'

James turns to face her. 'Of course, Kat. Of course you do.' He looks over to Susan, who hasn't moved since the final twists of her secrets unfolded. Since my response, since my anger. I watch him move towards her. I can see how he aches to reach out; I feel it too. But her barriers are back up. Despite all that she has said, Susan's still hiding.

James crouches down before her. 'I can take you, Susan. I can drive you back, and stay for as long as you need me to. We can talk, work out how we…' I don't know what he had in mind as his words trail off. She gives him a shallow nod, but she's vacant. 'Are you okay?' he asks, a note of concern in his voice. 'You look…' He looks up to Kat, the concern now etched across his face.

Susan gives a shallow nod, speaking so quietly we can barely hear her. 'I'm okay,' she says, breathless. 'I'm just…'

Her head lolls forward, then her body too. James reaches out to catch her. 'Woah, Susan? Susan!'

Kat rushes over, taking hold of her face as I come around to see her too. She's pale, almost blue, like a rag doll in his arms. Kat lifts her eyelids to check her pupils; her head falls back, then forward again. 'Susan, can you hear me? Rhys, Have you got your phone? Call an ambulance, tell them who it is, tell them I am with her. Get them to send it straight away.' I fumble with the phone, trying to dial. Kat is holding her head firm, talking to her calmly but urgently as I dial the numbers, waiting for the line to connect. I can't lose her. Not now that I've found her. Now she's found me. I can't...

'I'll take her,' says James, jumping up. 'It'll be quicker in the car.' He bends to lift Susan into his arms, losing balance slightly before he's quite got hold of her.

I cancel the call and rush over to help him. 'Let me,' I say, and James stands back. Ignoring the boundaries she's put between us when conscious, I lift Susan into my arms. She's light, barely there, so fragile. James runs to the door, holding it open with his foot as I pass through, careful not to knock or jolt her.

'I'm coming, hang on.' Kat runs into the kitchen to grab her phone, keys and purse then steps around me to run down the steps and over to the car. 'Sit her in the back with me, I'll keep an eye on her pulse and keep talking to her.' She catches sight of my face. 'Don't worry,' she advises, but there's a panicked look in her eyes that says I'm right to be feeling this fear.

I've just found them, and them me. This can't be happening.

Chapter Fifty-Two

KAT

'Follow me,' I say, opening my office door and inviting him to sit down. 'Do you want a drink?'

'Beer?' he asks, not quite looking at me.

'Tea…' I offer as a lame substitute, proven when he shakes his head. I can't blame him. It's moments like this a hip flask would come in handy. I perch on the edge of my desk. 'Is it a stupid question to ask if you're okay?'

He stretches out his arms and legs, then rubs his face. 'Yes, but there's not many other questions you could ask, so you're forgiven.' He looks up to give me the smallest suggestion of a smile. It's soon replaced by the distance he's been wearing since Susan told her story. 'It's funny,' he says, 'David and I used to talk about this. About if we would know, you know?' I wait for him to explain. 'Sheffield, it's tiny, isn't it? As big a city as it is, and with as many people, it's like a village. You don't need six degrees to find a connection, there's generally one next door.' I move to sit opposite him. 'He always thought he'd know if he bumped into one of his. He said there would be that connection and you'd see it.' He sucks his teeth together. 'I felt something with Susan, without a doubt, but I convinced myself I was being ridiculous. That it was all too obvious. That I was desperate for it to be true, clutching at any straw that came my way. I tried to convince myself it was just because of what she'd done.'

'And now?' I ask.

He looks out of the window. It's almost eleven o'clock, and light pollution from the hospital has chased off any chance of seeing the night sky, yet he keeps looking. 'It's like every question I didn't know I had has been answered. It's like I'm real. Like I was meant, even though clearly I wasn't.' He pauses. 'I never realised I was missing anything. Mum was Mum, and I didn't question that despite always knowing the truth. But this…'

'She's going to be okay, Rhys,' I say, and he lets out a cough of air, as if I've just given oxygen to a fear he daren't consider. 'She was just exhausted, after all she'd put her body and self through. She should never have left the hospital, never mind anything else. Her body just shut down to protect her. Sleep, food and patience, she'll be fine,' I reassure.

'And then?' he says, looking back to me. 'What then?'

'How do you mean?' I ask. I understand what he's asking, but I want him to say it out loud.

'I've arrived. In life, in truth, I'm suddenly and finally here…' He looks up pleadingly. 'I don't think I can do this if there's a chance she's going to give up again.'

I take his hands. 'Rhys, she gave up because she was frightened. Maybe she doesn't need to be anymore.' I shift to the edge of my seat, finding the facts of the situation give me a focus, some strength to work out what's required. 'Rhys, you don't have to rush anything. With her or with James. You don't have to become happy families overnight. You don't ever have to, if that doesn't feel right.'

'But it does. And that's the point. No matter how confused or angry I feel about what she did, it does feel right. I do want to know them. What if I want to build a relationship and she doesn't? Or he doesn't? He already has a family, why would he need me?'

'He drove three hours, picked you up and helped you try to find her,' I remind him. 'And now he's by her bedside, holding her hand until he knows she's going to be okay. Look, you're tired, and she'll be sleeping till morning. If I was you, I'd go home, try to get some rest, let your heart settle. Call me tomorrow if you like, let me know how you're feeling and what you want to do next. I'm here to help,' I say, squeezing his hand. He moves to hold my hands within his and we sit quietly for a moment.

'Thank you,' he says, quietly.

'Thank you?' I ask.

'For calling. For taking that risk. I wouldn't be here if it wasn't for you.'

'Don't blame me!' I joke, pulling my hand back.

'I wasn't.' He smiles. 'I owe you.'

I push my glasses back up my nose, running my hand through my hair. 'You owe me nothing,' I say, fiddling around with some papers on my desk.

I sense him get up and stand behind me. He takes my shoulders and turns me to face him. 'You've no idea how brilliant you are, do you?' I laugh, uncomfortable with his proximity and his words. 'Whatever broke you, needn't have.'

'Broke me!' I say, surprised.

'I saw it. I can still see it. You care about everyone else. Your focus is on Susan. On me. On reassuring and fixing, and yet I've seen how you've watched us. There's a pain in this for you too, isn't there?'

I sigh. I try to always give him the Kat he needs to see, the one in charge of a situation, of her patients, the one trying to ensure that this mess is mended by me, for them, to the best of my ability, and I can't admit to him that between him and Susan, I've begun to see myself as someone choosing to opt out of my future.

'Why do we hide from the things that might make us?' he asks.

'Because they can just as easily break us,' I answer, easily. 'Because we're too tired to cope. Because we don't want to feel pain again like we've felt before.'

'And yet we risk not feeling anything ever again,' he says. 'Is that better?'

'I don't know.'

He looks at me for a moment, before stepping forward suddenly and taking my face in his hands. 'Risk the pain, you deserve to be happy,' he says, a look of focus and intensity in his eyes that I've not seen before. Then, out of the corner of my eye, I see Mark through the glass, watching us. I want to move and tell him to come in, tell him what's happened, but before I can, he's stepped out of sight. I pull out of Rhys's hold and go to the window.

'What?'

'Nothing.'

'Oh God, sorry, was that a bit…' He stands back, ruffling his hair, colouring slightly.

'No, it's fine. It was just a colleague…'

'Go, if you need to,' he says. 'Like you say, I should probably go home.'

'It's fine.' I shrug it off. 'He's… I don't know.'

'I mean it though,' says Rhys, moving towards the door.

'What?' I ask, occupying myself with papers like I do every time someone risks reaching inside of me and making me listen.

'If this situation has taught me anything, if Susan has, it's that we all deserve to be happy. You deserve to be happy. To believe in yourself. Letting people in isn't easy, I know. God, I know! But imagine what might happen if you did...'

I give a shallow nod, biting my lip. 'Look, you should go, get some sleep. I'll call you in the morning and let you know how she is. Or you can come in. Whichever, just get some rest,' I instruct, nurse status fully reinstated.

Rhys yawns and nods.

'I'll talk to you tomorrow,' I shout after him, trying to regain authority yet feeling distinctly like someone has just opened me up and seen inside. My door slowly clicks shut and I drop back behind my desk, lifting my glasses away to run finger and thumb across my eyes till I see stars.

Maybe he's right. Maybe we can all learn from Susan.

Chapter Fifty-Three

RHYS

It's late, almost midnight, as I pull up to Mum's. Maybe I should have just gone home. I don't know that I want to talk to her about this yet. Or even how I feel about it all. It's everything I wanted that day I asked for my papers and everything I thought I'd lost when I saw what they said.

It's everything our David wanted too. And there's nothing I can do to change things for him. Why couldn't this have been him? His story? Perhaps then he'd still be here. Maybe.

Mum opens her front door and Derek steps out. I reach for the keys to restart the engine but my hand stops before I turn the ignition. I think about Susan, and the near on forty years of pain she buried deep inside. I think about James, and the same years of not knowing. I think about the baby, left for the church to find him, to rescue him, to give him a new life. To give me a new life. I look back to Mum, the woman who took on that responsibility. Selflessly. Against the odds. More than once. I think about the pain she feels every day knowing David is no longer here.

And how Derek has helped her smile again.

I get out of the car. Mum looks up. 'Rhys,' she says, looking at her watch. 'It's late, is everything okay?'

'It's fine, yeah… I was just feeling… I just needed to come home,' I say. 'Is that… I could leave, if not.' I motion to the van, crossing my fingers that she'll say it's fine.

'Of course it's okay,' she answers without question. 'Come in, love, Derek was just leaving.' She gives him a look and he nods.

'Yup, on my way home. Totally lost track of time.' He smiles.

'Derek,' I say. As I get closer, something inside makes me hold my hand out to shake his. He returns the offer and we share an unspoken moment. Acceptance?

'Your Mum says she wants her beauty sleep. She won't believe me when I tell her she doesn't need it.' She playfully hits his arm and he catches her hand to kiss. 'I'll call you tomorrow,' he says. 'Goodnight, Rhys.'

We watch in silence as he walks down the road, around the corner and out of view. 'No car?' I say.

'Bus,' she answers, and we fall back into a heavy silence. In the distance, I can hear the main road. Some kids larking about a few streets away. The sky is clear enough, a few stars glinting above, and I am reminded how tiny we are. How insignificant.

'I put clean bedding on yours today. I must have known,' says Mum, stepping back into the house and waiting for me to follow. I step inside, inhaling the familiar smell and sensation of home. And Mum. And security. It all envelops me, wraps me up. 'You want to talk about it?' she asks. I realise I don't. Not because I can't, or won't ever, but because I need time to digest the news myself before I tell her. I need to see how I feel. I need to believe and trust what I know and feel. I shake my head. 'Tea?' she offers. I shake my head again.

'I think I'll just…' I half motion upstairs, my energy fast depleting.

'Okay, love,' she says. I bend into the hug she pulls me in for, squeezing me tight like she did when I was a kid. She kisses my shoulder, then reaches up to ruffle my hair. 'I'm very proud of who you are, Rhys Woods,' she says as I climb the stairs.

I push open the door to my childhood bedroom. Everything about it remains the same. The poster of a Hutchence-years Kylie above my bed; Wendy James over on the other side. The half spent bottle of Kouros our David used to nick until his teenage girlfriend bought him CK One. I climb inside the single bed, my body heavy with the weight of the day, of the past week or so. When I close my eyes, my thoughts rush from Susan to Kat to James to Michelle, and then to Mum. Downstairs. Like she always has been. Whatever I might have thought.

Chapter Fifty-Four

KAT

THREE WEEKS LATER

I carefully place the book of fairy tales into the bag, where it rests on top of her clothes. I brush my fingers across it, its significance giving it a beauty I hadn't seen before. I zip up the bag I've brought for her things, checking around her bed for anything I might have missed. 'I think that's everything.'

'Thanks,' she says, her voice quiet in contemplation, but present at least, as it has been since we found her in the park, there being no need for her to hide her words any longer.

'What time did James say he'd be here?' I ask, checking my fob watch against the clock on the wall. 'Two?' Susan nods. I wonder how she feels, whether my nerves are only a slice of her own. I offered to go to her house with some food to fill her fridge, a few bits to make it feel less sterile when she got back. I was worried she'd walk in and the atmosphere, how she left things, would make it too hard to re-establish her life there.

'I'm going to be okay,' she says, pre-empting my thoughts, her voice small but not uncertain.

I step around the bed and sit down carefully beside her. 'Do you promise me?' I ask, our shoulders just touching.

'I promise,' she says, looking me in the eye. 'Life feels brighter when you begin to forgive yourself.' I understand exactly what she means. A nurse brings James to her bed; Susan looks up at him and I'm sure I detect just a fleck of sadness in her eyes. Sadness that the man she loved is back in her life, but not there to stay? Maybe I'm overthinking it.

'Come on, then,' he says, taking her bag from me, hefting it up onto his shoulder and offering Susan his arm. 'Time to go home.' She reaches up, wincing slightly as she adjusts her balance and threads one arm through his, the other into her crutch.

They start to walk, slowly at first, until she finds her rhythm. I walk steadily behind them, feeling a sense of sadness myself. Patients come and go, but Susan was different somehow. 'Would it be okay to call you, Susan?' I ask, before she leaves the ward. 'Maybe in a few days, just to see how you're doing. You'll be an outpatient now, but I'd like to…' She nods, stopping me from having to explain why I'm not quite ready to let go of her.

James holds the door open, but she stops to look at me. 'Thank you,' she says. There's a look on her face that makes me feel the words don't quite convey how she really feels. As if it's all too big to describe. I get it. 'Thank you for everything.'

I clasp my hands to my chest and smile at her. Because I can't find the words either.

The door closes and I watch Susan and James take their time as they head for the lift. A buzzer goes in one of the private rooms, and whilst I don't want to walk away until I know she's gone, I'm on duty. Life on the ward goes on, so I turn on my heel.

'Hey, Kat.' Mark approaches from the opposite end of the ward. He's undoing the top button on his shirt, loosening his tie. 'I'm glad I caught you. Was that Susan? Has she gone?' he asks, peering towards Susan's empty bed.

'Yeah, she's gone. Another one bites the dust.' Though I say it with a smile, my eyes sting and blink.

'You did a great job,' he says with a shuffle and a cough.

'Thanks.'

Mark looks up and down the corridor, then back to me. 'So look,' he says, with a half-smile. 'I have a transfer.'

'What?'

'A transfer. To Loughborough. There's a great opportunity for me down there, a new challenge and…' He looks around, suddenly nervous. 'I guess there's not much keeping me here at the moment.'

'I didn't realise you were… I thought you said you were staying?' I realise my voice sounds more bothered than I probably need to be. He's just a consultant. They come and go. It's no big deal.

'Yeah.' He adjusts his tie looser still. 'I guess things… change.'

'Right,' I say, stunned, searching for something to say. 'Well, I guess the nurses can get on with their jobs if you're not here to distract them.'

'Pardon?'

'Nothing.' I colour.

'Right.' He stuffs his hands in his trouser pockets. 'Anyway, this is my last shift so I just thought I'd…'

The buzzer in the private room goes again. 'I need to…' I say, looking around for anyone who might be able to answer it. 'You can't get the staff!' I joke, then swallow, despite my mouth running dry. 'Well, good luck then, I guess.'

Mark looks at me and it feels as though he sees deep inside of me. My stomach flips and I cross my arms. 'Maybe we could keep in touch?' he offers, taking a paper with his number on from his pocket. 'If you fancy…?'

'Sure,' I say, taking it, unclear why this has suddenly got so weird.

He goes to say something, then stops himself and instead drops a clumsy peck on my cheek. I can feel my colour deepening.

'Bye, Kat.'

'Bye.'

He walks away, not with quite the swagger he's had in the past. He throws a final glance in my direction before heading down the stairwell. There's a pause, an echo of his footsteps coming back up the stairwell. 'Kat,' he says, poking his head back through the door. 'One more thing.'

'What?' I ask, smiling to myself at how often he does that.

'I just wanted to say, if you ever get to a point where you're, you know… ready…'

'For what?' I ask, and he stares at me for a moment.

He shakes his head and smiles to himself. 'Never mind,' he says, and this time when he leaves, he doesn't turn back.

Chapter Fifty-Five

RHYS

I loosen my top button, pulling at the neck of my shirt while wondering whose idea this was. It's September, the weather hasn't yet broken and I am attempting to be a grown-up, all suited and booted.

It was Mum's idea, that we should go somewhere nice. Apparently a menu that includes roast breast of squab pigeon will impress her. I've no idea what a squab pigeon is – God knows whether she will. I look at the flowers I've brought, their heads beginning to wilt slightly, despite not being from the garage this time.

A taxi pulls up and my heart leaps to my mouth – but a middle-aged couple get out. They take a selfie outside the front door and I get the impression their date night is about to be announced to his Facebook nation. The part of me that cringes is quietly challenged by the part of me that envies what they have. As I check my watch to see just how late she is, the crunch of heels on gravel stop me. I almost daren't look in case it is her, but a waft of familiar perfume makes me certain.

'Wow,' I say, as I look up. 'I've never seen you… You look amazing.'

'Thanks,' she answers shyly. 'You too.'

We stand facing each other, both oddly uncomfortable in each other's company. I don't really know how she feels, but I know that

I am way out of my depth. Apparently, Derek said, I should feel the fear and do it anyway, but as she stands here before me, I wonder if she'd notice me run in the other direction.

'Shall we?' she asks, and I nod. She loops her arm into mine. We take a half look at each other, glancing away when our eyes meet.

'Table for two. Woods,' I say to the waiting maître d'. He ticks off our arrival. 'This way, sir, madam.' He takes us past a room with what looks like a small wedding party in it. We are led through the narrow Victorian corridor to a dining room. My grown-up shoes, which Mum bought for me as a stamp of approval for tonight, click on the room's original floorboards. We are led to a table nestled in a floor to ceiling bay window. A small vase of white flowers – I've no idea what they are – sits in the middle of the crisp white linen tablecloth, the sun reflects off polished cutlery. The maître d' pulls out her chair and I wish I'd thought of that.

'Thank you,' she says in her politest voice, watching intently as he pours her some water from a freshly iced jug he collected on the way. No sooner has he filled up her glass does she reach for it and empty it in one go.

'I'll give you some time to peruse the menu, but I can tell you that the roast fillet of saddle of wild fallow deer with walnut forcemeat comes recommended. It's served with a crushed butternut squash and potato gratin, alongside a cranberry and ginger compote. I'll give you a moment.' He finishes by laying out our napkins and asking a waiter to bring us fresh rolls before disappearing into the fabric of the building like some kind of restaurant superpower.

I look down at my menu, trying to fathom what any of it means. After a few seconds, I look up to see if I can sneak a glimpse of her. She looks different. The make-up, maybe. And her clothes. We both look like we've dressed up as other people.

'Are you as nervous as I am?' she asks, leaning forward yet looking over her shoulder.

'Me? Nah, I do this all the time.' She turns to face me. 'Or yes, I'm shitting it, is the other answer.' And that's when I see her, the Michelle I know and… I stop myself before thinking it. 'Yes. I am terrified.'

'It's nice though.' She smiles. It's a much sweeter smile than I've ever noticed before. Her whole face lights up, despite only the corner of her mouth turning. It's in her eyes.

We go back to our menus. 'I've never heard of half of this stuff,' I admit.

'And I thought you were a connoisseur of fine dining!' she teases.

'Is it bad that my knowledge starts and stops at the kebab menu?'

'Yes. It is. It's a good job I'm here.' She winks. When the waiter returns to take our order, she orders for both of us in word-perfect French. I stare, open mouthed at her.

'What?' she asks flirtatiously.

'I didn't… I didn't know you could…'

She leans in. 'There's a lot you don't know about me, Rhys Woods.' I loosen my collar.

'So,' she says. 'What are people like us doing in a place like this?'

'They shut down Wimpy,' I joke, still a bit hot under the collar.

'Shame,' she answers, buttering her bread and biting it with more sex appeal than is strictly necessary. There's a break in conversation, a pause that I sense she wants me to fill. 'Really though,' she pushes, 'what is this?'

I put my glass down, taking a deep breath whilst I work out how to answer as honestly as I can. 'I don't know,' I say. She sits back. 'But, whatever it is, it's something I can't ignore anymore.' She looks at me, perfectly composed. 'I have fought it, I have tried to feel differently, but I can't, I don't…' She reaches for her magically refilled drink, taking a sip. Her lips leave a pink stamp on the side of the glass, which I watch as she places it back on the table. 'I've had time to think. The last month or so, it's been… full on, and…' Lost for words, I reach for my own drink now.

'What does your mum think?' she asks.

I think about the conversation we had last week, when I sat down and told her everything – about my drive up to Ambleside, to finding Susan, to the truth I'd suspected which finally unravelled that night. Mum said hardly anything, just listened to the lot, her face beginning to crumble as I got to the end of my story. Then she sat and silently cried on the sofa, a picture of David and me as kids on the table beside her. She'd picked it up, running her finger down his face first, then mine. She held me, letting her sadness pour into our hold. Then she stepped back and told me she was happy I'd found Susan. That she was blessed to have raised me. That she would one day like to thank Susan because, despite the pain behind her choice, they both had a son they could be truly proud of.

When I told her how I felt about Michelle, she quickly, without pause, told me that my happiness was paramount. As was Michelle's. And that she was certain David would have felt that too. 'She says that we don't choose who we love.'

Michelle nods. I'm not sure if it's in agreement or just to allow her to process my response. I'm not sure if she really heard what I said. About love.

She's composed. Controlled, even. She is the Michelle I've always admired, but stronger somehow. And in reverse, I feel like a schoolboy, all butterflies and unfinished thoughts. She takes another sip of her water and smiles. I take the opportunity to look at the woman before me, instead of seeing our David's girlfriend. Her flame-red hair is brighter than before. Her eyes are an intense green, like emeralds. Her lashes are thick and long, and when she blinks, she looks like a Disney drawing, only better. Because she's real. And here. 'I feel like I'm seeing different things in you, noticing little details,' I say.

There's a pause, a sudden fracture in her confidence. She looks to her lap, smoothing her napkin down. 'Rhys,' she starts, her voice uncertain. 'You need to know that I can't do this, if it's a one-off. I'm not saying I want to eat out at fancy restaurants all the time…' Her plate arrives and she raises a perfectly shaped brow. 'Although…' She looks back up at me and smiles, before carrying on. 'I've already lost one Woods brother. And I lost him long before he left, but still… I don't think I could go through that again.'

'I don't want to hurt you, Michelle.' I say, picking up where she left off. She looks down at her plate so I try to catch her gaze again. 'Honestly, I promise. I've learned some things. About myself, about life. I want things to be different.'

'How different?'

'Well, maybe not frequent visits to Michelin-starred restaurants different, but different.' I search for a way to lighten the mood. 'I don't even want to have sex with you tonight.'

She smiles wryly. 'Wow, thanks. I thought I scrubbed up okay.'

'You do, Michelle. Oh my God, you so totally do. I just, I want us to get to know each other. Properly, I mean, as Michelle and Rhys, not David's girlfriend and David's brother.' I pause. 'I mean, don't get me wrong, you… I could… but—'

'You're assuming I'd want to,' she teases. But I also notice she runs her tongue across her lower lip and there's a feeling in my belly that I'm not alone.

I reach across to take her hand, and immediately take it back because I can't bear the physical shockwave that runs up my arm, down my spine and through my body.

'Okay. Let's give it a month.'

'A month?' I check.

'Yes. A month. We have a month to get to know each other properly. To see if this is real or grief.'

'A month…'

She winks, running her foot up the inside of my thigh, making me squirm in my seat.

'Okay. Done. A month. Now get your foot away from my crotch, you hussy, I've got a pigeon squab to explore.'

Chapter Fifty-Six

KAT

'Right, hang those up there. Put that on ice. Run the bath and open the chocolate!' Lou squeals and giggles as she runs around the largest room in the hotel, setting mood lighting and making her mark. I struggle to hang up the giant, white dress bag that contains her most precious item in the world. Apparently. Then I take my own dress bag and rest it over a chair. 'Not there!' Lou says, picking it up. 'It'll crease!' She sweeps it up and hands it straight back to me. 'GLASSES!' she shouts.

'STOP!' I say, dress down, hands up. 'If this is going to work, you need to step back from Bridezilla and breathe.'

Lou stands in the middle of the room, hands on hips, deep breathing. All she needs is a brown paper bag and we've got ourselves a scene straight out of a romcom: wedding dress, champagne and a hyperactive bride to be.

'We have all the time in the world,' I say. 'We have everything planned to the last detail. I have the Gantt chart you so carefully drew up and I am as crystal clear as those glasses about what you want, when and where. Also, those glasses – are they not the ones you inherited? Is it wise to bring them here? I'd have drunk this out of a mug, you know.'

'I am not drinking out of a mug, Kat!' she says, then drops her hands and retreats. 'And besides, they were used at Grandma's wedding so they should have a role in mine too.' She eyeballs me before relenting. 'Okay, okay, Bridezilla is climbing back in her box.' She falls dramatically onto the bed, letting her head loll in the luxury of crisp white Egyptian cotton sheets. 'I'm just sooooo excited,' she says dreamily. I pop the cork and spill the champagne into the glasses, impressed I manage not to lose a drop on the carpet. Lou takes her glass, watching the bubbles disappear, which quickly depletes the liquid in her glass from almost full to barely a thimble-full. She looks at the glass, then to me, but chooses to get up and top up her drink herself.

'I can't believe this is happening, Kat.'

'Me neither. It's surreal isn't it?' I look around at her room. The George in Hathersage. Right beside the little church they'll marry in and the only place she could book that would let her have the entire hotel for the whole weekend. Like she's some kind of celebrity. Plus, Lou has plans to walk the long route back to the hotel, via the village, as opposed to the little pathway that leads straight between the two. Not that she was keen to draw attention to herself at all. Not for a second.

She pulls out her overnight bag, which may as well be a suitcase, and starts taking out all the things she needs for tomorrow: products for the hairdresser, her own designer make-up for the make-up artist, lotions and potions to lift, separate, smell nice and glisten. I look in my own bag: toothbrush, toothpaste, Bio-Oil for my face and a few discarded toothpicks.

'You okay?' she asks me.

'Course.' I smile, knocking back the fizz and pouring us both some more. 'Just setting the alarm. Are you sure we need to be up at six?'

'Absolutely. And when I say are you okay, I mean are you *okay*?'

'Yes. I'm fine. We are all set; I'm looking forward to tomorrow. This is your big day – I can't wait to be part of it.'

'I know but…' She wrinkles her nose. 'I don't want you feeling shit because it's not you, you know?'

'My, Lou, you have a real empathetic take on this.'

She smacks me. 'You know what I mean. Not that long ago, this was going to be a forerunner to you getting married. He was supposed to be here.'

'I know, I know. But he's not.' I take a sip of the champagne. 'And I'm fine with that. In fact, I'm glad.'

'Really?'

'Really, Lou.' She eyes me up. 'I'm a new woman,' I say, taking my glasses off and putting them on the table. 'It's not just these and the hair that's changed.'

'I totally love it,' she says, running her fingers through my new cropped pixie do.

'Are you sure you don't hate me for having it cut off before your big day?'

'Nope. You look like you've found yourself, and I like it,' she says. 'You look smoking!'

'Thanks. I feel… Well, I feel like I'm just beginning to learn who I am.'

'I can tell you,' she says, clinking my glass, 'you are my amazing, brilliant, smart, funny, kind friend, with a sparkling career and total control over your future.' I top up her glass. 'And I'm set to become an old married witch who anticipates feeling all jealous of this independent you and the fun you're going to have! Now pass me the chocolate.'

I slice my nail into the gold wrapper and the sea salt and caramel smell wafts through the air. 'I've never thought of myself as an independent woman before,' I say, popping a piece in my mouth.

'Well, you are, and I love you,' she says, wrestling the box off me.

'I love you too.' She fiddles with the wrapper, so I take the chocolate back off her to open it up. We stand facing one another, both of us blinking back sudden tears. 'It won't change anything, all this, you know,' she says to me. 'We'll still be the same.'

'Best friends with added husband.'

'Exactly. And he is great, so, you know, everyone wins.'

'Indeed they do.' I smile.

Lou goes into the bathroom and turns on the taps. She goes quiet for a moment, before sticking her head around the door. 'All that independent stuff noted, did you ever hear from him?' she asks.

'Who?'

'That consultant bloke. Mark. Did he get in touch?'

'Yeah,' I answer, climbing into bed with the remote control.

'And?'

'We talk. From time to time. I don't know if he *likes me* likes me or just…'

'Does it matter?'

I think for a moment, unwrapping another chocolate. 'Yes,' I answer eventually. 'Yes, it does matter. I don't know what the future holds. He seems nice…' She doesn't manage to raise an eyebrow through the newly topped-up Botox, but I've known her long enough to know that's what she's trying. 'Okay, I liked him. I didn't realise it with everything else that was going off, but yes, I did like him. I do… But you know something? I like me too. And I think I need to nurture that a little bit.'

'Not too long though, eh? The good ones don't stick around, look at my Will!'

'They'll stick around if they're meant to,' I say. I pick up my phone and read the last message he sent me. He's coming up in a month for a long weekend, to pack away his old flat. Did I fancy meeting up? I tap out a long-overdue response: 'I'd love to. Tell me when and where when you're back.' Then I click send, my heart jumping a little at the prospect of a secret meet-up. I know I'm not ready for a relationship yet. I know I want time to myself. But I also know that my future might hold one or two surprises. And finally, I feel ready to embrace them.

Chapter Fifty-Seven

RHYS

Three weeks after our 'first date', I wake up with her arm across my face and her taste across my lips. The bed sheet barely covers her as she stretches and I hold back the urge to reach out to her. 'Morning,' I say, brushing her hair from her face as she begins to stir. 'Look, you're here in my bed.' I grin like the teenager she makes me feel like inside.

She turns over and lifts her arm to rest on her elbow. 'I am. And look, so are you.'

'Is it weird?' I check.

'Nope.' She leans across to give me a lingering kiss. 'Wasn't quite four weeks, mind, was it?' she says accusingly.

'True…' I tuck stray hair behind her ear. 'We could pretend it didn't happen and wait another week if you like?' I trace my finger across her collarbone, hoping she doesn't agree.

She takes my fingers to her mouth, kissing them. 'I'm good, thanks,' she says.

I lean forward to kiss her. 'Bacon sandwich? Red sauce?' I ask, as she pulls me back towards her.

'That right there is proof you still have much to learn, Rhys Woods,' she says, pulling the sheets up over me and locking them down with her arms. 'As if there is anything other than brown to have on a bacon sandwich.'

'Brown! You are all kinds of wrong!' I tease, but she wraps her legs around mine and I decide I'll probably forgive her that one.

Half an hour later, I'm spreading butter on Michelle's home-baked bread. I flick on the radio and search out her favourite station. The sound of the shower fights with the sizzle of the bacon in the pan. There's something beautiful about her being here. Something right. When I told Mum how I felt about Michelle, she said, 'There are two types of love, Rhys. That which you can't live without and that which you choose *not* to live without. Only you can work out the kind you feel, either are perfectly valid.' And I realise that, although I don't know which kind of love this is, I know, without a shadow of doubt in my mind, that it is definitely one kind. I love her. Everything about her. Even the fact she has brown sauce on a bacon sandwich when we all know it should be red.

Michelle pads back through to my kitchen, towel wrapped and with wet hair falling over her shoulders. I pass her breakfast as she flicks the kettle on. The mundanity of our actions sends a shiver of contentment up my spine. 'You all set for today?' she asks.

I take a bite of breakfast to buy time to mull over my thoughts. 'I think I am,' I say, butterflies creeping back into my belly with thoughts of the day ahead. 'I think I am.'

She pauses, watching me, waiting for more.

'It's time to get to know each other properly,' I say of Susan. 'We've talked a little since she went home. I know she's been trying to ease herself into life again. She tells me she no longer feels the need to read the fairy stories out loud. She says she's thinking about moving, finding a home of her own.'

'How do you feel about that?'

'Honestly?' I think for a moment. 'I feel like I want her to stay close by.'

'Do you want me to come with you?' she asks.

'No,' I answer. 'Pick Mum up as you planned. I need to do this on my own.' She leans across, wipes ketchup from the side of my mouth and gives me a kiss. 'I love you,' she whispers into my ear.

I turn to face her, blown away by how life shifts. 'I love you too,' I say, with absolute certainty. There's a tiny tap on the window, making me look up. A tiny robin red-breast pecks at something on the sill, dotting about before us. 'Mum always told me robins were loved ones, letting us know they're okay.'

Michelle looks at it with the faintest sadness in her smile. 'He'd better be,' she says. 'He'd better be.'

Epilogue

SUSAN

I run my duster along the mantelpiece, adjusting the vase stuffed full of cornflower-blue irises I picked up at the market. They brighten the lounge, giving it life.

In the kitchen, a Victoria sponge cools on the side. I take out a teapot, swapping it for a larger one, then decide to use them both. I reach into the back of the sideboard to get out Mother's best china, laying it out on the lace-covered dining table.

I climb the stairs, letting the discomfort in my leg dictate the speed at which I go. When I eventually make it to the top, I take a breather. I move into my new bedroom, the large one at the front that for so many years was off limits. A room I wasn't allowed to go in until such time as I had to, to help one or other of them into bed, to get them up in the morning, to let the undertaker in when their final moments came. It still feels odd, like it isn't mine. But then sometimes the whole house feels that way. I suspect it always did. That's why it's time to sell. To make a change. To live my own life. I discounted it immediately when the subject came up with my counsellor. My counsellor, something I never thought to seek out and yet with whom I am just beginning to unpick the pain and anger I have nurtured within myself. Perhaps support like this was all I needed in the first place. Support, forgiveness, acceptance that I'm not okay.

But I am now, or I will be, in time.

I freshen up, pick up the book of fairy tales, and steadily make my way back downstairs. As I reach the final step, a nervous knock sounds at my door.

I open it and there he is. My son. The man who I could never have raised as his mother has, but to whom I intend to take every opportunity to make it up to for each day I live until my natural last.

'Come in,' I say, standing back as he steps in the house. It's the first time he's been here since I came home. He looks around – I suspect he's as nervous as I am – before finally leaning across to give me a kiss, handing over the flowers he clutches in his hand.

'Thank you!' I say, taking in the scent of delicate yellow freesia. 'Come through.' I nod in the direction of the lounge and watch as he wanders through.

'It feels a bit more like you're here this time,' he says, reaching for the new book I've been reading each night before bed. 'You like poetry?' he asks, flicking through the pages.

'I like all sorts,' I say. 'I've found a new love for reading since I stopped…' I look down at the book in my hands. 'I don't know if this is appropriate,' I say, stepping towards him, book outstretched. 'But I want you to have this. I don't know if you ever plan to have your own children, but—'

'God, can you imagine me as a father!' he says, taking the book from my hands.

'I can.' I smile.

'That would make you…' He cuts himself short, as if finishing the suggestion is a step too far, and I realise that each time he thinks about our relationship, he must also think about his mum.

'That would make me the family friend who you can visit whenever you have time,' I offer, by way of escape route for him.

'That would make you a grandmother,' he says simply, making my heart swell with a love I never knew I deserved. 'Just think how lucky any child I had would be: two grandmothers on my side, an extended family spreading far and wide.' He smiles. 'It could almost make up for all the mistakes I'm bound to make should Michelle ever do me the honour of having my babies!'

'Mistakes can be learned from,' I say. He nods, opening the book up and flipping through its pages. His hands shake. 'You nervous too?' I ask.

'Terrified.' He smiles. 'But excited too, you know?'

'Totally,' I agree. 'Rhys, before they get here, there's something I need to say—'

'Susan…'

I hold my hands up to stop him. This is too important. And long overdue. 'Rhys, I know I have said it, but you will never understand how deeply sorry I am for the choice I made. For a long time, I believed it was cowardice. I would never judge another woman's decision in the same way, and yet, for years I could not forgive myself. I couldn't accept that it might have been the right choice. Even now, the strength to accept it comes because my survival depends on it. I owe you that at the very least.' Perhaps in time I'll see I owe it to myself.

'Susan,' he tries again.

'I will never be able to thank your mother enough for all she did for you. She has raised you to be a kind, thoughtful and brave human being. A man I am blessed to have the chance to build a relationship with.'

'She is amazing, it's true, and had you not made your choice to leave me, I might not have her in my life,' he says. 'You were no more a coward than I was to blame. You felt you had no option, and it breaks my heart to think you believed that, but I get it. It wasn't your fault.'

'I couldn't do it,' I say quietly. 'In the park.' He drops his eyes to the floor, but I carry on, because he needs this final piece of the jigsaw. 'I went to the place you were born because I thought that was the place I should end it. And yet, when I got there, I could feel you. I could hear your cry. I felt the same wind in my hair that I felt the night I gave birth to you. And I couldn't do it. I couldn't do to you again, what I'd done once before. And then you turned up to save me, you and James and Kat, and, well...' I try to catch his eye so he knows I mean what I say. 'It made me realise, without doubt, that being too weak to take my life might have been the very thing to save me.' Rhys swallows, rubbing away a wobble I see on his chin. He takes me in his arms, holding me tight, and for a moment I wish he'd never let go because I suddenly feel like I could live forever.

'How lucky we are to have found one another,' he says finally. 'Despite all that kept us apart.'

Before I can find any words through the rush of love I feel for him, a knock at the door makes us both jump. 'Shall I go?' he asks, and I nod, following just behind him. Slowly, he opens the door wide. 'Come in,' he says, reaching out his hand. He turns to face me, reaching out for me with his other hand. 'Susan,' he says, pulling me closer. 'This is my mum.' I look at the woman who raised him, who took on the job I could never have done. 'It's a pleasure to meet you, Susan,' she says, politely, squeezing my hand. 'Rhys has told me so much about you. It's lovely to put a face to the name.' And I instantly know where his warmth comes from.

'The pleasure is all mine,' I say. 'Truly.'

I take in the moment, feeling a sense of what is in the air. As Rhys guides Michelle into the house too, with a soft kiss on her cheek, I realise I am surrounded by love, and a family I never dreamed I might have. And with that comes strength. And a future that, thanks to a combination of Kat and Rhys, I now realise I deserve.

James will be here soon, with his wife and his daughter.
The summer was indeed a long one.
I'm so grateful I was here to see it.

A Letter from Anna

Hello!

Thank you so much for taking the time to read my debut, I really hope you've enjoyed it. It's been a long time in the making and I've learnt loads in the editing process.

In case you're interested, I wanted to share how the idea for this novel came about. I've long been interested in the idea that some people 'opt out' of life. I don't mean physically, necessarily, but often just emotionally. They plough on from day to day but don't live it. Like James says in the novel, 'living and breathing doesn't mean [Susan] survived, just that she [was] alive. It's not the same thing.' That idea really interests me. What makes us feel we aren't deserving of the very best in life? What happens to stop us wanting to make the most of every chance life can offer?

And then there are those who do opt out physically. Those who feel they can no longer go on. I once knew a man who was possibly the most beautiful, generous and intelligent spirit I've ever met. A real giver with the kindest heart and the most forgiving nature. The day I heard he'd taken his own life, I was devastated. I couldn't understand how someone so generous could not work out how to forgive himself.

The only way I could rationalise it was to believe that, perhaps, taking the choice he did was actually his greatest act of self-forgiveness. He couldn't continue as he was, and he valued himself enough to put an end to his innate sadness. That those around him couldn't make a difference was the hardest lesson to learn, but the truth was, only he could ever have made the change. And I believe that is true of us all.

In Susan, Rhys and Kat, I have tried to create three people who've opted out of aspects of life to protect themselves. That they learn from each other how to mend their broken hearts is a love letter to those who fix themselves in whatever way they see fit.

True life is as dramatic as fiction, often even more so. If any of the themes in the book have touched on your own personal experiences, I hope you have found the support you need to lead the best life you can. In our real world, mental health challenges don't only come about because of regretful decisions, or experiences we face; adoption doesn't come about because somebody doesn't care, so often – in both instances – it's entirely the opposite. The following are just two of the many resources that can help: http://www.adoptionuk.org/ and http://www.mind.org.uk/

If you feel able to, I'd love you to review the book. It really does make a difference to us as writers. And if you wanted to drop me a line too, feel free. I'm on Twitter @annamansell or Facebook at AnnaMansellAuthor.

And finally, Bookouture can send you information on my next book if you take the time to sign up to my mailing list http://www.bookouture.com/anna-mansell. We promise not to spam you and we'll reward you with hot-off-the-press news of my next book, due out later in 2017.

Thanks again for reading, you've made my actual day!

Anna

Acknowledgments

I'm sat at my desk, staring at the laptop, wondering where to start. Acknowledgments? That's what actual, bona fide authors write, isn't it? I've dreamed of this moment… but where to begin?

Well, I suppose I could start by thanking the person who was first prepared to stick her neck out and not only say that I could do this, but offer me a contract to prove it: Kirsty, I am eternally grateful and hope you love the end result. Thanks also must go to Olly, Abi, Claire, Lauren and all the brilliant team at Bookouture. I am so proud to write for a publisher that places warmth, support, patience, guidance and total commitment alongside the importance of business and building the author brand – as a debut writer, this approach has been invaluable. Working with my editor, Celine Kelly, has been a total joy. She understood what I was trying to achieve and guided me gently, carefully and skillfully to achieve something of which I'm very proud. Thank you, Celine! And to all the ladies and gents in 'the lounge', led by Lady Kim of Nash, thank you, thank you, thank you. Laughter, support, occasional filth – who could ask for more? (Possibly real life puppies or gin, if I was being picky.)

To early readers: Lian, I'm nothing without your wind. Clare C, thirty years plus and you're still on my side. Mel, any medical errors are mine and mine alone! Jo M, your support was just what I needed.

Kerry, with that SWOT, you TOTALLY got me! Dad, you have read, proofread, printed and posted so many pages, thank you! You are all brilliant and supportive and I appreciate the very bones of you... Even those friends and family (Mum, now is finally your chance!) who haven't yet read it, the ones I've known forever and those known barely a few years, that you are all so proud and generous in your encouragement of my dream-chasing makes me thankful every day. Let's schedule a night in which to enjoy our body weight in cheese and Prosecco!

Is this all a bit Oscar winner? Having done several drafts of these acknowledgments, I can tell you it's tough to be anything other. Because, whilst my books are written by me, they don't fully come to life without those people who recognise what they could be and nurture them into existence.

And with that, I suppose I should really end on the biggest thanks of all, to my lovely family. Andy, my 'him-in-doors', who has never questioned whether I could do this. Or if he did, he never let me once suspect that was the case. He is a top catch, we make a good team, and I love him very much... I'm not sure I'll ever be able to buy him a boat though, which may or may not change his level of support. To our latest arrival, Olive: you won't let me go far without you, which is fine, because why would I want to? And last, but by no means least, the kids, Harley and Maggie. You've both been published before me, and you are therefore my inspiration. I hope that one day, with this, you might be as proud of me as I am of you.

And to you, dear reader, if you got this far, thank you! And if you didn't, that's a shame... because I was just about to thank you, too.

CPSIA information can be obtained
at www.ICGtesting.com
Printed in the USA
BVOW06s2008130217
476076BV00013B/302/P